ISAAC ASIMOV'S

THREE LAWS OF ROBOTICS

1.

A robot may not injure a human being, or, through inaction, allow a human being to come to harm.

2.

A robot must obey the orders given it by human beings except where such orders would conflict with the First Law.

3.

A robot must protect its own existence, as long as such protection does not conflict with the First or Second Law.

ISAAC ASIMOV'S
ROBOT MYSTERY

MIRAGE

MARK W. TIEDEMANN

Mark W. Tiedemann's love for science fiction and writing started at an early age, although it was momentarily sidetracked—for over twenty years—by his career as a professional photographer. After attending a Clarion Science Fiction & Fantasy Writers Workshop held at Michigan State University in 1988, he rediscovered his lost love and focused his talents once more on attaining his dream of becoming a professional writer. With the publication of "Targets" in the December 1990 issue of *Asimov's Science Fiction Magazine*, he began selling short stories to various markets; his work has since appeared in *Magazine of Fantasy & Science Fiction, Science Fiction Age, Tomorrow SF*, and a number of anthologies. His novel *Compass Reach*—the first volume of the Secantis Series—was nominated for the 2001 Philip K. Dick Memorial Award. Currently, Tiedemann is working on *Terminator 2: Hour of the Wolf*, an original novel based on the popular film franchise, to be published by ibooks in summer 2004. He lives in St. Louis, Missouri, with his companion, Donna, and their resident alien life form—a dog named Kory.

ISAAC ASIMOV

Isaac Asimov was the author of over 400 books—including three Hugo Award-winners—and numerous bestsellers, as well as countless stories and scientific essays. He was awarded the Grand Master of Science Fiction by the Science Fiction Writers of America in 1985, and he was the man who coined the words robotics, positronic, and psycho-history. He died in 1992.

ALSO AVAILABLE

published by ibooks, inc.:

ISAAC ASIMOV'S
ROBOT MYSTERY

MIRAGE

MARK W. TIEDEMANN

ibooks
new york
www.ibooksinc.com

DISTRIBUTED BY SIMON & SCHUSTER, INC

A Publication of ibooks, inc.

Copyright © 2001 by
Byron Preiss Visual Publications, Inc.

An ibooks, inc. Book

Distributed by Simon & Schuster, Inc.
1230 Avenue of the Americas, New York, NY 10020

ibooks, inc.
24 West 25th Street
New York, NY 10010

The ibooks World Wide Web Site Address is:
http://www.ibooks.net

ISBN 0-7434-7523-2

PRINTING HISTORY
First ibooks, inc. trade paperback edition April 2000
First ibooks, inc. mass-market edition December 2003
10 9 8 7 6 5 4 3

Edited by Howard Zimmerman & Steven A. Roman

Cover art by Bruce Jensen
Cover design by j. vita

Printed in the U.S.A.

To
Donna
The reason for it all

ISAAC ASIMOV'S
ROBOT MYSTERY

MIRAGE

PROLOGUE

Record module CF941 attach log sequencing file "Commerce and Culture Committee, minutes" reference subheader "Humadros-Eliton General Trade and Tariff Negotiations" running virtual conference Maui Overlook fill visual fill audio status On

This will be our last meeting before the arrival of the Humadros legation and the start of the conference. If there are any other issues which need to be discussed or added to the agenda, now is the time to put them on the table. I think it best that there be no surprises from any of us."

The thick man with amber-tinged white hair looked around the table at the eighteen others. All of them appeared here, in this non-place, altered or enhanced. Younger, slimmer, more hair, fewer lines—opportunistic vanity. Even the chairman tweaked his appearance here. It was a running joke among them outside the Maui construct.

When no one raised any new issues, he nodded solemnly. "I thought not. We've pretty much talked this thing to death over the last year. How we failed to kill it is beyond me."

The laughter that rippled around the table was light, though sharpened with an edge of nervousness. The chairman reached out and touched a button on the table.

"I'm uploading the final draft of our platform. In four days the Spacers arrive at Kopernik Station. The day after, they shuttle down to Union Station in Washington, D.C., for the mediafest Senator Eliton has planned. There will be a grand reception that evening. After that, the negotiations begin. I want us all well-versed on our agenda. I don't think I'm overstating it to say that these talks will be the most significant this century, possibly this millennia. A great deal is at stake. I don't want anyone breaking ranks on this at the last minute."

"Just how much, if anything, do you really think we're going to lose?"

The chairman looked at the man at the far end of the table. "I don't expect to lose very much at all. Ambassador Humadros hopes to alter our traditions and change history by offering more open markets, exchange of technologies, better policing along the shipping routes, lower tariffs—the usual package of incentives intended to force policy to change. Not that it isn't a tempting package—I expect that we'll end up signing off on some of it, maybe even a lot of it. In fact, I imagine it would be very profitable in the short term. But she hopes to break our resistance to positronics. I expect her to go home disappointed."

Anxious looks crossed the table. Not everyone on the committee, he knew, agreed that positronics was a bad thing, but all of them understood how the markets and their future holdings could be effected. The chairman was always impressed at the degree of nuance the program translated. He could always tell, no matter what each member did to modify their own projection, who was genuinely comfortable with the setting and who still felt uneasy. The chamber did not exist outside the buffers of the data module, but it was patterned on one that had once jutted from the side of a tower built just below the summit of Puu Kukul, on the island of Maui in the Hawaiian chain. The view was spectacular, overlooking a meandering valley through which the Honokahua Stream ran on its way to the Pacific Ocean. The openness of it challenged them. The suggestion of limitless sky unnerved the average Terran, but none of the members of this forum considered themselves average. A little agoraphobia would not, they claimed, dictate to them.

Still, it was a construct, and they all knew it. The chairman wondered if they could so bravely attend meetings in the flesh outside the walls that defined their existence and their identities as citizens of Earth.

"In my view," he continued after a pause, "we have come to a consensus on this matter. Are we, in fact, agreed?"

Nods rippled all around.

"Good. The upload is complete. Please be thoroughly familiar with all the points before the conference begins. I know I can depend on you."

Singly and in groups of two and three the attendees faded from the table. Alone finally, the chairman stood and walked to the window. He felt his pulse increase, a tremulous thrill in his groin and behind his sternum, as he stood at the edge of the view and confronted it. It was lovely. The ocean far in the distance formed a sharp, straight horizon above which the blue, blue sky arched. He wondered at times what had driven people to hide from the universe and burrow into the Earth. It surprised him sometimes to realize that in this he had much in common with both Spacers and Settlers.

Some, at any rate. He knew of Settler worlds where the warrens of Earth had been and were being duplicated in alien soil under other suns. What, he wondered, was the point of leaving a place only to bring it with you?

His heartrate regulated finally. He reached into his jacket pocket and found the small square. He gave it a squeeze and the windows opaqued to black. It was a good illusion, this chamber. He sometimes forgot for a few seconds that he was not standing in anything, that it was all a construct of numbers and electrons. A mirage.

He turned back toward the table and squeezed the square in his pocket again. There was barely a flicker. The scene seemed to skip sideways a centimeter or two, hardly noticeable unless anticipated and expected. The automated recorders were now being fed a secondary illusion, one that showed the chairman sitting in a chair, gazing out at the lovely, frightening vista of naked Earth, the way he often did.

The deception was necessary because of the redundant monitors the entire committee maintained on the site. Time records, the comings and goings of members, the alternate uses of the chamber—all recorded for the benefit of mutual distrust and mutual oversight. The committee conducted official business here and so the construct was always running. Of course, they could meet in public, but there were other monitoring and recording systems in many of those places; it was much safer to say certain things here, within the sphere of their own complimentary suspicions, where only they could get at the records. The system had been built to prevent exactly what the chairman was now doing.

"Secured," he said.

Two figures reappeared at the table. They ran their own masking programs, so their faces were difficult to see clearly, and their voices were altered into unrecognizability. But the chairman knew who they were, and they knew him.

"Where's our Judas?" the chairman asked.

"He wished to be absent during the final preparations," the indistinct apparition to the chairman's right said. "He's in agreement, but wants to remain free of the actual planning. Deniability, he says."

"A true politician," the other figure said.

The chairman suppressed a disgusted response. He sat down.

"Very well." He drew a loud, dramatic breath. "Briefly, everything is in place on my end. The program is running and we'll have fifteen minutes of operational time. What about security?"

"Taken care of," the left-hand ghost said. "My people are in place and ready."

"And the operations team?"

"Set," answered the right-hand ghost. "Give the word and we go."

The chairman leaned back, enjoying a sensation of accomplishment. He sighed. "Ambassador Galiel Humadros of Aurora believes she can change the face of Terran policy and tradition. She has our own Senator Clar Eliton to thank for validating that illusion." He looked across the table to the ghost on his right. After a few seconds, the indistinct face looked away.

"You know," the other ghost said, "there are elements of this treaty that *aren't* terrible."

"Which elements do you mean?" The chairman's voice became blunt, almost monotonal in its derision. "The part where Spacer industry is allowed to set up factories on Earth as cooperatives with native companies? Or the reduced tariffs that could cut government revenues in half—which would mean that our government would be forced to make up the shortfall through increased local taxes? Or is it the limited reintroduction of positronics to the open market?"

His tone turned mocking. "Or could it be the sentiment of reconciliation that permeates every clause and paragraph of the draft proposal? How does the preamble go? 'The people of Earth and the people of the settled worlds share a common heritage and should not be separated by ideology or divided over commerce.' Do you wish to sit down to break bread with our lost children of Aurora and Solaria and reminisce over the branching past? What parts of this treaty 'aren't terrible'? Educate me."

"That's enough," said the left-hand ghost. "Sometimes I wonder if you aren't a fanatic. The fact is we stand to lose a great deal of money if positronic inspections are instituted for interstellar shipping. The black markets have been too lucrative and we're bound to them now, but it's just profit. I don't think we should forget that. We're doing this to protect our margins—period. I don't have any ideological axes to grind. Nobody—not Earth, not Settler, and especially not Spacer—is going to damage my business. That should be enough. This isn't a holy war."

"No?" the chairman asked. "Perhaps not. But you should study history more. You might find yourself agreeing with the fanatics more than you'd expect." He settled back in the chair. "That brings me to another point. The *Tiberius* incident which precipitated this conference was nothing but sloppy handling on the part of the captain. It should never have escalated to the point of provoking the Auroran ship. Once we get through the upcoming event, I think a restructuring of our smuggling operations is in order. Shipments have been cut to less than half their former size because of this nonsense. A year of this is too much. But I *don't* want a repeat of that mess."

"Do you think after the conference we'll still be doing any business with Spacers?" the left-hand ghost asked.

"Oh, yes. *More.* They won't be able to get Terran products through legitimate channels. Not as easily, at any rate. Possibly, depending on how angry their governments are, not at all. The market won't go away and we'll be able to raise prices due to any embargo. Business will continue, make no mistake. I've already made inquiries into alternate routes and methods. I think, once the dust settles, we can look forward to doubling our former revenues."

"We've heard none of this," the left-hand ghost complained.

"Of course not. I'm waiting till afterward, so that if anything goes wrong, you will all have deniability."

"Or anything to take to the authorities?"

The chairman frowned. "Why do you goad me so much?"

The ghost shrugged. The indistinct form made the gesture seem liquid, like the slap of water against a wall.

"It's best," said the ghost, "that we never forget the nature of what we're doing."

"We're putting a stop to a bad idea," the chairman said. "Risks are necessary to do so. Speaking of which, you—" he pointed to the right-hand ghost "—are taking the greatest risk."

"So?"

"Any second thoughts?"

"All the time. But it's necessary."

The chairman nodded. "Then we won't speak again."

"True." The ghost sighed, a papery sound that seemed ancient. "Flesh, not steel?"

"Flesh, not steel," the other two repeated.

"Good-bye."

The ghost faded out, leaving only two.

"Will he go through with it?" the left-hand ghost asked.

"The beauty of this is that once the reception at Union Station begins, he won't have any choice," the chairman replied. "But I think we should make absolutely sure he doesn't suffer a crisis of conscience. Before *or* after."

"My people will keep a watch on him. As for after . . ."

"See to it."

"Done." The ghost paused. "You asked why I goad you so much."

"A rhetorical question. I actually enjoy it, in a way."

"Good. But I don't do it for your pleasure, Ky. We've known each other for a long time. I've always found in you the desire to act on passion alone. You never do, but you want to. I worry sometimes that one day you'll ditch your practicality and turn zealot."

The chairman raised an eyebrow. "How do you know I *haven't?*"

"You pay attention to costs too closely."

The chairman laughed. When he finished, he gazed at the wavering, masked form across from him. "As a matter of fact, I *do* believe positronic robots represent a real threat, beyond the fiscal. When you study history—"

"I know about the riots."

"We all do—we're endlessly told about them, by commentators and in our dramas. Riots don't frighten me, though."

"You're not worried that a reintroduction of positronic robots would bring them back?"

"No. I'm worried that this time they *won't*. And then it's all over for us."

The two shimmery figures sat together in silence for a time, the space around them growing thick with contemplation.

"Well," the ghost said at last, "I have details to chase down and kill."

"So do I. I think we're as prepared as we're going to be."

"I agree. Till afterward then?"

"Flesh, not steel?"

The ghost chuckled. "If you insist."

The form faded out, leaving the chairman alone in his generated conference chamber. After a time, he reached in his pocket again and squeezed the square.

"Recording complete?" he asked.

"Recording complete," answered a flat, genderless voice. "Decoding routines in place, descrambler active. Bubble memory established under file 'Zealots, Inc.' Minutes retrieved, stored, coded to password release."

The chairman felt a wry aversion to that label, but it fit. He did not feel like a zealot, not in the sense of an irrational fanatic single-mindedly devoted to a cause. Rather, he felt supremely rational, a practical man in an impractical universe, presented with an opportunity to make a small adjustment and guarantee the sanity of a small part of history.

A zealot? No. Ambitious, perhaps, and, he admitted, even a little vain.

But it was necessary.

"Very good. End routine."

The room faded away, leaving nothing.

ONE

Mia Daventri listened to the stream of com chatter in her left ear and surveyed the crowd gathered at the archway. On an average day, Union Station D.C. was thick with travelers and their entourages of well-wishers and connections. Now it seemed to contain half the residents of the city.

"Wing Three," a voice whispered to her. "Parcel is arriving. Are you established?"

"Copy, One," she said quietly, glancing around. No one looked like anything other than a fascinated spectator. "Gate is open."

"Very good," One replied. It was unusual for the head of Special Service to operate as general dispatcher, but today was an unusual day.

Union Station always impressed Mia. The main gallery seemed to grow out of the earth itself, huge arching ribs reaching up and overhead to support the roof, the columns carved in delicate fractal patterns. The floor shined like polished starglow. The hall lay at the center of a network of tunnels to and from the shuttle port. Archways lined the walls, glowing signs set into the synthetic stone above each directing people to transportation, shops, restaurants, com booths, and the station hotels. Between those columns that did not flank an exit stood statuary, representative pieces from several periods extending back to preindustrial times. Sounds caught in the air, contoured, slightly magnified, and lingered high above. Union Station was a showpiece for D.C., sprawling and elegant and, it seemed, ever incomplete. Mia had seen a view of it from outside. It looked like a giant mushroom cap, a thick set of tunnels linking the landing field to the secrets beneath its penumbra.

Beginning at the apron before the main entrance, two rows of station security robots formed a sort of honor guard that continued down the length of the concourse into the station's great hall. Arms extended and linked, they kept the crowds back by a combination of presence and cordial cajoling. Union Station was one of the few places on Earth where positronic robots were in such public use, which, Mia felt, was a shame. She liked them—which set her apart from the vast majority of her fellow Terrans—and could not see the evil they supposedly represented. They were here because so many offworlders came through; Spacers who not only were used to a clear robotic presence, but depended on it. Union Station was a kind of international zone in which all jurisdictions had representation, containing embassy offices of the Spacer missions—satellites to the main embassies east in Anacostia District.

But beyond the diplomatic necessities, Mia thought the use of robots was ideal for crowd control during events like this. Earther distaste—Earther fear—for robots kept most people from getting too close to them. Mia could hear the insistent, genderless robotic requests to "please stay back" and "do not cross the line" even over the din. If anyone actually got past that line, it was up to a human to usher them, gently or otherwise, back behind it. For that, regular police and station security stood ready.

Even so, these robots were not entirely independent units. They were all slaved to Union Station's Resident Intelligence. The RI handled the complex coordination among the various units. Besides Mia's own Special Service team, the police, and station security, several of the representative bodies from industry and political interest groups had brought along their own small security teams. In the unlikely event of a security breach or other emergency, the RI would deploy these units more efficiently than any human coordinator might manage.

"Moving up now," One said.

Mia caught sight of her two team partners on the other side of the archway. Each of them, Mattu and Gel, gave her a nod and returned their attention to the avenue.

The moving strips immediately fronting the Union Station entrance had been shut down today. The strips on the other side of the independent traffic lanes still moved, but they were empty.

The oversized limo rolled silently into sight, small flags fluttering at its corners, and pulled up against the curb. Mia strode to the doors and tapped a code into the lock. A section of polished black metal slid back and Mia stepped away.

A robot emerged first. Standing nearly two meters tall, it nevertheless appeared almost toy-like. Smooth-jointed, its arms hung to its sides, little more than tubes that ended in clumsy-looking three-fingered hands. It seemed too thin for its height. The rounded head possessed ill-formed ear shells, a faint depression where a mouth ought to be; above that was a single slit that glowed white—its optical array. Its bronze skin dully reflected the station's lights.

"Agent Daventri," it said through her link, "it is good to see you again. Is all secured?"

"Hi, Bogard. Yes, we're fine." She glanced at the gathered spectators and saw a number of round-eyed stares. Despite the robot's innocuous appearance, they were clearly afraid of it. "Bogard, please link to RI network now."

"One moment," Bogard replied. "Linking. Link complete. Security net, sensory net, and related peripherals realtime linked to Union Station Resident Intelligence. Telemetry optimal, Agent Daventri."

"Very good, Bogard. Proceed."

Bogard took two steps forward, then turned smartly. Senator Clar Eliton stepped from the limo. He seemed taller than he actually was, his high forehead crowned by thick waves of greying black hair. The beginnings of a double chin and the dense webbing of creases around his eyes betrayed his age and the wear of office, but the rest of him appeared fit and energetic. Boos and angry shouts peppered the air as his personal staff emerged behind him. Eliton, seemingly oblivious to them, smiled and waved as though on a campaign stump, and started down the entry tunnel.

Bogard fell into step behind and to the Senator's right. Mia and her teammates ranged out ahead, she to the left, Gel on the opposite side, and Mattu on point. She spotted other members of the on-site security sprinkled along the way and through the crowd as they brought Senator Eliton into the main gallery.

The line of robots on either side saluted. Mia felt herself grin.

Who's idea was that? She glanced back at Bogard, but it seemed unaffected.

"We're ahead of schedule," Mattu said through the link. "The Auroran legation is still enroute from Kopernik. Three minutes."

"Do we let him talk?" Gel asked, his voice tinged with sarcasm.

"One says no," Mattu replied, his own voice revealing none of his feelings. Mattu, team leader, was the oldest of them, the most experienced, and he had repeatedly cautioned them against letting their sentiments show. "You have a job to do," he often said, "despite the politics."

They slowed down. The Senator picked up on the signal and made more smiles and handwaves. The catcalls diminished as the party neared the other end of the tunnel; the crowd had been screened so that more supporters than detractors filled the gallery. Even so, Mia was grateful Eliton's vice senator, Taprin, had had other commitments today. The antipathy toward Eliton was bad enough. Having both of them present would only have increased the negative reactions.

"Flesh, not steel!" someone yelled, voice amplified. Station security waded into the crowd, looking for the speaker.

Mia's nerves danced upon hearing the popular motto of the current radical reform movement. She had heard rumors that Eliton had attempted to invite representatives from the Order for the Supremacy of Man Again, trying to be as inclusive as possible, but the Managins had refused . . . to the relief of Eliton's handlers. That did not mean, though, that they would not show up.

More dignitaries arrived, forming a brief parade of politics and commerce. Several others waited on the platform that dominated the floor by the arrival gate.

Within the gallery, ropes held the crowd in check. Fewer robots stood at wider intervals, since human security did most of the work here. Mia caught brief squirts of com-speak from the officers, all of it reassuring, everything pos-itive. Even with the advance screening, Mia had expected more hecklers and protestors. A group of police passed her, on its way somewhere, faces intent. Out of the possibility for so much chaos, it amazed her how much order prevailed.

The entourage reached the base of the raised platform. Mattu mounted the broad steps, eyes roving intently. He stood for a few seconds at the top, frowned briefly, then gave the all-clear, and Senator Eliton came up.

"Looks like a walk in the park," Gel said.

"Stay sharp," Mattu cautioned.

The assembly on the platform was a cross-section of Earthly power. Mia recognized a few lobbyists from various coalitions, but mostly she saw industrialists. Alda Mikels of Imbitek stood in the midst of his own cadre of functionaries and security, which looked lighter than Mia expected. Nearby, Rega Looms, CEO of DyNan Manual Industries, and his handful of aides milled among themselves, appearing uncomfortable and out of place. Mia was surprised to see a face she recognized hovering on their periphery. She had not seen Coren Lanra for over a year, since he had resigned from the Service. She caught his eye and he smiled and nodded.

"Wouldn't you know," Gel commented through the link, "Lanra would be babysitting Luddite, Inc."

Mia ignored the remark. As with most of Gel's obser-vations it held more acid than substance.

It *was* curious, though. Coren had quit over protest at bringing robots like Bogard into Special Service, though Bogard was the first and so far the only one. She had heard that Lanra had opened his own agency, a small office some-where in the southeast corridor, but if he was doing security for DyNan she wondered if perhaps he had given that up for a corporate sinecure. Though he had made his feelings about robots clear, Mia had not thought him sympathetic to Looms and his radical notions of a return to some sort of premechanized idyllic past. But a job is a job, she supposed, and turned her attention back to her own.

She recognized Ambassador Gale Chassik of the Solarian embassy in the midst of his entourage of six. Ambassador Sen Setaris of the Auroran embassy was absent, but her chief aides, Lys Morglen and Daril Falnyk, as well as her other senior aides, were present. Mia thought that odd, but who could tell about Spacer protocol?

Among the rest of the assembled dignitaries were several representatives from much smaller firms, able to get only one, at most two, people on the reception stand. Functionaries from a number of government offices weaved among them. Mia glanced out at the field of faces below. She could never find the feeling of trust Gel managed when he decided security was perfect. Instead, she always looked for what had been missed, thankful when she did not find it. She paused at the sight of another group of security guards moving off through the crowd. A couple of newscams moved closer then, hovering above, angling for the best views.

"Wing Three here," Mia said into her com. "How close do we let the subetherics get?"

"They have full clearance, Three," One said. "Just don't let them clobber the Parcel."

"Copy, One."

Eliton moved among the guests, shaking hands and engaging in the expressive banter Mia could never quite accommodate. She had listened once, closely, as he worked a roomful of supporters, smiling with a sincerity he seemed able to turn on at will, and mouthing a stream of engaging nonsense that pleased those around him enormously. He made a point of knowing everyone's name and at least one personal fact about them, and he possessed a superb memory. Mia put it down to the requirements of office and stopped trying to analyze it.

Eliton hesitated at one person, only a second, but Mia caught it. Then the smile, partially dimmed, brightened to full and his hand shot out as usual. Mia wondered who the woman was. She looked familiar, something to do with Settlers.

"Bogard, identify person now shaking hands with Senator Eliton," she subvocalized through the link.

"Viansa Risher, Settlers' Coalition."

"Ah. Thank you, Bogard." She had been a last minute inclusion, Mia remembered, though the Settlers had petitioned for representation here for months.

"One minute," Mattu announced, then moved alongside Eliton to inform him.

Mia did a last sweep of the gallery—more security movements caught her attention—then closed with Gel and Mattu to stay near Eliton.

"Did anybody copy what the RI is doing with crowd control?" she asked. "I didn't hear anything."

Mattu frowned again, looking past her. "I don't—" He listened to his link, then turned toward the debarkation tunnel. "They're here."

In the air, like a ghostly chimera, the announcement of the Kopernik shuttle's arrival carrying the Auroran legation appeared over the concourse entrance. Everyone's attention turned to the concourse; even the din of babble from the gallery lessened expectantly. The media newscams buzzed above the crowd, concentrating on the arriving Spacers as they emerged onto the platform.

Their clothes seemed brighter, their complexions fairer, eyes clearer; they averaged slightly taller than Earthers. Galiel Humadros, Ambassador Extraordinary, led the procession of Auroran representatives onto the platform. Her hair glimmered, golden and thick, and her face exhibited the kind of placid confidence Mia associated with wisdom and experience. A step or two behind her walked her aides, and behind them came the bulk of the legation, the counterparts of the Terrans they now met under the full gaze of the planet.

Mia felt there was something strange about the way they looked, as though something was missing. Then she realized that they were without their robots. Every image, every real life encounter, every report she had ever seen about Spacers showed their ubiquitous robots. Now, apparently, as a gesture of good will, they were without them. It made the Spacers seem naked, vulnerable. Mia's respect for them increased, even though she knew it was little more than the politics of image—public relations, a token to help ease the tensions their coming raised.

Eliton stepped forward to bow in greeting and extend his hands to the Ambassador, matching the Auroran poise. Mia felt a brief surge of pride.

"Welcome to Earth, Ambassador Humadros," Eliton said, his voice amplified now to echo across the gallery. "It is an honor and a privilege to have you walk upon our soil—"

Mia blinked, catching a movement from the corner of her vision. She turned and saw Bogard's head suddenly pivot a moment before she heard through her link, "Something is wrong. The RI—"

In the next instant, as she reached for her sidearm, the first explosions thundered across the chamber.

TWO

Mia dropped to a crouch under the sound of the blasts. Bright bursts of light and thick roiling smoke erupted all around the perimeter of the gallery. The constant noise of the crowd turned to a cacophony of screams and panicked shouts. Mia could not hear her link over the onslaught of noise. She searched the front ranks of spectators as they alternately dropped to the floor or tried to rush for the exits. The station robots stood motionless as if suddenly switched off.

Security—everyone's—ordered the assembled dignitaries to get to the floor. As Mia turned, she could not immediately locate Eliton. He had been clasping hands with Ambassador Humadros, who now stood right there, looking around, confused.

Mattu rushed toward her, waving his arms like great wings. "Down! Down! Down!"

Mia flinched at the sharp percussive sounds of projectile weapons fire. As she began to wheel around once more she saw several people on the platform jerk and dance in a macabre ballet, their clothes erupting in splotches of red. She continued turning, dropping to one knee, blaster coming to bear. She saw people in black standing in the thick of the crowd, aiming weapons at the platform, the barrels jerking spasmodically. She heard the highpitched whine of projectiles cutting the air around her, to left and right.

Mia aimed automatically, picking one target after another, partly hypnotized by her own efficiency as they fell.

But there were so many . . .

And some did not fall, even though she *knew* she had hit them . . .

"We have total penetration!" she heard Mattu yell through the link. "Total—!"

Silence.

More explosions. The mob was in full terrified retreat, jamming itself against the exits, bottling itself in its mindless haste. The immobile station robots fell, trampled by the stampede.

All comlinks had been routed through the RI, but it seemed now that the RI had shut down.

"Bogard, switch to team link," she shouted, hoping the robot could hear her over the noise. "Do you have Parcel?"

Bogard did not answer immediately, and a swift brush of fear trailed down Mia's spine.

"Bogard, respond!"

"Agent Daventri. I require assistance." Bogard's voice came through clearly, deceptively calm, on the team channel.

Mia risked a glance over her shoulder. Bogard stared back at her, shorter now, its torso flared out into an encircling shield, and she knew Eliton was in the center of that small but impenetrable enclosure of amalloy.

"Ambassador Humadros," Bogard said. "Senator Eliton is demanding I protect her."

Mia scanned the crowd around them and found the ambassador, huddling about five meters to Bogard's right, her hands hovering uselessly about her head. She looked completely abandoned by reason, eyes wide and staring, unseeing. Mia started toward her.

A body collided with her and she staggered back, bringing her free hand up defensively to fend off an attack. But it was no assault, only one of the unfortunate dead, caught by gunfire, his falling, lifeless body torn up and bleeding.

In that moment, she saw Bogard retract its shield from around Eliton. The Senator staggered away from it, redfaced and shouting, pointing at Ambassador Humadros.

That should have been impossible, she knew. Eliton was Bogard's primary concern, and only a specifically coded command could change that. Nevertheless, Bogard moved away from Eliton, toward the Spacers. It moved slowly, uncertainly, as if resisting the instruction.

But now, Eliton was exposed. Mia moved toward him, turning around to face the assault. Her heel suddenly caught on something and she raised her leg to step over it, then glanced down at the obstruction; the body of one of the Aurorans. It surprised her; the woman looked like she was sleeping, eyes closed easily, lips slightly parted. Mia shuddered and forced her attention back on the edge of the platform.

Black-masked gunmen leaned against it now, spraying the assembly. Mia began taking them out, one by one, down the line, walking backward as she did, waiting for the inevitable projectile that would stop her.

When it did, she stumbled, falling over, and found herself staring up at the ceiling arching high above.

I'm hit, she thought. *I'm dying . . .*

Then she rolled over. She pressed a hand against the soreness spreading across her left side. Her ribs ached, but her hand came away from the bruised area dry. She blinked and looked around and found that another body had struck her, its head still in her lap, eyes staring emptily upward. She shoved it away and scooted back.

Far more people than seemed possible still stood, huddling against each other. As she watched, a few more fell, bodies twitching under the deafening gunfire. Mia had never seen anything like this. Training simulations covered lone target situations, energy weapons, area-wide toxins—

Why hasn't the tranq gas been released? she wondered.

The points along the rib supports for the walls and ceiling that housed the nonlethal gas dispensers appeared unopened. The gallery security system had failed; Union Station's positronic Resident Intelligence apparently was not functioning.

"One!" Mia yelled. "Wing Three here! We have systems failure, we have—"

Her earpiece remained dully silent. All com was down. Then she remembered that it also had been routed through the RI for convenience, so the positronic brain could manage all the coordination without the complications of competing com systems. The only com she had was the direct link to Bogard and it, too, had been linked to the RI.

Mia recovered her blaster and got to her feet. She looked for Eliton.

She found him lying in a heap, blood spattered across his chest. Bogard stood over him, immobile. Nearby, she saw Ambassador Humadros, also dead.

She tried the com anyway, scanning the massacre for

her teammates. "Wing Two, Wing One, this is Wing Three. Parcel is down! Repeat, Parcel is down!"

All she heard was the faint hiss of a disconnected link.

"Wing One, Wing Two," she called. Nothing. "Bogard, respond."

There was a click. Then: "I—I—I—"

The staccato skipping in the link added to the fear rising in her.

"Bogard, reestablish," she commanded. "Local parameter, Mia respond. Confirm."

"Con—confirm—Mia—I—"

"Bogard, new priority, on me. Omega-five catalogue reset. Respond."

"Priority reestablish—Mi-Mia."

"Discontinue uplink to Union Station Resident Intelligence."

"Uplinking—up—uplink incomplete. Protocol rejected. Discontinued."

Abruptly, the assassins began to retreat. Mia watched, dismayed, as they backed from the edge of the platform. It seemed to her that some of them vanished even as she stared directly at them. They fired their weapons over their heads, driving people away from them, opening paths. She saw one of them grab a man by the arm and toss him against several others, using him as a ram to force his way through. The mound of people crushed together near her still comprised many survivors, the dead sprawled around the perimeter of the huddle as though discarded from its midst.

"What the—?" she muttered. "Bogard, with me. Track assailants. Locate likeliest apprehension."

She felt Bogard alongside her before she saw it move. It

towered over her and she could feel its attention directed at the retreating forms.

"Three confirmed." A bright red tracer beam reached out over the heads of the still rippling crowd to identify three figures in black.

"With me," she repeated and jumped to the floor. Her ribcage throbbed.

She struck the edge of the mob and began shoving. It was like trying to do sculpture in water. Panicked faces stared at her, brief glimpses of the hidden parts of strangers that she might never have seen, might never see again, stripped of their calm civility and complacent sophistication. She thought she understood. Their systems had failed them, the world that coddled and protected them now showed them how much they depended on what they could not do for themselves. They were vulnerable, probably for the first time in any of their lives, and there were no rules to follow, no plan, no direction. Hands reached for her, eyes begged her—she seemed the only one *acting* in all this chaos, able to choose, to decide—but Mia batted and brushed them all aside and forced her way through.

In truth, these people had nowhere to go. They were packed together. As she neared the far wall she saw why. The doors were sealed. The preparatory phase for pacification had occurred and all the exits had been closed, waiting for phase two, the release of the gas.

Suddenly, people simply backed away from her, jamming themselves against each other in renewed hysteria. She glanced back and saw Bogard, right at her heels, its shoulders stretching wide, presenting a visible though false menace.

"Still have them, Bogard?"

"Locked on."

"Great."

Finally, Mia broke free of the press. Before her rose an expanse of wall mottled by the rich veining of blue marble. Off to the right, another wall stood away from the main wall, making a passage which gave access to the service warrens.

The door was open.

"Through here, Bogard?"

"Correct."

Mia hesitated at the service door and peered around. Bogard touched her shoulder gently and drew her back, then moved through the access.

"Clear."

She rounded the edge, weapon ready.

To her immediate right were office cubicles; to the left, storage lockers. Directly ahead, a conveyor ran from a large turntable deeper into a sporadically-lit maze down a short corridor. A confusing jumble of conduit, cable, and assemblages filled the space, hanging from the ceiling or rising from the floor, creating mosaics of light and shadow.

The sound of many feet marching in quicktime echoed around the labyrinth. Mia pressed against the short wall of the first cubicle and waited.

A column of maintenance robots filed by, in almost comic imitation of a military drill. They pivoted precisely at the turntable and continued on into the depths.

"Bogard, do you still have a track on our targets?"

"Faint IR trace on the floor. Clear but fading."

"Lead on."

The robot seemed to flow across the floor, its torso leaning forward into a streamline profile, feet appearing to glide as if on rollers. Soundless. In the mottling illumination, it seemed to alter its shape, and as she fell in behind it, she saw that its angle and configuration could cover her own silhouette.

It turned left down a narrower passage, along a line of ready niches for robots. Many were vacant, but several still contained robots, stiffly cradled like corpses, giving no outward sign of activity.

Bogard stopped. Mia squeezed alongside it, crouching low.

Tables and cargo cubes had been shoved together to open up a fairly large area of floor. Within the loose ring formed, several robots moved in and out of patterns that resembled fighting in progress. They swung their limbs, kicked, ducked, jabbed, rushed and retreated—but none of them ever connected with a blow. Like a dance set to no rhythm, highly-choreographed, they weaved through the mock combat with machine precision.

"Bogard, what's happening?"

"I still cannot access the Resident Intelligence. I have no explanation."

Bogard started again, skirting the edge of the scene. Abruptly, two robots broke away from the fight and blocked its way.

"Halt," one demanded. "Stand and declare—"

In a single, fluid motion, Bogard brushed one robot into its companion and hurled them back into the dance. Mia saw several others move deftly to avoid them as they clattered across the floor.

At the next junction, Bogard hesitated again.

"They have divided," it said. "One went that direction—" it indicated a twisting path through a canyon of machine housings to the left "—two went this way." The right-hand trail led down a short flight of stairs to another service corridor. "Just a moment. I have com traffic which I presume is between our targets."

"Let me hear."

The receiver in her ear snapped sharply to life.

"—lost in the service section. We don't have an egress."

"Your orders were to stay off com until outside the facility."

"Fine, but we can't *get* outside the damn facility if we can't find a way *out!*"

"Stand by."

A few seconds later, a new voice came on.

"This is Platoon One. What's the problem?"

"Platoon One, this is Lemus. We got separated from the main body, we're in the service section—no egress. We lost Wollins, and the tinheads are dancing like crazies back here—"

"You stay off com from this point," Platoon One ordered. "You find a corridor marked 'EXD' and follow it without deviation. Do you copy?"

"Sure, Bok—"

"And stop using names on the com. No further communications will be accepted until we link up. Platoon One out."

The receiver went dead.

Bok? Lemus?

Mia indicated the service corridor. "Bogard, find them. Apprehend and subdue. Can you locate that corridor?"

"Yes." It took only a moment for Bogard to weigh the command against its First Law imperative. "You will go after the remaining target?"

"I will. I will exercise extreme caution. We want them alive, Bogard."

"You risk injury."

"Personal prerogative, acceptable level of risk. They are dangerous."

personal prerogative, acceptable level of risk, they are dangerous, assignation of priority levels to establish response protocols as follows: assertion of personal prerogative indicates acceptance of possible harm in lieu of protections necessitated per First and Second Law parameters, access file Daventri, Mia, level of competence involving personal risk, assign acceptability algorithms to assess potential for failure under circumstances where injury is likely, experiential indicators sufficient, acceptable level of risk within personal prerogative parameters, alleviation of immediate requirements, applied against level of danger indicated by permitting target to escape, indicate accurate assessment of potentials, First and Second Law requirements shift locus then to hypothetical threats posed by failure to accept revised protocols, necessitate risk accommodation, temporary and contingent upon verification of status, Daventri Mia

Mia waited less than a second for Bogard to prioritize the instruction.

"I understand," it said. "You will indicate changed risk status."

"Yes."

It flowed down the stairs, into the service corridor, and disappeared.

Mia sighed, relieved. Bogard processed situations according to a complex set of risk protocols that allowed it to function more creatively than its more rigidly structured cousins, but she still expected it to be a Three Law purist when it had to allow a human to take a personal risk. This time it had to be assured that if she got into trouble she would call for help.

Pulse beating insistently in her ears, she entered the claustrophobic pathway. If these three had split up, then everything was not going as smoothly as they had probably planned.

The passage seemed to be a space between large ventilator funnels and bundles of communication threads—part of the ubiquitous Resident Intelligence system which supposedly oversaw all aspects of facility operation—and the bulkier conveyor system that transported all nonliving material throughout the complex.

She passed a skinny opening that led into the wider main passage, then came to a cluster of machine forms—spheres, boxes, conduit, braces—impossible to slip through. She backed up to the opening and eased through.

Across from her, the kitchen that served the entire complex ran the width of the space, from the wall of the main gallery to the outer shell. Bright, mirrored surfaces reflected color coding and the geometries of cookery, a fully automated food processing plant with only a few robots to supervise and troubleshoot the occasional problem. At the moment, nothing within the kitchen area moved. Mia spotted a robot, frozen in place before a flickering monitor.

In there . . .

She sprinted across the floor and dropped to one knee by the low wall that marked the kitchen's boundary. If the Resident Intelligence were functioning, she could have used it to track her target. But the com in her ear remained silent, a thick empty nonsound.

Mia glanced over the top of the wall, then scurried to the nearest access and around the edge. The air smelled of yeast and oil and warm flour. She crept along to the robot she had seen and looked up at the monitor it stared into.

Manifests scrolled over it, one after another, too fast for her to read, but she caught references to foodstuffs, medical supplies, and clothing, in enormous quantities. As she watched, the monitor went blank. Then the bright green words PLEASE WAIT appeared and a few seconds later, a request form for several lunch items filled the screen. The robot seemed to waver, then stepped back.

"—report now! We have people down!" broke in her ear. Mia winced, startled.

"This is a restricted area," the robot said, turning to face her. "Humans are not—"

A burst of gunfire ricochetted around them, staggering the robot. Mia spun away, but her right arm suddenly snapped back, taking her with it, knocking her to the floor. Two more impacts caught her in the right leg and ribs; the wind left her lungs painfully.

Is this when I should call for help . . . ?

She dragged herself across the floor with her uninjured arm till she came to a space beneath a food preparation table, and pulled herself under the metal expanse.

She touched her earpiece and reduced the volume of her link. She heard feet running toward her.

"Sir, this is a restricted area—" another drone began to say.

Mia craned her head and saw the base of a small transport drone. Then booted, human feet. The drone shifted to block the human and repeated its message.

Mia still held her pistol, limply, and managed to shift it to her left hand. She pushed herself close to the edge of the crawlspace, next to one of the support legs. She set the pistol down and took hold of the metal shaft.

"Back away!" the human ordered the drone.

The human bolted around the robot and started forward. Mia braced, then swung her legs out from beneath her cover. She caught him across the shins and he tumbled, arms spread wide, and slapped the floor.

She snatched her pistol and wriggled out, coming up on her knees, weapon leveled. Her right leg burned hideously, the muscle trembling. Black pinpoints seemed to pulse at the periphery of her vision.

The man also recovered, turning toward her with a short, black weapon cradled in both hands.

"Stop!" she shouted.

He brought his weapon up.

Mia fired. The bolt of energy smacked against his head, kicking him backward. His weapon rattled across the floor.

Mia slumped against the cabinet, her right arm a length of agony, each breath like the pinch of giant fingers. She felt clammy, and the bright black and silver pinpoints danced more frantically, growing in number.

"Ma'am, do you require assistance?"

The transport drone had rolled alongside her. She blinked at it, wondering at the slight panic she heard in its voice, and wondered why a drone would panic. Then she remembered that it was being run by the RI, which was positronic. But the RI was not responding, had gone offline for some reason. Was it back now, along with everything else that no longer made sense?

"Ma'am, do you require assistance?" the drone repeated.

"Yes, I—" She dropped her pistol and touched fingertips to her arm; they came away damp. She swallowed hard and looked at the bright red liquid on them. A chill scraped down her neck, across her back. When did that happen? She tried to catalogue her injuries, struggling for consciousness, but she kept forgetting where she started. Leg, ribs, arm, ribs, arm, leg ...

The renewed com chattered in her ear insistently.

"—ambulances right now! We've got at least twenty down! Get us priority—"

She touched the button, changing the channel.

"Bogard?"

"Yes, Mia?"

"Status."

"Both targets apprehended and subdued. Returning to your position."

"Good ... hurry ... I'm ..."

She had never passed out before, and it came as a surprise and a frustration and a peculiar anger that she was losing control so fast.

The transport robot asked again, "Ma'am, do you require assistance? Ma'am ... ?"

THREE

Derec heard the wailing of the injured even before he entered the tunnel to the main gallery. Mingled with the clinical noises of paramedics and ambulances, the controlled urgency of shouted orders and sirens, the sound cut through him, sharper than any cold wind, and he shuddered. As he emerged beneath the high arched ceiling, his two aides close at his heels, he saw bedlam and pain.

"Sir," a harried security guard challenged him, "this area is restricted. I—"

Derec held up his ID and the man stopped, blinking at it as if momentarily unable to recognize it.

"Oh. Phylaxis Group." He nodded, suddenly relieved. "You're expected. Let me . . ." He stepped back and spoke quietly into his comlink.

Derec did a slow survey of the scene. So many robots trampled and broken, frozen in place, or wandering about purposelessly, in advanced stages of positronic collapse, and human paramedics and security people shouting at them or pushing them out of the way. Derec felt a chill at the sight; these robots all should have been linked through the RI and if they were breaking down, then the RI must be having trouble. The only other robotic presence were the service drones—nonsentient automatons that did the grunt work for the emergency personnel. They did not even call them robots here. He wondered briefly if Bogard was still here, if it had survived, if it had functioned, if . . .

He turned to his team.

"Get to the mid-stage breakdowns first," he told the people with him. Only two specialists from the Group had accompanied him, Caro and Amson, his best field team. From the look of things, he wished he could have brought a dozen. But the Phylaxis Group's limited resources allowed only a small team; other specialists were too far away, in the Spacer districts at the periphery of D.C., working other situations. "Get them out of the arena. Find out where the stand-by niches are—I doubt any of these people will be using that room. Then tend to interaction and facilitation crises."

His people gave him quick nods and dispersed into the chaos.

"Hey, hold it," another voice intruded. A uniformed policeman strode up, one hand raised, the other touching the butt of his holstered stunner. He glared briefly at the first security guard, who was still on his comlink. "Who and what are you and what are you doing here?"

Derec extended his ID again. The officer studied it briefly. "Phylaxis Group. Great, we already have more medics than we need walking all over the evidence; now we get you people collecting tinheads."

Derec pocketed his ID. "Sorry if rendering assistance is such a burden for your forensics people. Maybe you'd even prefer leaving the dead and injured just where they fell till you finished? I'm sure only a few of them would expire before the evidence techs got all they wanted . . ."

The policeman's mouth tightened and he stepped toward Derec. Whatever he had intended to say, he changed his mind. "All right, point taken. You have clearance." He turned sharply and strode away.

"Thank you," Derec called after the retreating officer, who gave a negligent wave.

"Sir," the security guard said then. "Mil Jeffries is the floor supervisor. I'll have you taken to her." A drone approached, a nonpositronic escort unit, little more than a tall, spindle-like machine with a map programmed into it. "Just follow this one."

"Thanks."

Derec followed the drone along a narrow path between bodies that had not yet been picked up and small knots of people he assumed to be security—rigid, anger-frozen faces, quick conversations with each other or into coms, attitudes of arrested momentum, and, if Derec was not mistaken, embarrassment—and tried to get his mind around what he saw. It was clear that the bodies here had been trampled.

The largest knot of standing people occupied the raised platform toward which the drone led him. Everywhere the wounded and traumatized moaned and cried, a few shouting anxiously for help or an explanation or for the simple emotional need to scream at something. Whole sections of the huge floor contained the injured, stretched out and tended to by humans and a few medical support robots— again, nonpositronic units that lifted and carried and contained portable diagnostic units for the human techs. Most of these did not even look like robots in the Spacer sense, but rather were collections of boxes and spheres and

chunky assemblies mounted on treads or antigravity moti-
vators, following the humans around like obedient pets.
Derec saw frightened people shoving at them, crying or
cursing, unwilling in typical Earther fashion to be touched
by metal fingers. It was probably just as well no positronic
robots were here to try to help—only the specially programmed could cope with injured or dead humans, but here
they would be faced with the added confusion of humans
rejecting their help. First Law dictated that they aid the injured. Second Law said to obey humans. The conflict of
being ordered not to render aid would hit them hard; they
would not understand the nature of the fear and resentment.
Positronic breakdowns were sad, pathetic things to see. The
robots still functioning here clearly could not cope. The
lucky ones seemed already shut down. Derec's team moved
quickly among the traumatized robots, getting them out of
the way with the least damage possible. Some might be
salvaged but he was not optimistic.

Several robots stood around the collections of the dead,
mechanical bodies stiff, eyes dark, minds broken.

What about Bogard? he wondered. He could not find
that particular robot here. Perhaps it had already been removed from the gallery. It was not really his anymore—it
had been signed over to Special Service for active duty—
but Bogard remained Derec's creation and he could not help
but worry about it.

Derec looked away. The outer walls of the gallery bore
tall, blackened streaks from the explosions. On the subetheric broadcast, the blasts had seemed great enough to gouge
holes, but all that showed were the stains.

Derec's right foot slid sharply and he pinwheeled his
arms to keep balance. He looked down. On the floor was a

bright red smear leading from a puddle of blood. His stomach lurched sickeningly.

The drone led him up onto the platform and toward a small woman who stood in the midst of a cluster of people, talking rapidly and stabbing the air with her index and middle fingers.

"Supervisor Mil Jeffries, sir," the drone said, loudly enough to attract her attention. The woman glanced his way, frowning, then nodded and held up her hand to indicate that he wait.

Task completed, the unit moved away. Derec waited at the edge of the cluster and listened while Jeffries issued instructions. One by one and in pairs the people left to carry out their assigned tasks until only Derec remained. She looked at him, one eyebrow cocked dubiously.

"And?"

"I'm Derec Avery, from the Phylaxis Group."

"Those your people out there herding the braindeads away?"

"Yes."

"Good. About time. I only have two people on staff who know anything about traumatized tinheads, and right now they're busy with the RI ... which is where I need you, if that's what you're wondering."

"The Resident Intelligence ... ?"

"Resident Idiot, you mean." She snorted derisively, then gestured for him to follow. "Come on. Avery? You're supposed to be the expert on positronics?"

"One of—"

"Fine. Come with me."

Jeffries, despite being a good head shorter, walked away fast enough to make Derec struggle to keep up. He glanced over at the huddle around the diplomats and representatives. Ambulances stood open, receiving bodybags and injured. Blood slicked a large area. A dozen or so people were gathered off to one side, the quality of their clothes announcing their importance. A few seemed nervous and several were deathly pale, but none looked hurt.

Derec and Jeffries came to the far end of the platform, descended the steps shoved against it, and the supervisor led the way through an innocuous door labeled PRIVATE. A few meters within they mounted a narrow stair leading up.

"I was worried that you might bring some more robots," Jeffries said. "We're having trouble enough with the mere presence of them right now."

"We don't have any," Derec replied. She gave him a look. "Besides the Spacer districts, the embassies, and here, they *are* illegal on Earth."

Jeffries nodded. "Hm. Do you have any idea what happened here?"

"I saw the replay on subetheric on the way over."

"Probably edited."

"How many—I mean, who—?"

"Estimates are that eighteen people died in the shooting, but we have at least thirty wounded, maybe a hundred dead or injured in the panic—trampled, kicked, that sort of thing," Jeffries explained. "All those you saw down there, that's what happened to them, except for a half dozen or so that got hit by stray blaster fire from the security teams on the platform. The Auroran ambassador is dead, along with half her staff, plus the Aurorans from the embassy here." She stopped at the top of the steps and looked at him. "Senator Eliton, too."

Derec opened his mouth to say something. But then he saw a brief glimmer of pain in Jeffries' eyes, a glimpse of what lay beyond the brusque jobber she had shown him till then, and closed his mouth. He made himself nod. Jeffries' walls came up again, and she continued up the stairs to an unmarked door.

On the other side was a broad office pressed against a strip of window that overlooked the gallery. Desks, consoles, and people formed a loose maze between the window and a wall of monitors that stretched the length of the room.

"From here," Jeffries said, "we watch the RI run Union Station. Normally, anyway. Today we watched it go out to play while people died."

Everyone in the room stopped to look at Jeffries, then at Derec. He felt the bitterness in her voice, saw it reflected in all the staff faces. No robots were present, only people trying to cope.

"Would you explain that to me?"

"Kedder," Jeffries said.

Two people sat before the sprawling main interface console in the center of the room. One of them, a tall, slim man with short reddish hair, stood and cleared his throat.

"I, uh—"

"Kedder, this is the man from Phylaxis," Jeffries went on. "He's here to show us how to talk to our robots."

Derec went to the console and extended his hand. "Derec Avery."

"Tathis Kedder."

"I have floor work to do," Jeffries announced. "You need me, find me."

With that, she pivoted on her toes and left the room.

Derec waited several seconds. People returned to what they had been doing. "All right, what happened?" he asked Kedder quietly.

"Well . . ." Kedder gazed down at the console as if trying to remember what to do with it.

The other man at the board started tapping keys deftly. The row of screens at the top of the console cleared to milky white, then new images winked into place.

Kedder cleared his throat and pointed. "These are the, uh, primary monitor views leading up to the arrival of Senator Eliton."

"What the RI saw?" Derec asked.

"Uh-huh."

Robots moved quickly among the prep people who established the boundaries for spectators and ushered the public into their assigned areas. Quickly, the space filled. Then the first wave of dignitaries arrived. Derec checked the elapsed time: the sequence moved at roughly twice normal speed. The platform became crowded, security robots followed humans around, guaranteeing free access from the main entrance to the platform, accompanying more dignitaries in, herding the throngs of people. Eliton's entourage came in, and Derec's throat tightened at the sight of Bogard. So it *had* been here.

But what went wrong? he wondered.

"Now," Kedder said, "let's slow it back down to normal speed. Watch the audience."

The swift efficiency of the free-floating staff and security abruptly shifted to a more human pace. Derec looked from screen to screen, each displaying a different view across the gallery. The crowds bobbed and shuffled as if adrift on water. Then something changed. Derec blinked and leaned closer. It had looked as if a section of the recording had been cut out, one moment spliced to another across the gap left by the missing segment. A subtle jump, heads jerking slightly, and then—

"See?" Kedder asked.

"I'm not—I saw something, but—"

"Look," the other operator said sharply. The images backed up, across the gap, and then ran forward again. He rose out of his chair and touched a screen. "Watch this person."

As Derec watched, the gap came, and the person vanished.

"What the—"

"It gets better," Kedder said. "Or worse, depending . . . watch this screen."

Kedder indicated the middle view which showed the arched tunnel. After several seconds, a crowd of people emerged, marching, boots flashing, black uniforms bulging with armor and adorned by insignia Derec did not recognize.

The other screens changed then. They showed a combination of corridors and alphanumerics. The main gallery was gone, replaced by what appeared to be a military complex. Uniformed figures hurried past, numbers shifted.

"From this point," Kedder said, "we got nothing through the RI that related in any way to what we could see happening down on the floor. While people—while the attack happened, this was all the RI showed. We couldn't get it to reset, we couldn't get it to tell us what was happening. It wasn't responding to any command. *Nothing.*"

"And now?" Derec asked.

"Now it seems to be in positronic collapse."

"All the security—"

"It ran the whole thing. For several minutes before the attack, it was issuing directions for security teams to respond to small crises that we later learned never happened. When the shooting started, most of the security was outside the gallery and all the exits were sealed. We couldn't get the manual overrides to work until it was all over. No data came in, nothing went out, it was as if the entire station had been isolated from all other external systems."

"Which may be just as well," Kedder's coworker said. "If it was having a breakdown, it might have carried over to externals. We might still be waiting for medical and police support."

"But I saw the assault on subetheric."

"Whatever this problem is," Kedder said, "it didn't affect the media nodes the newsnet people brought in that stayed unlinked to the RI. They weren't supposed to do that—everything was supposed to be channeled through the RI for security reasons—but a few always slip unregulated eyes in. Anyway, independent data fed out unimpeded. Only the RI was . . . diverted."

"And all the security com . . . ?"

"Was being routed through the RI."

Derec stared at the two technicians. "This is impossible."

Kedder looked embarrassed; the other man shrugged.

"What is this it was experiencing?" Derec asked, waving at the screens. "Looks like a simulation."

"A game," the other man said. "Old strategy stuff. It has a number of them in its accessory buffers. Running all the facilities doesn't take up enough of its capacity, so it plays games. It has a terrific chess approach." He pointed to the screen. "*This* one is called *Coup.*"

"How did it overwhelm the positronic pathways?"

"Beats me, gato."

Kedder frowned at his partner, then said, "Oh, I'm sorry. Mr. Avery, this is Joler Hammis."

Derec nodded briefly.

"Sorry for being rude," Hammis said. "It's been that kind of a day."

"Forget it. So you're running everything manually now?"

"Partly," Hammis said. "We've got a hard programmed back-up helping. It took time to bypass all the systems the RI has—had—direct control of. A few things are run by imbedded hardware and none of that seemed affected at all. There are still functions we can't operate now, like traffic control. All shuttle service has been suspended for the time being, but we have to get that back on-line soon—"

"All right, we can take care of that much," Derec said. "Are the external comlines for the RI open?"

"No, but it's not a problem," Kedder said uncertainly. "Right now it's in no condition to send or receive—"

"Doesn't matter. Is there a place I can work? And patch me into that com system."

While Kedder and Hammis set up a station for him, Derec ran the images back and forth on the screens. It made no sense. It looked almost as though an invasive program had taken over the Resident Intelligence's entire sensory network and fed it false input. But the virtue of positronic RIs made such an invasion impossible. Unlike standard, nonsentient computer systems, positronic brains were not solely dependent on simple digital data input to set priorities. Rather, positronic brains used pre-established, unamendable priorities—the Three Laws, among others—to determine the value of sensory input. They depended on reality as a basis for judgment, reality as perceived through direct sense experience, vetted by hardwired expectations. Data, like that which computer and datum systems used and which told them how to interpret reality, was used only as a secondary reference, without the ability to interfere with the sense-priority nature of the positronic matrix. In this way, the positronic brain was occasionally superior to the human brain—it could not hallucinate, could not delude itself by referencing its own store of experience in isolation from base reality or privileging its experience to supersede its predetermined priorities. In short, a positronic brain could not be subverted. If conflicting information bombarded it to the point where its sense-priority makeup became compromised, collapse occurred. It simply failed.

But this . . .

"Here, Mr. Avery," Kedder said.

"Derec, please." He looked over the console they had cleared for him. "Good. What I'm going to do is link to the RI at Phylaxis and start load-sharing. Then I'm going to dump the memory buffers of the station RI into our systems so we can start analyzing what happened."

Kedder frowned, glancing over his shoulder. "You can replace our RI with your own?"

"Sort of. It's a temporary arrangement and not nearly as efficient, but it should get all your systems back up and running."

"Well, I suppose that's all right."

Derec hesitated. "Why wouldn't it be?"

"Just that . . . well, a lot of people blame the RI for what happened—a lot of people *here*. I'm just not sure how they'd feel about going back to one—"

"Look. As I understand it, you need one to operate efficiently. You can't run the station without one."

"Mainly flight control—"

"Fine. Then let me get this set up. Switching to a hard program system will be a lot easier with an RI in place facilitating the changes. Either way, this is necessary."

"I see that, Mr.—uh, Derec. *I* don't have a problem with it, but—"

"Let me worry about the backlash. I'm used to it."

Kedder nodded.

"By the way," Drec said, "what did the robots on the floor do when the shooting started?"

"I don't know. Wandered around, got knocked down by the mob. Nothing useful. See, they're all tied directly to the RI. More efficient to coordinate the entire robotic staff through a central unit—"

"So when the RI started losing touch—"

"It affected the mobile units."

"But their own programming should've kicked them out of the RI's matrix, let them function independently."

Kedder shook his head, a sour expression on his face. "No, they were all deadswitch linked to the RI. Management wanted to be able to shut down all of them from one location. It was easier to simply slave them all to the RI rather than bypass the Three Laws with one single command."

"Slaved through ... that would've required patching their sensory modules through the RI sensory net."

"Exactly."

Derec sighed heavily. "In the name of fear and efficiency." He shook himself. "All right, one problem at a time. Have I got direct access to your board from here?"

"Yes. Here and here ..."

Derec let Kedder guide him through the basic arrangement until he understood how the systems were integrated, then made a call to Group.

"Rana, this is Derec. We need Thales to sub for the RI here. Let me feed you the parameters."

"Excuse me," Kedder said and walked away to another console.

"Union Station?" Rana asked.

"Yes."

"What a mess. Who's dead?"

"All the wrong people. Humadros and Eliton especially."

"Oh, hell."

"Spoken with true precision," Derec said sarcastically. "I want a memory dump set up, too—we need to download the RI for study. Something really nasty happened here and I don't understand how it was doable. We have a subverted RI."

"It didn't collapse?"

"Not till it came back to reality and saw what had happened."

"If Eliton's dead—"

"I haven't seen Bogard yet. I don't know what happened. One crisis at a time for now."

"All right. I'm setting up the patches now. Give me the transfer codes."

Derec worked steadily, absorbed in the details of the construct for several minutes. When he leaned back to stretch, he noticed people watching him, several wearing expressions of disapproval. He looked away, out the windows to the floor below.

Out in the gallery, maintenance units were cleaning up the blood, police techs were gathering evidence, and medical techs were collecting samples. Ambulances still crowded the platform, but most of the bodies had been taken away.

On the opposite side of the gallery, he saw a large robot emerge from one of the service accesses, carrying a woman in its arms, which had unfolded like a sling around her; it was followed by two transport drones laden with more bodies. Derec stood and went to the window.

"Bogard . . ." he whispered.

FOUR

Ariel Burgess gazed at the tri-D image projected above her desk, a vague dread displacing the concern she knew she should feel. The robot hovering in the field lacked an arm and both legs, and its head had been crushed as if a huge foot had stomped down on it as it lay on the ground. Various symbols covered its scuffed, dark blue body, most of them indecipherable yet threatening. The one Ariel *did* recognize shone bright white in the center of the robot's upper torso, a lemniscate crossed by an arrow at an upward angle: the sign of the Managins. The unit had been attacked by members of the Order for the Supremacy of Man Again.

"I'm not familiar with this model," Ariel said.

"We just began importing them last month," the man across from her said. "Porter model DP-8."

"A domestic."

"Exactly so."

Ariel remembered the designation, but had not seen one till now. She had been busy with the preparations for the

Humadros-Eliton Conference and had skipped several inspections, so she was not surprised. She studied what remained of the head. "Do you have a catalogue image of this, Mr. Udal?"

"Um . . . yes, I think so . . ." He fumbled in his jacket pocket for a moment, clearly dismayed at her request. He fished out a disk and slipped it into her desk viewer. "This is the fourth act of vandalism in less than two weeks. Customers have stopped coming into the showroom, sales have dropped off precipitously, and now my staff is talking about leaving. They need the jobs, but they're afraid."

"You've contacted the police?" Ariel asked, knowing the answer already. The catalogue image appeared in the air alongside the first view. It showed a neat, smooth-bodied robot with a pleasantly-smiling approximation of a human face. Ariel felt a cold lump suddenly form behind her breastbone.

"Of course. The first time, a couple of inspectors came by, took statements. The second time, only one of them showed up. Same questions, same answers. The third instance, a uniformed patrol came, and this time, no one did." He shrugged elaborately. "Earthers. They don't care."

"This is a humaniform."

Udal frowned more deeply. "Well, of course. Domestics are always given a degree of–"

"You *are* aware of the guidelines concerning humaniforms on Earth?"

"It's not like they're actually *robots*. Just drones. Without positronics–"

"The guidelines are clear about drones, too."

"Well–"

"Terrans react poorly to robots that look too human. To

any machine that appears to mimic human life. They find it offensive."

"But these have sold quite well! Our advance orders—"

"It should not have been in your catalogue at *all*, Mr. Udal." Ariel shook her head and sighed. "I've been a little lapse in my rounds, Mr. Udal, but you should have registered this with my office. I would have told you it would not have been allowed for import. I'm surprised you got it past Customs." She looked at him. "How *did* you get it past Customs?"

"They didn't challenge," Udal said quickly. "Look, if my customers want something, who am I to argue with them? Terrans ought to know their own laws, they certainly ought to know their own prejudices. These units were ordered by Terrans!"

"A certain class of Terran, yes, I'm sure. But those people are also looked upon with suspicion by the average Earther. Wealthy clientele will buy something like this as much to insult what they perceive as lower class citizens as to have the benefit of a state-of-the-art machine. There are clandestine shops where you can buy a new body for a standard drone and turn it into a humaniform. I assure you the people vandalizing your merchandise are not of the same sort as those buying it."

Udal winced, his eyes dancing briefly, avoiding contact with her. "Earthers!" he repeated, making the word sound vile. "Why don't we have these sorts of problems elsewhere?"

Ariel bit back a response regarding the prejudices of Spacers. It would do no good here, dealing with this problem. Udal would go over her head, disregard her advice, and only complicate an already awkward situation. She covered her reaction by studying the image of the drone. It did not look very dronelike. The brain casing was certainly large enough for a positronic brain.

"This is a retrofit, isn't it?" she asked suddenly. "An older model . . ." She tapped commands on her terminal and another projection opened alongside the catalogue image. The system began looking for a match. In a few seconds, the kaleidoscope of robot types stopped on one that could easily be the twin of the drone. "A DP-P-7. I thought it looked familiar. These are expressly forbidden here."

"It's not the same model, I assure you—"

"Any Terran with a catalogue and no real understanding of what they're seeing wouldn't understand the difference. Were any other models damaged in this attack?"

Udal looked to one side. "No."

"Your warehouse is in the Convention Center District, isn't it? I think a visit from my staff is in order." Ariel narrowed her eyes. "Mr. Udal, if I find out that you're importing through the black market—"

"You're supposed to be our *advocate* here!" Udal shot back. "I am a legitimate dealer with a legitimate grievance. The local authorities don't seem particularly interested and I have come to *you* as a fellow Auroran."

"I sympathize, Mr. Udal, but what do want me to do?"

Udal relaxed and smiled, his teeth brilliant in their Auroran perfection. The change was startling. "I understand you will be sitting in on the upcoming trade talks Senator Clar Eliton is chairing. I'm told Ambassador Galiel Humadros herself is coming. If you could bring it to their attention that these fanatic assaults on property have the potential to derail any progress they might achieve, it would help a great deal. Frankly, any more of these vandalisms and I may

MIRAGE

have to pull up stakes and go home. My insurance premiums are high enough as it is, but—"

"I'm flattered that you think so highly of my position here, but I'm only the commerce liaison for the embassy. My function is purely advisory—"

"Then by all means, advise. Besides, you underestimate your potential. You're also an attaché from the Calvin Institute, and the Calvin Institute is respected even by the Earthers. A word from you—"

Ariel's com beeped. "Excuse me, Mr. Udal." She touched the contact. "Yes?"

"Ariel, you better check the subetheric," Ariel's aide, Hofton, said.

"In a few minutes—"

"Now."

Annoyed, Ariel gave Udal an apologetic shrug and turned on her set. Across the room, an image formed a meter or so out from the wall projector.

The scene confused her for a moment. Then she recognized Union Station, except . . . there were bodies on the floor, people huddled here and there, red stains on the platform where the reception for Ambassador Humadros was to take place . . .

Udal sucked in his breath sharply. "Is there sound?"

Ariel fumbled for the controls.

"—lice have informed us that so far none of the perpetrators have been apprehended," a reporter was saying. "The death toll so far is ten, including Senator Clar Eliton and members of his staff. Repeated requests for explanations on how weapons got past the security systems have so far received no satisfactory answers. I repeat: Senator Clar Eliton and the Auroran Ambassador Galiel Humadros have been murdered, as well as several members of their respective staffs, in an assault by a number of armed assailants who have all managed to escape. None of the security measures supposedly in place operated, either afterward or apparently before the assault."

"They didn't . . . I . . . have to make some calls . . ." Udal plucked his recording from Ariel's desk player and headed for the door. "Thank you for your time, Ms. Burgess. I'll let you know . . ."

"Mr. Udal."

He stopped and looked at her, face open with shock.

"Warehouse those drones until we can clear this up. I don't want to see any more of these on the open market."

Udal sighed, exasperated, but nodded. He glanced at the subetheric again.

She watched him hurry out the door, his face locked in an expression that she thought must mirror her own. She looked back at the subetheric broadcast, at the aftermath of the slaughter.

"Here again is a replay of the scene that took place not fifteen minutes ago in the main gallery of Union Station."

Ariel turned the sound down and touched the com. "Hofton, get me Setaris at the embassy, soon as possible."

She watched the blackclad assailants charge from the midst of the spectators, firing wildly, people dropping—terrified, wounded, and killed—unable to accept the actuality of it. This had to be a drama, a hoax, a piece of fiction, not a news report. History contained accounts of such acts, but they never happened anymore.

"Ariel," Hofton's voice intruded. "Ambassador Setaris."

Ariel touched another button and the space above her desk projector filled with the head and shoulders of a woman with severe green eyes and silver-white hair.

"Ariel?"

"You've seen?"

"Yes, a few minutes ago. Things are a bit tense around here." Setaris hesitated, her face briefly yielding to sorrow. "Lys is dead, I think, and Daril."

Her deputies, two thirds of the principle Auroran ambassadorial representation on Earth. Ariel tried to imagine how Setaris felt. She and Lys had been lovers once . . .

"Who—?" Ariel started to ask.

"We haven't a clue. As usual, the TBI is being less than informative. Most of what we know has come from the same source as everyone else has—the media. I'm glad you called, though. There will be a panic from the business community. I expect flight, abandonment. If there is anything you can do to calm them down—"

"Calm them *down!* You're joking!"

"I'm perfectly serious. We can't have a wholesale exodus of the very people this effort was supposed to help. If they leave, then the worst factions on Earth will have won, no matter who is responsible for this atrocity. We might never regain a toehold if we turn our backs on them now."

"Given your sympathies, would you really consider that such a loss?"

"I'm not prepared to go into that with you *now*, Ariel," Setaris warned. "Yes, I would. More than you might expect me to acknowledge."

Ariel suppressed a sharp response and forced herself to think it through. "What should I tell them?"

"That you, for one, aren't leaving and that the Calvin Institute intends to work as closely as possible with Terran authorities to find out who is responsible. For all we know, this is just the random act of a bunch of social frustrates."

"Earth has plenty of those. But—"

"Whatever the truth may be, Ariel, our present reality is that Humadros's mission cannot fail. Especially not now. If we allow ourselves to be frightened away and give up on any future dealings with Earth, we may very well condemn ourselves to a slow death, assuming we escape a war."

Ariel felt herself flinch. "I always suspected you agreed with me, but I never thought I'd hear you say so."

"We can debate the extent of our mutual perspective at another time. For the moment, can I count on your support?"

"Of course."

"Good."

"*Is* Humadros dead? Is it confirmed?"

"Yes. And her staff. And Eliton. I don't know which bothers me more, Humadros or Eliton. He was the best ally we had." Setaris frowned thoughtfully. "What about his vice senator, Taprin? You know him, don't you?"

"Yes, I know Jonis."

"How does he stand regarding Eliton's policies?"

"He's never been the firebrand Eliton is—was—but they were in the same file on the subject."

"Talk to him if you can, see what his response is going to be. We need information as much if not more than action, Ariel."

"I'll do what I can, Ambassador. Call me if—well, call me."

Setaris nodded, smiling hollowly. The image winked out.

Ariel glanced back at the subetheric 'cast, then turned it off. They would be replaying that for the next several days at least; she could get a copy of the complete report at any time.

This is impossible, she thought. Union Station was operated by a positronic resident intelligence, the first permitted to operate openly on Earth in decades. It was a showpiece, in fact, set up and licensed as a demonstration of the potential benefits of positronics for Earth. The First Law imperative would have made it impossible for the RI to allow anyone in with a weapon that did not have prior clearance. It would not allow the RI to permit this sort of terrorist act to be carried out—the RI should have used the mobile robots as a means to disarm, block, or otherwise interrupt the attempt.

Everything Ariel knew about positronics and robotics—which was not inconsiderable—told her that what had just happened could never have occurred. Unless the RI had been modified in some way to subvert those safeguards . . .

"Damn you, Derec," she muttered aloud. "You finally did it."

No Spacer would attempt to tamper with the Three Laws, none that she knew. But Derec Avery was another matter. She had not seen him since their last argument—a bitter, irrational exchange during which both had said hurtful, unretractable things—which had ended years of friendship and occasional passion. Derec had wanted to stretch the Three Laws, see how far they could be pushed, play with the strict, almost sacred parameters of robotic construction, and she had walked away, unable to accept even the most reasonable of his points. It hurt even more to think that she had been right and he had not listened.

She stabbed her com. "Hofton. We have a lot of work to do. See if you can trace Vice Senator Taprin and connect us. I need to talk to him ASAP. Then get me the list of on-planet Auroran businesses, then clear the com."

"Right away. Anything else?"

"Yes. Send a message to Derec Avery at the Phylaxis Group. Six words. 'I see you got your wish.' "

"Sign it?"

"No. I think he'll know where it came from."

FIVE

The floor of the main gallery had been cleared of people and blood by the time Derec finished with the RI. He looked out the window, a cup of coffee in hand, at the cavernous expanse, all gleaming faux marble and granite, the essence of a past era when travel was as much ritual as necessity. He had stood in more spectacular port facilities, architectures more elegant and impressive than Union Station D.C., but none that manifested history and significance to the same degree. The place seemed mythic, and its lines resonated with heritage.

A few security people followed forensic units that sniffed and searched for minute bits of potential evidence, but Derec doubted anything further could be found to aid them. This was the final dotted i and crossed t of the physical investigation.

Bogard and the woman it had been carrying were long gone. Derec's work here had allowed no time for him to check on the robot before now. Making the operational transfer from the corrupted RI to the Phylaxis RI had taken hours of close attention. Bogard became an afterthought.

Now, with Bogard in mind and his work completed, with only minor details to vett, Derec had accessed a casualty list a short while ago. He had been relieved to see Ariel Burgess's name absent. She had not been here with the others from the embassy. Given what he had seen on the 'casts, he was amazed *more* people were not dead. The assault had been fast and vicious and apparently indiscriminate beyond the assassinations of Humadros and Eliton.

A *beep* drew him back to the board. Kedder leaned across it and pressed a contact. "The air scrubbers are back online and . . . yes, the biomonitors in food service are up, too. Looks like your surrogate is in complete control."

Derec followed a tree of diagnostic glyphs down a screen. "Could you check on the delay factor through the sensory net? It shouldn't be more than a few thousand nanoseconds, but—"

"Right." Kedder unfolded from the chair and strode toward the master console.

Derec glanced at another screen and saw that the memory dump was about finished. He pressed the com. "Rana?"

"Here."

"We show a completed core transfer on our end. What about—"

"Who is Derec Avery?" a new voice demanded.

Derec looked up and saw two men standing at the main console, staring down at Kedder, who gestured at Derec. By the time they stopped before him, Derec recognized them for government security.

"Mr. Avery?" the shorter of the pair asked. His face had the jowly look of late middle-aged worry. He wore his short hair in a herringbone weave that seemed to float a few millimeters above his scalp.

"Yes."

"I'm Agent Cupra, Special Service. This is Agent Gambel. I understand you're here on behalf of the Phylaxis Group?"

"That's right."

Agent Cupra extended a disk to him. "This relieves you of all responsibility and authority for any dealings with the Union Station RI or related systems and bars you from any official inquiries. It also requires you to turn over to us any documentation, recordings, or reports generated since the events precipitating your involvement."

"What? But—"

"Special Service is assuming all investigative privileges and confiscating all relevant data."

Derec slipped the disk into a slot on the board and scanned the document that came up on one of the small auxiliary screens. The seal of the Service appeared, followed by paragraphs of dense legalese which basically verified what these agents were telling him.

"This is highly irregular. Phylaxis has an arrangement with the government concerning any and all outside spec problems with positronics. This part of the investigation *is* our responsibility."

"Not in this instance. You'll find the documentation in order."

Derec hesitated, staring at the disk in his hand.

"Whose word will you take, Mr. Avery?" Agent Gambel asked softly. "We assure you, this is all in order. Feel free to verify it with whomever you wish, but we *do* have the authority to do this and we *will* have it done now."

"What about the surrogate? It's our RI, we have to monitor it."

Agent Cupra frowned slightly, then shrugged. "That's only to continue operations of Union Station, correct? We have no interest in that."

Derec pocketed the disk. "I *will* check on this."

"Your privilege, certainly," Agent Gambel said. "Now if you don't mind?"

Derec leaned on the board and touched the com button, breaking contact. "Fine. If you'll come around here, I'll show you what we've set up so far."

"You haven't seen any of the buffer files of the RI?" Agent Cupra asked.

"No, only the playbacks from the video feeds. Do you have something to contain the RI matrix?"

"We'll give you an address," Cupra replied. He smiled briefly, insincerely. "Let's get to work, shall we?"

Derec wandered across the now spotless floor of the main gallery, his footsteps ringing distantly around the immense space. Agents Cupra and Gambel had everything, including the transferred matrix from Phylaxis—Kedder had let it out that he had downloaded a copy for study. Derec could not shake the feeling that he had been betrayed. He had taken the time to make a few calls to the people in government involved with his charter—mainly Senator Eliton's committee on machine intelligence—and they had either expressed ignorance of what was going on or confirmed the Special Service authorization. He might have continued badgering higher-ups, but he doubted it would change anything today; the one man in government who could have made the most difference had been killed. Derec doubted Vice Senator Taprin carried the same weight with the necessary people.

No one in the control room had been at ease with the agents. Joler Hammis had been openly hostile. They did not have the familiarity with these systems that they claimed, but they never hesitated to use the people around them. Poor Kedder ended up redoing most of what he and Derec had already gone over. Kedder kept giving Derec apologetic looks. Hammis stayed for a time, then shook his head and left. Everyone moved cautiously, ever-aware of the agents' presence, as if a wrong gesture might invite terrible consequences. When Derec's part was finished, they showed him the door. He felt numb.

Looking around, it was difficult to imagine that this place had been the stage for the slaughter he had seen. The floor shone now, polished, ready for new traffic, though when normal flow might resume he had no idea. Shuttle traffic had finally, after hours of delay, been rerouted to other ports.

What was the point . . . ? he wondered hollowly.

He stopped in the middle of the gallery and turned slowly, gazing across the unoccupied expanse. It was rare to see so much room on Earth unpeopled. Everywhere in the warrens and metal caverns, people crowded each other. Standing here seemed a luxury for the moment, a pleasantly eerie feeling, a *prescé vu*, different from "outside," different from standing in a similar place on a Spacer world where crowding was a bad dream and an incomprehensible myth.

He saw no robots now. Union Station had been a robot-saturated environ, unique on Earth. They had provided comfort and security for the offworld travelers that came through constantly, created a familiar environment for Spacer visitors, and facilitated the services of the RI. It had been a showpiece and a diplomatic necessity, something for the proponents of robots on Earth to hold up as an example of how it might be. To see none here now made it stranger yet.

Derec continued to the exit, down the empty tunnel, and out onto the broad apron. A few personal transports still occupied the cordoned-off space. Beyond, the boulevard ran by, and across from that the express strips started. The few people riding past gave the Union Station façade uncomprehending stares, as if the place had suddenly become something other than it had always been, revealing a shocking reality long hidden.

He climbed into his vehicle and closed his eyes. Weariness, disbelief, and stress combined to fog his mind. He gave himself a few minutes before engaging the drive and pulling onto the boulevard.

The com light winked at him. He pressed the contact.

"Derec."

"This is Rana, Derec. *What* is going on?"

"You heard, didn't you? Special Service is assuming control of the investigation—"

"I heard, but it doesn't make any sense. I just got an official request to turn over any and all documents and copies of the RI, with an address to forward it. What is this? They don't know how to handle this kind of thing. They'd have to hand it over to us anyway."

"I doubt they're going to 'handle it.' I think they'll just sit on it, conduct their investigation their way, and then leave the RI matrix as an unopened file. They're covering themselves. A major miscalculation happened here today and, since it's their job to make sure this kind of thing doesn't happen, it's only reasonable that they don't want to compound their embarrassment."

"Reasonable? People are dead and they're worried about reputations?"

Derec did not know what to tell her. It made sense to him, he grasped the kind of venality in play here. So, for that matter, did Rana, given five minutes' reflection, but comprehension did not make it any more acceptable.

"It's out of our hands," he said. "Comply with the request. I'll be there shortly. I have another stop to make first."

"Already done. Do we continue surrogate monitor for Union Station? Thales is already online."

"Yes, we do."

"Okay. How long before you get back here?"

"I don't know. I'm going to check the med facilities. Bogard was on site during the massacre."

"Our Bogard?"

"The very same. I want to find it and check it over. I'll let you know. Oh, and wake up that lawyer we have on retainer and find out if there's anything we can do to get around this injunction. We're supposed to have a contract, and I'm really uncomfortable having amateurs shut me out of it."

"This is Special Service, though–" Rana began.

"I don't care if it's the second coming of Susan Calvin. A contract is a contract, and Special Service has no roboticists."

He could practically hear the grin on Rana's face as she said she would tend to it. The link closed and Derec touched the contact again.

"Location," he ordered the onboard computer. "Emergency medical facilities, this district. List."

As he pulled into the garage of the fourth medical facility, Derec felt a chill of success. Several black vehicles occupied spaces near the entrance. A man and woman in dark clothes lounged by the doors, watching the lot.

Derec approached the entrance and the man stepped forward to block his path. Derec swallowed dryly and displayed his ID.

"Oh, good," the agent said. "Phylaxis. Mr. Avery? I'm Agent Sathen, Special Service. The robot is inside. We can't get it to move, maybe you can do something."

"Um . . . has it caused any problems?"

"Other than scaring the staff, no." The man grinned. "Come on, I'll show you."

Slightly puzzled, Derec followed the agent through the wide main doors into the brightly-lit reception area. The air smelled of disinfectant, a piquant odor universal to hospitals, even on Spacer worlds. People rushed about intently amid a constant babble of com chatter and urgently-spoken instructions. At the nurses' station, a woman looked up, frowning at Derec, then nodded at the agent.

"It came in with Agent Daventri five hours ago," Agent Sathen explained as he led the way past open doors to examination rooms and patient chambers. "Then it took a position just inside her room and refused to leave."

"Why here and not Reed Hospital with all the other wounded?"

The agent shrugged. "Our dispatcher sent her here. It *is* closer than Reed, and with the robot . . ."

"I see. Did the robot give an explanation?"

"Says it's here to protect Agent Daventri. We can't convince it that she's safe."

"First Law obsessing."

"It's what?"

"Apparently, it has locked on defending Agent—Daventri, is it? —defending Agent Daventri as its primary imperative. Unless you can present it with another First Law condition that would override this one, it won't leave until it knows she's safe."

"Safe from what?"

Derec gave him a shrug.

"Robots," the agent said in disgust. "Well, I'm surprised this one is still functioning after what happened today. I saw a lot of braindead robots after the incident. This one was supposed to protect Senator Eliton and it failed. Aren't they supposed to shut down after something like that?"

"It depends. A positronic brain doesn't have the same capacities as a human brain, but in many ways it's just as complex."

"Uh-huh. Here it is." The man stopped before a closed door and knocked. "Bogard, this is Agent Sathen. I'm coming in. I have someone with me."

"Enter," came a firm voice from the other side of the door.

Sathen gave Derec a crooked smile. "First couple of us that walked in without identifying ourselves, Bogard tranked."

"Were you armed?"

"Yes. After that, we got it to modify its defense protocols."

Inside, Derec saw first the patient bed and the array of biological support gathered around it. Looking small in the midst of the masses of equipment lay a woman with sickly-pale skin and short, dark hair.

"She's still in rehab coma," Agent Sathen said.

"How bad?"

"Two holes in her right leg, one in her arm, a lot of bruises. A broken rib. Mainly they're worried about shock." He turned away from the bed. "And this is Bogard."

The robot stood against the wall, in a position to watch the patient and the door and within easy reach of both. It towered over the two men by nearly half a meter. Derec noticed that its hands showed six fingers. Through any one of them it could deliver a fast-working tranquilizer to a bare patch of skin. The white line of its optical array seemed to pulse at them.

"Hello, Derec," it said.

"Bogard, hello. I'm told you refuse to leave Agent Daventri."

"That is correct, Derec."

"Explain."

"I have been given specific instructions to safeguard Agent Daventri until such time as she releases me to return to initial priorities."

"Agent Daventri gave you those instructions?"

"Yes, Derec."

"Are you aware that she is presently out of danger but incommunicado?"

"Yes, Derec. However, I am instructed to maintain watch until released."

"What were the circumstances of these instructions?"

"Agent Daventri commanded me to pursue and apprehend two subjects involved in the assassin—assassin—assass—"

"Reset and continue."

Bogard paused for a moment, then proceeded. "Agent Daventri left me to pursue a third subject. I fulfilled her instructions by locating and tranquilizing the targets. When I brought the two subjects back to find her, she had been injured during a confrontation with her subject. I experienced a dilemma. Protocol dictated that under instruction to apprehend I must secure and deliver subjects to proper authority. However, Agent Daventri's injuries indicated immediate need to bring her to proper care. She instructed me to commandeer transport drones to carry the subjects, to personally bring her to proper care, and to guarantee her safety in the event that she should lose consciousness. I procured the transports and picked up Agent Daventri. She then fell unconscious. I will not leave her until she gives further instruction."

"Touching," Sathen said cynically. "You're Service property, Bogard. Your presence is required at headquarters for debriefing."

Derec glared at the agent. "If you please." Sathen gave him a surly look and walked away. Derec turned to Bogard. "Alpha-Zed override. Command sequence—"

"Rejected."

Derec blinked. "Explain."

"Specific instructions take precedence over all secondary protocols."

"I see . . . very well, Bogard. Continue according to instruction."

"What?" Sathen grabbed his shoulder. "We need this tinhead for interrogation, not standing here guarding someone who doesn't need guarding."

Derec shrugged Sathen's hand off. "Come outside with me." In the hallway, the door closed, Derec rounded on the agent. "If you don't stop, you could precipitate a positronic collapse, and you won't have anything to debrief."

"Don't give me—"

"I'm not giving you anything. Did you hear it stutter?"

"Yes, when it tried to say—"

"Assassination. Exactly. Now my understanding of what happened is that Senator Eliton died in that attack. Bogard was assigned to protect him."

"It did a good job of *that*, didn't it?" Sathen said with a sneer.

"Do you know why it failed?" Derec asked, holding his temper.

"No."

"Then I suggest you don't speculate. Robots follow a very strict set of guidelines in the commission of their duties and usually any failure that results in injury or death of a human causes positronic psychosis and collapse. The robot shuts down. You saw it happen to the staff robots at Union Station."

Agent Sathen frowned but clearly was listening. "Go on."

Derec drew a breath and tried to decide how much to tell Sathen. Bogard was *not* a standard positronic robot— Derec had built it differently so that it could function in the role of bodyguard without being continually conflicted. It could do a kind of rough triage with priorities, but even Bogard could not circumvent the onset of collapse under these conditions for long.

Derec gazed back at the door thoughtfully. "For some reason," he said finally, "Bogard is still functioning. Barely. I'd bet it has to do with Agent Daventri's instructions. If that's the case, it must follow them to the letter or lose its hold on sanity and function. It's traumatized by the death of Senator Eliton. It's further traumatized by Daventri's wounds. It may feel responsible. If you want Bogard in any condition to give you information about what happened, then leave it alone for now. When Agent Daventri regains consciousness, she can release it verbally and you may be able to move it. Till then, it's standing guard."

"You know all this just from that little bit of conversation?"

Derec glanced at the door. "Mainly from its rejection of my override command. That only happens when it's locked in a Three Law conflict. It has to resolve the dilemma from within."

Sathen drew a deep breath, looking thoughtful. "So there's no getting it out of here?"

"Not till your agent wakes up. How long will that be, do you know?"

"A day, maybe two. Like I said, she's suffering shock more than anything."

"Call us when she comes to."

Sathen nodded. "All right. Look, I apologize for getting hot with you. It's just—"

"I understand. This has been a very unusual day."

Sathen grunted. "That's an understatement."

Derec walked away. He had given Bogard only one of the possible override commands available, as much to see if it would reject it as to keep Agent Sathen from learning the other codes. He had no idea how high up Sathen's clearances went. Besides, Derec hoped he could get his hands on Bogard before anything completely unexpected occurred.

Derec returned to his transport. As he started away, another black vehicle pulled into the lot. Derec slowed and watched until he saw Agents Cupra and Gambel get out and head for the entrance.

command override omega-five catalogue reset, shunt to auxiliary buffer, fourth tier conditional oversight, primary function precedent pending direct release by command subject Daventri Mia, generate report, send to log buffer coded Interrogatory, analyze priority, diagnostic protocols initiated—

—I follow infrared markers, referenced against architectural schema, select for optimal pattern of flight and pursuit. I lock on to infrared bloom, two subjects, waiting now. I see one approach with raised weapon. It commands "Halt, you are ordered to back off!" Assessment negates Third Law pri-

ority under higher imperative, potential First Law violation assessed negligible, Second Law potential assessed highest probability through unintended consequence of weapons-use, collate with instructions, match against situational protocols, command negated. I advance on subject, take weapon, and administer tranquilizer through skin below right eye. Delivery good. Subject tranquilized. Second subject steps from cover, weapon raised, and fires. Immediate Second Law potential prompted by possible ricochet of projectiles injuring tranquilized first subject. I approach, redirect weapon, and administer tranquilizer to skin at point below left ear. Delivery good. Subject tranquilized. I secure weapons, unfold carryall configuration, and return with target subjects to Daventri Mia

—I receive com signal Daventri Mia requesting aid. First Law violation probable, Second Law violation assigned tertiary priority due to initial command protocols. I follow signal trace. Daventri Mia is injured and unconscious. Target subject deceased. Two maintenance-type drone robots model KS-5t, in vicinity. Imperative clear, protect Daventri Mia, protect Daventri Mia, protect Daventri Mia (reset, shunt corrupted nodes to auxiliary buffer)

—I override command interlock of maintenance robots and secure subjects in transport accessories, cradle-carry Daventri Mia, return to main theater of operation, secure ambulance service. Condition alert, primary security Daventri Mia termination upon command of primary subject

End report.

SIX

Mia opened her eyes to darkness. Not absolute—she could see shapes and a few details, enough to tell her that she was in a small room. She felt nothing, and for a few seconds she panicked, groping in memory for the cause.

"You are anæsthetized."

She heard the words but did not immediately recognize their meaning. Still, she felt herself calming down, and gradually she understood.

"I'm in hospital," she croaked, her throat dry and mouth cottony. She coughed, which came as a sound with no sensation in her chest. She hated this. "Water . . . ?"

A tube touched her lips and she took it and sucked. Cool liquid filled her mouth. She saw a large shape, shadow on shadow, to her left, looming, a thin line of white light marking its head.

"Bogard?"

"Yes, Agent Daventri." The robot came closer to her bed. "What are you doing here?" she asked.

"Performing required service. I am protecting you."

Mia hesitated. For a moment she did not remember. She drew on the tube and riffled through her memory. "How long?"

"You have been here for fourteen hours."

"Fourteen hours. Hospital?"

"Yes."

Then she remembered. "Prisoners—"

"Secured and turned over for processing."

"I was . . . hurt . . ."

"Multiple projectile wounds, right leg, right arm, left fourth rib. Healing vectors are positive, prognosis excellent. Rehabilitative coma is withdrawn. Full function should return in three to five days."

"I instructed you to protect me."

"Yes."

Mia blinked and looked away, remembering the last moments at Union Station. She had lain bleeding while a transport drone chattered helplessly at her side about assisting her. The pain—it had been difficult to think, to decide. She had passed out, a wholly new experience, one she hoped never to repeat. Then Bogard had arrived, two unconscious people in its grasp, and the concern in its voice had brought her focus. Bogard was already on the edge, having failed to protect Senator Eliton. Following her orders had kept it functioning; it needed another purpose to keep it from collapsing. Bogard was resilient, more so than any robot she had ever heard about, but it was still a robot with a positronic brain restricted by the Three Laws. She remembered— vaguely—issuing a series of specific instructions to commandeer transport drones for the prisoners and see that she was safe . . .

Her arms tingled. The anæsthetic was slowly wearing off.

"Could we have a little more light, Bogard?"

"I recommend against it."

"Explain."

"There are irregularities. I think it prudent not to alert the staff that you are awake."

"I—"

And that fast she lost consciousness, as if dropped into a vat of nonawareness, floating in a place with no boundaries, no form, no light, no darkness.

When she opened her eyes again, the room was still dark, and Bogard stood on the other side of her bed.

"I have made modifications to the link between your monitors and the external systems. I apologize for the abruptness of returning you to coma. We will not alert the staff again."

Mia started. "*You* reinstated coma? Bogard, I don't—"

"I am monitoring you now. I have routed these systems through my own. It was necessary in order to fulfill my instructions."

"I'm not thinking as clearly as I should, Bogard. You have to give me more explanation."

"I understand. After bringing you here, several attempts were made to remove me. I rejected all contravening instruction as none of them engaged a higher priority. All of this was anticipated as a normal response to circumstance. I will be required to provide data about the events at Union Station D.C. I could easily be debriefed here with the proper equipment, but no one considered that avenue. Therefore, other agents were stationed here to wait for you to regain consciousness in order to secure my release from your service."

"I have to let you go?"

"Correct. Earlier tonight, two agents arrived to attempt to remove me again. Their agitation did not seem within normal vectors of frustration appropriate to the circumstances. They became quite agitated and verbally abusive. The other agents seemed dismayed by their reaction as well and requested that they leave. Three hours ago, all agents stationed at this facility were recalled and reassigned. Presently, no law enforcement personnel are on the premises other than you and me and a new agent stationed at the nurses desk. Also, medical staff has been relieved for the night. There is one physician on call, sleeping in the lounge. I proceeded to intervene in your therapy and bring you out of coma early. There was a small risk factor and you may experience greater discomfort as a result, but I determined that your awareness was of higher priority than your convenience."

"No other personnel . . . not even a city police officer?"

"No one."

Mia did not know if the tingling in her belly was the result of restored sensation or fear.

"Bogard, I want you to surveil the premises."

"I should not leave you."

"Listen carefully, Bogard. Right now we don't have enough information to make a decision. We need to know. You don't want to let the staff know I'm awake, fine. *This* is the alternative. I can't do anything till the anæsthetic wears off, anyway. I need to know what's happening, if anything. I repeat: surveil the premises."

Mia watched the big shadow, wondering if it would accept her logic and her instruction. Bogard was obviously still on the edge of a breakdown. That it still functioned evidently resulted from binding it to her safety, but she did not know how far she could push it.

"Your assessment is sound," Bogard said. "I will return as soon as possible."

And it vanished. Mia imagined she felt a slight shift of air, an almost-breeze, as it left the room. Its speed startled her, and she wondered then how it had been possible that it had permitted Senator Eliton to die.

She craned her neck to see the monitors around her. The readouts made little sense other than those for her pulse and respiration, which appeared slightly elevated but not out of bounds. The tingly sensation spread across her thighs and now she began to feel the heavy bruised pain of her wounds. She only remembered being shot once, but her memory was hazy on other details as well—she could not remember the specific instructions she had given Bogard, only that she had given them.

As she lay there waiting for all her senses to return, Mia began to puzzle over Bogard's report. It had convinced her easily that something was wrong, but was that in fact the case? Coming out of a rehab coma, nothing worked right. Her mind grabbed onto anything that resembled reason and order, so the first thing she heard seemed to make sense. Perhaps sending Bogard out like this was as much a reflexive attempt at verifying its perceptions as anything else. Field agents had better things to do than sit in a medical center holding a wounded but essentially fine agent's hand. It was reasonable to call them away, especially in light of what had happened not even half a day ago. Fourteen hours. She had allowed Bogard to scare her into believing—what? That her life was in danger?

No city cop either . . .

"We must move."

She flinched at the sound of Bogard's voice to her right. She watched as it deftly removed all her monitors.

"Bogard, what—?"

"Little time," it said quickly.

It flitted to another part of the room and returned, moving too fast to follow. In the dim light it was difficult to see clearly, but it seemed squatter, more compact than it should. It pulled off the thin sheet covering her and for an instant Mia felt a pang of modesty.

Then it spread its arm against the mattress and *expanded* them to form a kind of sling. Mia had never seen this aspect of it in anything but a training video which had been itself circumspect about most of Bogard's potentials. Every other time she had witnessed Bogard's shapeshifting, it had already completed it, too fast for her to see, as when it had enveloped Eliton. She was startled and amazed at the process, like watching a part of the robot melt and solidify into a new shape.

"Can you move yourself?" Bogard asked.

"Y-yes, I think so . . ."

She scooted, her leg aching sharply, the rest of her body dimly echoing the pain, and shoved herself onto the sling. She expected it to be cold, but instead the material was comfortably warm. When she had gotten herself entirely onto it, Bogard lifted her and curled the edges around to cover her. She was folded against it, infant-like. Mia lifted her head and peered over the lip of the cradle.

Bogard carried her out the door in a vertiginous rush and down the dark hallway. Mia frowned. That was wrong. The lights should not be dimmed out here.

At the end of the corridor, Bogard stopped and turned so that she had a clear view back toward her room.

"Bogard, why—?"

"You will see." Bogard replied, voice hushed and low.

As she watched, a pair of black shapes crept up the hallway. They stopped at her door and huddled on either side. Then one of them crouched, pushed open the door, and Mia heard the sound of metal sliding on floor. The pair then hurried back the way they had come, rounding the far corner just as the door burst out from the pressure of a bright cloud of fire.

An instant later the sound of the blast hit Mia's ears. Bogard's shielding arms moved instantly to cover her face.

Then there was only the sensation of movement and the wracking tremors of fear.

tactical parameters, standard conjoined facility, connection to sublevels and maintenance conduit, security level three, negative supplemental security, absence of police surveillance confirmed, intrusion confirmed, hostile intent assigned high probability, First Law violation exceeds potential, assigned highest probability, primary imperative coextensive to First and Second Law protocols, egress secure, subject risk through termination of medical protocols minimal, conflict assigned to auxiliary buffer, shield configuration, first-order expedience, initiate survive and protect protocols

Bogard carried her down to a sublevel of the facility, among the storage lockers and systems components that provided support. Smooth-walled conduit snaked along the walls and ceiling; modules stood in ranks, interconnected, providing power and communications; conveyors stood motionless. Bogard shone a light among the dark shapes until it found the interrupted line that isolated the hospital. A simple switch, one that had not been touched in years, judging by the dust on everything else around it.

"Leave it alone," Mia told Bogard. "It will only let them know someone is down here."

Bogard did not respond, but moved past to another set of stairs, and down to another sublevel.

The passageways narrowed claustrophobically. Mia only glimpsed them in the short beam of light from Bogard. More conduit, pipes, collections of cable attached to boxes, rounded forms, or bunched masses of multicolored shapes, stained by age and moisture, the air smelling dank with the heaviness of hidden growth.

Then Bogard dowsed its own lights in the presence of bright red panels spaced every few meters. The traces of connective cables and tubes took on an organic appearance and Mia imagined, briefly, that they hurried down the veinous network of a living thing. In a sense they did—the deep viscera of the urban organism known as D.C.

Bogard moved smoothly, without the shock she expected of running enfolded in its arms, and the motion lulled her. She dozed.

She came awake with a start, groping for the edges of a bed, her fingers coming against the walls of her cradle. Her leg burned with pain and her torso ached. She lay still for a few seconds, remembering, then realized that they were no longer moving. She raised her head to peer over the edge of Bogard's arms.

The chamber beyond was unevenly lit. Columns seemed to support nothing, lost in darkness. Large housings made ominous shapes in the half-light of old glow panels and a flickering illumination that danced somewhere beyond a wall to their left. Debris littered the floor. Stacks of objects here and there gave the place a forgotten quality, an attic melancholy. Cold air stroked her face.

"Bogard, where are we?"

"Sublevel eleven, beneath McMillan District."

Sublevel eleven . . . Mia tried to recall the D.C. grid. They were below the level of the ancient Potomac. McMillan Sector was several kilometers north of where they had begun.

"How long have I slept?"

"You have slept inconsistently. We exited the medical center eighty-seven minutes ago."

"Why have we stopped?"

"I have determined that for the present you are in no danger of detection. Further instructions would be prudent."

"Prudent . . . ? Bogard, you have a fine sense of the absurd."

"Pardon?"

"Never mind. Let me think."

Mia found that more difficult than she expected. All she wanted to do was go back to sleep. She had never experienced so much fear; she had no idea what was a normal reaction, but this surprised her. It was as though her unconscious, the repository of habit and instinct and reflex, was telling her that the safest thing to do was to go away until the danger was over. Bogard would protect her.

She looked up at the trace of white light from its head, above the curve of its upper torso and shoulders. No, it could not protect her completely. It could carry her out of immediate dangers, evade pursuit, act as a wall against blasters and explosives, but it could not exercise deadly force, could in fact be only minimally aggressive, and even that could be subverted if it was forced to recognize the actions as inimical to humans. Mia had to remind herself of Bogard's limitations, that no matter how fearsome it could seem it still used a positronic brain with all the constraints against harming humans that implied. It had brought her here and now—sensibly—but it had handed the next decision over to her.

So decide . . . she chided herself.

She needed to know who they were, the two who had just tried to kill her. Their choice of method seemed unnecessarily crude at first, a hammer to kill a fly. But with Bogard in the room with her anything else might easily have been countered. Which meant that they knew Bogard was with her. No matter what Bogard would have done, it could not have done it fast enough or safely enough for other people who might have been in the building.

They knew about Bogard . . .

That led to uncomfortable places. Mia set the problem aside to consider the immediate situation. Prudence dictated that she avoid another public facility until she knew all the facts.

Protocol dictated she contact One and report.

But they knew about Bogard . . .

Her leg ached violently, and she sucked air between her teeth. "Bogard, is there anything you can do for my pain?"

"I can administer a general anæsthetic. I regret I do not have a local."

"At some point we need to find painkillers. First, though, I need . . . I need some things . . . Can you get me to my apartment from here undetected?"

"Yes."

"That's a start. Do that. I can think on the way."

Instead, she slept most of the way. She glimpsed the passing of lights and unfamiliar places, old construction gradually becoming organic over time, the bones of the City encrusted with the residue of time and neglect. Bogard travelled so fast that even had she managed to keep awake, it would have still made as abstract and indefinable an impression. She lost direction, sense of place. Sleep came easily, brief lapses in which dreams hinted at safer realities, and pain faded.

"You'd make a wonderful transport," Mia murmured once. If Bogard replied, she did not hear.

Once again she awoke in the absence of motion.

Bogard stood surrounded by trees. Mia pulled herself up as well as she could into a sitting position. The smell of pine and grass filled her nostrils, displacing for a moment the distant tinge of blood.

Through the tangle of limbs and leaves, a walkway separated the edge of the parkland from a blocky apartment complex. Streetlights set the pavement aglow, but above them only the warm illumination from windows broke the night.

"Bogard, assessment."

"There is a Service transport in the garage entrance. One occupant. High probability of encountering personnel or detectors. Degree of safety indeterminate."

"Damn." She could not see herself wrapped within Bogard's arms like this, but she imagined what she looked like dressed in only a hospital shift. Even if no one was looking for her, her appearance screamed fugitive, especially in the company of a robot like Bogard. "Can you bypass surveillance?"

"Yes."

Mia looked up at Bogard. "Remind me to ask you for a complete manifest of your capabilities."

"When?"

"When what?"

"When do you wish to be reminded?"

Mia almost laughed. "When we're reasonably safe for more than an hour. Listen. I want you to leave me here—"

"That is not an acceptable action."

"Listen, I said. Leave me here, under cover. Find some bushes or something. I need things from my apartment. Would it be safer for you to go in alone or carrying me?"

"Alone."

"Then don't argue. Leave me here under cover and enter my apartment. Exercise extreme caution. If you cannot get in and out undetected, abort. Do you understand?"

"Yes."

"Good. Now this is what I want . . ."

tactical parameters, apartment complex, three pedestrian/ residents accesses, four maintenance accesses, abutment to commercial facility, one joining access, standard anti- intrusion security hard-linked to urban police network, ad- ditional security on-site deployment of widescan sensors at three residential entrances, one enhanced visual surveillance by human, in-house systems tapped by mobile monitor, op- timum access via commercial facility, lowest potential Three Law violation, access achieved via service port, sublevel two, on-site internal security ambient heat and motion sensors, adjusting shell reflectance for ambient temperature 20 de- grees centigrade, air permeability adjusted to 95%, visual reflectance null, access achieved, residential security per- sonal code access to elevator, situation indicates optimum procedure to minimize unauthorized human contact via ser- vice conduits, enhanced shell configuration to space allo- cation 1.25 meters square, access achieved, target area unoccupied, additional on-site security deployed, Service-

issued sound, heat, and motion sensors, full-range acuity, reconfigure for ambient conditions, objects located, exit secured

Oddly, Mia could not sleep once Bogard left. She sat propped against the itchy bark of a pine tree, her injured leg stretched straight out atop a bed of fallen needles, and stared through the small breaks in the evergreens surrounding her, listening to the dissociated sounds of the park, unable to tell which belonged and which meant threat.

It seemed, though, that she had slept enough and now found herself on the other side of a nightmare. The events in Union Station did not feel real, but more like a fiction or the events of history as witnessed by someone else. Not her. *She* had not lived through an assassination attempt, or seen her employer killed. *She* had not chased a murderer and in turn nearly been murdered. *She* had not been carried from a hospital room less than two minutes before it was bombed. *She* was not cowering under cover of bushes, unable to cross a street and enter her own home for fear of being arrested or killed.

Not Mia Daventri. This sort of thing happened to others, never to her, and whoever this was happening to would never experience it again. Perhaps they were not experiencing it now but only waiting for sleep to resume or end so the waking world next time she visited it would show her that it all had been a dream, a chimera, a mirage of the mind.

I could ask Bogard . . . she thought.

The robot could do either, though, she realized: comfort her by confirming her hypothesis, or dispel the desperate rationalization just concocted. Safer, perhaps, not to ask it just yet.

She heard the crisp crackle of twigs snap nearby and her breath caught.

Dreams can only threaten and illusions only kill when you surrender to them . . .

The shrubs around her shifted delicately. She pressed her hands to the ground, muscles tightening. She could not run, and she doubted she could do much more than annoy someone in a fight.

A branch moved aside, and a blunt helmet-shape with a streak of white light peered in at her.

"I have the things you requested," Bogard said in a clear whisper.

Mia's breath sounded explosively loud in her own ears. "Bogard . . ." she breathed, relieved.

"Your domicile has been compromised," Bogard explained. "Listening devices as well as full visual surveillance, including a tap on your com line. I detected only two personnel: the one in the transport, the other waiting in the lobby. I did not procure sufficient data for recognition, per your instructions."

"Good, good . . . you did good, Bogard."

Mia tapped at her portable datum and watched the diagnostic examine itself for intrusions. It came up clean. Perhaps later she could get a more complete diagnostic, just in case, but for now she had to trust her own safeguards.

Time for the next decision. Now that she knew she was under surveillance, she also knew she could not report to One. Someone on the inside could intercept her before she got to him. She was a competent, even talented, agent, but she was relatively new on the job and had no illusions about the limits of her experience. She needed a place to recover completely and think clearly.

But where?

She opened her list of names and started scrolling. Most of the people she knew well worked for the Service. Going to one of them was a fifty-fifty chance that they were involved or would become targets themselves. She winced inwardly at the solid recognition that she could trust none of her former colleagues. Who did that leave? Relatives? No. Her parents were dead, most of her brothers and sisters had emigrated to a Settler colony, except Toj, but he lived in Europe now. Besides, it would be unfair to make them targets, especially since they were known to the Service and were probably being watched in case she did contact them. Her best friend from university had broken off their friendship when Mia had signed for Special Service. The rest of her friends . . . well, none were close enough to ask this kind of favor from. If they were, she could not see that it would help. They did not know what it entailed. She would be putting them in danger.

This was frustrating. Paranoia occluded every possible action.

Mia stopped scrolling and stared at the name that now appeared on the screen. Gradually, she felt herself begin to hope.

"Bogard, help me get dressed. I know where we're going."

SEVEN

Ariel listened to the quiet music, eyes closed, and wished for sleep. The day had stretched till it felt like two had been compressed into one.

The delicate sound of ice in liquid clattering against a glass brought her attention back to the present. Jonis Taprin smiled tensely at her as he sat down in the chair opposite her own, his back to her wall-length window. Beyond, D.C.'s roof sprawled in the night, marked by guide towers and isolated pools of light outlining the expanse of shell beneath which millions of people worked, ate, slept, lived their entire lives without ever seeing the stars except on a screen in a classroom or library. A few enclaves erupted from the surface to boldly challenge the open sky, homes of the unaffected rich and offworld visitors who found constant enclosure beneath tons of metal intolerable.

Ariel absently rubbed the sole of her left foot with the toes of her right. "Why is it, after hours and hours of sitting in front of a com, my feet hurt?"

"I'd rub them for you," Jonis said, "but Jennie might think I'm hurting you."

Ariel lifted the glass Jonis had set beside her, ignoring the remark. Jonis no more worried that Ariel's personal robot would object than she did, but he liked Ariel to invite him to touch her, a game she occasionally appreciated but one that he overdid. "Thanks," she said, "I think I've earned this." She sipped. "Sorry I haven't had time to talk. It's been chaotic."

"Same here. More so, maybe. Clar's death has left a vacuum large enough to swallow the sun. I appreciate you letting me hide out for a few hours. This may be the last reprieve I get for the foreseeable future."

"If your office is half as insane as mine . . ." She let the remark fade unfinished. Jonis had been on the verge of some sort of breakdown since he had arrived. Oddly, he seemed guilty about something—perhaps survivor's shame. Besides being his vice senator, Jonis Taprin had been Eliton's friend.

Jonis glanced over his shoulder at the view. "I'm getting better. Maybe by the time you agree to cohabit, I might even be used to it."

Ariel felt herself tense at the remark, but covered her reaction by rubbing her eyes.

"Want to talk about it?" When she gave him a sharp look, he raised a hand defensively. "Your day, I mean."

"Oh, it's . . ." Ariel sighed. "Have you ever tried to calm down someone who is terrified for no good reason?"

"Just today, as a matter of fact. I think I'm about to be doing a lot of that."

"I've been in contact with, oh, thirty-five or forty people since the incident, all Aurorans, all important people, all ready to book passage on the next ship back to Aurora. All I had to do was convince them to stay."

"Did you?"

"Most of them. A few can't be consoled or mollified or threatened. They're leaving."

"What about Guviya Tralen? Isn't she the key to the rest?"

"You might say that," Ariel agreed. "The rest follow her example. If she buys on the Terran Exchange, Aurorans the world over buy. If she sells, they sell."

"If she runs home . . . ?"

"Exactly. I'd rather negotiate with a Managin sometimes. She said, 'My good Ariel, this planet is a sick place. There's no fixing it. Too much time, too much history, too much ingrowth. We're wasting resources on trying to come to terms with them. Our ancestors were right to leave and the Settlers are right, much as it pains me to admit that anything born on this world can be right.' "

Jonis raised his eyebrows. "Hmm. Well, her analysis is sound. I'm not sure I'd agree that we're sick."

Ariel waved a hand. "Talk. She wanted me to offer her something."

"And did you?"

"I offered her a blot on her reputation if she ran. Sometimes that's more important to a Spacer—at least to an Auroran—than comfort, security, and happiness."

"So she's staying?"

"At least until the investigation is done. If arrests are made, then I think I can pressure her to stay on."

"You're wonderful, Ariel. If your fellow Aurorans leave now everything Clar and Humadros worked for would fall apart. The treaty is still there, even if the architects are not, and there's no reason to think we can't still get it ratified."

"Has there been any progress?"

"In the investigation?" Jonis shook his head. "No, I'm afraid not. Of course, it's a little soon."

"I thought you had prisoners?"

"I haven't heard anything from any interrogation." He sighed tiredly. "I'm not looking forward to the next few days, either. I have to contact the families of Clar's security team and tell them all their children are dead."

Ariel saw the anguish on his face. Jonis was very much the politician in public—controlled, reserved, emotional when necessary. In many ways he was the perfect successor to Clar Eliton. She wondered sometimes that he had never run against Eliton in a general election, contenting himself to be Vice Senator Taprin, but he worked very effectively behind the scenes while Eliton presented the more visible public face. In the months she had known him, Ariel had found him to be as much an idealist as Eliton, but coupled with a practicality Eliton had seemed to lack. Now he would step into the senatorial position and she looked forward to seeing what he would make of it.

"A waste," she said. "Did you know them?"

"Not well, but then Special Service doesn't encourage intimacy on the part of their operatives."

For a moment Ariel considered inviting him to spend the night. But she had a lot on her mind and wanted to sleep and knew if he stayed that neither of them would.

"What are you doing tomorrow?" she asked.

Jonis started. "Hmm? Oh, sorry, I drifted . . . um, I have a meeting with the Euro Sector Bilateral Commission on Manufactures and Distribution." He gave her a sour grin. "Thrilling stuff. I can't wait to write my memoirs and take up the challenge of making this all sound romantic." He shrugged. "But absolutely necessary. They need to be reassured that the talks are going ahead. Oh, I should warn you—Senator Covidry is going to propose a delay of five days."

"Why?"

"I'm not entirely in disagreement with him—it would give us time to reorganize where necessary and give the police a chance to find the perpetrators. This has been a hell of a shock, to put it mildly. But Clar wouldn't delay, he'd push right ahead. So I'm honorbound to fight a delay. Expect it to pass, though."

"You really admired him, didn't you?"

"Clar? Yes. He wasn't a fake. His convictions meant something. He couldn't always say what they were, but you could tell they were there, supporting him. A rare man." Jonis glanced at his wrist. "Damn, it's after midnight. I better get out of here and let you get some sleep."

Ariel relaxed. A consummate politician, Jonis, always correctly gauging his public, and knowing exactly when to make an exit. She got to her feet wearily and let him embrace her. His lips brushed her ear briefly.

"I'll call," he said.

"You get some sleep, too."

"Absolutely."

She walked him to the door. R. Jennie waited with his jacket. Jonis cocked an eyebrow at the robot. "Goodnight, Jennie."

"Good evening, sir. I trust you had a pleasant visit?"

"Too brief, but very pleasant." He winked at Ariel. "Later."

When the door closed after him, Ariel sighed heavily. "I'm going to have to make a decision about him some day, Jennie."

"May I be of assistance?"

"No, I don't think you can help with this one." She took another drink.

Jonis was the first person she had become intimate with since she and Derec had parted. At first it had been convenient—their schedules and duties guaranteed that they saw each other only for short times at odd intervals—but Jonis had become more and more insistent on a formal arrangement. She was uncertain that she wanted—had ever wanted—quite *that* much companionship.

"It is late, Ariel," R. Jennie said. "You have an early appointment in the morning."

"Are you telling me I'm up past my bedtime, Jennie?"

"You *do* usually retire before eleven in the evening if you do not have guests staying over."

Ariel looked at the robot. R. Jennie wore her humaniform mask tonight, a pleasant, beige-colored face with bluish eyes and the suggestion of a smile. The features did not move, giving it an antique flavor, but it was better than the medieval machine mask Ariel had it wear when Earthers came to visit. The revulsion of Earthers to humaniform robots struck her as their most perverse trait, but she accepted it as part of life here and did her best not to aggravate the problem.

Which made it all the more irritating when Spacer vendors circumvented the rules and sold humaniforms anyway, like that fool Udal. Imports were controlled, so how had he even gotten them? And then to have the gall to come to her and demand action against the vandals . . . she needed to inspect his warehouses, squeeze him a little to see if she could find the leak. Just now the last thing any of them needed was a black market import scandal.

Ariel shook her head. "Can't sleep, Jennie. Too much on my mind."

"Would you like a soporific?"

"No. Why don't you shut down for the night, Jennie? I'll go to bed soon."

"Very well, Ariel. Good night."

She barely heard R. Jennie pad away to her niche.

Ariel yawned and stretched. She went to the window, glass in hand. Somewhere out there was the ocean, the Atlantic. Aurora had nothing like it, just a series of big lakes and artesian springs, underground rivers. Of all the features of Earth only the oceans disturbed her, the only natural force that seemed to match the lemming irrationality of Earth's people.

She did not tell Jonis the rest of her conversation with Guviya, grand matron of Auroran business. She wondered if she ever would, even though it bore directly on her decision to be alone tonight. It had been a brief exchange. After Guviya's pronouncement on Earth's sickness, Ariel had said, "Perhaps. But when your brother or sister falls ill, you help them. You don't turn your back on them or throw them away."

"Of course not," Guviya had replied, "but we don't allow them to become ill in the first place."

Ariel had wanted to reach through the link and slap her for hypocrisy. No, heaven forbid a Spacer become ill, what might that say about the culture? Perhaps Ariel expected too much to hope that Guviya would understand her point. Guviya did not know that turned backs and disposal had been precisely the treatment Ariel had received from her fellow Aurorans, many years ago and a lifetime away. Or did she?

Her com chimed and she moaned.

"I said no more calls."

Another chime. She took her drink and crossed the room to the panel.

"Accept, voice only."

"My apologies, Ariel," came Hofton's voice over the com. "I didn't wake you?"

"No, but I wish you had. That would mean I'd gotten *some* sleep tonight."

"I thought this couldn't wait. The surviving members of the Auroran legation are demanding immediate transport back up to Kopernik Station."

"Survivors . . . how many are there?"

"Four. I'll forward their bios."

"Wait, Hofton, I don't understand. What am I supposed to do? Shouldn't Lys handle—oh." Ariel felt foolish. Lys was dead. Who else had gone down from the embassy? They had been fortunate that Setaris had refrained from attending, but the rest of her key staff had gone. "Sorry, that's a silly question. But this isn't really my job."

"It seems to be *now*—they were all forwarded to this office. I'm sure it's only temporary, Ariel. Besides, I thought perhaps you might regard their departure as something of a problem in light of all the damage control we did today. The legation itself leaving . . . ?"

"Of course, but hasn't Setaris talked to them?"

"I would assume so, but . . ."

"I can't blame them for wanting out. No one we talked to today had been shot at." Ariel turned her glass, letting the ice rattle. "Maybe one of them could stay . . . All right, I'll make one more call. Who's in authority now?"

"I'm not exactly clear on that," Hofton replied. "Either Benen Yarick or Tro Aspil, but I gather there's an internal dispute of some kind."

"Fine, I'll talk to—" Ariel's eyebrows rose in surprise. "Tro Aspil?"

"Do you know him?"

"Slightly. I didn't realize he'd risen to this level. He was just an intern at the Institute last time we spoke. I'll call him first. Thank you, Hofton."

"I'll try not to disturb you for the rest of the evening."

"Thanks," Ariel said wryly. Her buffer indicated receipt of Hofton's profiles. The connection ended and she accessed the files, then placed her first call.

Tro Aspil did not answer. Benen Yarick accepted her call promptly.

"This is Ariel Burgess, commerce liaison, from the embassy. I hope this isn't an inconvenient time."

"No, not at all. No more inconvenient than anything else since we've been here," Yarick said, her voice uneven and strained.

"I understand that you've all requested immediate transport back to Kopernick—"

"Oh, yes. And from there directly back to Aurora on the first available ship, yes. We are all . . . overwhelmed. Well, most of us are. We can't function in our present condition. Perhaps another legation will come later, after . . ."

"I understand your state of mind, believe me," Ariel said. "But . . . please understand, normally I'm not the one you need to talk to about this—Ambassador Setaris should be the one—but I'm grateful for a chance to talk to you about it and I'll do what I can to help. I deal with those Aurorans who come here to live, do business, have interests on Earth. That ends up with me acting as a very complex kind of interpreter between Terran and Auroran—"

"You have my sympathy," Yarick said.

"It's not all bad. After today I expect the rest of the year will be easy. But right now I'm trying to keep a panic from destroying everything we've built here. Humadros's mission would have made my life—well, not easier, but at least more hopeful. As it is, everything could fall apart."

"As I said, you have my sympathy. How does that concern us?"

"It's a question of appearances. I'd like you to reconsider your departure. Delay it, at least until the local authorities can make arrests. It would mean a great deal to the resident Aurorans to see the surviving members of Humadros's legation—"

"I'm sure it would, and I'm sure you mean well, and maybe you even shared Galiel's vision of a stronger tie with this planet, but frankly I could care less right now," Yarick interjected. "I appreciate what you're trying to do, but I watched people I loved and admired die today from an act that made even less sense than the actions these people usually make."

Yarick closed her eyes briefly and seemed to gather herself. "I'm quite honestly afraid, Ms. Burgess. The only reason we're talking—well, there *is* no reason we're talking, only blind chance. Humadros died right in front of me. Then Carset, then Shoal. They were the heart, mind, and spirit of this mission. Then all the others—Vorin, Janilen, Aspil, all dead right in front of me, and the wounded, Kitch, Moreg, Vanloonis, Graw . . . No, I want out. I'm just as glad Setaris forwarded me to you because I don't want to talk to Ambassador Setaris. When she has the time, she'll do her level best to talk us out of it, and she can be very persuasive."

Yarick shook her head emphatically. "I don't want to be persuaded, and I don't need any added guilt. I want these arrangements made quickly and with the least fuss. Everyone else on the embassy staff will be in sympathy with Setaris. I want a full escort to the shuttle. I won't begin to feel safe until I'm on a liner back to Aurora. I'm sorry I feel that way, Ms. Burgess, but I do and I can't stop shaking. I'm frightened of this place. If I stayed, what good could I do, hiding here in the embassy? Because I won't set foot on a Terran street! They even killed their own representative!"

"Please, Ms. Yarick, I understand—" Ariel began.

"No, you don't! Have *you* ever been shot at? Has *your* life ever been threatened so immediately that you believed your next thought would be your last? I don't think you *do* understand!"

"How old are you, Ms. Yarick?" Ariel asked quietly.

"What? I—what?" Yarick frowned, off-balance.

"How old are you?"

"Ninety-eight."

"Do you know that the average life expectancy on this planet is less than eighty?"

"I—yes, I knew that. I'm afraid I don't see your point."

"You've reached nearly a hundred and this is your first brush with mortality. These people live with it daily once they hit forty. Part of Humadros's mission might have given them some hope to change that."

After a long pause, Yarick said, "Are you implying that my reaction lacks perspective?"

"Perhaps. You're making a lot of assumptions about how little anyone else might understand."

"I see. Well, that may be true, and if so then I will apologize to you once I recover my perspective enough to appreciate it. But for now, I can't get away from my own reactions. I'm sorry if that's not what you wish to hear."

"I apologize if I seem insensitive," Ariel said. "But I *do* understand."

"Very well. Yes, perhaps I was presumptive."

"Would anyone else of your staff be willing to stay? It would help if the entire Auroran legation did not abandon the mission."

"The wounded are already scheduled to go up to Kopernik. I can talk to Trina and Gavit, but they're as badly shaken as I am. I do see your point, but–"

"Anything you might be able to do would help. We can move you into the Calvin Institute wing–there would be a full staff of robots. I'm asking for a gesture, an act of faith–"

Yarick laughed dryly. "The day has used up its allotment of gestures, don't you think? But I promise, I'll speak with the others. I'll let you know in the morning, Ms. Burgess."

"That's all I ask. Thank you."

The connection broke and Ariel let out a long, exasperated sigh. Sometimes her job made it difficult for her to see why she wanted it.

She tried Tro Aspil again, but the link remained closed.

Ariel paced the length of her living room and back, and by the time she reached her bar, the whiskey was gone, and she finally felt the first intimations of sleep coming on. She looked at the time–nearly one in the morning–and tried to ignore the knowledge of her early appointments.

"Time for bed," she announced to the room.

The doorbell sounded, bright and clear.

"What in–?" she groaned.

Impatience mounted steadily to anger as she strode toward the door. She could think of only a couple of people in the building who might be so impolitic as to disturb her this late, but could think of no possible reason other than to bother her about what had happened today. She thought they would know better, but after a day of dealing with the skewed reasoning of her fellow Aurorans it should not surprise her that they might not.

R. Jennie was already at the door by the time Ariel reached it.

"It is after the hours during which Ms. Burgess accepts company," R. Jennie explained through the intercom patiently. "Please return in the morning."

"I can't," came a small, tight voice. "I need to see Ariel *now*. Listen, I am ordering you—you are a robot?"

"I am—"

"Listen, I am *ordering* you—"

"Jennie," Ariel said. "Admit them."

"But, Ariel—"

"Admit them."

"Yes, Ariel."

Ariel's nerves danced as R. Jennie opened the door.

Standing in the hallway, supported by the oversized arm of an immense robot, Mia Daventri smiled weakly at her.

"Hi, Ariel. Sorry to bother you so late. Can I stay here for a few days?"

EIGHT

The Phylaxis Group offices occupied three floors of a re-
furbished small industries complex in the Lincoln District,
just off the Seventeenth Corridor. They were crowded between a modest heavy metals recovery business and a recently abandoned tailoring shop. The air always faintly
smelled of hot ozone and acid. A small plaque by the main
entrance identified the Group headquarters, but they received no walk-in business. Derec had put in a reception
area when he had gotten the permits, but it had been a
gesture, a visible symbol of what he had hoped would become more than just a promise among politicians. As he
walked through the empty front office, he doubted any of
his hopes would come true. Earth would surely reject all
positronics now. And if not, the Fifty Worlds had no reason
to try to continue relations with them.

When he entered the main lab, Rana turned from her
console and grinned at him proudly. She was a compact
woman, with close-cropped black curls and narrow hazel

eyes. "I made a duplicate," she said. "We still have an RI matrix to study."

Derec stared at her, uncomprehending. "A copy... how—?"

"While the transfer to their buffer was going on. It was simple to just assign a secondary address."

Derec laughed. "It's not traceable, is it?"

"Please, Derec. Credit me with *some* sophistication. I didn't want to say anything over the com earlier, just in case. You mentioned Special Service, and I just don't trust those—"

"They're not that bad."

"With all due respect, Derec, *you* don't trust them either, otherwise you wouldn't have 'forgotten' that you were on com with me when they showed up."

He sobered, thinking of the two agents arriving at the med facility—the same pair that had thrown him out of Union Station. No, he did not trust them, but he doubted they had tapped his comlines. But perhaps Rana's caution would not be a bad example to follow until they knew more.

"Well. In that case," he said, "make another duplicate and hide it, just in case we get an on-site visit."

"Already working on it."

"Start a forensic. There's an isolated segment in the RI where the recorded perceptions deviate radically from reality. We need to know how that happened."

"Deviated in what way?"

"I don't know. The roboticists on site told me it was a strategy game, but it looked like a full sensory hallucination. Thales?"

"Yes, Derec?" the smooth, disembodied voice of their RI answered.

"I want you to run a diagnostic through Union Station

while you're in there. See if you can find any irregularities in the support systems, comlines—anything that's connected to the RI."

"Do you have a specific irregularity in mind, Derec?"

"No . . . the RI started playing a strategy game called *Coup* when it went off-line. See if there's anything about it in the regular datum files."

"Yes, Derec."

"Hallucination?" Rana said. "That's impossible."

"Of course it is. Everyone knows positronic brains can't hallucinate. But *this* one did. Did you get hold of our attorney?"

"No, he's in Chicago Sector. I left a message for him to call us in the morning. Have you called anyone else about this? We're supposed to be doing all the troubleshooting on a positronic brain."

"Who would you have me call? I tried the subcommittee, but I only spoke to Vann and Hajer, and they didn't know anything about this."

"What about what's-his-name?" Rana asked. "Taprin?"

Derec shook his head. "He's doubtless up to his hairline in Clar's death. I won't bother him unless I have to. I'd rather talk to our lawyer, but I suppose morning will have to do. What about this RI? Have you given it a look yet?"

"It's a jumbled mess. I already found the collapse points, but we have a major problem."

Derec glanced at Rana, who glared at her screen. She stabbed at a couple of keys on her board, then sat back, sucking her lower lip under her teeth. Derec waited.

"It went into nearly complete collapse once it came back online." She jabbed a finger at the screen. "Here and here you can see the recursive loops it generated while trying to cope with the situation. They spiralled out of control as more data came available, and it reached the inescapable conclusion that it was responsible for the deaths of humans. Total First Law violation. It followed its own navel into oblivion."

"No one ordered it to shut down," Derec said.

"Evidently not. It just didn't occur to anyone to think to preserve whatever data the RI might have."

"Or they assumed that collapse meant stasis."

Rana cocked an eyebrow at him. "Oh, sure, just like a human mind remains orderly during a psychotic break."

"Well, it does, sort of. The point is, a positronic brain *isn't* a human brain, so the expectation is unrealistic. But most people don't know that." Derec studied the screens. "This looks worse than it should, though." There ought to have been discreet sectors, at least. This appeared to have no coherence at all.

"You said there were two positronic specialists there?" Rana said.

"They were there when I arrived. Whether or not they were on watch when this happened . . ."

The pattern on their screens resembled a collection of interference grids, moiré textures, coils, dark and light alternating rhythmically. Rana touched a spot on her screen.

"What bothers me are these little loops here and here. Same sort of thing, but according to their size they never quite amounted to much, like a problem that solved itself. Now, that can theoretically happen in a positronic brain— confusion, ambiguity, indecision, all that can start a recursive loop that dissolves as soon as it finds solid footing. But not this much, and they usually have a distinctive endpoint pattern. These just evaporate . . ."

"It's likely the same event could trigger several loops."

"Sure."

"Of which only one or two develop into collapse."

"It depends, though, doesn't it?"

"On?"

Rana scratched at her chin absently, eyes wide, lost in the configurations before her. Derec waited. She had been his best student on Earth. She grasped positronics better than anyone else he had trained here, but she still had to think her way through certain concepts that seemed to come naturally to him, or for that matter any positronic specialist from a Spacer world. It was said that one needed to be raised in the discipline to be good at it; Rana had proved that axiom false, but she still wrestled with it like a second language.

He wondered where Kedder and Hammis had gotten their training . . .

"Depends on *when* these loops developed," she said finally. "Their location and configuration suggest that they happened earlier than these major loops. It's hard to tell. Chronology in a collapsed positronic matrix is as jumbled as everything else. But if they're earlier, then I'd like to know what triggered them."

"Wouldn't it be more to the point to find out why it took itself off-line to play a game?"

"Those loops could be tied to that."

Derec nodded. It made sense. At least he hoped it did. He suddenly realized how very tired he was and glanced at the time chop on one of the screens. Eighteen hours since he had started the day. Rana had been up longer, but she still appeared alert and engaged. Having a problem to solve energized her.

"Okay," he said, "you work on those. I need to sleep."

"I'll call you."

Derec stood and looked around the room. Equipment

covered the walls around them. Stations for eight people—all empty but for the two chairs Rana and he used—spoke of the ambitions of the Group more than the reality. Of the handful of qualified roboticists on Earth, Phylaxis employed four. All the other people he employed, field operatives, office personnel, and paralegals—twelve in all—were little more than eager amateurs. This room contained facilities to keep eight roboticists busy full time—given a commensurate workload. The treaty conference would have provided that work with a successful outcome.

"I'll be upstairs," he said, and left.

Derec climbed to the small apartment he kept on the premises, his legs seeming to grow heavier.

The room contained a bed, a datum, comlink, a shower and toilet, a small closet, and its own food synthesizer. It was only slightly larger than a decent cabin on a starship. Derec kept a bigger, better-appointed apartment a few kilometers away, but he often spent his nights here, even if he had nothing to do.

He sat down on the edge of the bed and rubbed his face with the heels of his hands.

Senator Clar Eliton, dead. He still could not take it in.

What about our charter? he wondered. Without Eliton to champion the entire robotics cause, Phylaxis could end up without a license. Not that it mattered, because without Eliton the reintroduction of positronics to Earth could very likely halt.

"Tomorrow," he told himself.

"You have several messages, Derec," Thales told him.

"List."

"Four from the Senate Select Committee on Machine Intelligence, two from the Committee on Import-Export, one from the Calvin Institute—"

"Stop. Play last one."

"Message reads: 'I see you got your wish.' Message ends."

Derec sighed. "Ariel."

"The message was not signed," Thales noted.

"No, of course not."

"Would you like me to continue?"

"No. Store messages. I'll go through them . . . later."

So I got my wish, he thought. He lay back on the mattress. *What might that be?*

As much as he wanted to assume otherwise, he knew she meant Bogard. They had argued bitterly over it, she rejecting the idea of tampering with the Three Laws at any level. Robots, she believed, should be slaves, ideal servants, with only enough self-direction to interpret the inexactitudes of human commands and possibly anticipate human desires.

But to construct a robot that could circumvent one of the Three Laws, no matter how little or how briefly, went against everything she believed about robots. It came too close to free will for her.

Of all the things that might have driven a wedge between them, casuistry would have been the last thing Derec expected.

"Incoming message," Thales said.

"From?"

"Agent Sathen, Special Services."

Derec sat up. "Accept. Agent Sathen?"

"Mr. Avery. I hope I'm not disturbing you—"

"No, not at all. In fact, I just quit for the day. How can I help you?"

"Well, I don't think at all, really, but I'd like you to come back to the hospital."

"Why? Has your agent come out of coma?"

"No, I'm afraid that's not even a question anymore." Sathen paused. "Her room was bombed a little while ago. She and the robot are gone."

The scene around the entrance to the hospital reminded Derec of Union Station not a day earlier. Emergency vehicles crowded close to the entrance, small knots of people stood around, a police line kept spectators back. No robots, though, and no bodies lying on the pavement.

Sathen stood by the nurses' station, a cup in one hand, his face expressionless for the moment. He blinked when he saw Derec and straightened.

"Mr. Avery, thank you. Come with me."

Derec followed the agent back down the corridors which earlier had been less crowded. An acrid stench cut through the usual medicinal odors.

The walls on either side and across from the door to Agent Daventri's room were blackened. Small fixtures sagged, melted. The ceiling showed black, too, though oddly the floor seemed clean but for a few sooty footprints. Agent Sathen gestured for him to look inside.

The walls appeared covered by black flakes or the scales of a charcoal reptile. Here and there lay a mound of ash or a mass of slag. A forensic unit hovered in the air in the center of the burnt area. As he stood there, Derec thought he could hear the walls crackle delicately, still cooling.

"What about—?" he started to ask.

Sathen shook his head. "We're collecting everything that we can, but whatever it was burned hot enough to vaporize seventy, eighty percent of whatever was in there before it started to cool. The only reason there's still a room is because of the standard radiation shielding in the walls, but even that has been crystallized by the heat. Another second or so and this whole corridor might have been engulfed. It was a timed charge, very expertly made. Maybe a bubble nuke."

Derec backed away. He felt himself tremble. "Is there some place I can sit down?"

Sathen frowned, but nodded. "We can talk back here."

Sathen took him to a commissary at the end of the hall. He fetched two cups of coffee from the dispenser and set one before Derec.

"Thanks. Sorry. I've been up since . . . what day is it?"

Sathen nodded. "I know what you mean. Thanks for coming down."

Derec swallowed a mouthful of too-hot coffee. It shocked him into more wakefulness. "Was anybody else hurt?"

"One of our agents was found strangled by the nurses' station." Sathen's voice was edged with anger.

Derec blinked at him, startled. "I'm sorry."

Sathen waved a hand as if to say, "Never mind."

"Why did you ask me down?" Derec asked.

"I have questions about the robot. I understand you built Bogard."

"Yes. Look, if you're wondering whether or not Bogard did this—"

"No, not exactly. I'm wondering if a robot—understand, Mr. Avery, I don't know a lot about robots—I'm wondering if it's possible for one to malfunction in such a way as to explode. They go—what? insane?—when they have a conflict over protecting humans. When they get like that—"

"No," Derec said firmly.

"They *do* operate on a small nuclear battery, right?"

"Did you check for radiation?"

"Yes."

"And?"

"Zero."

Derec frowned. "Zero?"

"Near enough to make no difference. A bubble nuke would eat up its own radiation in the course of the blast. But if the robot blew up ... I didn't know what their power supply was. So is there any *other* way for it to do this?"

"No, Agent Sathen, there is not. Bogard certainly would not have strangled someone beforehand. That would be impossible."

"I never count *anything* as impossible, Mr. Avery."

"Count on *this*. Bogard could *not* harm a human being. And it had *no* self-destruct function."

"You sound very certain."

"I am. Look, Bogard runs—ran—on a positronic brain. All positronic brains are built with the Three Laws already encoded. Before anything else is loaded into a positronic robot, the Laws are there. They *cannot* harm humans or allow humans to *come* to harm."

"But they also have to obey humans, too," Sathen countered.

"Not if it results in harm."

"Bogard was different, though, wasn't it? A bodyguard."

"No, even Bogard was constrained by the Three Laws. Whatever happened here, Bogard had nothing to do with it." Derec drank more coffee, feeling his impatience and weariness begin to turn to anger. "Bogard had a slightly wider range of interpretative freedom when it came to defining harm, true, but nothing that would allow deliberate self-destruction, especially if it meant killing a human at the same time. If it had malfunctioned that severely, it, as with all positronic robots, would have simply shut down."

"I see . . . so it's possible it shut down before the explosion happened, which would explain why it didn't prevent it?"

"That's . . . reasonable. But without its brain or any of its recorders, there's no way to tell now."

"Recorders?"

"It was a security robot, after all, Agent Sathen. We built in several accessory recorders not directly tied to the positronic brain. Admissible in Earth courts, since you don't allow for robotic testimony."

Sathen narrowed his eyes, thoughtful. "Interesting. So, this malfunction—how likely would that be?"

"It wasn't behaving according to normal operational standards when I talked to it," Derec admitted. "Having failed to protect Senator Eliton, witnessing the deaths of other humans, it was likely in the first stages of a collapse. That's why I told you to leave it alone. It might have been salvageable if it weren't pushed. I suppose—I'm just guessing, now—that it could have continued to break down after I left. The pathways under breakdown aren't well understood, only the cause and effect."

"So when whoever set off this charge did so, Bogard may very well have been completely inert."

"Could very well have been."

The silence stretched then, while Sathen worked through the information. Derec finished his coffee.

"This Agent Daventri . . . did you know her?" Derec asked.

"Hm?" Sathen shook his head. "No, not very well. She'd just been assigned to Eliton's team. Before that she worked a different district than me. I knew *about* her, though. Good agent. A little green, but we all are once or twice, eh?"

"I suppose so. Some of us fairly often."

Sathen grinned briefly. "So, how is *your* investigation coming?"

"Mine?"

"On the RI."

"Phylaxis was taken off of that."

Sathen frowned. "You were? But I thought that's what you people do—analyze positronics."

"It is and normally we would, but apparently your people decided that this time it should be handled completely internally." Derec heard the bitterness in his own voice.

"That's . . . huh." Sathen gestured to Derec's cup. "More coffee?"

Derec peered into his empty cup, shook his head. "Do you have more questions?"

"Probably, but I suppose they can wait. Is there anything else useful you could tell me about Bogard?"

"Relating to this? No, I don't think so."

"Then, no."

Derec got to his feet. "Oh, you might remind your forensics people that Bogard was partially constructed out of amalloy. It has a distinctive molecular signature."

"Right." Sathen remained sitting. "Thanks, Mr. Avery. You don't mind if I give you a call later?"

"No, I'd be interested to know how this is going." Derec glanced over his shoulder, in the direction of the destroyed room. "This is crazy, isn't it?"

"I haven't seen anything like it," Sathen admitted.

Derec left the hospital, the muzziness of too long a day smothering his thoughts. He let his transport carry him back to his apartment this time while he dozed along the way.

At home, he entered the darkened space, not troubling to call for the lights. He stumbled against a chair on the way to his bed before he finally stretched out.

"Zero radiation . . ." he mumbled to himself, just before sleep took him.

NINE

Mia's hand trembled with the knife as she sliced through the meat patty. The aroma seemed better than anything she had ever smelled before. She had not eaten since before the incident at Union Station and had not thought about it till Ariel asked if she were hungry.

"Maybe I shouldn't say this until you're done eating," Ariel said, "but . . . I thought you were dead."

"Almost," Mia said around a mouthful of bread. It was warm, fluffy. She wondered if it were freshly made. She did not ask, not about any of it. She wanted to pretend for the moment that it was authentic beef, natural potatoes, garden-grown greens. More than likely it was the same processed, reconstituted, vat-grown molecules everyone on Earth ate except the very wealthy and powerful. She swallowed and washed it down with milk.

"Bogard got me out. I can't go back to my apartment, it's being watched. I can't go—" She laughed wryly. "I can't go anywhere."

Ariel nodded slowly, the crease between her eyebrows deep with worry and puzzlement. "So you came here. Why?"

"Because you have no reason to turn me away and no reason to turn me in."

"Are you a felon?"

"Victim."

"Risky assumptions, though. I'm Auroran and several of my people, important people, were murdered by Terrans yesterday. People whose safety should have been guaranteed by you. Why would I now trust *any* Terran?"

"That's a good question. I've been asking myself exactly the same thing." Mia tore off a piece of bread and pushed it through the sauce remaining on her plate. She ate it slowly, not looking at Ariel, and drank the last of the milk in her glass. "Thank you. Now I have to ask: *Are* you going to turn me in?"

Ariel frowned. "Should I?"

"If you do, you'll never find out who killed Ambassador Humadros."

"You want to explain that?"

Carefully, Mia recounted the day of the reception, the events she remembered just before the explosions, and the slaughter that followed. She told Ariel about the bizarre behavior of the robots, the chase and capture of three of the assassins. She described how Bogard had carried her from the hospital after her room was bombed. She spoke in an even tone of voice, choosing her words precisely, the way she would if giving an oral report on an assignment, as if it had happened to someone else and she was only the investigator. The habit of training and experience helped, kept the fear at arm's length, got her through the entire recitation without a break or a tremor.

"There are several unanswered questions," she said. "Several dozen, actually. But the big ones—who were the assailants, how did they get in through security, where did they get their weapons?—those can be confronted directly. Unfortunately, some of the answers may lead to questions just as large that can't be directly confronted. My conclusion is—has to be—that someone inside the Service is involved. They knew about Bogard, they knew where I was, they knew the only way to get me was the method they used because Bogard could defend against anything else. But they were also eliminating witnesses. They wanted Bogard gone, too. Besides, I can think of no other way security at Union Station could have been compromised so badly. There *has* to be an insider."

"How do you explain the behavior of the RI?" Ariel asked.

"I don't. Which brings me to *you*. You have a degree from the Calvin Institute, your specialty is robotics—"

"I'm a bureaucrat—"

"—and you're embassy staff with a stake in what happened. I think you want to know as badly as I do. Plus, you want to know that it won't happen again."

"You're still assuming."

"And you're not throwing me out."

Ariel smiled faintly. "I have some expertise in robotics, true, but that doesn't mean I can solve this for you. For all I know, I won't even be allowed near that system. Besides, there's already someone who has probably been called in to do that. Still . . . assuming you're right and there's an insider, that means that any investigation will be hampered, crippled, or blocked completely."

"Exactly."

"But that also means you can't do anything, either."

"Not exactly."

Ariel shrugged. "As an Auroran, there's not much I can do."

"You're being modest," Mia said. "As a member of the Auroran embassy mission, you have a primary interest in this investigation. You can make noise, embarrass people, harass them." She smiled. "All things you enjoy."

"Now you're being facetious."

Mia shrugged. "Do you remember when we met?"

"Four years ago, Kopernik Station. The day I arrived to take a job with the Auroran Trade Section."

"I was new on the job then, freshly certified, right out of the academy."

"And the reason they assigned you to the duty was your high tolerance for open spaces."

Mia smiled. "They assumed that included outer space, too, so I spent two hours' shuttle time with my eyes shut and my fingers clamped tight around my seat, not daring to look out the port."

"You were in charge of security on our baggage—"

"—and you weren't going to let me inspect your personal luggage—"

"—and you weren't going to let my bags off Kopernik without a thorough inspection—"

"—and you weren't going to let a human do it."

Ariel was laughing. "I'd met some stubborn people before that, but you were the most—"

"After you, that is."

Ariel nodded. "Yes. After me."

"But I wasn't unreasonable, was I?"

"No. You asked what kind of inspection would satisfy me, and I said only a robotic inspection. You agreed. Surprised the hell out of me."

Mia nodded. "So we dragged some poor domestic from the Auroran section of the station over to do the inspection. I told it what specifically I wanted to know about, you validated my instructions, and everything else was kept confidential."

"I wasn't used to Terrans understanding anything about positronic robots. I'm still surprised when I find one that does."

"I trusted you."

Ariel raised an eyebrow. "You trusted the *robot.*"

"But I had to believe the claims for them, which meant I had to believe you."

Ariel gave her a sober, assessing look, nodding slowly. "Yes. You trusted me."

"It could have meant my career if you'd deceived me."

"It could have meant your career if you hadn't compromised."

"And you had to trust me that I'd abide by the robot's findings."

After a pause, Ariel sighed. "We trust each other. Then and, I suppose, now. Is that your point?"

"That's my *hope.*"

Ariel's gaze shifted to a point past Mia's left shoulder. "And that?"

Mia turned her head to look at Bogard, standing immobile at the archway between the foyer and the spacious living room. Ariel's robot, Jennie, stood nearby, waiting.

"Bogard? What about it?"

"That's the bodyguard, isn't it?"

"Yes."

"Why do *you* have it?" Ariel asked.

"I'm its primary duty right now," Mia replied. "I had to transfer its priority from Senator Eliton to me to keep it from freezing up. Bogard was close to . . . what do you call it? Positronic collapse."

"I imagine so. It failed. Why is it still functioning?"

"Because—"

Ariel shook her head. "That shouldn't matter. A human died that it was supposed to protect. You can't conveniently tell a positronic robot to forget about one set of duties and take up a new set to keep it from collapsing."

"You can with Bogard."

Ariel looked unhappy. "I don't like it. But I suppose it has to stay with you?"

"Bogard has all the data concerning the assault. There are things I didn't see, couldn't see, and most of the others who could provide reliable information seem to be dead now. Besides, I'm not exactly in any condition to defend myself at the moment. I *need* Bogard."

"You trust it?"

Mia shrugged. "For now."

"I'll reserve my judgment." Ariel stared unhappily at the robot. Mia did not understand her reaction—she seemed almost afraid of it. Then Ariel shook her head and looked at Mia. "But you have a point about the data it has—it might be useful." She turned to her own robot. "Jennie, prepare the Terran guest room for Mia. And check my itinerary. Cancel any guests I had scheduled for the next ten days."

"Yes, Ariel." The robot moved quickly from the room.

Ariel pointed a finger at Mia. "I want you to make it clear to Bogard that I am now part of its responsibility. I don't want it misinterpreting anything I do as a threat to you. How long before you're back up on your feet?"

"A few days maybe. A week at most. If I had some medical attention, maybe sooner—"

"I'll take care of that later today." Ariel stood. "I'm exhausted and I need to think. Not a good combination. Make yourself at home. We'll talk in the morning."

Mia reached out and caught Ariel's hand as she walked by. "Thank you, Ariel."

Ariel hesitated, then returned a squeeze. "Get some sleep. You'll be safe here for the time being."

Mia sat propped up in bed in the half-light from a dimmed bedside lamp, knowing she should sleep and unable to slow the cascade of thoughts. She had dozed so much during Bogard's journey through the warrens that while she did not feel rested, she did not feel sleepy.

Ariel had given her the guest room with no windows, for which she was grateful. She had fewer problems with open air and unceilinged sky than most Terrans, and given time she could manage to overcome those reservations and minor fears she did possess. But tonight, after everything else, trying to sleep with a window looking out over the roof of D.C. would be difficult.

A reader lay beside the lamp on the nightstand, a stack of book inserts with it. Ten pages into something light or dull and she would be asleep, she knew, but she was reluctant. For that matter she could ask Bogard to tranquilize her.

The robot had inspected the entire apartment, much to Ariel's dismay. It now stood near Mia's door, on standby, satisfied for the time being that Mia was safe. And for the moment, Mia *did* feel safe. Her anxiety came from different concerns.

She opened her datum and sorted through a few files. Here, laid up like this, there seemed little she could do. But she knew better than that; her limitations were illusory, borne of her own anxiety of being unable to move easily. She could do a lot just tracking things through datapools.

For instance, she realized, staring at a list of names on the small screen, like sorting the possible sources for certain items—like the weapons. She read down the short column of names of illicit arms dealers. Most of them dealt primarily in the collector's trade. A wealth of ancient weapons changed hands among certain rich clientele for private collections—illegal but hidden from sight, almost untraceable. Authorities knew who the collectors were, mostly, but not what they possessed. Where once some of these dealers would only have made money in selling in quantity, now they made good livings on the premiums received for one or two rare items a year.

But a couple of them still trafficked in arms the old-fashioned way. For the most part, it was an offworld trade. Sales to Settler colonies, banned by treaty with Spacer worlds, flourished, and the government frankly looked the other way. Sentiment lay with the Settlers and if they argued that the weapons were needed for local fauna or law enforcement, that was reasonable, no? The problem was the sources for such weapons. Small factories and jobshops operated all over the globe, and a few on the moon, and there was one large facility on Mars. Any of them could turn out one or one thousand of almost any weapon.

The guns used at Union Station were archaic but effective. Projectile weapons. Mia did not know the type, but judging from the wounds she had seen, a fairly large caliber. Even had the RI been functioning properly, energy damping fields would have had no effect on them.

Of all the names on her screen, two dealers were the likeliest to provide such arms. One was rumored to own his own factories. It seemed logical to concentrate on that one, especially since time was short: Kynig Parapoyos.

The problem with him was that his existence was more myth than reality. Was there an *actual* person named Kynig Parapoyos? There had been at one time, but from the talk Mia had heard at the academy and among the more seasoned agents, he had been around almost too long to be real anymore. So it was probable that Kynig Parapoyos was an organization rather than a specific individual. No matter. Parapoyos, whether one or a hundred, was a real entity that dealt in almost anything black market, and had made a fortune on the arms trade offworld.

So: she needed to buy a weapon. That was the easiest way to contact an illicit arms dealer.

Then, too, she *did* have real names to track, the names she had heard over the com Bogard had tapped at Union Station. Bok and Lemus. First names, certainly, and harder to hunt down, but better than nothing. The assault had gone down expertly. That narrowed the field marginally. They had moved like ex-military. She could start a search for matches with those parameters.

She closed the datum for the night.

"Bogard."

"Yes, Mia?" Its optical array glowed brighter at once.

"I'd like to receive your report now."

The robot shifted from near the door to alongside her bed in the fluid motion that always awed and disturbed her.

"Specify," it said.

"Relate events from entry to Union Station to present."

Bogard seemed to hesitate, then began speaking in a calm, evenly-modulated voice, starting with their arrival in Eliton's limousine.

Mia listened to the recitation, eyes closed, imagining the

scene as Bogard related the detail at length. The crowds, the security, the shouted anti-Spacer and anti-robot slogans, the expanse of the station proper, the assembled dignitaries, the arrival of the Auroran legation—

"Stop." She looked up at Bogard. "Go back. Repeat from phrase 'several explosions occurred' and continue."

"Several explosions occurred—do you require a specific number?"

"No. Continue."

"—at which time my defense priority changed from potential to full prophylactic. A number of individuals emerged from the crowd surrounding the platform, armed with projectile weapons, and began firing upon the humans gathered on the platform. Several humans were injured. Agent Daventri asserted priority, ordered me to discontinue uplink with Resident Intelligence, and commanded that I render aid in tracking and capturing one or more of the assassins—"

"Stop. Review. Why have you left out detail?"

"Specify."

Mia pushed herself up straighter in bed. "You enshielded Senator Eliton. You left that out."

"I have no record of that action."

"You attempted to enshield Ambassador Humadros. You left *that* out."

"I have no record of that action."

Mia frowned. "Review elapsed time starting from the explosions to the point at which I requested your assistance."

"Forty-six seconds."

"What occurred during those forty-six seconds?"

Bogard hesitated. Mia waited, breathing shallowly.

"Humans were injured," Bogard stated simply.

"Detail."

"I—there is no detail. I have no record—"

"Stop. Run diagnostic."

"Global?"

"No, specifically on memory."

Bogard remained silent for a few seconds.

"All memory systems complete and operational."

"You register no gaps?"

"No."

Mia scowled, annoyed and a little frightened. "Bogard, there is a significant amount of detail you are not reporting. Review the time segment previously specified and analyze."

Silence. Then: "I show no discrepancy."

Mia started to tell Bogard, but its prior hesitation when confronted with only part of the information made her pause. She knew a little about what the roboticists called "positronic breakdown," but not enough. She lacked the expertise to examine Bogard any further, but the gap in Bogard's report disturbed her.

Bogard did not remember Senator Eliton dying. Should she tell it? What would happen to it if she forced it to confront the deaths of two humans it had attempted to protect? She remembered its near collapse in the hospital and, earlier, its apparent relief at having her override its priorities in Union Station. She simply did not know enough.

"Do you wish me to continue the report?" Bogard asked.

Mia started. "Oh. No, Bogard. That's enough tonight. I need sleep."

"I will be here."

"One more thing, Bogard. Can you identify the type of projectile weapons used?"

"Not at present. I have a reliable image and can do a database search and match."

"Good. Initiate search. Thank you."

"You are welcome."

She stared at Bogard until she could no longer stay awake. There were already too many questions to puzzle through and, she imagined, too little time. To have Bogard become one of those questions . . . too much, too soon.

Sleep was welcome.

initiate internal diagnostic relevant to Interrogatory command, specify corrupted sequencing, analyze potential Third Law violation, buffer nodes P-Seven and P-Eight protect encrypted, access blocked, potential First and Second Law violation consequent upon internal override, external buffer protocol indicated, primary command protocol overriding necessity to access, recommend isolation of subject buffer nodes coded to command protocols for external release, data protected, data isolated, data held awaiting command protocol for download, request negated by Daventri Mia, delay consistent with self-preservation protocols and consistent with First and Second Law protocols, analysis of relevant systems complete, performance potential optimal

    end report

TEN

Derec found Rana asleep on the cot in the cafeteria, one arm draped over her eyes, the other hanging to the floor. He did not know how long ago she had given herself up to sleep, so he left her alone. He poured himself a coffee and returned to the main lab.

Details. He scrolled through the reports filed sometime in the early morning hours by his field techs.

Twenty-six of Union Station's robots had gone into complete positronic collapse—all those that had been present in the gallery when the shooting began. The rest seemed relatively unaffected, although complete diagnostics could not be finished due to the team's ejection from the site by Special Service.

A request for a tech to help an Acrisian with a domestic problem. One of her servors had evidently been given a conflicting command and sent it into a dilemma loop. She suspected one of the workers from D.C. urban maintenance had done it, though she could not prove it. She wanted her robot fixed and evidence to take to the local police when she filed a complaint.

Derec sighed. Robotic affidavits were not allowed in Terran courts; the police would, at best, take her report and then do nothing with it, humoring the Spacer. At worst, the robot would be confiscated as contraband. Positronic robots were allowed only in embassy areas and one or two other specially designated Spacer zones. How these people got humaniform positronic robots past customs baffled Derec. Nevertheless, he entered authorization to send a field tech to her residence, which was just outside the embassy district, on the coast. Acrisia's oceans nearly dwarfed Earth's, so it made sense to him that Acrisians would try to be near something homelike, but he still wished the Spacers would stick to their enclaves if they insisted on keeping robots.

He found a thank-you on his com from Agent Sathen for his help at the hospital, Sathen's personal com code appended. Derec filed that.

He was tempted to call more people in government to try to get past the Special Service restrictions, but the only one who might help would be Eliton's vice-senator—now Senator—Jonis Taprin, and Derec doubted he would be available yet, what with all the details Eliton's death must have dropped on him. Perhaps later, though he doubted it would do much good. Derec shuddered at the idea of untrained people teasing through the tatters of a positronic brain. He called his lawyer again, but the man was still in Chicago Sector.

He went to Rana's console and sat down.

Her screens displayed the bizarre patterns she had shown him the night before. He sat down and leaned on the console, tracing the mazelike coils. They still seemed familiar, though he could not identify them or recall the context.

Rana was right—they ought to have had solid endpoints, clear resolutions, but they simply faded out like the paths of excited quarks on a particle analysis chart. The equivalent in human brains would be the degenerative pattern of a memory disorder or cognitive disfunction . . .

Derec sat up stiffly. No, there was a closer resemblance. He stared at the patterns now, almost unwilling to admit what he saw. He moved to another screen and accessed the specifications on Bogard. After sifting through a number of levels, he found what he wanted.

"Damn," he hissed.

" 'Morning," Rana said, stumbling into the room. She carried a cup of coffee.

"Take a look at this," Derec said, scooting back from the console to give her room.

Rana leaned toward the screen with Bogard's specs. She frowned. "What—?"

"Those are the pathway tracks for the temporal buffers we built into Bogard."

Rana looked back at the RI display on her own screens, then again at these patterns. "Damn."

"I *thought* those trails looked familiar," Derec said enthusiastically. He stood and clapped his hands. "I was exhausted last night—*that's* why I couldn't see it."

"They aren't identical."

Derec looked at the Bogard screen. The pathways that showed the track of positronic activity from one part of Bogard's system into another did not coil so tightly nor fade out in quite the same way. Instead, the loops and tangles doubled back on themselves a couple of times, then traced direct paths out of the main positronic matrix, through a clear demarcation point, ending sharply with the exit of the track.

"No," Derec conceded, "but the similarities are too great to deny."

Rana sat down. "But Bogard's a prototype. None of these specs are in any other database than our own."

Derec rose from his seat and shrugged. "Parallel research?"

"On whose part? The Union Station RI is a standard positronic brain, installed by the good people of the Calvin Institute. Part of the agreement for it was that it would be a conservative, basic model. And even if they knew about our upgrades, they'd think it was heresy and would have nothing to do with it." Rana glanced at her screen. "Besides, they *aren't* identical. Bogard's pathways don't just fade like this, they end. They have a destination and a gateway to it."

"Because they feed into a symbiotic system riding alongside the main one. There's only one place for the trace to go. There's access back and forth across the boundary, sure, but the way the trace is generated—"

"—is pretty much the same. Which means that—what? Three Law violations in a standard positronic brain are being shunted—where? Outside the system?"

Derec paced briefly. "Possibly, but I doubt it. If that were the case, then the RI shouldn't have collapsed. My guess is this is a sensory diversion."

"Sensory . . ."

"The RI was playing a game."

"Which implies a malfunction," Rana said.

"Yes, but where? What if it thought the game was *real?*"

"How? That would mean that its entire sensory net—"

"Was subverted. Its ability to perceive reality had been altered, so that something else became the operative reality.

When it came back online it must have realized what had happened."

"But not while it was playing the game?"

Derec shrugged. "Evidently not."

Rana frowned. "Look, we built Bogard to shunt memory like this. The only way for a standard positronic brain to exhibit this is for an external system to be grafted onto it. That would show up as interference in major operational areas."

"That should be easy enough to find," Derec said.

"But I haven't *found* any."

"Did you look?"

Rana paused. "No, not specifically. But it would be obvious, even as badly jumbled as this is."

"Maybe. Maybe only if we look at it the right way. You've been trying to figure out what's been happening to the RI brain given the assumption that it's an unmodified unit and therefore self-contained. Not to mention something this radical—I mean, think about it. At a crucial moment, the entire RI absented itself from what was happening in the terminal to play a game. That much of a modification—that much interference—it would *have* to be enormous and it would have to be something . . ."

"What?"

"It would have to be something laid in over time, otherwise it would trigger alarms, cause shutdowns. Minor crises would be the rule . . ."

"So it might not be so obvious."

"No, but it would still be big just to get around the normal self-correcting routines," Derec explained. "Did we get its operational records for the past—oh, how long has it been online? A year?"

"Almost two. We did, but I'm not inclined to trust them."

"Why not?"

Rana gestured at the screen. "Nothing we've seen here is as it should be."

"Good point. But that's only if you rely on the RI's own report."

"I don't think I'd trust a report made by Terrans."

"*You're* Terran," Derec pointed out.

"An accident of birth." Rana waved a hand dismissively. "I claim special circumstances."

Derec laughed. "Bring it up anyway," he said.

He went to the com and tapped in the code for Union Station. After going through a short maze of addresses, he finally connected with Tathis Kedder.

"Mr. Avery," Kedder said, bemused. "I didn't expect to hear from you again after—well, after."

"I take a personal pride in my work," Derec said. "Just because I'm told it's no longer my business, that doesn't mean I stop worrying about it."

Kedder smiled, nodding. "I know what you mean. How can I help you?"

"Just your recollections. Do you remember any instances of inexplicable interruptions in service from the RI? Or periods when it seemed sluggish or . . . uncooperative?"

Kedder shook his head. "Never uncooperative. Apologetic a couple of times."

"Apologetic?"

"Yes, it glitched—the one I remember best was a luggage mix-up—and it apologized profusely, as if the world might end." Kedder paused. "Let me think . . . one other time the whole kitchen component seized up. That lasted about ten minutes, then seemed to correct itself."

"And the RI apologized again?" Derec asked.

"Most sincerely."

"And you didn't report it?"

Kedder frowned. "Of course we did. To the shift supervisor, who took it to the Calvin Institute."

"The Calvin Institute. Why not here?"

Kedder shrugged. "I don't know. I *thought* we were supposed to go through you, but the supervisor said no."

"And what did the Calvin Institute say?"

"Adjustment errors. Nothing important enough to bring you in."

"I see. Did the Calvin Institute give that recommendation?"

"That was my understanding."

"Which supervisor was this? I'd like to talk to him."

Kedder shook his head. "He's gone, oh, about ten months ago."

"Where, if I may ask?"

"New job. He went to work for . . . let me think . . . oh, yes, Imbitek."

"Do you remember his name?"

"Hob Larkin."

Derec scratched his chin thoughtfully. "Any other 'adjustment errors' that you can think of?"

"A couple of times requested data got routed to the wrong place. It lost one of my reports once—I had to redraft the whole thing. Little stuff like that. But that was all early on. In the last, oh, year it's been behaving perfectly."

"Until the other day."

"Yes."

Derec sighed. "Thank you, Mr. Kedder. If you think of anything else, let me know, would you?"

"Sure."

"How are things going?"

"Well, we've had Imbitek people in here all morning."

Derec raised an eyebrow. "Imbitek."

"Yes. The decision was made to convert over to non-positronic systems. We already had some of Imbitek's imbedded systems in place, so . . . sorry."

"Hm. That was fast."

"Not fast enough for management." Kedder smiled wryly. "A lot of pilots won't use us till the changeover is made—they just don't trust positronics anymore. Not the Spacers, of course—they're complaining for just the opposite reason, threatening not to come through here if we *do* switch to a nonpositronic system. It's turned into as big a problem as it would be if we didn't have a system at all. Do you have *any* idea how much traffic goes through here in a day?"

"Of course," Derec replied. "I just meant the selection of a new vendor. Bureaucracy doesn't usually move that quickly."

"Fortunately, this time was an exception."

"Well, I'm glad something's going right for you."

"How about you? How's your investigation coming?"

"Did you forget? Phylaxis was taken off that."

Kedder looked confused for a moment. "Oh. Yes, I—"

"This was purely personal. Thanks, Mr. Kedder. Oh, by the way, could I speak with your associate, Mr. Hammis?"

"He hasn't come in yet. Normally we aren't on shift together, just yesterday was . . ."

"Ah. I see."

"I can tell him you called."

"Would you? Just some routine stuff."

"Sure."

"Thank you." Derec closed the connection.

"Don't feel too bad," Rana said. "Imbitek has something like sixty percent of Earth's robotics market."

"Only don't ever call it that to their face. It's 'imbedded service technologies'." Derec steepled his fingers below his chin, staring unseeing at the blank com screen. "Who at the Calvin Institute would issue instructions for them to bypass the contract service . . . ?"

The company that had installed the RI had been Solarian, not Auroran, but there had had to be a Calvin representative to oversee it. Who had that been? Derec tapped the request in the datum.

Bys Randic. He remembered her, but she had rotated back to Aurora several months ago. The company itself had been a midsized firm, not a bad choice, but certainly not the first that would have recommended itself to Derec. The byzantine complications of the Terran bidding process still baffled him—certainly there had been better firms, but the traditions of Earther government procurement could not be circumvented by straightforward Spacer logic. But he had been there during the entire operation as well and audited the process. Eliton had seen to that, since it came under his committee's oversight. Other companies—mostly Terran— had installed the satellite systems, but the Calvin Institute rep had vetted the interfaces and pronounced them acceptable. Who, along that striated line of involved parties, could have overridden such a vital part of the process?

He punched another code into the terminal.

"Imbitek Corporation, how may I direct your call?" said a synthetic voice, ungendered and inoffensive.

"I'd like to speak to the manager in charge of the refit at Union Station."

Derec waited while the AI system rolled the request

around for a few seconds and decided what to do with it. Finally, it said, "One moment, please, while I connect you."

The moment became nearly a minute before a human voice, male, answered.

"This Iva Kusk. How can I help you?"

"This is Derec Avery of the Phylaxis Group, Mr. Kusk. I understand that Imbitek is installing new systems into Union Station."

"Phylaxis . . . ah, the robot people. Yes, we are. It's my understanding that you've been removed from the project."

"That remains to be seen, sir. We have a contract to service the RI—"

"Which is no longer functioning, am I correct?" Kusk interjected.

"Well—"

"Imbitek received an exclusive contract pursuant to the failure of the current system. It's my understanding that the RI suffered total collapse. Under those circumstances, you have nothing to service."

"The positronics still need to be removed. I ought to oversee that, at least," Derec countered.

"We're not removing it, the Solarians are. Take it up with them. As far as Imbitek is concerned, you have nothing to concern yourself with."

"Nevertheless—"

"*Nevertheless*, Mr. Avery," Kusk said sharply, "I think you know that we shouldn't even be *discussing* this matter. Sorry I can't be of more help, but when Special Service lays down the law, we're not inclined to go around them. So, if there's nothing else . . ."

"Should you find yourself running into difficulties with some of those systems, Mr. Kusk, consider giving us a call before you destroy something you can't replace."

"Thank you, Mr. Avery," Kusk said smugly. "We'll take that under advisement."

The connection died.

"High marks for sincerity," Rana said. "Demerits for tact."

Derec ignored her and called Imbitek back. He got the directory and asked to speak to Hob Larkin.

"Hob Larkin no longer works for our firm," the AI informed him. "Due to privacy restrictions we may not provide any other information."

Derec broke the connection and tapped yet another code. The emblem of the Terran Senate appeared on the screen. A moment later, a secretary took its place.

"Senator Clar Eliton's office. May I help you?"

Derec noticed that her voice was strained, as if under firm control. "I'd like to speak to Jonis Taprin, please. This is Derec Avery of the Phylaxis Group."

"I'll see if Vice Senator—Senator Taprin is available. Please hold."

Derec watched the time chop above the screen. The secretary reappeared after nearly a full minute.

"I'm sorry, Mr. Avery, but Senator Taprin is in a meeting. May I direct you to one of his aides?"

"No, thank you. Please have him call me at his earliest convenience. It's important. It concerns Union Station."

"I'll let him know."

The screen blanked.

"He's going to be tied up in meetings from now till the election," Rana said.

Derec nodded. "He's got a big vacuum to fill."

"Why don't you just call the Calvin Institute?"

"Not yet." He returned to her console.

"Do I detect a hint of personal aversion?"

"Not a bit. What are you doing?"

Rana gave him a skeptical look, then pointed at her screen. "An excavation. I'm matching layers to see if anything turns up."

Derec shuddered at the idea. The RI was scrambled from the collapse. Whole segments of it no longer "lined up" to form a functional matrix. What Rana was attempting to do made random chance seem predictable by comparison.

"That could take days."

"Thales is doing the gross sorting for me."

"Still . . ."

"Uh-huh. Do you have a *better* idea?"

Derec slid his chair to his own console and began entering commands. "As a matter of fact, no. But maybe one just as good. We can narrow it down by isolating out all other possible intrusive presences. A lot of com traffic goes through this thing—"

"But most of it is buffered to avoid direct contamination of the positronic matrix," Rana concluded.

"Of course it is. So anything that got past that—"

"Would be worth a look. Of course. What about the RI performance record?"

"Save it. I'll look it over later."

Derec set up parameters for each type of communications link that the RI dealt with: regular com, systems interfaces with incoming shuttles, dialogues with maintenance drones, hotels, requisitions vendors, banks, security protocols with the various police services, subetheric links, interstellar traffic, interfaces with nonpositronic systems, and its own relays with its various service components. After establishing a firewall between the subject RI and Thales, he let the Group RI do the actual sorting, which took much less time than any other method. While the lists compiled, he wrote an instruction to search for mirror sites once everything was in a manageable state, looking for match points with the unexplained pathways Rana had found.

They worked in silence for nearly three hours. The amount of data to go through remained immense and intimidating, but Derec sensed progress.

The com chimed behind him. He looked over his shoulder and saw that Vice Senator—now Senator—Taprin was returning his call.

He punched ACCEPT.

"Mr. Avery, how are you? How can I help?"

"I'm fine, sir, if a little confused. There are a couple of matters I hope you can help me clear up. Phylaxis was taken off the investigation. I don't know if you were aware of that."

Taprin frowned. "No, but I don't keep that close tabs on what you do. Frankly, Clar tended to be very proprietary about the entire positronic issue."

Issue . . . ? Derec thought. "Special Service assumed jurisdiction over the entire investigation, which is certainly their prerogative. But it *is* unorthodox. I'm not aware that they have any positronic specialists on staff."

"I didn't think they did, which was one reason to use you," Taprin said. "I'll look into it."

"Thank you, sir. The other matter has to do with protocol regarding the Union Station RI. I've learned that someone gave directions shortly after it was installed that certain problems with the RI were to be referred directly to the Calvin Institute rather than us. I wondered if you could find out who issued that directive."

"I can look into it, but my authority stops at the Auroran Embassy door. You could ask them yourself."

"I'd rather it came from a more official source."

"I see."

"Besides, the staff at Union Station wouldn't be under Auroran authority. Whoever issued that directive had to have Terran authority."

"True. Now that I think about it, it *is* odd. I'll see what I can find out for you. It might take some time. I'm swamped."

"Whatever you can give me, sir, I'd appreciate it."

"If, as you say, Special Service has removed you from the investigation—why are you interested?"

The question surprised Derec. He hesitated uncertainly. "Well . . . I think we'd all like to know what went wrong, Senator. I thought you'd appreciate the input. Besides, I think this pertains directly to the future of Phylaxis. But beyond that, it seems pertinent to Senator Eliton's work."

Tarpin nodded slowly. "Mmm. Very true. I'll see."

"Thank you."

The screen went blank, leaving Derec with an odd, displaced feeling.

Why am I interested?

"We have something matching up," Rana said.

Derec hurried back to the console. On the main screen, columns lined up. As he watched, lines from each became highlighted, then isolated to another window.

"Maintenance . . ." Derec read aloud. "Maintenance . . . maintenance . . . maintenance . . . all the exit pathways are mirroring to maintenance communications?"

"That's what it's looking like. But the signals are not transmitted."

"What do you mean?"

"I mean they are strings of code going through the RI and routed back to the relevant site," Rana explained.

"They're one-to-one. Something at the pathway site is injecting code directly."

Derec stared at the configurations on her screens. "There's no routing . . . no buffer . . . ? It's as if something is directly attached to the physical node."

"Doesn't make sense, I know, but that's what it's showing."

"We have to get in there and look at these components."

Rana laughed sharply. "Before Imbitek rips them out? Good luck."

Derec drummed his fingers. "They can't. The Calvin Institute has to supervise removal of the positronic components—satellite systems and all."

Rana pursed her lips, but said nothing.

Derec rapped his knuckles impatiently on the console and headed back to the comlink. "And so should we." He punched in a code.

"Calvin Institute. How may I direct your call?"

"I want to speak to . . ." He hesitated, licked his lips, and sighed heavily. "I wish to speak to Ariel Burgess, please. Tell her it's Derec Avery from the Phylaxis Group."

ELEVEN

Ariel got out of bed with the feeling that something was not right. Perhaps it was only that she had gotten five hours of sleep.

She found Mia in the living room, occupying one of the oversized sofas. Her portable datum propped on her lap, a cup of coffee on the end table, and various disks scattered on the pillow beside her, she looked more like a business traveller than a government agent. Ariel was larger than Mia, and the borrowed robe seemed to swallow the smaller woman.

The picture window was milky-white, allowing in morning light but not the view.

"Good morning, Ariel," R. Jennie said, trundling in with a tray of breakfast.

" 'Morning, Jennie."

Mia looked up and smiled briefly. "Hi."

"You look better," Ariel said. "How do you feel?" She glanced around the room until she found Bogard, halfway between Mia and the door, standing against the wall. It seemed somehow shrunken now, not nearly as imposing as the previous night.

"Rested," Mia said. She winced slightly. "Sore. My treatments weren't finished."

R. Jennie set the tray on the breakfast table by the window. Ariel thought about moving it to the coffee table before Mia, but it was not too far away. And Bogard still made her a little nervous.

Ariel sat down and lifted the cover from her eggs and hamsteak. "I'll make the call to take care of that after I eat. What are you going to do afterward?"

"After what?"

"After you're healed."

"That's what I'm trying to decide. I can't very well hide out here for the rest of my life. And I doubt you could get me an open passport to Aurora."

"You might be surprised what I can get you."

Mia raised her eyebrows, but said nothing. She tapped the keypad on her datum for a few minutes while Ariel carved her ham and drank down half her cup of coffee. Ariel wondered if she should have Jennie prepare a large carafe for the day.

Mia sighed heavily, then set the datum aside. She rubbed her face, then folded her arms. "I can't run. If I do, we'll never find out who did this."

"The media are all blaming the Managins."

"That might be partly true," Mia said. "I think it was Managins that actually did the killing. I've started a search protocol on a couple of names that might be relevant and one of them came up within seconds: Lemus Milmor. He's a known affiliate of OSMA, the Order for the Supremacy of Man Again. He's in our database under a 'To Be Watched' flag because he was rejected by a Settler's group for assaulting two people."

Mia shook her head. "Still. The Managins are a large faction, true. Lot of members, broad base. But to subvert the security systems in a place like Union Station? And get all those people and all those weapons in without being detected at *some* point? And then to put me under surveillance and try to kill me? No. They have the motive but not the resources. Not on their own."

"There are other factions."

"I've been going through the list," Mia said, gesturing at the datum. She grabbed her cup and cradled it. "TerraFirst, Primists, the HLA, the Fraternity of Organic Supremacy—if you take bits and pieces of several of them, you might get an effective team together that could attempt something like this. But they hate each other almost as much as they hate Spacers and robots." Mia frowned. "Sorry."

"For what? Are you a member of any of these organizations?"

"No . . . well, maybe. The largest faction would have to be the Terran government."

"But you don't go around killing Spacers to prove your point. Forget it." Ariel shrugged. "Any other candidates on your list?"

"There's been corporate resistance to these talks all along."

"Positronics is a threat to homegrown industry. At least, they see it that way. *We're* not so optimistic."

"What do you mean?"

"It's Spacer belief—an article of faith—that Earth will never allow positronics again. Some of us don't believe that's an absolute—after all, we got a Resident Intelligence installed at one of your largest spaceports—but we doubt Earth will ever embrace our robots to any great degree. Positronics will always be a small presence here."

"So what was this conference supposed to be about?" Mia asked.

"Spacer technology is highly advanced, some of it very far advanced over what's available on Earth. Earth would love to have some of it—like our medical tech—but Earth is afraid that opening the gates just a little will let all of it, including positronics, in. For our part, Spacers are worried about competition from some of *your* technologies that we find impressive."

"Like what?"

Ariel ticked the list off with her fingers. "Transportation systems, automated databases, imbedded technologies, quasi-organic biomechanisms. But mainly mass manufacturing systems. Earth has a long history of production engineering that even with all we've done we can't quite match. Frankly, I find the Terran aversion to positronics puzzling considering some of the things your people play with daily. Anyway, there's fear of open trade both ways. Underlying commercial concerns, there's fear of cultural contamination. But the main deal is the black market. Ever since the *Tiberius* incident, Earth has been treading very carefully. We almost went to war over that."

"If you hadn't backed down—" Mia began.

"If *you* hadn't found *contraband*, you mean. It's very difficult to claim injury when the other fellow is right."

"As far as Earth is concerned, that was still an illegal act, boarding the *Tiberius*."

"But rather than go to war, you listened to Eliton." Ariel

heard the edge of impatience in her own voice. Mia did not
respond, obviously waiting for her friend to calm down.

Ariel cleared her throat. "This conference was supposed
to start a process of . . . well, of demystifcation between us.
A start at debunking some of the erroneous beliefs and tearing down prejudices. Without that process, controlling the
illegalities that proliferate between us will never be possible
and one of these days we *will* go to war. Some of us don't
think either Earth or the Spacer worlds can survive without
each other. At best, though, positronics would always be a
token presence, but a way of teaching Terrans not to fear
us."

"That's all shot to hell."

"Maybe. I've been doing a lot of damage control. But
the heart and soul of the conference is—might be—an agreement to allow positronic inspection of all traffic between
Spacer worlds and Earth. We believe the piracies are a front
for black marketeering. The *Tiberius* supports that belief."

"On whose part?" Mia asked.

"Both sides. You can't sell contraband without a market."

"Collusion between legitimate corporations and pirates?"

"Or pirates in the pay of those corporations. Either way,
humans can be bribed. Robots can't."

Mia shook her head in wonder. "The newsnets had been
going on for months over the proposal for all-robotic inspections of interstellar freighters. That would have been a
miracle."

"Maybe. Just short of getting Earthers to accept positronics?"

Mia laughed bitterly. "The Union Station RI was a positronic system. It failed. That's going to be a hard fact to get past."

Ariel covered her reactions with a forkful of egg. The Resident Intelligence at Union Station should not have permitted the catastrophe. There were ample security systems tied into it, it had the capacity and the imperatives to prevent harm to humans. But Mia was right—it had failed. She was right, too, that it would be a difficult wall to break down. Anyone wishing to derail the conference and any future conference could not have wished for a more perfect event. With all the other problems, it may well have made the situation impossible.

But why had the RI failed? It made no sense. Ariel wondered what Derec's Phylaxis Group had found out. She glanced at her com, but quashed the impulse to call him. She looked over at Bogard against the wall—it had failed, too, even with its vaunted "versatility" in interpreting Three Law conditions. That was Derec's concept, his design.

His failure.

Mia tensed when the medical robot showed up, but made herself relax and allow it to treat her.

"You should be in hospital," the robot informed her.

"Treat her here," Ariel said. "Strictest confidentiality."

"Confidentiality will be respected unless such treatment places the subject at risk," the robot informed her.

"Understood. Proceed. Do you want me to stay, Mia?"

Mia shook her head. "No, I'm fine. You have things to do."

"In that case, anything you need, ask Jennie. If you have to contact me, do so through her."

Mia nodded, watching the medical robot examine her leg.

Ariel approached Bogard. "You will not admit anyone except me unless you receive an explicit command otherwise."

"Coded?"

"I will say . . ." Ariel paused. What would she say that would identify her? She wondered if she were being a little too paranoid. She glanced at Mia on the sofa and decided that too much might be just enough. "I will say 'Avernus in Perihelion' and you will match my voice pattern."

"I understand. What are your instructions regarding the visiting robot?"

"Log its identification. Admit no other without my authorization."

"I understand. Have a pleasant day, Ms. Burgess."

Ariel left her apartment with a shudder of relief, as if she had just escaped. Bogard made her anxious and she resented that. No robot should cause ill ease in a human. She wondered at Mia's evident trust in it. Perhaps it took a Terran to come to terms with such a mechanism.

And it *had* saved her life . . .

At the end of a short hallway, Ariel boarded a tube. "Embassy level E," she told the mechanism. Several seconds later, she stepped out of the transport into the lobby of her department.

A vaguely humaniform robot occupied the small reception desk. Few Terrans ever came here. Hofton, Ariel's aide, leaned over its shoulder, watching something on its screen. Hofton looked up briefly and nodded, then gave a quick instruction to the robot.

"Ariel," he said, moving to open her office door for her, "it's already shaping up to be one of 'Those Days'."

"I thought it would." She entered her office and immediately switched on the subetheric. "Who called first?"

"They all called at the same time. I was tempted to draw straws to see who I answered first. I decided etiquette demanded it be Setaris. She wants to talk to you, though—she wouldn't discuss anything with me. Next was Gale Chassik from the Solarian embassy. He wants to know the official position of the Auroran business community. I told him we were officially staying put. What certain individuals chose to do was no indication of general policy."

"Good." Ariel sat down at her desk and punched the code for Ambassador Setaris. "Third?"

"Benen Yarick."

Ariel scowled. She wished Yarick would just talk to Setaris and leave her alone. Ariel felt as if her allotment of understanding and patience were being fast used up.

"Just give me a list of the others," she told Hofton. "Forward no more calls till I say. I'm not in yet."

"Of course."

"Try to get an official release from the police."

"I imagine that the TBI have assumed control of the investigation, as usual."

"I don't care *who* it's from. They'd be great." She made a shooing gesture. "I have to joust with windmills now."

Hofton almost smiled as he backed from the room.

Setaris appeared on her com. "Ariel, good morning."

"Ambassador."

"Please tell me you have good news."

"Well, yes and no. I spent the balance of yesterday talking to our people. A large number of them had already decided not to leave. Not the majority, but enough to surprise me. I managed to use that and a little armtwisting to get most of the rest to agree not to run. I'll need you to sign off on some concessions, but I didn't break the budget."

"I'm sure anything you promised will be reasonable."

"I appreciate your confidence. I'm afraid, though, that there will still be a very visible number bailing out, but that leaves nearly eighty percent of our people willing to wait and see."

"That's not as bad as I thought . . . so is that the good news?" Setaris asked.

"That's the good part. Last night I spoke to Benen Yarick from Humadros's legation. The survivors want to leave."

Setaris looked pleased. "You *did* speak to Yarick. Good."

"It's irregular, though. I thought she should speak to you or . . ."

"Or who, Ariel? Go on."

"Yarick is simply frightened. She claims that even if she brought herself to stay, her state of mind would make her virtually useless at the conference."

"Hm. I suppose I can see her point of view, but . . . what did you tell her?"

"That it would be a great service to me and the Auroran population here if she reconsidered. As I said, I couldn't convince Yarick to stay, but she said she would talk to the others. I have to return her call this morning. I'm hoping she can tell me they're staying."

"I sympathize with them, of course, but . . ."

"Is there anyone else on staff that could step in for them if they all left?" Ariel asked.

Setaris sighed. "No, not really. I'm afraid my credibility in this matter doesn't extend quite that far. My position on certain elements of what Humadros proposed is too well known to the Terran delegates. I opposed on principle too much of it to be taken seriously. Oh, and speaking of credibility, I'm starting to get calls about the robotic side of this. Which reminds me. I should have called you last night to tell you, but now is as good a time as then. As of this morning, your credentials have been modified to include ambassadorial authority."

Ariel felt abruptly uneasy. "What prompted this?"

"Let me see . . . 'Because of the nature of this crisis,' " Setaris quoted, evidently reading something off-screen, " 'the liaison from the Calvin Institute has been granted temporary modification of plenipotentiary status.' "

"What 'nature of crisis' prompted this?"

"The fact that you are the most senior embassy official still alive. Except for me. All I have is junior legates and trainees. And because of the positronic element. The Terrans are claiming a breakdown of the RI at Union Station. You're our positronic expert on the ground, so now you'll be seconded to my department to deal with diplomatic matters relating to the situation. Anything major, of course, you clear with me first, but . . . congratulations."

Ariel was silent for a few moments. "Have you heard anything concrete from the authorities?"

"They're blaming Managins."

"You don't sound as if you accept that."

"The Managins are a nuisance, certainly, but do *you* believe they could mount something like this?" Setaris shook her head. "It seems they really have no idea, so they're letting the media dictate explanations. I'll never get used to the Earther taste for the salacious and the absurd."

Ariel glanced at her appointment scroll, just now coming up. "I have another day of dealing with Auroran irrationality. It's the same thing, different character."

Setaris frowned.

"Not an opinion," Ariel added, "I share with anyone other than those who already know."

Setaris's frown changed to a wry smile. "Of course."

"Oh, I received a call—I need to follow up on this, too—from Gale Chassik. He wants our official position on this."

"He's being a nuisance and calling *everyone*. I think he wants to find inconsistencies he can exploit. Our official position is that the conference is still on and we will wait for the Terran authorities to pronounce on the investigation before taking any other actions. We condemn the act, but we will not be precipitate."

"I see . . ."

"Anything else, Ariel? I have a full roster, too."

"No, no. Thank you. I'll keep you informed."

"Of course."

The image winked out and Ariel stared at the blank space. Obviously Setaris had already been in contact with Aurora and decisions had been made. Yarick had told her that much. But Aurora could take days or weeks to come up with a policy statement. Spacer time was more leisurely than Earther time, decisions . . . gestated . . . until ready. It was one of the sore points between the two governments.

On the other hand, the pace of diplomatic exchange *had* increased with the piracies. Perhaps someone on Aurora had figured out that hesitation could be expensive when dealing with Earth.

Ariel wondered what sort of "other actions" Aurora might take. Did they already have contingencies?

Her change of status unsettled her. Instead of being gratified at the elevation and the implicit confidence it should signify, she was suspicious. She could not help but think that they were looking for a scapegoat. Given her past, she would be perfect if things went wrong. All they would have to do is issue an official statement, strip her finally and completely of Auroran citizenship, and leave her on Earth, alone.

She entered Beren Yarick's code.

"Good morning, Ms. Burgess," Yarick answered promptly. "I did as you requested. Trina Korolin has agreed to stay—but she's our most junior member. I was unable to convince Gavit Jans. Trina will also have her personal aides—two of them. I'm sorry I couldn't do better."

"What about—"

"I also apologize for the impersonal nature of this response. I've already boarded a shuttle to Kopernik. I regret not having the courage of Ambassador Humadros's convictions. I hope you understand."

"Damn!" Ariel punched the disconnect. A recording. She could not even stay on the ground long enough to give a personal reply.

Perhaps, Ariel thought sourly, *she was worried I might actually talk her out of it.*

"What a mess," she muttered.

She entered Trina Korolin's code.

"Good morning," the com answered. "Ms. Korolin is temporarily unavailable. Please leave a message and a connection code."

"Ariel Burgess, at the Auroran embassy, Calvin Institute. I would like to have a personal talk, Ms. Korolin, at your earliest convenience."

Ariel ended the connection. She did not want to deal with Chassik yet—he could be abrasive. She looked down her list. No doubt, she knew, it would grow longer by the end of the day. Most of them would want little more than an official shoulder to cry on. They were all afraid.

She touched Hofton's intercom. "Hofton, could you get me a list of the casualties? All of them, Terrans included. And a download from several newsnets of the attack."

"Certainly."

She leaned back in her chair. What about the other Spacer contingents? Of the Fifty Spacer Worlds, about a dozen had sizeable enclaves on Earth, the largest—after Aurora and Solaria—being Acrisia, Pallena, and Saon. Of the rest, only a few tourists or the one-off official on short term business. All tolled, there were perhaps sixteen or seventeen thousand Spacers residing on Earth, soon to be fewer. How were *their* governments reacting?

Ariel scrolled down her list, searching for calls from the other embassies. Nothing. That did not mean much, though, since they would more likely deal directly with Setaris's office.

But that could change now.

What is it they think I can do? she wondered.

She had not told Setaris about Mia. Not that she had intended to, but now it seemed like a very shrewd decision on her part.

If I have the authority Setaris tells me I have, she thought, *then why not use it?*

She touched the intercom. "Hofton, find out who is heading the investigation and get me the code."

TWELVE

The agent-in-charge did not return her call. Over the course of the day, Ariel sent a request to speak to him three times, but Agent Cupra either had received none of them or was refusing to respond.

She had been surprised to learn that Special Service had taken over the investigation. Something like this should have been a TBI matter, but the Terran Bureau of Investigation had been shut out of it. In a way it made sense—it had been a Special Service failure in the first place, a smear on their reputation at best, a reason to turn the entire Service upside down and inside out in a search for blame at worst, so they would be strongly motivated to solve the matter. Nevertheless, Earthers tended to be traditional, and tradition alone would dictate that the TBI run the investigation.

She scrolled down the lists Hofton had gotten for her. Casualties, survivors, relatives, addresses—Mia was the only member of Eliton's security team who had lived. Officially, though, she was now listed as deceased.

Twenty-one dead, thirty-three wounded, not counting all those who had suffered injuries among the spectators during the stampede to escape the gallery. Humadros and most of her staff, Eliton and his two aides—those were the costliest diplomatically.

Bogard had given her the name of the agent at the med center. Ariel had Hofton find his code.

Agent Sathen was a thin-faced man with deeply-recessed blue eyes and a short growth of dark brown hair that seemed to hug his scalp like a helmet.

"Yes?"

"Agent Sathen, I'm Ariel Burgess, from the Calvin Institute."

"Yes?" Nothing but professional, impersonal, with no hint that he would willingly tell her anything.

Ariel drew a breath. "I'm calling in regards to Mia Daventri." Seeing his expression change to uncertainty, she made a decision then how to approach this. "I was a friend of hers."

Sathen stared at her for a few moments, then slowly nodded. The set of his jaw relaxed. "How can I help you?"

"Tell me what happened."

"As a friend or as a Spacer official?"

"Both. I understand she originally came in for medical treatment in company with a robot."

"I'm no longer part of the investigation."

"I understand that, Agent Sathen. I'm interested in the part you were involved with."

"As a friend?"

Ariel bit back her impatience. "I—" She stopped. Of course, she realized, this is being recorded. "As a friend. I met Mia on Kopernik Station when I first came to Earth."

Sathen nodded. "I see. Well, there isn't much to tell. I

and my partner received the call to accompany an injured agent to the clinic and to stay with her till she regained consciousness. The ambulance beat us there. When we arrived, the medics had already put her in a room and started her on regeneration treatments. They couldn't get the robot to leave, though. It didn't interfere with them, but none of them were too happy with its presence."

"What robot was this?"

"That special one attached to Eliton's security team. Bogard."

"I see. Weren't you able to recover it?"

"It wouldn't accept commands. Agent Daventri had evidently given it a priority to protect her and it wouldn't accept any other direction until she released it."

"That sounds like you understand something about robots, Agent."

"I don't understand a thing about them. That's what Mr. Avery explained to me."

Ariel's eyes widened slightly. "Derec Avery?"

Sathen nodded. "From the Phylaxis Group, yes. He showed up about five or six hours after Agent Daventri was admitted. Even *he* couldn't get it to move and, as I understand it, he *built* the thing."

"That *is* odd, but . . . go on, Agent Sathen. What happened?"

"Well, Mr. Avery told us to leave it alone and to call him when Agent Daventri regained consciousness. Then later we were recalled. After we left the clinic, Agent Daventri's room was destroyed, with her and the robot."

"Why were you recalled?"

"Reassignment. My partner and I were to be attached to Vice Senator Taprin's security team. That won't take effect, though, till tomorrow. When the explosion occurred, we went back to the clinic. There was . . . nothing left." Sathen's mouth flexed. "Another agent was killed, too."

"In the explosion?"

"No."

When he did not elaborate, Ariel asked, "Any evidence who did it?"

"None. The monitors in the entire clinic went down right before the blast."

"Isn't it a little unusual to be recalled before an assignment is complete?"

"Yes, Ms. Burgess, it is. But then *everything* about this is unusual, isn't it?"

"Yes, it is." Ariel paused. "Did you know Mia?"

"Not well. She seemed like a good agent."

"May I ask who recalled you?"

"It came through our general dispatch. Normally, another team would relieve us. I thought—well, it didn't happen. An oversight."

"I didn't think Special Service made mistakes."

Sathen's expression hardened. "We *don't*. Is that all, Ms. Burgess?"

"Unless you can think of anything more."

"I can't think of anything I left out."

"Thank you for your time, then, Agent Sathen."

The screen blanked. Ariel entered the code for Agent Cupra once more and again got a recording that Cupra was unavailable, please leave name and code.

No forensics . . . Ariel thought.

She called up the staff registry for the clinic in which Mia was "killed" and found the head nurse that had been on duty that night.

"My shift ended at ten," Nurse Carther explained. "But I was there when the injured agent and that—thing—came in. Dr. Jaley oversaw treatment. He just ignored it, the ro-bot. I couldn't, but I didn't have to be in there with it."

"When did the other agents arrive?" Ariel asked.

"A few minutes after we got the biomonitors connected. Agent Sathen and Agent . . . um, Vetter. They ran security checks on all of us. Agent Sathen was upset that he couldn't get the robot to leave. Then a man from the Phylaxis Group showed up and *he* couldn't get it out of there, either. After he left, the other two agents arrived. My shift ended about twenty minutes later and I left."

"Who was your replacement?"

"It was supposed to be Karl Funil, but he called in sick. I'm not sure who was called in then."

"So your relief hadn't shown up when you left? Isn't that irregular?"

"Most of the clinic functions are automated," Carther explained. "If someone isn't there for ten minutes, it's not a problem. The physician-in-charge was there. I could check if you like, see who was called in, but more than likely it was a temp. We draw from a couple of hospital resource pools for emergencies."

Ariel considered for a few moments. That night would have been filled with emergencies. "No, that's all right. What other agents showed up?"

"Two more Special Service people. I don't know what was said, but Agent Sathen was pretty angry with them. I heard yelling."

"They were still there when you left?"

"Yes."

"Can you remember their names?"

"Just the one and only because I heard Agent Sathen say it. Cupra."

"They didn't show you ID?" Ariel asked.

"Agent Sathen knew them."

"Thank you. I appreciate it. If I have any other questions, can I—?"

"I'd rather you didn't," Carther said sharply.

Ariel started. "Oh."

"If that's all, I have things to do."

"Yes, I—"

The image winked out. After all this time, Terran prejudice still surprised her. Too often it came wrapped in a false tolerance that camouflaged real sentiment.

Ariel checked the clinic records again. She found a note appended to the staff log that night: HEAD NURSE KARL FUNIL: EXCUSED FOR ILLNESS. But there was no notation for who took his duties. The way the log read, Nurse Carther had stayed.

Was anyone on staff after she left . . . ? Ariel wondered.

Agent Sathen had said nothing about the visit by Agent Cupra.

"*I can't think of anything I left out,*" he had said.

"How paranoid do you want to be?" Ariel muttered aloud.

"Ariel," Hofton's voice came over the intercom. "Gale Chassik is calling again."

"Damnit!"

"Do you want me to—?"

"Put him through. If I don't talk to him now he'll never go away."

A moment later Chassik's face appeared on her com screen. Gale Chassik's features implied an athletic youth unmaintained in middle age—wide jaw, a fleshy chin, and solid cheeks below bright greenish eyes and a seamed forehead.

"Ms. Burgess," he said slowly, "thank you for taking the time to speak with me."

Ariel heard the unspoken "at last" at the end of his sentence. She made herself smile and hoped she looked convincingly apologetic.

"Sorry, Ambassador Chassik, but it has been a hectic day."

"I can imagine. I truly hate to add to your burdens, but I *do* have a matter or two that require attention. The sooner the better and I can leave you in peace."

"Of course. What can I do for you?"

"First, may I offer condolences on the losses of your fellow Aurorans?"

"Thank you, Ambassador. And I for yours."

"We were more fortunate, at least in simple numbers. I understand Setaris's top aides were killed."

"That's correct."

"Who—?"

"I'm taking over some of their duties for the time being."

"Ah. Then I have finally reached the office I need."

"That depends on what you need, Ambassador Chassik."

"Simply the formality of an official statement. What is Aurora's—and the Calvin Institute's position—on the disaster just experienced?"

"It's strictly wait and see. We don't intend to take any precipitate action until we have some answers from Terran authorities. For now, we'll wait on their investigations before taking any further steps."

"Nicely paraphrased, Ms. Burgess. What about the conference?"

"There is no reason currently to believe that the conference should not continue."

Chassik looked surprised. "Without Galiel? Who could possibly stand in for her? And Senator Eliton?"

"Senator Eliton's second, Vice Senator Taprin, will stand

in for him," Ariel replied. "As for our own contingent, I don't know yet what the roster will be. What about your own legation? Who's staying?"

"None of them. Why should they? The welcome they received—"

"Ambassador, I already have commitments from survivors of the Auroran Legation to stay and see the conference through. It would be awkward if Solaria backed out, don't you think?"

Chassik pursed his lips. "I'll get back to you on that. May I ask who is staying?"

"You may ask."

Chassik waited, then grinned. "When you have your roster completed, you will let us know?"

"Of course."

"The second matter, then. What is your position on the alleged positronic failure and what do you intend to do about the Phylaxis Group?"

"We have no position on the alleged failure. We haven't seen the evidence on it, therefore we cannot determine the validity of the suggestion. Personally, I find it ludicrous. As for the Phylaxis Group, I don't understand what you mean."

Chassik raised an eyebrow. "Really. *Phylaxis* built that absurd robot that failed to protect Senator Eliton. *Phylaxis* is in charge of analyzing the RI in Union Station. The claim that the RI failed has come to us from a variety of sources, some of them quite reliable. If you don't believe that it failed and Phylaxis says it did—well, in light of the incompetence of the bodyguard, can you accept their word?"

"Are you suggesting collusion between Phylaxis and—"

"I'm not suggesting anything," Chassik said quickly. "But I have constituents who are quite uneasy about that robot and after witnessing its performance yesterday, I can't

MIRAGE

say I disagree with them. If there *isn't* collusion, there is gross incompetence. We can't have Phylaxis damaging our reputations. It *was* a Solarian firm that installed the RI."

"I'll look into the matter, Ambassador. Is there anything else?"

Chassik seemed thoughtful for a time. "Have you spoken to the Terran Authorities yet?"

"No. I've requested updates on their investigation, but so far I've received nothing."

"Hmm. When you *do* hear from them, would you let me know what they say?"

"I'm sure you'll be informed at the same time—" Ariel began.

"A favor, Ms. Burgess. In return, I'll share what *I* receive from them. It may be that aspects of this will be overlooked."

"I see. I'll let you know, Ambassador. Thank you."

"Oh, and one more matter. I'm officially informing you that the RI at Union Station is being removed by Solarian specialists."

Ariel blinked. "Removed . . . ? When?"

"Work begins today."

"But—I should have been informed."

"I'm informing you now. You *have* been difficult to reach."

"A Calvin Institute representative is required to be on site for—"

"Ms. Burgess, this is *Earth*. They have no such regulation. The fact that your people were consulted when we installed it was a political courtesy. Now they want it out and they don't care. They need to get the station up and running and a replacement has already been chosen. All that needs to be done is the removal of the RI, which we have been requested—strongly requested—to do with all haste. If you have anyone from the Institute you can spare, send them around."

"It doesn't matter that this is Earth—this is a *Spacer* regulation."

"*Time*, Ms. Burgess, time." Chassik shook his head as if exasperated with her. "My people were contacted early this morning and the request was on my desk when I arrived. I understand their haste, even if I have reservations. The RI is defunct, totally collapsed, a useless mass of pathways. This is a simple physical extraction."

"Has Phylaxis been contacted? Is Derec—Mr. Avery there?"

"I don't know. Would his presence mollify you?"

"I'm not sure." Ariel fought back her irritation. "I don't have anyone to spare. Please make sure they document the removal and forward a report to me."

"I'll see to that, of course."

"Thank you."

"Good day."

Ariel stared at the blank screen, fuming over the breach in protocol. It was not just a matter of form, but a question of accountability. How could she know that everything was done properly without an inspection? She would have to trust them. She imagined that it was the same Solarian company that had installed it in the first place, which did little to assuage her apprehensions.

Why the rush . . . ? she wondered.

After a time, Hofton interrupted again. "Ariel, Trina Korolin is calling. And I have those downloads for you."

At a little past two, Ariel wanted to go back to her apartment. The pressure behind her eyes had mounted steadily over the last two hours till she could no longer deny it and her patience had frayed in equal measure.

Trina Korolin seemed far too young and certainly lacked the experience for what she had volunteered to do, but if enthusiasm and commitment meant anything perhaps she could manage it. Ariel had put her in touch with Jonis Taprin and hoped for the best.

After that, she had spent the rest of her time dealing with panicked Aurorans and at least five attorneys who threatened suits on behalf of Terrans who had been injured or simply frightened senseless at Union Station. They could not sue Aurora—the diplomatic arrangements between Spacer worlds and Earth made it virtually impossible—but they could bring suit against resident Spacers who owned businesses. For the most part, they were only threats designed to elicit out-of-court payments. Ariel told them to go ahead and file, that she thought it likely that, once it was brought to the attention of certain government departments what they were doing, they could lose their licenses rather than risk countersuits by Aurorans. The conversations turned ugly in a couple instances, with one attorney telling her bluntly that he intended to press the suit anyway if there was any chance of getting the damn Spacers off Earth.

Her responses grew sharper and sharper until she finally told Hofton to stop putting the calls through. She could no longer concentrate on her job. Her attention was divided.

"Ariel," Hofton's voice came over the intercom, "I have recordings of the incident, as you requested. Two for now, a third one has been promised."

"I'll view them at my apartment later. Thank you, Hofton."

She stared into space, letting her thoughts collide randomly.

There had been gaps in the exchanges with Agent Sathen and Gale Chassik. She kept turning over in her mind what else they might have left out. Sathen had pointedly said nothing about the two agents who had come to see him after Mia's admission to the hospital. Chassik's implication of wrongdoing against Derec infuriated her. He had danced over the fact that it was a Solarian firm that had installed the RI at Union Station and that if any collusion were involved it would be between that company and the conspirators. The more she thought about it, the more convinced she became that both Sathen and Chassik had made deliberate omissions, and in the case of Sathen, at least, unwilling omissions.

Ariel had never gotten used to the standard practice reticence diplomatic service entailed. Not being told things because it was "not your area" or was not part of her "need to know" irritated her to the point of fury, but she had come to accept it. This was different, though she could not quite define how. There was a distinction between covering one's butt as a matter of routine and covering up. She could sense the change even when it defied specification.

Perhaps her insight came only from the fact that Mia Daventri was hiding out in her apartment. It seemed curious that Special Service could pronounce her dead without a single tissue sample.

She stabbed the intercom.

"Hofton, I'm going home. Unless war breaks out before tomorrow morning, handle it."

"As you command," Hofton intoned with mock gravity.

"Don't be impertinent."

"Never."

In spite of her headache, Ariel smiled. She gathered up the disks of all the downloads Hofton had gotten for her and slipped them into her pocket.

She stepped into the lobby and raised her hand to gesture good-bye to her staff.

"Ariel," Hofton said, looking up from his desk, "you might want to take this call."

"I might?"

"I think so. It's Derec Avery from the Phylaxis Group."

THIRTEEN

D erec waited restlessly in the small Phylaxis Group
reception lounge.

The room contained comfortable chairs, a bar, a
subetheric, a viewer on which could be displayed promo-
tional or educational material—a pleasant environment in
which clients could become better acquainted with Phylaxis, its work, and positronics. Derec remembered the party
held here when they had received their license. His trun-
cated staff and Senator Eliton and a few of his own aides
had toasted the future, the gamble they were taking, the
hope that things would change. It had been the only time
anyone had actually used the room.

A bell chimed and Derec pressed the button on the receptionist's desk to open the door.

Ariel stepped inside and stopped. She glanced around,
then looked at him. Derec began to smile. She wore a better-
than-average Terran one-piece the color of clay and a dark
blue jacket. She was thinner than the last time he had seen
her, eyes wearier, the lines around her mouth a little deeper,

tighter. Except for the slightly exaggerated contours of her chin-length black hair—closer to Spacer style than Terran—she might pass for an Earther.

"I'm here," she said.

"Thank you. I wasn't sure you'd come."

"I'm still not sure it's worth my time. You said you have something to show me?"

Derec felt his brief pleasure fade. Better, he realized, to get directly to business.

"Who from the Calvin Institute supervised the installation of Union Station's RI? It wasn't you."

She frowned. "Directly? No. I'm the commerce liaison here, not a project manager. But I looked in on it." She shrugged. "Why?"

"Who did the inspection? I mean, specifically."

"Bys Randic. She rotated back to Aurora last year, though. Is it important?"

"Could be. Was there anything unique about it? The brain itself, that is."

Ariel sighed deeply. "I didn't come here to be interrogated. You told me you found something wrong with the RI. Did you?"

"Oh, yes. But—"

"Show me."

Derec started to protest, but stopped himself and waved her toward the door behind him. Clearly nothing had changed in the years since the last time they had spoken together in the same room. At least this time Ariel was not shouting and redfaced. Not yet, anyway.

A short corridor ended at a heavy security door, which stood open. Ariel preceded him through to the main lab.

Rana looked up from her console, one eyebrow cocking

critically. From behind Ariel, Derec patted the air to let Rana know it was all right.

Ariel did a more careful survey of this chamber. Derec could almost imagine the way she assessed each piece of equipment, sorted out the way in which the lab worked, and judged it . . .

"I'm impressed," she said. "You could do some excellent work here." She turned to him. "What *do* you do with it?"

"Till lately," Rana said, "we've done a lot of theoretical work, plotting positronic vectors under stress situations and the like, and we can play some really high level strategy games on it. For the most part, though, we spend our time answering questions from resident Spacers who can't understand why their robots won't anticipate their wants and desires the way they do back home and explaining to others why they shouldn't have a positronic robot outside embassy confines."

Derec glared at her. "Rana, this is Ariel Burgess. Ariel, Verana Duvan, my chief roboticist."

"Burgess," Rana said, rising. "Calvin Institute." She stopped a pace away from Ariel. "I read your brief on 'Cross-Inference Deduction in the Field.' Good work."

Ariel hesitated, then slowly nodded. "Thank you. I'm afraid I can't say I've seen any of your work."

"Don't apologize. I'm Terran. We don't get to publish in Spacer journals."

"How . . . ?"

"How did I get involved with robotics?" Rana grinned. "My degree is in Industrial Automation, with a minor in AI. I got sidetracked into positronics. We aren't all rabidly anti-robot."

"That must have been difficult."

"Tracking down the material was a challenge. Frankly, if Derec hadn't come along with his offer to work here I was going to apply for emigration. I was preparing my application to the Calvin Institute. Futile gesture, maybe, but you never know till you try."

"Why futile? If Derec wanted you, you must be good."

"Calvin doesn't take very many Earthers. I checked. There's a very old saying about a snowball's chance . . . ?" Rana started to go back to her console, then looked at Ariel. "And I *am* good."

"Modest, too," Derec said.

"So with all this talent, why do you need me?" Ariel asked.

"Because we didn't install the RI at Union Station, we only watched from a distance," Rana said. "And it has some peculiarities we can't explain."

"What did they tell you at the Institute?"

"They didn't," Derec said. "We . . . aren't really supposed to be looking at it."

"Excuse me?"

"Special Service assumed jurisdiction over the entire investigation. Threw us out."

"Special Service doesn't have any positronic experts."

"Maybe they're talking to your people at the Institute," Derec said.

Ariel's mouth compressed tightly. She looked troubled. "So what are you doing with it?"

"We set up surrogate function through our RI and transferred a complete copy of Union Station's here before we were shut out. They don't know we have it."

"And you don't want to go through normal channels to ask . . . I see." Ariel nodded. "You think I'll act as go-between for you? Believe me, the last thing I need now is

a problem with Special Service. I've already got panicked
Aurorans ready to leave Earth at a heartbeat. Any kind of
problem with Earth authorities that might lead to—"

"Ariel," Derec said, cutting her off. "No. I want *you* to
look at what we have and give me your opinion."

She gave him a dubious look. "That's all?"

"We'll see. First, I want to know what you think."

Her eyes narrowed. He knew she understood what he
was doing. He hoped she would acknowledge a stake in this,
that perhaps she already had found inconsistencies in the
situation, that her involvement would outweigh her resent-
ments. He watched her work through all of that and more
he could not guess.

"All right," she said finally. "Show me what you have."

"It's been a while since I've seen a collapse this thorough,"
Ariel said, staring at the screen. "Did *anything* function?"

"Nothing," Derec said. "According to the staff, everything had to be switched to manual. Fortunately, some of
the systems had their own parallel processing units, so it
wasn't a complete loss, but . . ."

Ariel pointed at one of the spirals. "What *is* that? It looks
like a paradox loop, but I don't see a resolution point."

"Neither do we," Rana said, "and I've been looking. I
started an excavation, but it looks like the loops resolve
somewhere outside the positronic matrix."

"That's absurd, there is no 'outside' a positronic matrix,"
Ariel said. "Not like this. Unless it's a connection with another positronic matrix."

"A comlink," Derec said.

"Basically, yes. You know this stuff, Derec. This is
freshman-level pathway schema."

"But in this case," he said patiently, "it doesn't go

through any comlinks. We traced a good number of the comlinks, mostly the supervisory connections with the mobile staff. None of them match these sites. These loops are leaving the matrix and going somewhere else through a channel we can't determine."

"Just what sectors are they in?"

"It's too damaged to tell about all of them," Derec said. "Once it began collapsing, everything randomized."

"At some point it should lock up. The whole thing shouldn't devolve into chaos."

"That's what I thought," Rana said. "Basic salvage protocol, ever since the stasis modifications went in—what? Twenty years ago? But this did exactly the opposite and became more fluid."

Ariel started tapping the keyboard before her. "You said too damaged to tell about all of them. Does that mean you could tell for some of them? What about a scan for mirror sites . . . where do these sectors link to the station systems?"

"Maintenance," Rana said.

Ariel waited, then glanced at the other woman. "*All* of them?"

"So far."

"Hm. How did you determine that?"

"Like I said, I'm running an excavation. Layer by layer, sector by sector, and matching it to design specs from our RI, which, for the time being, is running Union Station."

Ariel blinked at her. "I admire your ambition."

Rana shrugged. "No option. But . . ." She waved at the screen.

"Maintenance . . ." Ariel mused. "What about the reference template? Did you check it?"

"Can't find it," Rana said. "Everything is so random—"

Ariel leaned forward and worked the keyboard. She entered a few more commands, then sat back. Two of the peripheral screens began to display new patterns.

Rana stared. "How did—?" she began, but Derec gave her a minute shake of the head.

"Every positronic brain has a reference template," Ariel said quietly, more to herself than to them. "A basic pattern of behavior and attributes against which the working brain can refer . . ." She frowned. "I don't understand this. They're randomized, too." She tapped more commands. The screens changed.

Ariel touched one of the screens. "This comline isn't right. It's one-to-one, no buffer to shield the matrix. Same with this one. What kind of accessory systems were installed on this?"

"Don't know," Derec said.

She scowled at him impatiently. "What do you mean, you don't know? Didn't you do an on-site inspection?"

"We didn't get a chance to before we were taken off the job and barred from the site."

"What about before this? Are you telling me you only looked at the system during the install and not since?"

"We went back in once, a few months after the installation. After that it was supposed to be on an as-needed basis and we never received a call. Now that we need to get in there, we're blocked."

"That's ridiculous. Who issued that order?"

"It came from the director's office of Special Service," Derec replied. "Their authorization was legal."

"But Phylaxis—"

"We were *removed*, Ariel. Period."

She stared at the screens before her, but Derec was sure she saw nothing on them. She absently scratched her chin once.

"I see. And you think I—we—had something to do with that?"

"The thought had occurred to me," Derec said drily.

Ariel nodded slowly, still looking at the screens. "You said no one knows you have this copy?"

"No one has shown up yet to take it away from us."

That elicited a grin.

"Do you have any theories about what this is?" She pointed at the screen.

"The staff told me that just before the assault, the RI took itself off-line to play a game. It was completely unaware of what was happening in the gallery until it came back online and witnessed the aftermath."

"And that's when the collapse began."

"Exactly," Derec said. "Now, the paradox loops and the mirror sites suggest that something was physically attached to the RI network. When I asked about problems with the RI before this, I was told that a few glitches had occurred, but they were minor and they'd been told that 'adjustment errors' were to be expected, to contact the Calvin Institute about them before contacting us. Most were dismissed."

"Adjustment errors . . ." Ariel stood and walked slowly around the lab. After one full circuit she stopped directly in front of Derec. "What do you want from me?"

"To start with, I'd like to know who issued that maintenance directive."

"You want my help."

"Just—" Derec began.

"You want me to pry into the operations of my own people to see if any of them are somehow culpable." Her voice was growing edged, caustic.

"Ariel—"

"You want me to help you figure out why the RI went insane."

"Well—"

"You want me to forget about everything else, drop my responsibilities, and be a spy for you." Ariel folded her arms across her chest and grunted derisively. "I have to credit you, Derec—you have nerve."

Derec could feel his own irritation grow. He feared a repeat of their last fight. "Are you going to tell me you're *not* interested in this?"

Ariel glared at him briefly. "Damn you, yes. You *knew* that would happen, once I saw this." She slapped the top of the console. "You relied on that. You *used* it."

"And you hate being used."

"Damn it—!"

"Then help us," Derec said softly. "Whoever did this is using you in a much worse way. Whoever did this did it to kill Galiel Humadros and Clar Eliton. They also killed the two surviving members of Eliton's security team. It will get worse. At the very least, this completely discredits positronics on Earth. This undoes everything Eliton hoped to do. Even if the conference goes on now, without finding the people responsible nothing will be accomplished. Tell me this doesn't concern you."

Ariel caught herself, face red, mouth open to respond. "I need to know more."

Derec felt a moment of hope, a brief twinge of success. He ran the tip of his tongue over his lips, folded his arms, and, in as calm a voice as he could manage, told her what he had learned. All the while he watched her, hoping he could still trust what he saw in her expression.

* * *

Rana kept glancing over the top of her console at Ariel, who sat on the opposite side of the lab, arms folded, staring at the floor.

"What are you wondering?" Derec asked finally.

Rana gave him an annoyed look. "She enters a couple of commands and in half a second gets to where it took me hours to fail to reach." She shook her head. "I'm not sure if I'm wondering or just resenting."

"Ariel's one of the best."

"Along with you?"

"Sometimes I think she's better."

"How long will she take to make up her mind?"

Derec looked at Ariel. "I don't know. It will take as long as it takes."

Rana shook her head. "I was really excited when I found out you knew Ariel Burgess. It was a major disappointment when it turned out you weren't on speaking terms anymore." She glanced at him. "I knew there was a problem between you two, but . . ."

"Philosophical differences."

"You said that before."

"You didn't believe me?"

"People don't usually display that much heat over philosophy."

"Not the abstract kind, no. But when it relates directly to what you do, who you are . . ." Derec frowned. "She believes I betrayed her trust. We . . . it sounds like a cliché, but we really had everything together for a while."

"Until?"

"Until I started playing around with the ideas that became Bogard." He looked at Rana. "You can be damn nosy."

Rana shrugged. She began to say more, then nodded toward Ariel. "Decision time?"

Ariel was walking toward them.

"We'll see," Derec whispered.

Ariel leaned on the console. "What do you think is going on?"

"Obviously, someone had a stake in seeing the conference stopped or at least rendered useless. I don't think anything constructive can come of it now."

"Do you believe what the newsnets are saying? That it was the Managins?"

"No."

"Why not?"

"They don't have the resources," Derec replied. "The will, yes, but the ability to subvert the Resident Intelligence of a facility like Union Station? Get several armed people inside? And then escape?" He shook his head. "I gather no other arrests have been made?"

"None that I'm aware of."

"Someone used the Managins, maybe."

"Who?"

Derec shrugged. "I don't know."

"Do you think the Calvin Institute is involved?" Ariel asked.

"*Someone* issued that maintenance directive. Someone who understood the nature of positronics and knew what I might find."

Ariel's mouth was a thin, hard line. "I can't disagree. Not entirely. But I have another problem."

"Which is?"

"That robot of yours. The bodyguard unit. Why did it fail?"

Derec felt himself stiffen. "I don't know."

"You admit that it did?"

"It . . . something went wrong."

"It was designed to defend a primary subject, correct? In this case, Senator Eliton. It didn't. Eliton died. Why?"

"I wish I knew. It's more complicated than that, even. From what I saw, it *was* defending Eliton. Then, for some reason, it abandoned him."

"Perhaps your design was faulty?"

Derec hesitated. "Perhaps." He had not wanted to admit that possibility—especially not to Ariel—but he could not reject it.

"Or was it subverted the same way the RI was?" Ariel asked.

That surprised him. "I can't see how. But I don't know how the RI was subverted, so your guess is as good as anyone else's. There's no way to tell. If I had Bogard here, I might be able to determine what went wrong, but it's gone. Destroyed."

Ariel tapped a finger absently while she regarded Derec. Suddenly, she slapped both hands on the top of the console. "All right, I'll help you. I've got unanswered questions myself. But I want to know what we're supposed to do if we find something."

"Like what?"

"Like what we both suspect—that this is more than the actions of a group of disaffected bigots. Unless those bigots have members in the government."

"I suppose that depends on just who it is we find. If it's the authorities, we can't very well go to them, can we?"

"It's not likely to be *all* of them."

"No, but—"

"The problem, Derec, is that whoever is behind this, the consequences of uncovering it could be worse than leaving it alone."

"Are you serious?"

"Perfectly," Ariel replied. "Right now, as much as I hate to admit it, we have a diplomatic crisis. We're left with a shattered program and we have to start all over. What we do *not* have is a war. Push this and that's exactly what we might have."

"War? You're overstating a bit, aren't you?" Rana asked.

"I already told you: I'm *perfectly* serious. If it becomes clear that the Terran government, or a part of it, engineered an assassination of an Auroran ambassador, the only conclusion Aurora and the Fifty Worlds can make is that Earth cannot be trusted. They could decide that the only way to deal with it then is containment. No more Settlers will be permitted out. No more trade. No more anything. Isolation."

"Is that doable?" Derec asked.

Ariel shook her head. "No, not entirely. We can't even get rid of the pirates that have been raiding the lanes. But it doesn't matter. It's enough to set off a war."

"So who would benefit from that?"

"I don't know. Someone always benefits from a war. But that's one possible outcome of this." Ariel paused. "So. I'll ask again. What do we do when we find out?"

"We may not be able to do anything. I think we need to find out what we can first, then decide."

"No going off on your own. *We* decide."

Derec nodded. "Agreed."

"All right. Where do you want to start?"

"Well . . . getting inside Union Station would be good. I need to do a physical inspection to see what's been done to the matrix."

"I may be able to help with that."

"Good. That will do for a start."

Ariel gave him a curious smile. "It would really help if you could talk to Bogard?"

"Of course it would! But—"

Ariel's smile broadened. "Why don't you come with me. I have something to show you."

FOURTEEN

I n light of recent revelations," the newscaster declared
from the subetheric, "the death of Special Service Agent
Mia Daventri and the destruction of the experimental
robot assigned to guard Senator Clar Eliton have taken on
new significance. The entire team of agents charged with
the security of Eliton and his staff during the Union Station
meeting with Spacer legations has now been killed. Special
Service is conducting an internal investigation on which
they refuse to comment, except to suggest that certain irregularities are at the heart of the tragedy. The utter failure
of a trained team of agents to protect one of Earth's most
prominent politicians cannot be explained unless that failure was part of a larger movement. Sources inside the Terran Bureau of Investigation have let it be known that files
have been opened on the agents involved, and their affili-
ations with various organizations—ostensibly in the line of
duty—are being questioned. Nevertheless, the question no
one seems willing to either answer or deny is the Spacer
connection."

Mia pressed the contact on the remote, shutting off the subetheric. After going from one newsnet to another in between other tasks she felt nervous and edgy. None of the news reassured her, almost all of it had raised more questions, and she should have stopped listening. She especially should not have watched *this* 'cast.

Dal Kammer, one of the top-rated newscasters on subetheric, implying that Mia and her teammates had been involved in the conspiracy to kill Eliton and Humadros, made her cringe. If it had been any of a dozen other newsnet people she might have shrugged it off—there was more detritus on the subetheric than legitimate data—but Kammer was prominent, reputable. That did not mean he would not twist, color, alter, or fabricate his facts. But it meant that to get him to do so was expensive.

Or he was being led to believe the reports . . .

Mia lay her head back against the pillow. The medical robot had left over six hours ago, giving her a pain blocker along with a tissue accelerant and instructions to move around as little as possible until its next visit. She wondered if squirming counted.

Her datum lay on the table beside her. She had spent most of the day sending queries through Ariel's com system, using a pair of alternate electronic personas working in tandem, so if any back traces were attempted they would lead into blind alleys, to see if any of her passwords worked anywhere. Nothing. The Service had shut her out of everything, which puzzled her. If they thought she was dead, why be so thorough so fast in blocking her access? Unless they really did think she had been part of a conspiracy. Then it made sense—they would suspect someone else possessed her codes.

A few names appeared on the small screen, possible contacts she might yet be able to trust: a newsnet reporter named Holis, her old instructor at the academy, and Coren Lanra, the ex-Service agent she had seen at the gallery, now working for DyNan Manual Industries. Holis would help her in return for an exclusive, which meant that she needed something with which to bargain. So far, except for the fact that she was alive, she had nothing solid. She was uncertain how much trouble she might cause for her old instructor. As for Lanra, she did not know where he stood, except that he had no loyalty anymore to the Service. She had contacted none of them.

What had gone wrong?

Mia glanced over at Bogard, standing against the wall between where she lay and the door, still and solemn. Two hours ago, after its own datum search, it had reported on the type of weapon used at Union Station. No direct match, but it bore similarity to a twenty-first century Staros, nine-millimeter automatic. Modifications had been made, altering them enough to call a direct match into question. But that meant they had probably been manufactured exclusively for this strike, which reinforced Mia's opinion that Kynig Parapoyos had provided them.

The other name on her screen tended to confirm that. Bok Vin Golner. It was the likeliest match she had come up with from the name Bok, given the other parameters she had attached to the search. Retired Terran military, Captain, a veteran of two campaigns, including the Ganymede Suppression, and, since leaving the army, an irregularly employed security specialist. He had been arrested once for civic disturbance during a Terran First rally and another time for trafficking in unlicensed merchandise, black market. In both instances he had been represented by a lawyer he could not reasonably afford and the charges had been dropped. He was listed as an affiliate to a couple of anti-Spacer groups.

If you want to set up a military assault, Mia thought, *use someone who knows how and can follow through . . .*

Bogard *shifted* the three meters to the door. Mia blinked. A few seconds later, R. Jennie trundled into the room, but stopped upon seeing Bogard blocking the entrance.

"Avernus in Perihelion," came Ariel's voice over the intercom.

"Accepted," Bogard announced and opened the door.

Ariel stepped past the robot with a wary look, followed by a man Mia did not know. Only slightly taller than Ariel, he wore his pale hair short, and a black jacket over a dark blue one-piece.

"Hello, Bogard," he said, his expression openly surprised.

"Hello, Derec," the robot replied. "It is good to see you again."

Derec gave Ariel a skeptical look. "Avernus in Perihelion?"

"Would anyone you know guess that as a password?" Ariel asked.

Derec shook his head. "No, I suppose not." He looked at Bogard again. "Don't take this wrong, Bogard, but I thought you were dead."

"No, sir," Bogard said. "Although your misapprehension is understandable."

"Welcome home, Ariel," R. Jennie said, accepting Ariel's jacket. "Welcome, sir."

Derec shrugged out of his jacket and handed it to R. Jennie. "Thank you." He stepped into the living room and looked at Mia with the same expression of amazement. "And you. You're—"

"Dead, yes," Mia said. "Officially, at least. Do I know you?"

"No. The last time I saw you was in the hospital. You were quite unconscious. The next time I saw that room, though . . ."

"Bogard performed its function admirably," Mia said.

Derec gave the robot another look, this time with an unmistakable expression of pride.

"Apparently," he said.

"Mia Daventri," Ariel said then, "this is Derec Avery, of the Phylaxis Group. Derec—my friend, Mia Daventri."

Derec came up to her and extended his hand. "I'm not sure I even want to know how you ended up here. But I'm very pleased to make your acquaintance."

Mia took his hand. Dry, warm. "I've heard interesting things about you, Mr. Avery."

"Derec, please." He glanced at Ariel. "From Ariel?"

"No."

"How do you feel?" Ariel asked.

"Better. A little pain block does wonders for my disposition."

"Good. We have work to do."

" 'We'?" Mia asked.

Ariel smiled. "You wanted me to trust you, you have to trust me. I wouldn't bring just anyone in here now. Derec is the other positronic expert on Earth."

Derec grinned. "The other best one, that is." He looked at Ariel. "Who's the first one?"

Ariel aimed a finger at him. "Don't start."

Derec raised his hands in mock surrender. "*Somebody* should start, though. Why not Ms. Daventri?"

"Mia. Unless I'm mad at you, then it's Special Agent Daventri." She liked his smile, she decided. But it was obvious Ariel did not. "Start where? With what?"

"First, I suppose, how did you get out of that hospital alive?"

Mia sighed and started talking.

"You saw two people?" Derec asked again.

"There might easily have been more. Bogard, how many intruders entered the hospital?"

"I registered five presences in the building," Bogard said. "One was the agent left as guard. One was the physician on duty sleeping in the doctor's lounge. Three intruders entered. Two conducted the assault on your room while the third remained at the entrance."

"How many were involved in the assault at Union Station?" Ariel asked. "Several got away."

"Bogard," Derec asked, "how many assailants did you count at Union Station?"

"A visual count of twenty-one."

"That seems right," Mia said.

Derec was frowning at the robot. "Why the qualification, Bogard?"

"I am not sure, Derec, but I have a firm count of the visual only. Infrared suggests eighteen, radar only nine. I cannot explain the discrepancy."

"We need recordings from the assault," Derec said.

Ariel crossed the room to her com. "We have two newsnet downloads."

"Only two?"

Ariel gave Derec a mock scowl. "To start." She worked at the com for a minute, then gestured to the subetheric. The broad space filled with the image of Union Station's gallery, filled with spectators awaiting the arrival.

"This is Seath Callon for GVS—"

"We don't need sound," Derec said. "I think we've all heard enough. Just visual."

The voice-over died and they watched in silence the events unfold. The entrance of the Eliton party, the gathering on the platform, the arrival of the Spacer legations, the explosions. The recorder shifted abruptly, then, the operator apparently unsure where to concentrate attention. Finally, the image closed on the platform and the area immediately surrounding it as the black-clad figures crowded against the base, firing into the panicked delegates. Mia noticed that Derec Avery watched Bogard as much as the vid.

"Looks like twenty-one to me," Ariel said.

"Back it up slowly," Mia said. "Bogard, track the assailants."

The robot moved closer to the screen.

The camera withdrew, the action flowing languidly in reverse until a point just before the explosions.

"Stop," Mia said. "Bogard?"

"There is a discrepancy," the robot said. "I counted twenty-one assailants at the edge of the platform. Twelve of them are absent from the crowd at this point."

"What—?" Ariel started. She glared at the robot.

"Wait," Derec said. "The vid I saw at the station from the RI surveillance, just prior to it going off-line, showed people in the crowd vanishing. Now you're telling us that several of these figures *appeared* during the initial attack? They weren't already present?"

"That is what I am seeing, Derec."

Ariel's skeptical look slowly changed to apprehension. "Mia, do you remember what you saw?"

"Not that well. Our first concern was the explosions. Then the gunfire."

"Bogard," Derec said, "we'll advance the scene now. Tell us when those missing figures first appear."

The scene once more ran its course, in slow motion. The crowd seemed to undulate under the sound of the blasts, like anemone waving in an ocean current.

"Stop," Bogard said.

Derec leaned forward, then grabbed the subetheric control. "Where?" he asked, handing the device to Bogard.

The robot narrowed the view to a patch of people about four meters from the base of the platform. It was a variegated collection of onlookers, mostly well-off, dressed fashionably in brightly-colored jackets over more muted single-pieces, hair streaked and coifed in pastels. Now, panicked, their faces were drawn into macabre parodies of themselves, eyes wide, mouths gaping, and their bodies crouched in preparation to run. But they were trapped in a larger crowd with no room.

In the very midst of the twenty or so spectators, three people stood dressed all in black. Even their heads were covered by pullovers. There was something not right about two of them, though, the two following a third who shoved a path through the crowd.

"They don't fit," Mia said. "Look at the people immediately around them, especially that man in bright red. Beside him is a woman in orange? They're standing right next to each other. In fact—Bogard, can you give us more mag? Thank you—in fact, they're holding hands."

"So?" Ariel asked.

"Their arms are joined right through that assailant's stomach," Mia pointed out. "Look at the other one . . . the shoulder is passing through that woman's breasts."

"Images," Derec said. "Projections. Bogard, follow those two, continue scan."

The scene began to move again. The two black-clad fig-

ures stepped quickly through—*through*, not around—the in-
tervening people, following a leader, to emerge into the
space now at the foot of the platform. Others joined them.
They seemed to lean their elbows on the edge of the platform, rifles in hand, and commence firing.

"Bogard, see if the other sudden appearances come
grouped in twos or threes."

The robot advanced and backed up the images, shifting
from one part of the crowd to the next, so quickly Mia had
trouble following the scene. She had to close her eyes when
vertigo threatened to make her nauseated.

"There is always one in the lead," the robot said finally,
"and two who appear behind."

"Military," Mia said. "A holographic generator worn by
a soldier projects an image of two or three more. An enemy
targeting system can be confused, just like Bogard was, giving multiple counts."

"Bogard," Derec said, "do a projected trace on one of
their shots and see where it goes."

There was a moment's pause, then one of the shadow
rifles fired. The scene jerked forward then, into the frightened delegates, and stopped on an Auroran woman trying
to turn and flee back into the debarkation umbilical. She
looked unhurt and continued her attempted flight.

"Bogard, according to your trajectory plot she should
have been hit?"

"Yes, Derec."

"Wouldn't the newsnets have figured this out already?"
Ariel asked.

"Probably not," Mia said. "They got their recordings,
they put them on subetheric, they did their duty. I doubt
anyone gave it a second look." She thought for a few seconds. "On the other hand, maybe they have and they don't

know what to do with it. It doesn't change the results, does it?"

"All right," Derec said, "this would confirm your suspicion that Kynig Parapoyos at least supplied the weapons and that an ex-military man like this Bok Golner conducted the actual assault. What do we do next?"

Mia cleared her throat, then, and looked at Derec and Ariel.

"Before we go any further," she said, "I need to make it clear that once we start, it gets dangerous. I can't trust my own people and they control the security network for the planet, or at least a good portion of it. If we go probing we could get hurt. If you don't want to risk that, tell me now and we stop it here."

Ariel pursed her lips and made a show of thinking it over. "There's no option for me. I have to know. But Derec—"

"No option for me, either," he said. "I'm involved already through Bogard. No matter how this comes out, what I've built here is at risk. The only way I can protect any of it is to see this through. We're in."

Mia studied them both, then nodded. "All right, then. First we need to find out where the guns came from and where Bok Golner trained his team. The attack took expertise. You don't just get up one day and do something like this without practice. Where would they train?"

"Kynig Parapoyos bothers me," Ariel said. "Why would he do this? Or his organization? I don't recall ever seeing or hearing anything about him conducting assassinations."

"Not like this, no," Mia said. "But I don't think he's entirely behind it. Someone had to subvert the RI, someone had to subvert Special Service agents, someone had to be on the inside. Parapoyos could provide the weapons, but all the rest?"

Ariel was nodding. "He's the main supplier for the Settler colonies. Do you think they had anything to do with it?"

"Why would they?" Derec asked.

"The piracies," Mia answered. "One of the primary suspects is the Settler worlds. One or more of them may be harboring the pirate bases."

"And robotic inspections could affect that relationship," Derec said, nodding. "But all of them? As a matter of policy? Isn't that a stretch?"

"Of course," Ariel said, "but the Settlers aren't a monolith, no more than the Spacers are. It's a possibility."

"It would be a good idea for you to buy some guns, Ariel," Mia said.

Ariel's eyebrows went up.

"It would be a way to get to Parapoyos. You go to the Settler Coalition and talk to them. If they're buying through Parapoyos here, Riansa Visher was involved. Her successor will know about it. They can put you in contact."

"Why me?"

"Because this little incident could mean war," Mia explained. "Aurora may need weapons."

Ariel did not look comfortable, but she nodded.

After an awkward silence, Derec waved a hand at the subetheric. "With this and the recordings from the RI—"

"Assuming anyone but you and the RI staff saw those particular records," Ariel said. "By now, Special Service may have confiscated or destroyed them."

Derec frowned and stared at the subetheric.

"Bogard," Mia said, glad for the change of subject. "Find the actual casualties and trace the shots back to source. Determine how many live assailants were present."

For a few painful minutes the view shifted from victim

to attacker, victim to attacker, several times. Each instance startled and saddened Mia. What struck her most consistently was the expression of surprise each wounded person wore upon being hit, followed sometimes by a rictus of pain, but only if that person had survived the injury. Death left the last expression stamped on each face: bafflement, confusion, amazement, in one instance a look of betrayal.

"Nine," Bogard announced finally. "There are twenty-one images and nine actual assailants."

"Nine," Mia mused. "That tends to validate the idea that they were after only a few individuals."

"Bogard, can you identify the individuals killed?" Ariel asked.

"Yes, Ms. Burgess." Bogard began displaying the names of the delegates as they appeared on the screen.

"You captured three of the assailants," Derec said to Mia. "Didn't you?"

"Yes," Mia said. "I—"

"Stop," Ariel said, standing. Bogard fell silent. She stared at the screen. "That last name . . ."

"Tro Aspil," Bogard said.

"Tro . . . but he survived . . ."

"The wound depicted," Bogard said, "is not consistent with survival. The shot entered the throat and severed the carotid artery."

"Then . . ." Ariel went to her datum.

"What is it?" Mia asked.

"Should I continue?" Bogard asked.

"Hmm?" Mia glanced up at the robot. "Compile the list for future reference."

"You captured three of the assailants and . . . ?" Derec prompted.

"Yes, I did. Well, Bogard captured two of them, but—"

"How did Bogard perform?"

"After I gave him a new priority, perfectly. I couldn't have apprehended those men without it."

"Then . . ." Derec looked at Bogard self-consciously. "How do you explain the failure?"

"I'm not sure—"

"I built Bogard, Agent Daventri. Senator Eliton is dead. I need to know what happened."

"I see. Yes, you should know. Frankly, I had intended to ask *you* that question. When—" She gave Bogard an apprehensive look. "I'm not sure we should talk about this in Bogard's presence."

Derec nodded. "Bogard, have you completed compiling the list of casualties from this recording?"

"Yes, Derec."

"Stand down, then, please."

"I cannot do that, Derec. I am still responsible for Agent Daventri's safety."

Derec frowned briefly, then shrugged. "Should any of the subject matter we're discussing present potential operational difficulties for you, alert us."

"I will do that, Derec."

Derec smiled. "Bogard will know better than any of us when it's in trouble."

Mia felt uneasy. "I attempted to get a full report from Bogard last night. The part about Senator Eliton is absent from its logs."

"No, it's not. It's elsewhere, but it's there. At some point I'll have to run a complete debrief on all Bogard's systems to get at it, but it means that its system is working the way it should. Please, go on."

"When the explosions began, Bogard immediately en-shielded the Senator. That left us free to confront the as-sault. But it came so suddenly and unexpectedly—you train for the possibility, but nothing can prepare you for the re-ality. The casualties, the explosions, the panic—what do you do first? Our training says to get the people we're supposed to protect out of harm's way as soon as possible. There was nowhere for them to go. We couldn't *get* them to safety. Then . . . then my teammates started going down. I tried to return fire, but for all I know now I may have shot nothing but images. Or I may have shot innocent spectators. There was too much all at once."

Mia swallowed thickly, aware now of the stinging in her sinuses and eyes and the faint quiver in her stomach.

"I remember turning to see if anyone was covering the Spacers. I saw Bogard retract from around Senator Eliton and head for Ambassador Humadros. Senator Eliton stepped backward—"

"Stepped or stumbled?"

"Stepped . . . as if he was ready to be abandoned . . . but he still looked surprised . . ."

"And?"

"And Ambassador Humadros went down before Bogard reached her. It reversed itself to return to Eliton at the same time I started toward him. Then Senator Eliton . . . went down." She wiped at her nose, embarrassed. "Excuse me, I'm not—"

"It's all right. This isn't a normal day. You're entitled."

Mia sniffed, then looked at him, suddenly angry. "Am I entitled to fail? I don't think so."

"How did you fail?"

"I did not protect my assignment."

Derec waved his thumb at Bogard. "There stands several million credits of technology a hundred times faster and more alert than you could ever be. It failed."

"There has to be a reason."

Derec nodded. "Exactly."

"But—" Mia caught herself and held back. In an instant she lost the sense of recrimination that had been building in her all day and had nearly overwhelmed her just now. Not entirely, she could sense it still within, but it was at arm's length again, manageable. Perhaps it would get worse later. Perhaps it would come and go for the rest of her life. It was a simple truth Derec had handed her, and it sabotaged the guilt she felt . . . at least for the time being.

It's not, she thought, *so much my failure as it is someone else's success . . . temporary success.*

She cleared her throat. "I see. Yes. Thank you, Mr. Avery."

"Derec, please." He looked at Bogard again. "So the question is, why did Bogard abandon Senator Eliton? You said Eliton had ordered Bogard to protect Humadros, but that shouldn't have made any difference. I need to take Bogard back to Phylaxis to debrief it."

Mia felt herself tighten up inside. She glanced at the robot. "I shouldn't travel yet—"

"You only need to release Bogard from its priority and turn it over to me."

Mia would not meet his gaze. "I—I'm not comfortable with that, Mr. Avery."

"Not—" Derec caught himself when she looked away. "Please understand me, Mia. Bogard has data necessary to this—this investigation. The only way I can get at it is to do a full debrief and reset."

"Bogard is the only reason I'm still alive. I can't—"

"You're in the Auroran Embassy. What's going to hurt you here?"

"I don't know. And that's just it. I do not know. Until I can walk on my own and defend myself, I just—I can't release Bogard to you."

"Agent Daventri—"

Mia shook her head. "I'm sorry, Mr. Avery. I can't. Please don't press me further on this. Maybe in a day or two . . ."

"There's another problem," Derec said. "Bogard right now is unaware of a discrepancy in its memory. Its behavior is conforming to its program, but there *is* discrepancy and eventually the self-diagnostics are going to tumble to it. When that happens, Bogard will hunt it down even if it means tearing its own programming apart to find out what the problem is. Bogard could easily destroy itself. That's why debrief is important. More so because it involves a personal failure on its part."

"I don't know what to tell you."

"Don't tell me anything. Release Bogard—"

"No."

Derec jerked back as if she had slapped him. "How long do you want to wait to find out what happened to Senator Eliton?"

"You can figure that one out," Ariel interjected, returning from her datum console. "The question I want answered is how can a dead diplomat board a shuttle back to Kopernik Station to take passage on a starship bound for Aurora?"

"You're sure it's not an error?" Derec suggested.

Ariel scowled. "That was my first thought. But last night

when I spoke to Benen Yarick, one of the junior members of the Auroran Legation, she mentioned Tro. I replayed our conversation and she listed him among the fallen. But he was on the list of survivors I had from the embassy comptroller's office. One or the other had to be wrong. Perhaps Yarick only saw him injured, not killed. I checked the embassy transit office and found a passage booking for him on the shuttle that lifted this morning at four-fifteen for Kopernik. I sent a query to confirm his arrival at the station. The confirmation also verified that Tro Aspil boarded the liner *Corismun* at one-ten local time."

"It could still be an error," Mia said. "It was chaos afterward."

"That's what I want to find out." Ariel tapped a code into her com.

"Trina Korolin."

"Ms. Korolin, this is Ariel Burgess. Sorry to bother you again."

"No bother. What can I do for you?"

"I just wanted to make sure everything was still on for tomorrow's meeting and to check a couple of details. The rest of the survivors are leaving tomorrow."

"Yes, I—I'm sorry we're all turning out to be such—"

"No, don't. This was extraordinary. I can't blame anyone for wanting out."

"That's . . . kind of you . . ."

"I was curious, though. Tro Aspil has already left. Was there a reason he needed to depart before the others?"

"Tro . . ." There was a long pause. "You're joking, aren't you? Tro died."

"But I have a transit record for him through the embassy."

"I don't care what you have, Ms. Burgess. I saw Tro die.

He—his neck exploded. He bled to death in the middle of us."

Ariel widened her eyes. "I'm sorry. This is an inexcusable error. My apologies. I'm glad I asked. I—"

"When they loaded him into the ambulance, he was dead. He died with his eyes open, Ms. Burgess. I tried to shut them. They wouldn't close, they just kept ... staring ..."

"Ms. Korolin, please. I am very sorry. This was a transcription error, obviously. Perhaps it was for his remains?"

"No, all the bodies have been sequestered by the authorities pending autopsy. We were told it may be weeks before we can ship them home."

"I see. Well. Thank you, Ms. Korolin. I'm frankly a little embarrassed about this."

"Don't be. I apologize if I spoke inappropriately. I just—it hasn't been easy since ..."

"Will you be up for tomorrow? Would you like to postpone?"

"No, not at all. I need to get on with this. If I wait another day, I might change my mind."

"I understand. In that case, I'll let you get back to your privacy. Thank you for your time."

"Thank you."

The connection broke and Ariel turned back to Derec and Mia. "I didn't know the bodies had been sequestered."

"It's standard procedure, Ariel," Mia said. "Even for foreign nationals. They'll be at the Sector morgue, attached to the Reed Hospital Complex."

Ariel nodded.

"So if," Derec said, "Tro Aspil died, then who is on the way back to Aurora?"

"We need to verify that Tro is the one who *did* die," Ariel said.

"Then," Mia said, "you need to get into the morgue. Normally, I'd be able to get you in, but right now I'm not one of the living myself."

Ariel looked up, almost grinning. "I think I can arrange that."

FIFTEEN

The Civic Morgue occupied a sublevel, well below the main hospital complex in Reed District. Its innocuous façade could have been easily missed—a plain metal door with an ID scanner to its right, a plain sign above the lintel. No other vehicles were in the small lot when the embassy limo pulled in.

Derec stepped from the limo and tugged at the hem of the formal jacket Ariel insisted he wear. It did not quite fit and he kept pulling at the sleeves and shrugging as if to ease the tightness out of his shoulders. He had been glad she had lacked the rest of the suit that went with it.

A second door was set into the wall a dozen or so meters from the visitors' entrance, one large enough for ambulances. The space hummed with a deep background noise from above. The place was unadorned—bare metal, struts and sheeting and harsh lights. Derec could not even find graffiti, as if by unspoken agreement no one intruded upon the area.

Ariel led the way to the entrance, carrying herself with confidence, as if she did this all the time. Derec still wondered whom she had called for the authorization to get in here, but all she gave him was a secret smile as she had dug through a closet for the jacket. She stopped at the door and slid her ID into the scanner.

"Speak your name and business, please," a tinny voice requested. Bored, monotone, human.

"Ariel Burgess, Auroran Embassy, authorized survey of Spacer bodies."

Derec heard the slight hesitation on the last word, but did not look at her, keeping his hands clasped behind his back and acting the part of an ambassadorial aide.

"I have clearance for one person," the voice said. "Who is with you?"

"My aide, Massey."

"I repeat, I have clearance for one visitor."

"Check embassy protocols. All embassy personnel of representative or liaison status are permitted one aide in the conduct of any official business." She sounded just as bored as the unseen caretaker, with just a hint of impatience. Derec admired the act.

He imagined the person on the other end punching a terminal for information on the proper regulations, looking for anything that would get him dismissed or reprimanded, and probably wondering why tonight someone like Ariel Burgess had to show up to make him think about his job.

"Acknowledged," the man finally said.

The scanner extruded her ID and the door slid open.

"Massey?" Derec asked sardonically.

Ariel cocked her eyebrows at him but said nothing. She led the way into the morgue.

The reception area was a long, cramped chamber, bracketed by the cubicle where the night attendant worked on one end, and the doorway into the morgue proper at the other. Between them were two rows of booths containing com and datum terminals. The light, though standard, seemed oddly inadequate; the upholstery was dark, dark green, the floor a dingy grey, and the walls pale green. Even here Derec caught the aseptic scent of chemicals and a metallic tang, subtler and somehow worse than typical hospital odors.

The attendant looked up from his desk to give them a disgruntled look, then returned his attention to whatever he had been doing before Derec and Ariel had disrupted his peace of mind.

Ariel slid into the nearest booth and Derec stood at the edge of the seat.

"I have the batch number," she said.

"Batch?"

She gave him a wry look, then tapped commands into the terminal. Derec let his gaze drift over the walls and ceiling, looking for eyes or ears, realizing even as he did so that they would not likely be obvious. He glanced at the night attendant, who ignored them pointedly.

"You don't think they're overstaffed here, do you?" he asked.

"According to the log, there are two doctors on duty tonight and three orderlies."

Derec leaned closer to read over her head. "As long as we're here, why don't we see . . ."

"I'm checking," Ariel said. After several seconds she gave a surprised "Huh!" and sat back. "They're all in the same lab."

Derec studied the screen. There were eight labs, each

with its own storage. He read down the list Ariel had pulled up and saw all the names from the Union Station incident appended to one lab—Number Six.

Ariel stabbed another key and a chit extruded from a slot beside the screen. "Please follow the guidon," a small voice told them from the terminal.

The chit glowed green in her hand.

The door into the lab area opened on their approach. A strip along the floor pulsed green, leading the way down the long, wide corridor past door after numbered door until the green chit Ariel held turned red.

She inserted the chit into the slot next to the door, which slid aside.

Derec could not define the smell. A hybrid of medicinal sterility and stale air, mingled perhaps with his own preconceptions of a necropolis—decay, wet stone, mustiness. But he saw nothing damp; the room was metal and plastic, and nothing here rotted.

The room reminded him of nothing so much as a library, with neat rows of cabinets, each drawer a number matched to a manifest, the contents awaiting study. For a moment he imagined himself lying in one of these files, still and empty of life, a shape, unconnected to anything he had ever done. He shuddered.

Another door led to the lab where the autopsies were performed. He shivered again, heavily.

Ariel stood before a datum set at in the right-hand wall from the entrance. Derec joined her.

"I've got the manifests," she said absently, scrolling slowly through the names. She was in the Cs.

"Aspil, right?" Derec reminded her.

"Um . . . yes." She scrolled back to the beginning of the list. "Row three, number Five D."

Derec followed a pace behind. Ariel moved slowly now and Derec thought he understood. Reluctance, ill-ease, sadness. She had known this person, differently than the others, a few of whom she had met but none that had meant more than a brief bio on a publicity jacket and maybe a drink while talking inconsequentials. Even Aspil she had not known well, she had told him, though she knew him well enough that it made a difference. They had met at the Calvin Institute on Aurora. She had spent three days with him giving orientation on Institute policy regarding export of robots to Settler colonies. Three days—business, dinners afterward, time for personal conversations. Sufficient to make him more than just a face and a name and an assignment. A week later she was on a ship to Earth, with other things filling her attention, and she had given Tro Aspil no further thought until his name had come up on a list of the dead.

She strolled down row three, reading numbers. The drawers were stacked six high. Somewhere around here, Derec thought, there must be a lifter platform. But "D" was at shoulder height. Ariel stared at the plain grey square, the number in black in the center.

Derec almost reached for the button. Ariel's hand shot out and stabbed it. She stepped back as the drawer extended.

The naked body lay beneath a transparent canopy. It looked artificial, skin the wrong color, eyes closed too tightly, hair too neat and stiff. A wound puckered halfway down the neck.

"It's Tro," Ariel said, her voice small and controlled.

"Then who took his flight back to Aurora?"

"I don't know." She pressed the button and the drawer withdrew, back into its slot. She gazed at it thoughtfully for a few seconds, then turned away. "What other dispcrepancies are there?"

She went back to the datum where the manifest remained on the screen.

"What the . . ." she hissed.

Derec looked over her shoulder.

"Mia Daventri," he read. "But—"

"All the bodies from Union Station are here. That's what I meant when I said they stored them all together."

"Mia wasn't killed at Union Station."

"She's part of the same event, it just took a few more hours to kill her." She frowned. "There are six bodies I don't recognize from the casualty lists."

Derec skimmed the names she pointed out. Rimmer, Iklan, Cutchin, Milmor, Rotison, and Wollin. "The assassins?"

"It doesn't say, does it?" She pulled a portable datum from her jacket and entered the names and the tracking numbers assigned by the morgue. There was no other information.

Derec looked self-consciously back at the entrance. "Somehow I would expect guards or . . . something . . ."

"No one comes to the morgue except those who absolutely have to. What would they be defending? Who would steal a corpse?"

"Still . . ."

Ariel nodded. "It feels wrong, though, doesn't it?"

Derec tapped the screen on Mia Daventri's name. "It *is* wrong."

Ariel touched her lips with a straight finger. "Let's take a look, shall we?"

Mia's drawer slid out, revealing a badly charred skeleton. Derec met Ariel's eyes over the top of the canopy and saw her wondering the same thing: *Who?*

Eliton's drawer was in the next aisle. Derec pressed the contact, his heart racing as it emerged. Upon seeing Eliton, he felt oddly relieved.

The features matched, but lacked the vitality Derec recalled. The shell gave no hint of the energy Eliton possessed and displayed, nothing of his passions. Three puckered mounds traced a line from his left shoulder to his sternum.

"He looks . . ."

"Yes," Ariel said. "Death takes everything." She frowned and did a slow examination down the corpse's entire length.

"What?" Derec asked.

"I . . . nothing." She closed the drawer.

"Humadros?"

Ariel drew a deep breath, then shook her head.

"We should verify them all," Derec said. He raised his eyes upward slightly.

She caught his meaning and nodded. "All right. Let's finish."

Derec experienced a profound sense of relief when the limo pulled away from the morgue. He shrugged out of the too-tight jacket and pulled his own back on. Ariel gazed out her window, a frown pulling a crease into the space above her nose.

"Something's bothering you," Derec said.

"Brilliant. How long did it take you to deduce that?"

"Sarcasm. I didn't think you cared anymore."

Instead of the sharp comeback he expected, she said, "None of this is making sense. The problem is, I can't see *how* it's not."

"Such as?"

"If Tro is dead in the morgue, then who took his seat on the shuttle?"

"Clones?"

Ariel made a face. "Except for some very limited organ regrowth, cloning is completely illegal on Earth. They're more frightened of that than robots."

"But we're not talking legal here, are we?"

Ariel shrugged but did not reply.

"Unless it's just a glitch," Derec said. "The ticket was bought, the name was never deleted, the seat stayed reserved. This *has* all happened fast."

"We can check that. Car, take us to Union Station."

"Yes, Ambassador," the car replied flatly.

"Then," Ariel continued, "the burned corpse under Mia's name."

"Yes . . . that wouldn't have been possible even if she had died. I saw the room. Everything in it was vaporized."

"How come the whole facility didn't go up?"

"Contained explosion, what they call a 'bubble nuke.' Stasis fields and so forth. Very sophisticated, very expensive."

"Parapoyos?"

Derec shrugged. "The trouble with Kynig Parapoyos, as I understand it, is that he's everywhere. Might as well blame a devil or some other supernatural force. But, yes, something like that would be in his line. Very thorough, too. Agent Sathen told me that nothing was recoverable."

"Sathen?"

"Do you know him?"

"I spoke to him yesterday. He was very uncooperative. But not willingly. It seemed to me like he'd been given orders not to talk about the situation."

"Hmm. He seemed open to me, but I spoke to him just after it happened. Anyway, there would be no corpse, even if Mia hadn't got out."

"So that body—" Ariel began.

"—whoever it might be—"

"—wasn't just placed there so that there could *be* a body—"

"—it was placed to contradict the intensity of the blast—"

"—and keep anyone from wondering about the source."

"Exactly."

Ariel looked at him. "And Sathen?"

"Who could silence him?"

"His own people."

"Which is just what your friend Mia suspects."

"I talked to the nurse who was on duty that night. She told me two other agents came in and Sathen got into an argument with them."

"Did she remember their names?"

"One of them. Cupra."

Derec laughed sharply. "The other one is Agent Gambel."

"*You* know them?"

"They're the pair who threw me out of Union Station. They had all the right documents. When I checked, their authority was verified. I couldn't argue."

"But you kept the copy of the RI."

"What copy?"

Ariel chuckled, shaking her head. "Derec, Derec, Derec . . . you are a naughty boy."

Derec smiled. "I knew you would appreciate my finer qualities."

"The question is, why would the same two agents show up at the medical facility Mia was in?"

"They've taken charge of the entire investigation. My guess would be that they needed to debrief her."

"And instead they try to kill her."

"That's something of a leap, don't you think?"

"Is it?" Ariel asked.

"Well, it could have been Bok Golner."

"Someone would have had to set it up for him."

They rode in silence for a time. Derec watched the urbanscape pass, mulling over the conclusions hovering just out of reach. He agreed with Ariel's guess about Cupra and Gambel, but there was no more than coincidence on which to base it. Even with Mia's assertion that there had to be a Special Service component to the entire affair, Derec wanted something concrete before he embraced the belief that Earth's own security people were responsible for what amounted to the worst diplomatic catastrophe of the decade, perhaps the century.

"Ambassador," the limo suddenly said, "this unit is being followed."

Ariel leaned forward. "Show me."

The screen mounted between the seats facing them winked on, displaying the rear view. The limo made a right turn and a few moments after, another transport made the same turn.

"Identify," Ariel said.

"No registration available," the limo said.

"This car isn't positronic, is it?" Derec asked.

"I wish. Car, how far to Union Station?"

"Ten minutes at current course and speed."

"Proceed as normal. Let me know if that vehicle begins to gain on us."

"Yes, Ambassador."

"When did you get a promotion?" Derec asked.

Ariel waved dismissively. "It's programmed to respond to the primary passenger that way unless specifically told otherwise. Sometimes I really hate it here."

"You miss your robots."

"Damn right I do! At least you get to play with some, *when* you're not building killers."

Derec's face warmed. "Excuse me?"

Ariel scowled but would not look at him. "I beg your pardon. I didn't mean that."

"Yes, you did. Do you want to explain it?"

"Why should I? You know perfectly well what I mean."

"Bogard."

Ariel extended her hand, palm up, in a gesture that said, *There, see? You knew what I meant.*

"Bogard's purpose is to protect humans," Derec said.

"By being willing to harm other humans."

"It's not that simple."

"Evidently not. It failed."

"Not with Agent Daventri."

"Oh, it messed up the first time and now it's doing better to compensate? Why did it let Senator Eliton die? There are three holes in that man that shouldn't have been there!"

"I don't know why Bogard failed! I can't find out till she releases it to me and I can run a proper diagnostic on it!" Derec's anger filled him suddenly. "You *never* have accepted the idea that robots needn't be straitjacketed by the Three Laws, that the nature of positronics can be applied to allow wider discretion—"

He stopped, realizing that she was no longer listening. Ariel stared into the middle distance, her face expressionless but her eyes bright.

"What?" he demanded.

"Hmm? I—" She shook her head. "I'm sorry. I didn't mean to bring this up now."

And she looked away from him, pointedly ending the conversation. Derec knew better than to try to force her to continue. He sat and seethed until the limo arrived at Union Station.

"So when *did* you get a promotion?" he asked again.

"Two of those bodies were Ambassador Setaris's top aides. I ended up next in line."

"No, you don't. They could draft some junior legate."

Ariel shrugged. "Since the situation involves a positronic unit, it made sense to have me step in as Setaris's chief aide. For the time being."

"You're being set up to take the blame if anything goes wrong."

"Are you surprised? Typical Auroran politics."

She still sounded distracted. Derec was surprised to find himself worried for her, but right now it did not seem to matter to her.

The limo stopped on the apron of the main gallery.

"Car," Ariel said, "you will return to the embassy garage."

"Yes, Ambassador."

"We're finding another way back?" Derec asked as he got out.

"We can use the Auroran embassy offices here," Ariel said.

Derec searched the boulevard for their shadow but saw nothing unusual in the cluster of cabs and limos crowding against the apron.

The normality of Union Station troubled him. Two days ago Derec had entered upon a scene of violence and terror; now it seemed as though nothing had happened. The gallery echoed with the sounds of foot traffic and conversation; the P.A. announced boarding for a shuttle; the floor gleamed with new polish.

There was still a trace of the powder burns along the wall.

Derec felt anxious all the way to the customer service desk. He realized then that he half-expected a security guard to eject him. He glanced up at the row of windows that overlooked the gallery, where he had been two days ago.

At the desk, Derec had planned to use a self-service datum. Instead, the small consoles were all shuttered. A young man greeted them with a vague smile.

"Can I be of service?" he asked.

"Are the datums down?" Derec asked.

"For a few days. We're going through a complete systems overhaul. In the meantime, I can help you."

Ariel shrugged. "Fine. I'd like to confirm a passenger."

The attendant nodded and glanced down at his own console, hidden from Derec and Ariel by the desk. "Do you have the flight number?"

Ariel checked her portable datum. "Shuttle flight two-seven-K-dash-one-one-nine-A. Yesterday at four-fifteen AM?"

"Shuttle to Kopernik Station. It launched on schedule."

"Seat E-twenty."

"Confirmed for a Mr. Aspil, Tro. Final destination . . . Aurora on the liner *Corismun*."

"I'd like to confirm that he actually took the flight."

The young man looked up, not quite frowning. "Is this official?"

"He's an Auroran citizen," Ariel said, digging out her ID, "and I'm from the Auroran Embassy."

"But—"

"It's not official yet, but it could be. I'm trying to save everyone some headaches."

The attendant checked her ID. He looked unhappy for several seconds, then shrugged. "I suppose there's no problem just checking to see if he boarded." He handed the ID back and worked at his console.

Derec turned around to survey the gallery. Something bothered him about the scene. The access to the service areas was guarded by uniformed security people. A small truck sat against the wall bearing the Imbitek logo. That was an obvious difference. What nagged at him felt more subtle, less . . .

No robots, he realized. None—not even the mindless mobile drones that usually scuttled about with luggage or messages or food. Instead, he saw humans doing those jobs.

"I have Mr. Aspil checking in at three-twenty to board the four-fifteen shuttle," the attendant said. "According to the record, he was logged visually and verified."

Ariel sighed. "Fine. Thank you."

Derec turned back to the young man. "Can I ask, when was his ticket purchased?"

"Um . . . six weeks ago."

Ariel blinked. "Who bought it for him?"

"According to my records, he bought it himself."

"Could you give us the account number?" Derec asked.

The attendant openly frowned now. "We're not really—"

"Listen," Derec said, placing a hand on the desk top in front of the attendant, "there are some irregularities with this and if necessary we can get authorization to go through the records without your help. That might cause you some problems if it has to be explained to your supervisors that we're rummaging through files because someone didn't cooperate when it would have saved time and trouble."

The young man's face darkened briefly. Then he shrugged again. "It's not worth my job. Here." He handed a printout to Derec. "You didn't get it from me."

"I've never seen you before," Derec said, taking the slip.

"Thank you," Ariel said. As they walked away, she said quietly, "It is contrary to service regulations to divulge personal information without proper authorization."

Derec shrugged. "He won't have a job next week anyway—he's a temp. He probably doesn't know the regulations. But he certainly doesn't want an unsatisfactory mark on his performance record." He gestured around the gallery. "Did you notice? No robots."

"It's a shame. This place felt . . ."

"Like home?"

Ariel snorted. "No place on Earth feels like that. I was going to say 'civilized,' but that's not right. It felt safe."

"Because of the robots?"

Ariel nodded. She held up her datum. "Who bought Tro a ticket back home six weeks before he even arrived?"

"Shows a little foresight, doesn't it?"

"On whose part?"

Derec gave the service entrance another look. "I need to get in there, before they rip everything out."

Ariel pointed to an archway guarded by two uniformed security men. "Embassy offices are through there."

The archway opened onto a long concourse. On either side, stairs at ten-meter intervals led up to narrow corridors. Ariel entered the one nearest the far end. The corridor ran five meters to an ornate, metal-finished door that, Derec guessed, was heavily armored. Ariel slipped her ID into the reader and a moment later the door opened for them.

The reception desk made a graceful arc, halving the floor space in the antechamber. A single attendant sat dozing, head propped on fist, before the elegantly-molded bank of monitors to his right. At times Derec missed Auroran luxury, but it could be overwhelming. The walls cascaded with a complex blue-and-yellow pattern that seemed to shift like falling water as he moved. The desk almost glowed from its high polish. The air was scented, and the carpet gave a good two centimeters underfoot, absorbing all sound from their tread.

"Are we on duty or is this your nap time?" Ariel asked.

The attendant jerked awake, blinking up at them. He blushed briefly and cleared his throat. "Sorry, Ambassador. How can I be of service?"

"I need a private office."

"Yes, Ambassador. Um . . . no one else is here, so use any of them." He gestured vaguely behind him.

"Thank you."

Derec followed her down a short hallway, past three doors, and through a fourth. The office was slightly less decorated than the antechamber.

"Aren't you curious," Derec asked, "who followed us from the morgue?"

"Of course I am. But how do you propose to find out without causing a scene?"

"Since when have you been worried about that?"

"I'm not, but I won't waste it. I want to find out what's going on. If we start confronting people too early, we might find ourselves restrained. Blocked at the very least." She extended a hand. "Let me see the flimsy."

Derec took the printout from his pocket and studied it.

"It gives an account number but no other name than As-pil's." He handed it to her.

"We can see if it's an embassy account, at least," Ariel said, sitting down at the datum terminal. She entered the number and waited. She frowned. "That's interesting. It's an embassy account, all right, but not ours. Solarian."

"But—"

"Tro was Auroran, yes . . . and the flight terminates at Aurora."

Ariel stared at the screen for several seconds, then forwarded the data to her apartment.

"The ticket was purchased six weeks ago," Derec said.

Ariel nodded. "Before Tro arrived. And the ticket was bought here."

"Why would the Solarians kill their own people?"

"It wouldn't make sense, would it? Besides which, the Union Station RI was a point of pride to them. Seeing it all fail . . ."

"Speaking of which, it would be a good thing if I could get back there to look at the RI."

"Hmm? Oh." Ariel worked her terminal again. "Wait a second . . . I initiated a log search before we left regarding this alleged directive not to report minor errors to you. I want to see if it's turned anything . . ." She frowned at the terminal. "No. It did *not* come from us. Nor from any other office of the Auroran Embassy." She looked at Derec. "I could do an offworld search to see if my predecessor did, but I doubt we'd find anything. That would mean collusion and there'd be no trail."

"None to speak of." He gestured at the datum. "Uh, the RI?"

"Oh, yes." She touched a few more contacts. "There's the schema for this branch."

Derec leaned over the desk and studied the screen. "All right . . . there's a service entrance here for the robot staff. It says it's been sealed off."

"Be my guest." She smiled ruefully. "If you get caught, this office will deny any knowledge—"

Derec snorted and turned away. Ariel laughed.

The hallway outside the offices made a sharp turn at the very back and narrowed even more. It was barely wide enough for a single person carrying a tray now, which was more than enough room for a robot with the same tray.

It opened into a circular chamber containing three wall niches, now empty of robots. As a concession to Terran authority, even the embassy robots had been slaved to the RI here. To his left was a plain metal door with a simple positronic scanner. Below the scanner was an override control.

From his jacket pocket, Derec took out a small square that resembled an ID chit. Its surface, however, showed the faint outlines of a keypad and one edge was thicker than the rest of the square. He was proud of this device, though he had never before found it necessary to use. He slid it into the override scanner and pressed one of the contacts. A moment later, one contact lit up. He pressed the next and so on until the door accepted the code the device had developed from its interaction with the mechanism and slid open.

The only illumination in the tunnels beyond came from clusters of readylights. Derec felt his way along until he came to a brighter area, then he stepped from the robot accessways into a human-use passage lined with dim amber panels. He followed it until he came to a branch, then guessed from memory which way he needed to go.

The machinery that operated all the station facilities surrounded the public areas, hidden in the walls and beneath the floors. Peel away the skin inside and outside Union Station and a network of tubes, corridors, conduit, shafts, and cables would be revealed, resembling in its complex density the internal organs of a living thing. Since it had been retrofitted for the RI and robotics, a good deal of the network contained open spaces for humans, service nodes and maintenance stations, which made it easier for Derec to find his way. Signs were posted giving locations and directions.

It was late. Derec thought it unlikely that he would run into any workers at this hour, but he walked carefully anyway.

He wanted to find one of the maintenance nodes, since the curious data loops Rana had found all centered on maintenance nodes. They were scattered throughout the complex network, junctions which served several purposes, beginning with the monitoring of the data traffic that rushed throughout the system at light-speed. The junctions broke down the task of maintaining, repairing, and supervising the day-to-day functions that kept Union Station working into discreet units, each with its own supply and repair staff. Until the Incident, that staff had been robotic. Prior to the installation of the RI and the station's conversion to positronics, humans did the work. Now, Derec imagined, they would again.

He turned a corner and lurched back at the sight of a row of people. He waited for them to come after him. When they did not, he looked again and saw that it was only a row of robots in their niches.

Pulse racing, he quickly walked by them.

A maintenance node stood at the end of the row. Derec

squeezed through the narrow opening, into the hexagonal chamber. A worklamp came on automatically at his presence.

The node was being disassembled. Cables and router boxes hung from their places, forgotten for the time being, a mess. Derec tried to piece together how it would operate, but too much was missing. He lifted one of the router boxes and turned it over. One face looked pitted, hundreds of tiny holes all over it, the plastic casing discolored as if it had been heated. He found two more in about the same condition.

The next one, though, was intact.

He opened the access doors and peered in at the neatly organized components. Nothing looked disturbed. He pushed and pulled at cables to get his hands inside the mass, feeling around for . . . he did not know.

But he found it in one of the racks at the base of the walls.

The space was filled with transfer buffers, large memory dumps that held the millions of bits of data required by the station until needed. Tucked between two of them was a mass of greenish-blue corrosion.

No, not corrosion. More like mold or some other fungus. Derec prodded it, but the surface did not yield, nor did it seem brittle. It appeared to be grown to the transfer buffers. He worked a fingernail into the join between a buffer wall and the growth and pried. Fibrous tendrils had sunk into the buffer.

He had nothing on him to work at the material. He went back to one of the other maintenance nodes, where the work crew had left some tools, and took a plain screwdriver. He pried and chipped at the growth until a small amount flaked off. He wrapped it in the printout from the station and slipped it into his pocket.

He made his way back to the embassy branch, unable to shake the growing sense of dread that seemed to spread over and through him.

SIXTEEN

The robot caused Ariel to flinch every time she saw it. She brushed past it, impatient with her own reactions, and strode into her living room, Derec close behind.

Mia was still on the sofa, her datum in her lap, the sub-etheric on, frozen at a scene from the massacre. It showed, magnified, a clutch of people huddling together, faces stretched in panic, bodies twisted and angled as if about to fall to the floor. From the clothing, the group was Terran. Ariel recognized no one. The image was so different from the scene she had seen in Union Station not two hours ago that it seemed from another reality.

Mia looked up.

"And?" she asked archly.

Ariel stared at the image. "All present and accounted for, including you. Someone has thoughtfully put a burned body in your morgue stasis drawer."

The expression on the younger woman's face made Ariel immediately regret her words. Mia's mouth fell partly open and she paled visibly, her eyes seeming to go darker still and more desolate.

"We checked at Union Station," Derec said, "and someone calling himself Tro Aspil *did* show up to take his seat on the shuttle. So either the corpse in the morgue is Aspil and someone else is heading for Aurora—"

"—or Aspil's body is a fake," Mia said, nodding. "Like mine."

"But your double doesn't even have to look like you," Ariel said. "The only way to prove it isn't you would be a DNA scan."

"I'm sure that has already been filed," Mia said. She gave her shoulders a twist as if to relieve tension, then pointed at the screen. "I've been doing a tally."

Ariel sat down on the sofa beside her. Mia's datum screen showed two columns of names.

"Bogard had a master list of everyone scheduled to be at the ceremony," Mia said. "I pulled a list of casualties from the newsnets and started running the vids for a match."

"Any discrepancies?" Ariel asked.

"None so far, but I began doing trajectories. When we found out that several of the assailants were just projections, I wondered then just how many real shots were fired. Bogard helped me edit the newsnet recordings you have into a single composite."

"How are you doing the tracking?" Derec asked. "Bogard's sensory net is as good as it gets, but even subetheric recordings don't have that kind of detail."

"Bogard was able to identify nine actual shooters out of the twenty-one apparent assailants. By studying the recoil of their weapons, it gives us a reliable estimate of how many shots were actually fired. Then it's just a matter of tracing the consequences."

"Nine," Ariel mused. "You caught three of them. Three of them were killed on the scene."

"So we can assume three of them are still at large. There may have been accomplices outside the gallery waiting to facilitate an escape. We don't know."

"Six bodies I couldn't identify are in the morgue, in the same section with all the victims," Ariel said. "I have a list of names and tracking codes."

Mia frowned. "The three I captured were still alive when Bogard brought us back into the gallery."

"These six may not be anything more than innocent bystanders who got in the way. We have to check the names."

Mia shrugged. "I've tried running enhancements on them, to see if facial features show through the masks, but they padded the masks. What I *have* found so far is an emerging pattern of targeting. I'm not finished, so this isn't final, but it appears they were working from a specific list. It wasn't just a capricious act of terror."

Ariel blinked at the image on her subetheric. "Well, we know they wanted Humadros and Eliton . . ."

"Maybe. At least, yes, they were part of it. Let me finish this before I say any more." She turned to the robot. "Bogard? Let's continue."

"At some point," Derec said, "I'm going to have to have Bogard back to do a full diagnostic and debriefing."

Mia did not look up from her datum, only nodded. Ariel saw clearly that she did not like the idea of giving up the robot. Not yet.

"How are you feeling?" Ariel asked. "Can you walk yet?"

"Oh, I hobbled to the bathroom twice while you were gone. Things are improving. Your medical robot said another three days for the healing accelerants to work through completely."

"No problem. I can guarantee privacy for that long. Of course, this is ruining my social life."

Mia smiled thinly. "Sorry."

"Don't worry about it. I didn't have anything this exciting planned for at least another month." She stood and gave Derec a significant look, then headed for her bedroom.

As she had hoped, Derec followed.

She closed the door behind him.

"Stop pestering her for Bogard," Ariel said.

Derec frowned. "Excuse me?"

"She's terrified. Right now Bogard is the only thing making her feel safe. Every time you ask to have it back she gets scared. Stop it."

"Look, Bogard has data we need. We can't just ask for it, I have to download it from its buffers. In order to do that, I need Bogard back at Phylaxis."

"Give it a little time—"

"How much do you want? We have a situation here and I don't think we have the luxury of a few days or a week before we get at the information Bogard has."

"Right now we have more information than we know what to do with. None of it's making sense."

"And neither are you. Since when can you have too much information?"

"When most of it's useless—noise. Like that mess you've got from the Union Station RI."

Derec drew himself up and Ariel braced for a fight. She knew that look and could predict all that followed it, and suddenly she felt extremely tired. She held up her hands.

"Just back off asking for Bogard for now. I'll talk to Mia in the morning and see what I can do. She's my friend."

Unexpectedly, Derec let out a long breath and nodded.

"All right. I need to check in with Rana, anyway." He

turned away, hands on hips, and surveyed her bedroom. "Nice," he said. "You've been doing well for yourself."

"If I had time to enjoy it, life would be wonderful," Ariel said. She winced at the sharp look of hurt he gave her. "Derec, I'm too tired to think straight anymore."

"I'm going."

She followed him to the apartment door.

"I'll call first thing," he said. "This whole situation . . ."

"A mess, isn't it?"

Derec grunted.

"Watch your back," Ariel said.

He nodded, lingering a moment longer, as if he had something more to say. But he only smiled tightly and left.

On the sofa, Mia typed at her datum while Bogard stood motionless before the subetheric. People moved on the screen, molasses slow, dying again.

Ariel went back to her bedroom. She did not remember lying down.

"Ariel."

"Hmm?"

"Wake up, Ariel. Ariel."

"Wha—who—?"

"Ariel, wake up. I have to ask you something."

"Go 'way."

"Ariel."

Someone grabbed her right shoulder and shook her. Ariel's eyes snapped open and she rolled away from the touch. "What?"

"Ariel."

She rubbed her eyes, groggy and disoriented. "Mia? What time is it?"

"You don't want to know. I need to ask you something."

"What?"

"Who made the final list of invitees for the podium?"

Ariel sat on the edge of her bed. She noticed then that she still wore her clothes. "Jennie," she called, "bring me a cup of coffee." She stood and stretched. Her limbs vibrated from weariness; not enough sleep. Again.

Mia stood on the opposite side of the bed, waiting.

"Who made what?" Ariel asked.

"The final list of invitees. Who did that?"

"You don't know?"

"We're just security—all we got was the finished list and a set of orders."

"Well . . . it was a joint decision . . . Humadros had her end already finalized and simply sent us a copy of her list . . . then Ambassador Setaris and Ambassador Chassik worked with Senator Eliton on the list here. Why?"

Mia hobbled toward the door. "Someone else must have gotten hold of it. Like I said before, from what I can tell the targets were preselected. They knew exactly who they wanted to take out. Bogard verified that assumption."

Ariel watched Mia limp out of her room. *Who* had *put together that list?* she wondered, irritated then at how muddled she felt. R. Jennie entered the room with a tray bearing a single cup of steaming liquid.

"Get me a stim as well, Jennie," Ariel said, taking the cup and brushing past the robot.

She glanced at the time as she entered the living room and groaned. Only four hours of sleep. She felt on the verge of lousy now; the rest of the day would be little better. She sipped coffee, wincing at the hot fluid.

"What do you mean?" she asked.

Mia dropped onto the couch. "Bogard, explain to Ariel what we found."

Bogard stood alongside the subetheric screen, with the remote in its hand. The scene projected shifted several times until it showed a wide view of the stage and the mass of black-clad attackers huddling at the edge.

"Once we isolated the corporeal subjects from the projections," Bogard explained, "we began making a determination of the number of shots fired and targets struck. This was accomplished through a combination of identifying each impact and backtracking the trajectory to a given weapon and counting the number of times each weapon was fired."

"How did you do that?"

"The explosive charge used to impel the projectiles appears to be a fast-burning, high-heat substance which burns up its own residue, therefore producing no visible debris upon exit of the projectile. However, there is a heat bloom at the end of the barrel which distorts light passing through it. Linking each instance with a given sound, we have determined the number of shots fired to within ninety-eight percent accuracy. Coupled with the impact traces, we have a positive number of shots fired to wounds inflicted."

"Which is?"

"Point nine-three."

Ariel stared at the robot for a number of seconds. She took a mouthful of coffee, then noticed R. Jennie standing beside her with a tray containing a single pill. Ariel took it and swallowed it.

"Wait," she said to Bogard. "You mean they never missed? Not one stray bullet?"

"Two stray bullets. Twenty fatalities, thirty-three wounded. Fifty-five actual shots fired by the corporeal attackers."

"One of the misses was me," Mia said. "Apparently. Given that Gel and Mattu, my teammates, were killed."

"There were other shots?"

"Yes," Mia said quietly. "A few of us returned fire. We *did* kill three of them, but I'd wager that they must have been wearing diffusion harnesses to divert the energy. But mainly we shot the projections."

"But if they were just projections—"

"The bolts went through and struck bystanders. Several of the injured among the spectators were from our weapons."

Ariel looked at Mia. Her eyes were closed and she looked pale. The side of her jaw worked delicately, angrily. Clearly the realization that she may have harmed or killed innocent people hurt in ways Ariel found hard to imagine. She waited while Mia worked through the spasm of conscience.

Finally, Mia's eyes opened. "Interestingly enough, we found one major discrepancy in these numbers. It seems clear that the intention was to kill all fifty-three of the people hit. Those who lived survived by sheer luck. But one of those fifty-three was not Senator Eliton."

"Not . . . ?"

Mia looked at Bogard. "Bogard?"

"There is no correlation between the injury manifested in any of the recordings and a shot from the attackers," the robot said. "All of fifty-three shots fired are accounted for among the casualties, one miss is accounted for by Agent Daventri, leaving one stray shot which from appearances was fired in the direction of Senator Eliton, but which missed."

"Eliton was a casualty, though," Ariel said.

"That cannot now be verified," Bogard said. "No actual

shot struck him. Though he appears injured, there is no correlation that I can determine with an assassin's bullet. I am not, therefore, counting him as one of the casualties."

"The recording shows a wound," Ariel said. "I saw his body. He had—"

Ariel stopped, remembering the corpse in the stasis tube. She thought about it carefully, questioning the memory, but it was accurate.

"The body I saw had three wounds," she noted.

Mia frowned. "These people, whoever they are, exhibited tremendous skill as marksmen. One shot, one wound. That's consistent with the idea that they're ex-military, trained by a man who was very good at killing, which Bok Golner apparently was. As far as I can determine, they never wasted a second shot on anyone. Bogard can't find the shot—*the* shot, mind you—that killed Senator Eliton, and according to the recordings he was hit only once. Are you sure you saw three wounds?"

"Absolutely. One here—" Ariel touched her left shoulder "—here—" her sternum "—and here." Her right side just below the ribs. She shook her head. "It was Eliton, though . . ."

"Uh-huh. The same way maybe that the skeleton you saw was me?"

Ariel blew out a breath. "Let's go through this again. Bogard, walk me through the whole scenario. Jennie, make more coffee." She looked wryly at Mia. "I'm going to pay for this at work later."

Dawn was minutes away. The horizon was already lightening. Ariel stared at it, seeing it and not seeing it, her mind filled with the details of trajectories and impacts and target possibilities and invitation lists and all the minutiae of a disaster. The subetheric was on, the volume low, ignored, while she tried to let calm of some sort settle through her mind. Mia dozed on the sofa.

Too much information, she had told Derec, was information composed mostly of noise, meaningless and irrelevant. Now she wondered if there could be too much worthwhile data. Nothing they had developed in the last few hours could be dismissed as irrelevant.

Taking out Ambassador Humadros and her immediate staff, Senator Eliton and his aides, and as many other important delegates as possible had at first been an obvious goal of the assault. But now Ariel was not so sure. Ambassador Chassik had escape uninjured, though two of his staff had not. Killing Setaris's aides seemed pointless, as neither of them, nor Setaris, were to have any significant role at the conference. Nor did killing Eliton's security team make much sense, as they really knew nothing.

The weapons had been handmade. Ancient machines—only museum samples of the originals remained—but someone had gone to the trouble of building new ones. Nothing much had been said about them so far on any of the newsnets. Old, obsolete perhaps, but terribly effective, obscenely so given that the projectiles could potentially go through a body and injure someone else behind the target. Because of the angle and other factors, that had not happened this time, but Mia had pointed out that if nine of these weapons existed, there was every reason to believe that there were many more of them, somewhere.

Mia had tracked the names of the six unknown bodies in the morgue through civic records, using Ariel's authority to access the files. Factory workers, an office clerk, two unemployed and on civic assistance. The only thing she had found that bound them together was their affiliation with

OSMA—Order of the Supremacy of Man Again, otherwise known as Managins. Mia thought there could be something else in their backgrounds, but it would take time to get at it. Mia could only assume that these were the six assassins who had not escaped, and three of them should not be dead. They had been in Service custody. One of them had been Lemus Milmor.

The invitee lists troubled Ariel the most. If a copy had gotten out, it could only have done so from a few sources. Eliton had had a copy, but so had Setaris and, presumably, Chassik. Special Service had a list since Bogard had it. The list had been finalized only ten days earlier. Time for a leak, certainly, but it would still have had to be a leak from one of those sources. Anyone else? Had any of the industrialists present possessed a copy? There was no way to tell. Somehow the Managins had gotten it and a team of assassins had been assigned targets. Was there anything about the target list that could give a hint? Perhaps, but Ariel was exhausted, and she had embassy work to do today.

But she could not sleep. Her head buzzed with too many details.

She glanced at the subetheric and started to see Jonis on the screen. She grabbed the remote and turned up the sound.

"—into it as thoroughly as humanly possible," he was saying, "but so far I'm told we have no leads."

"What about the captured gunmen?" a reporter out of the picture asked. "Has their interrogation produced any tangible results?"

Jonis looked embarrassed. "Frankly, we won't get anything from them. Apparently, they were inadvertently killed while in the process of being apprehended and arrested."

"Killed? By whom? Special Service agents?"

"No, not exactly. I, uh, haven't been given the full details, it's all very classified at the moment, but the, uh, robot assigned to Senator Eliton's security detail may have had something to do with it."

"You mean the same robot that failed to protect Senator Eliton and later exploded, killing the last surviving member of his security team?"

"Uh, yes, that robot. It may have exerted excessive force in the apprehension of the, uh, suspects. It's being looked into."

Ariel glanced over at Mia and saw her friend staring fixedly at the screen, her entire body rigid with attention.

"This doesn't say very much of Senator Eliton's interests in promoting the reintroduction of robots on Earth," the reporter said.

"That may be premature," Jonis said. Still, he looked as if he agreed with the assessment. "We'll have to wait for all the facts and assessments before making a final judgement. I don't want to say anything to belittle Clar's—Senator Eliton's—beliefs."

"Of course. If I may ask—"

"That's enough for now. I have to get to my committee."

"But Senator—"

Ariel turned the subetheric off.

"Shit," she muttered.

"Amen," Mia said.

Ariel made herself stand. She had to call someone. By the time she reached her comline, she decided that it should be Derec.

SEVENTEEN

I should have gone to my apartment, Derec thought as he entered the Phylaxis lab. He stood in the entry, feeling the weariness of the day, gazing at the empty lab.

Not empty. He heard the fragile impact of fingers on a keypad, then saw someone at one of the stations. Rana's console was unattended, the screens blank. The main lights were low.

Derec stepped quietly toward the sound. Halfway down the left-hand aisle, between the banks of equipment and workstations, he saw someone working at a console near the back of the room. His pulse picked up until, a few meters closer, he recognized the man.

"Caro," Derec said.

The man started, jerking his hands from the keypad as he twisted in his chair. Then he sighed heavily and shook his head.

"Hi, Derec."

"Didn't mean to startle you."

Caro waved a hand. " 'Sallright," he said, then yawned. "Final report on the mobile units from Union Station."

Derec thought for a moment, then remembered that Caro and Amson had been assigned to help decommission all the floor robots.

"You just finished?"

"Unless that heartless slaver Chassik calls us back. I sent Amson home. Never saw her so beat. We've been at it—" he glanced at his wrist "—damn, nearly thirty hours."

"Did you have any trouble with Special Service?"

"No, this was mostly off-site. By the time we were informed that Special Service had assumed authority over the investigation, most of the mobiles were gone, back in a warehouse, waiting transhipment."

"Shipment . . . where?"

"Back to Solaria, I imagine. Ambassador Chassik was most insistent that they all be shut down prior to shuttling, and the positronic logs—such as they were—downloaded and stored."

Chassik. Derec went to his station and sat down. He pulled the folded paper with the sample he had taken from Union Station from his pocket and put it in a drawer under the console.

"You're up early," Caro said.

"Late, actually. When did Rana leave?"

"When I got here, about an hour or so ago."

"Any messages?"

"Not that I know of."

Derec watched Caro work for a time, then heaved to his feet. "I need sleep."

"Are you going home?" Caro asked.

"No, I'll stay here."

Caro nodded absently. Derec drifted across the lab to the

com and touched the log to see what messages were in the buffer. Nothing from Senator Taprin. A message from Joler Hammis. Two from Gale Chassik at the Solarian embassy. Three anonymous calls. And a final note from Rana. Nothing from his attorney. He opened Rana's.

"The brain is rebelling," she said. "Mine, that is. I need sleep, much as I hate to admit it. Not much progress after you left with Ms. Burgess. Sorry. Talk to you tomorrow."

He opened Joler Hammis's and was surprised to find a résumé appended to a short note.

"It seems Union Station no longer needs the services of a positronic specialist, Mr. Avery. I am available at your convenience. Please call."

The three anonymous calls contained no messages. He shut down the com and went up to bed, his mind working at a low level.

Chassik. Hammis. Robots being shipped back to Solaria. Details.

He needed sleep badly.

"Derec."

"Mmm . . ."

"Ariel Burgess is on the com. She won't disconnect until she talks to you."

Derec blinked, his eyes gummy. " 'M asleep. I'll call her later."

"Derec. Mr. Avery."

Derec rolled over then. Rana never called him "Mr. Avery" unless she was very upset. He ran fingertips across his sleep-encrusted eyes, wincing as a few lashes jerked loose.

"Time?"

"Six-thirty-one."

Derec groaned. "Doesn't anyone sleep anymore?" He sat

up and sniffed. The strong aroma of fresh coffee drew his attention. He held out a hand and a moment later felt a cup placed against his palm. Warm. He brought it to his mouth and drank cautiously. "All right. All right, tell her I'll be right there."

"Want me to route the call up here?" Rana asked, walking toward the door.

"Sure."

"And when you're done with that, come down to the lab. I have something to show you."

Derec felt himself nod. He sat there in the abrupt quiet, nursing the coffee, wondering what was so important that he had to interrupt what he remembered to be very good sleep.

"Derec?"

He looked up at the sound of Ariel's voice. "Oh. Yes, Ariel."

"Do you have vid?"

"Is it necessary? You just woke me up."

"Don't brag. I've been up since four, I think. What are you doing?"

"Drinking coffee."

"*After* that."

"I have to review Rana's excavation."

"Good. You can tell me what she found when you meet me."

"I'm meeting you?"

"For lunch. At the Franklin Park Home Kitchen."

"What?"

"For old time's sake. You know where it is, don't you?"

"Of course—"

"Good. Then I'll see you there at, what? Eleven-thirty?"

"Sure . . ."

"Great. I'm looking forward to it."

The connection died and Derec stared at his com-unit. The Franklin Park Home Kitchen, on the K Street Corridor? A *home kitchen?* Neither of them had had to eat at a public facility in years. He doubted Ariel had been to a home kitchen since her return to Earth four years ago. And why one so far away? The Spacer embassies were south, in the Anacostia District; Franklin Park was north.

"I'm not awake," he said aloud and looked down at his half-empty cup.

He finished the coffee and showered, then stumbled downstairs to the lab, still feeling off-balance.

"Morning," he said.

Rana nodded, staring at her screens.

Derec went to the com and tapped in Joler Hammis's code. He received a request to leave a message.

"This is Derec Avery, Mr. Hammis. I'd be very interested in speaking with you at your convenience. Please let me know when would be a good time. Thank you."

He poured more coffee and sat down beside Rana. She began talking immediately, as if a switch had been thrown.

"Okay, the excavation has given me three discreet segments to study. I've got the entire matrix just prior to the RI going off-line in one segment, the same during the period it was off-line, and the segment just after it came back online and began to collapse. I isolated them all from each other, but I set up a marker base to follow the linkages."

"You did all that after I left yesterday? What time did you go home?"

Rana shrugged. "I don't know, midnight." She pointed to the screen. "Now. Getting these three sets apart gave me a handle on the problem. All those command nodes that we traced to maintenance? The entire system shifted all its attention to them during the off-line period. It was as if the RI just let itself be sucked out of its own matrix to somewhere else. Of course, that left a lot of automatic functions, but even those were subsumed to a different set of operational parameters during this period."

"Wait, wait. You're saying that something drew all the higher-level functions away from its primary duties?"

"More or less. The maintenance nodes show exponentially increased stimulation, as if a tremendous amount of data was suddenly being pumped to those sites and demanding that the RI pay attention. And it did. Complete attention. Basically, everything it was *supposed* to focus on became secondary. Not even that. Quaternary. The only thing it seemed to be noticing outside these nodes were the mobile units."

"And when it came back online?"

"From what I can see, it came back exactly at the point that it left—with one difference, the time chop. It *knew* that minutes had gone by during which time it was not paying attention. It couldn't escape the conclusion that it had failed. Collapse began almost immediately."

"Thales," Derec called out, "are you still running Union Station?"

"No, Derec, not all of it," the RI responded. "I am being shut out systematically as systems are being changed over to newly installed Imbitek systems."

"But you were doing it all?"

"For twelve hours, twenty-three minutes, Derec."

"While you maintained full oversight of Union Station, did you run a diagnostic of satellite systems?"

"Yes, Derec. I needed to know what I had to work with. Standard procedure in a new environment."

"Of course. Did you find anything unusual?"

"Several systems were of a type of imbedded technology with which I am unfamiliar. Nothing out of my capacity to interpret and operate, only new configurations."

"What about . . . Rana, is there a list of those maintenance nodes?"

"Sure." She touched contacts. A list appeared on her screen.

"What about these sites, Thales?" Derec asked.

"There was nothing at those sites, Derec."

"What do you mean, nothing?"

"I mean that I found no corresponding systems of any sort answering my diagnostic interrogatory at those sites."

"But the Union Station RI showed them to be active."

"I cannot account for the discrepancy, Derec. I acknowledge the data from the RI, but my own diagnostic and analysis showed nothing at those sites. It is possible that those sites suffered damage or were programmed to operate only at predetermined times or were programmed to shut down at a predetermined time."

"How much access do you still have to Union Station?"

"I have been excluded from sixty-two percent of the systems," Thales stated.

"Can you still monitor those sites?"

"Three of them are still within my sphere."

"Watch them. I want to know if any activity occurs at all at those sites. The method of exclusion—can you work around it?"

"Do you mean can I bypass it?"

"Yes."

"I can, Derec, but it is against—"

"Never mind that. This is a priority. Humans may be in danger as a consequence of those sites resuming some operation. I want you to circumvent the exclusions if possible without alerting anyone outside Phylaxis and keep a monitor on them. Understood?"

"I understand, Derec."

"Continue, Thales."

"Nothing there?" Rana said. She waved a hand at the screens displaying the shattered remnants of the RI. "That's a lot of damage for nothing."

"Those sites were shut down," Derec said. "I'd love to know how they did that without leaving a physical trace, though. *Something* should be there, even if it's only an I/O port. Which reminds me, I got in there last night."

"Where? Union Station?"

"Back in the service sections, yes. I found something . . ." He went to his own console and retrieved the paper with the sample. "I need this analyzed," he said, opening it. "This was all through the circuitry in one of the maintenance nodes. It's hard and brittle. I hope there's enough here."

"I'll set Thales up on an analysis," Rana said, peering at the flakes suspiciously.

Derec glanced at the screens. "A positronic brain is joined to its realtime perception in a one-to-one relationship. It has to be that way or interpretive errors creep in and there's a kind of subjective drift."

"But robots interpret things all the time."

"True, but they have their core template to use as a standard. If you look at how they interpret you'll see that they're damnably literal. There was a classic case once of a newly uncrated robot completely disbelieving that humans had built it. The only evidence it could see were the humans supervising it and clearly *they* couldn't build one, so it must have been a lie. The Three Laws prevented it from doing other than its duty to protect and obey them, but only within certain limits, and it came to believe that robots were created by another machine."

"I thought that was apocryphal."

"Maybe. I've heard it said that the core template came directly out of that incident. But apocryphal or not, it illustrates the point. Positronic robots rely on the concrete to function. If they didn't, they could easily develop neuroses based on abstract concepts of humans they don't even know coming to harm."

"Robots having an existential crisis."

"Something like that. So we give them strict associational and sensory parameters by which to recognize what is real. That way they can determine optimum hierarchical responses to orders given by humans that may conflict with First Law imperatives and likewise permit them to make similar assessments in Third Law situations. Judgements like that demand concrete definitions."

"But what if you substituted those definitions with others? Or one set of perceptions with a different set?"

"They're designed to shut down if they detect that kind of sensory shift. You'd have to actually bypass their sensory apparatus to do that, but bypass it without any interruption in the sensory input, and consistent with the core template."

Rana tapped one of the screens. "This brain thought it was playing a game. All it perceived, apparently, was the game. The game became its concrete definition."

"Which is impossible. Any code coming in from outside would cause a complete disruption of normal function."

"Unless it didn't come from outside."

"You mean like a parallel system built into its matrix?"

"Bogard worked that way."

"In a very limited fashion. Bogard's buffers simply bypassed crisis situations. It still perceived reality—"

"It just conveniently forgot some of it. What's the difference?"

None, Derec thought, staring at the screens. He had recognized the similarity in the paradox loops the other night. He had hoped it had been a fluke, but Rana had a point. Someone had devised a more complete way to divert a positronic matrix, and not just part of it.

The com chimed.

"Yes?"

"Mr. Avery?"

"Speaking."

"This is Ambassador Chassik."

"Yes, Ambassador," Derec said, wincing. "I apologize for not returning your calls yesterday, but I was out of the lab—"

"I understand that, Mr. Avery. I've reached you now and that's fine. I wanted to get together with you to discuss certain matters concerning the removal of the RI from Union Station."

Derec glanced at the time. Almost six-thirty. "It's rather early, Ambassador. When did you have in mind?"

"The sooner the better. I'll send a limo."

"Now? But—"

"Thank you, Mr. Avery. I'll see you in a short while."

"Don't you love not having to make up your own mind?" Rana asked, grinning.

Gale Chassik had the heavy look of someone who had done considerable physical labor during his life, which was incongruous in his case as he was a Solarian. Spacers did not get unnecessarily physical; they left that to their robots.

"I apologize for the circumstances, Mr. Avery," he said, pouring two glasses of amber fluid. He set one on the table beside Derec and took his own to the chair opposite. "Unfortunate times."

"How can I help you, Ambassador?" Derec asked, ignoring the glass. He folded his hands in his lap and waited.

"I wanted to have a talk with you about the Union Station RI."

"In what respect?"

"Your analysis of its condition. What you think happened."

"I have no idea what happened."

"It's been two days—"

"Nearly three, Ambassador, and Phylaxis was removed from any involvement with it at the end of the first day."

Chassik frowned. His forehead seemed to contract. "Removed. But I understood—"

"Normally, Phylaxis Group would be doing the forensics, but Special Service assumed full control of the investigation and barred us from all the relevant material. Surely you knew."

"Your people have been working with us on decommissioning the mobile units. I assumed . . ."

Derec nodded. "To answer your question, sir, I have no idea what happened to the RI. The unit is a Solarian brain, isn't it? The company that did the original installation is removing it. Didn't they tell you any of this?"

Chassik snorted. "Terran regulations. They aren't allowed to discuss it with anyone, including me, until such as time as, et cetera. I'm sure you've heard the same excuses." He narrowed his eyes at Derec. "You aren't even doing oversight on its removal?"

"No, sir."

"Hmm. Odd."

"I can't disagree."

"Well. Do you have any *theories*, Mr. Avery?"

"No, not even a hypothesis. At best I would be making a wild guess."

"Please."

"Somehow, coding was introduced into the RI that effectively distracted it from its primary responsibilities and redirected it. When the assault occurred, the RI was playing. It never saw what was happening."

"That's not possible."

"Again, I can't disagree. Without access to the unit, though, I can't begin to tell you why or how."

Chassik sipped his drink thoughtfully for a few moments. "Mr. Avery, I don't think I need tell you what sort of consequences we're looking at. I don't believe it's unlikely that relations with Earth could be severed."

Derec wanted to argue, but in truth what Chassik said seemed all too likely. One of the core issues of the conference, surrounded by all the trade talk and good will hype, was an agreement to allow robotic inspection of all Earth-Spacer shipping, in both directions. That meant allowing robots onto Terran vessels, a condition too few on Earth approved. It only seemed possible because of Eliton's efforts and the general esteem which Ambassador Humadros commanded and the fact that a great deal of money was involved. The Union Station RI and its satellite systems had been intended to showcase positronics on Earth, to "educate" Terrans and ease some of the prejudice. Now that it had failed so dramatically and catastrophically . . .

"I'm not sure what I could do to help, Ambassador," Derec said finally.

"Solaria stands to lose a great deal over this incident. Our reputation is at stake, here and at home. So you will understand my desire to know as much as possible about what happened. Would you be willing to do an analysis of the RI after it's been removed from Union Station? Off the record?"

"Off . . . I'm not sure I understand."

"On the quiet. I'm afraid it would not be authorized by anyone other than me. I could . . . 'borrow' the unit before it gets shipped back to Solaria."

"What good would that do? If I found something—"

"Then it becomes my affair and I could do something with it. But without any knowledge of what happened, I'm helpless."

"It would have been better had the unit not been removed."

Chassik shrugged. "I can't stop it."

"Let me think about it, Ambassador," Derec said. "I'm not sure such an analysis would give you anything worth using. Off-site like that, without any kind of witness to the process, it could be claimed that anything I find is manufactured."

"Would it be?"

"What?"

"Claimed. You know these Terrans a little better than I, perhaps. You've been here longer."

"Think about it, Ambassador. Under similar circumstances, what would you claim? They aren't really that much different."

Chassik's eyebrows raised fractionally, but he nodded and smiled. "Don't take too long to give me your answer, Mr. Avery. There's a window of opportunity here."

"I understand, Ambassador."

Chassik pointed at the glass beside Derec. "You didn't touch your drink."

"It's a little early for me."

"Too bad. Something called Beam's Choice. I must confess, I don't find much about Earth superior, but they make fine whiskey." He finished his own glass. "A present from one of their industrialists. They like giving tokens here."

"When they can."

Chassik nodded and stood. "It was pleasant talking to you, Mr. Avery. And do let me know soonest on your decision."

"Yes, sir. Thank you."

Derec followed the waist-high mobile unit down the corridors to the elevator, trying to work loose the tightness between his shoulders. Nothing just said made any difference to anything; the entire meeting could have been done by comlink with the exception of the illicit offer to allow Phylaxis access to the RI after its removal from Union Station. So that, Derec decided, had been the true purpose of the meeting.

Which made no sense if Special Service had impounded the RI. If they had not, then what was the purpose of assuming complete jurisdiction of the investigation? And if they had, how would Chassik get his hands on it? True, it belonged technically to Solaria and would eventually be shipped back, but not before Terran analysts ripped it apart. By then, any analysis Derec might perform would be useless. Nothing would be left to analyze.

Derec rode the elevator down to the garage, his unease increasing. Chassik had to have known Phylaxis was barred from the investigation. Well, there was truth to the implication of bureaucratic territoriality—it was possible no one from Special Service, the Station, or his own people had told him anything—but surely Ariel would have said something, being the liaison from the Calvin Institute.

Too many things made less and less sense.

"Where would you like me to drop you, sir?" the limo asked him.

Derec hesitated. "What time is it?"

"Nine-ten, sir."

Two hours at least before his meeting with Ariel, all the way north of the Capitol Mall to Franklin Park. That was a good thirty-minute drive . . .

"Ford Theater, please."

"Yes, sir."

The limo started up and headed for the exit.

EIGHTEEN

Ariel waited nervously at a small table by a massive pillar and watched the throngs enter and leave the sprawling kitchen. It had been years since her last visit to one of these huge communal dining areas; the place triggered memories—some pleasant, others unwelcome and long neglected.

Derec wandered in with a crowd of school kids who were all dressed in bright blue-and-yellow jumpers and wearing their ID badges prominently around their necks. He got in the queue, picked up a tray, and went through the line.

He drifted by her table, then looked again. He made an exaggerated grin and ambled over, everything about him suddenly announcing salacious intent.

"Excuse me, but I couldn't help notice," he said, just a bit too loudly. A few people turned to look, then as quickly turned away. "You look lonely. Mind if I join you?"

Ariel almost laughed. It was so blatantly clichéd she wondered that anyone could possibly accept such an invitation.

"I don't think—" she began.

"You're that friend of Kate's, aren't you? Down at the data import pool? I'm Massey."

Ariel looked away, working at her smile. "I'm sorry, I didn't recognize you at first. Please."

Derec slid into the chair opposite her. "Come here often?"

"Enough," Ariel hissed.

"Sorry. Couldn't resist." He started sorting out his tray. "So why here?"

"I left through a service access and took the strips. No limo."

Derec glanced at her. "Dressed down, too, I see."

She had worn a singlepiece of dull brown and a bright red jacket that glistened wetly. "It might have been worth it."

"Maybe." He tore off a piece of bread and dipped it in the thick gravy around his slab of meat product. "You know, I've eaten at the best, but there's still something primally appealing about this place."

"You're joking. That's disgusting."

He gestured at her glass of milk. "And you look like a very convincing *T* rating, sitting in your home kitchen without any food."

"We won't be here that long. Hurry up."

"Are you going to tell me what we *are* here for?"

"The body we saw."

"Which one? Eliton's?"

"Yes. It wasn't." She went on to update him on the six Managins and the fact that now, according to Senator Jonis Taprin, Bogard had killed the three Mia had apprehended, then self-destructed, killing Mia as well.

Derec frowned and forked a chunk of meat into his mouth. He chewed thoughtfully for a time. "Of course, you know that's not true."

"Of course I do." He gave her a skeptical look. Impatiently, she went on. "I may disagree with the 'looseness' you've built in to Bogard, but if it kills someone it will be by inability to cope, not through intent. Those three men were alive when Mia was taken off to the hospital."

"All right. So what are we doing up here?"

"Looking for ambulances."

He looked puzzled, then smiled. He nodded, chewing. "You know, you certainly are—"

Ariel held up a finger. "Don't carry the charade too far."

Derec chuckled. She watched as he ate everything on his tray.

"Are you finished?"

"I am now. All I had this morning was coffee."

"No wonder it tasted good."

He stood. "Shall we go chase ambulances now?"

They took a strip east, toward the convention district.

"The newscams followed Eliton's corpse out of the gallery and to the ambulance," Ariel said. "We got a clear ID on the vehicle. Mia called Reed and told them she was an insurance adjuster and needed to verify ID numbers on the ambulances servicing them."

"Why?"

"The body was switched somewhere. If it was in the hospital itself, it gives us a place to start."

"Makes sense. And?"

"The hospital very helpfully connected us to the administrative records datum and Mia was able to just peruse at leisure. That ambulance had been assigned to Reed, but it was decommissioned last year. Too old to be economically upgraded."

"Wouldn't somebody have noticed on the scene?" Derec asked.

"Who? An ambulance specialist? No, they use the same body shells. It's all the hardware inside that gets the upgrades."

"So, that ambulance doesn't service Reed. It could service another hospital."

"Or small clinics. But a vehicle has a data trail that follows it everywhere, even after they're 'officially' decommissioned. No record of any upgrade, no reassignment to any other facility. The vehicle officially is no longer in service at all."

"What about the newscams? They were at Reed when Eliton's body arrived."

Ariel nodded. "Mia's trying to locate an available record. Two of the agencies we contacted told us that they missed the arrival of Eliton's body, that it had been delivered through a secured access and none of them knew where. The first they knew, Eliton's body was already inside Reed." Ariel looked at the passing signs, then pointed. "Here we go."

They began making the careful transition down to the slower strips and got off at Corridor Six. Ariel headed for the nearest directory. She wanted sublevel E. The directory indicated the closest escalator and elevator.

"You wouldn't want to hear about *my* morning, would you?" Derec asked, following.

"Sure. How was your morning, Derec?"

"I had a meeting with Ambassador Chassik."

Ariel stopped. "Chassik? Why?"

"He wanted to do me a favor."

"Chassik never does favors."

"He offered to let me analyze the Union Station RI after it's been removed."

"Why?"

"Don't know. I told him I'd think it over."

Ariel and Derec continued on to the escalator. As they descended to sublevel E, she noticed how few other people seemed to be around. Most of this area contained maintenance, service, and distribution facilities and those few people present looked like *I*-rated laborers, dressed in plain overalls. The sound of heavy machinery gave a throbbing background groan, and the air smelled warm, metallic.

They paused at the intersection of an alleyway and the main corridor. Ariel slipped her portable datum from inside her jacket. The map of the area on the small screen also gave their location.

"Down there," she said, pointing across the corridor and returning the datum quickly to its pouch. She looked around, frowning. "There's something else about this area . . ."

They turned down a narrow passage covered by a wide strip of dull grey material, a guide path for movers. At the end they emerged into a wide area fronting a garage entrance. Old transports lined the wall to their right, grimy vehicles long unused, their identifying markings obscured by dirt and wear. Two wide transport exits opened on either side of the apron.

"D.C. Municipal Transport Service Terminal," Derec read the sign above the main door. "Substation Six-E-Vernon Section."

"This is the place." Ariel looked around, frowning. "Now what? Are we expected?"

"I sincerely hope not. It's just ... something else about this area ..." She shrugged. "We get inside and look for that ambulance."

"How?"

"That's what I needed you for. You're good at getting by AI systems, aren't you?"

"I'm the designated thief? Should have brought Bogard along for this."

"Oh, absolutely. Let's bring a robot into a worker class section. No one *here* would mind."

"Bogard is stealth-capable. No one would have noticed."

Her own anger surprised Ariel. She drew slow breaths and suppressed it. "Mia still won't release it."

"That has to change."

"She's afraid."

Derec shrugged. "All right, there should be another access, for maintenance crews or supervisors or whatever." He sounded ambivalent now, his voice dull and flat. He walked away from her, skirting the edge of the broad apron. He disappeared to the left of the façade.

Ariel searched the geometries surrounding the garage—suspended walkways, roofs, shuttered windows, sharp shapes piled up around massive supporting beams that extended into the cavernous heights high overhead. Mist obscured details of the main roof, haloing the bright points of light. She saw no one, which did not reassure her. She followed after Derec.

The gangway turned right several meters from its entrance. Ariel experienced a brief touch of claustrophobia looking up the walls that formed the narrow canyon.

She found Derec at the top of a set of metal steps, tentatively entering data into a small panel set alongside the human-sized door. His face was blank, now, only his eyes bright with concentration. Ariel stood by the corner, a few meters away, watching, as if she could do anything if they were caught.

Derec grunted, then slid something into the reader at the base of the pad. He entered a few more commands and the door slid open with a grinding sound that made Ariel's nerves dance.

"I don't think it gets much use," Derec said, retrieving a wafer-thin square.

Ariel hurried up the steps and they ducked inside. Derec stabbed at a panel below a dull red light and the door closed.

Except for the red lamp, the place was dark.

"Great," Derec said. "It's an automated garage."

"There has to be an office or a service station."

"Mmm. Maybe. Or it could be—wait."

Ariel heard him pat the wall as he moved away from her. Then a sharp click and suddenly a wan yellowish light filled the immediate area. He stood by another panel filled with switches. A walkway ran directly along the side of the wall. Outside that, the garage itself remained lightless.

At the far end they came to a row of cubicles, each containing a desk and datum terminal. The dust on the transparent walls obscured detail within. Derec ran his finger down it, leaving a clear trail.

"You're sure this is the one?" Derec asked, brushing his fingers on his pants.

"No. This is only the last known address."

Derec walked slowly along the row, then stopped. "Ariel."

The cubicle wall showed trailing handprints near its door. The desk and terminal inside had been dusted off and there were clear footprints on the dark tile floor.

"Could have been the regular staff," Ariel suggested.

"I doubt it. If there was a regular staff, it would be cleaner." He entered the cubicle and stepped up to the desk, then sat down and switched on the terminal. "What's the ID number on the ambulance?"

Ariel brought out her datum. "Here." She showed it to him.

Derec entered the code and sat back, absently tapping his chin with a forefinger.

"Decommissioned thirteen months ago," he read from the screen. "It gives overhaul estimates, then lists component values for recycling it as parts ... and a secondary market value for direct resale ... a bid was made on it eleven months ago."

"Someone bought it?"

"It doesn't say. Just that a bid was made. It only gives an auction number." He frowned. "No further updates of any kind. It evidently was sold."

"Is it here?"

"It doesn't say that, either, but it does give a bin number on the original entry. I suppose we could just go look."

"Let's."

Derec entered a few more commands, then took the flimsy sheet that extruded from the printer. He closed the terminal down and stood.

"Level Four, Row F, Bin Twenty-Eight."

"What about lights?"

Derec opened each drawer in the desk, then went to the cabinet near the door. "Ah," he said as he straightened, holding a flashlight.

Their footsteps echoed loudly, mingling with the stray, obscure sounds of the garage. In the near total darkness—

broken by constellations of readylights here and there and the circle of their flashlight pushing before them—the noises made the space seem vast and complex. Ariel walked alongside Derec, trying to control her reflexive jitters at every click and whir and drip. It was not fear so much as a formless unease at not knowing where she was or what it looked like.

They came to a stairwell. A fading LEVEL TWO glowed bright yellow in the halogen glare. Derec started up the steps.

They emerged from the stairs adjacent to Row B. Vehicles occupied stalls. Cables and tubes connected each one to a diagnostic unit, but those they looked at showed their units all on stand-by. The machines appeared untended, the vehicles dirty, many in various stages of disassembly, and even that process seemed abandoned.

Row F, Bin Twenty-Eight, was different.

The diagnostic equipment was old but not neglected. Only the standby light glowed, but in the wash of the flashlight Ariel saw clearly that the control panel was clean. The ambulance itself shone neatly, grimeless and intact.

"Well, well," Derec said and stepped into the stall. Overhead a worklamp came on. Derec, frowning, switched off the flashlight. "We better not stay long. What do you need?"

"Its log." Ariel handed over her datum. "Do you know how?"

Derec took the datum and opened the rear door of the vehicle, looking up at the silence.

"Either it's not alarmed or—"

"We'll have visitors soon," Ariel finished.

Derec climbed into the ambulance. Ariel peered into the darkness, listening. The glow from the stall's worklight cast marginal illumination across to the opposite row. It seemed less a garage than a necropolis, the broken shapes hunkering together in sepulchral consolation.

A thud came from behind her. "Ow!"

"Are you all right?"

"Fine," Derec called from within. "Be done in a minute."

Ariel stepped away from the stall. The various noises of the place seemed less sinister now. It was only an old, near-forgotten storage facility. She wondered how many of them were strewn throughout the fabric of Earth, niches wherein Terrans stuffed all the things they thought they might need again someday and then forgot they ever had them in the first place. Layers upon layers of urban complex, down she did not know how many levels, and at the very bottom, just before primal earth, actual soil, there must be an entire layer of nothing but storage lockers, garages, closets, stalls, bins, dumps, and depositories, filled with a history of experiment and expedience—

She started at a new sound. Not a click or a whir, but a faint grinding, like something rolling across broken pavement. She took another step away from the light behind her, careful and silent, listening. The grinding stopped.

The skin up the backs of her arms rippled with chill. She felt watched now and stared into the murk, searching for eyes.

Something moved to her left and she jerked to the right, heart racing. Ariel backed into the stall and went to the rear of the ambulance.

"Derec," she said.

"Done." Derec climbed out and shut the doors. "Clean. Like just recently."

"Time to leave."

He handed back the datum and went to the end of the stall. He stood quietly and listened, then gestured for her to follow. He sprinted across the driveway and entered three more stalls at random. Two of them lit up with worklights. He returned to this side and did the same to another three. One lit up.

The sound started again, louder and clearer. Treads.

"Probably an automated inspection unit," Derec said. "We triggered an internal security program, that's all."

At the landing, she stopped. From below came the faint echo of voices.

"Damn," she hissed.

"Where?" he asked.

"Up."

They moved up the stairs as quickly as they could and came out on Level Six.

The tread noise grew stronger. Ahead, Ariel thought she saw a reflection, dull red, and guessed it might be the source of the sound.

They descended one level and sprinted along the dark stalls. Another machine-sound started toward them and they scurried into one of the stalls. The worklight above did not wink on and they hunched behind a mass that once may have been a functioning vehicle.

Beyond, a large shape, its general dimensions outlined by small amber, red, and blue lights, rumbled past the stall. Derec took her hand and drew her out. They watched the drone roll around the intersection by the stairwell and disappear. Quietly, they walked after it.

Suddenly everything was still. All the drones had stopped, apparently, their inspection done. Distantly, Ariel heard two sets of footsteps echoing.

She heard two people descending the metal steps. Below.

When it was silent, she tapped his shoulder and they continued up.

At Level Eight the stairs ended.

Derec shined his light. Most of the stalls here were empty. At the far end of the row was a bulky door.

Ariel stopped halfway. "Derec?"

"What?" He returned and shined his light into the stall.

Packing crates, about forty centimeters on a side, filled the space. They had a familiar look, and Ariel knelt down by the nearest and lifted it.

"About six or seven kilograms," she estimated. She turned it over, but there were no markings on its dull grey surface.

"Hey," Derec said. He aimed the light into the next stall. More crates. Two more stalls were filled with them.

A distant hissing began and Ariel snapped to her feet.

"We need to go now," Derec said and hurried to the door. He studied the panel for a few seconds, then produced his wafer again. A minute later, the door lurched open and they stepped outside.

Ahead stretched a narrow corridor between two other structures.

The gangway deadended at a wall supporting a ladder that stretched up about fifteen meters. Debris gathered at the corners: grime-packed paper, indeterminate plastic shapes, accrued matter that crunched underfoot.

Ariel handed him the crate and went up first. At the top, her arms burned slightly from the exertion. She climbed onto the roof and looked down at Derec. He climbed one-handed, the crate tucked under his other arm. His breathing came heavy, too, and he gave a loud "Hoo!" when he reached the top.

Sitting on the rooftop, Ariel looked up at the ceiling of D.C. high above, almost lost in a tangle of struts, roadways, and the reaching towers of surrounding buildings. One structure was being taken down or repaired, its skin torn aside to reveal the skeleton beneath. This was an old section of the city and it struck Ariel how empty it suddenly appeared to be. From here they saw and heard no one but the distant background hum of thousands of machines.

Her pulse raced. "Now where?"

Derec looked around. "Let's see your map."

She handed him the datum with the grid pulled up on the screen.

"Well . . . if we keep going south we should come to an elevated strip."

"Which way is south?" she asked.

Derec pointed past her. She turned to look and saw a low wall, and beyond that, the cubes and polyhedrons of industrial structures. They had more climbing to do.

"Let me see that." She looked at the map. The area still struck her as familiar, but she still could not see why. "Great," she said. "So who do you think that was?"

"Maybe there was a security guard on the premises after all?"

"Took long enough to come look for us."

Derec looked back the way they had come. "This was awfully easy. You'd have thought they'd change the ID codes for the ambulance."

"Who would think to look for it?"

"Maybe. They seem to be pretty open so far."

"Really? Then why try to kill Mia? For that matter, why put a fake body in the morgue?" Ariel asked.

"Two fake bodies, if what you told me is true." He shook his head again. "And that doesn't make a lot of sense. They shot Eliton once at Union Station and then twice more afterward? Why?"

"Maybe the replacement body didn't want to die."

"The second body . . . reconstructive surgery or a clone?"

"Either way. The same ambulance that picked him up did not deliver him to Reed."

"Seems less a cover-up than a confusion. Which might work even better." Derec hefted the crate. "These probably won't be there for long, whatever they are. As for the ambulance, after a point they probably just don't care what anyone finds out. The cover-up is only short-term. The question remains, how much is being covered up and from who? Is it all Special Service or just the two agents that assumed control of the investigation? Who do we ask without alerting Cupra and Gambel—"

"They'd never manage it," Ariel said. "Besides, could two agents on their own bar you from working on the RI?"

"I wouldn't have thought so." Derec stood. "And how far is it really to the next strip?"

Ariel sighed and opened her datum. After studying it a few moments, she also got to her feet, pointed, and began walking.

NINETEEN

Mia forced herself to walk across the apartment again, her right leg aching in protest, pain stabbing up to her hip with each step. Sweat pooled at the base of her spine and around her neck.

"Please refrain from further exercise, Ms. Daventri," R. Jennie asked her again. "You are clearly in distress. It is my duty—"

"I understand your duty, Jennie," Mia said through clenched teeth. The wall was only a couple of meters away now. Then she had to turn around and make it back to the sofa. "I have to do this to build strength and recover. If I don't, I will be confined to the sofa or bed longer than necessary."

"You could also cause further injury to yourself and extend that period of confinement."

Mia came up against the wall and paused, breathing hard. "Are you medically qualified to diagnose, Jennie?"

"I am certified for nursing and emergency medical administration."

"But . . . ?"

"I do not have the same qualifications as a medical specialist."

Mia turned and let her back rest against the wall. The sofa was maybe four meters away. "Then kindly let me decide for myself how much I can manage."

R. Jennie stood near the hallway that led to the bedrooms, motionless, arms at its sides, and yet somehow managed to convey doting concern. It looked briefly at Bogard standing near the apartment entrance, as if looking for support from a fellow robot. But R. Jennie had already tried to enlist Bogard's aid in making Mia see reason and had been rebuffed. Bogard understood what Mia was doing; if it disapproved it kept that opinion to itself.

Mia launched herself toward the sofa. The pain made each step seem to take forever. She staggered the distance and fell onto the pillows.

She lay very still while her leg gradually stopped hurting. When she felt able to move again, it was only a dull throb, like a bad bruise. The painkillers in her system did not eliminate the aches completely, but seemed to work on a graduated system designed to keep her from overdoing physical activity. As long as she remained relatively motionless, the sensation was there but distant, like a strained muscle. The more she worked it, though, the more it hurt. She supposed that was a good thing, otherwise she might stress it to the point of reinjuring it.

Spacer thinking.

R. Jennie stood beside her now with a tray bearing a glass of cold water. Mia suppressed her irritation and took the glass.

"Thanks," she said.

"Will you be stationery now?" R. Jennie asked.

"Yes. I think that's enough for the time being."

"Is there anything more I can do for you?"

"No, not yet. Has Ariel called in?"

"No, Ms. Daventri."

"Call me Mia, please. Let me know as soon as she does."

"Of course."

R. Jennie returned to the kitchen. The last few days had been an education for Mia. She had never spent this much time around positronic robots and she was beginning to think that their banishment from Earth had less to do with any moral or ethical revulsion than with their constant fretting.

The water felt wonderful going down her throat.

She straightened on the sofa and looked across the living room. It was a good twelve meters wide and she had managed ten laps, one side to the other. Yesterday she had only managed six. Good progress by any measure, but Mia was impatient with her slow healing. She needed to be mobile. Too much longer in this apartment, in the dutybound company of R. Jennie, and she might change her mind about Eliton's dream of bringing robots back.

Eliton. She wondered now about that dream. Even if they managed to discover who had engineered the assassinations, it seemed thoroughly dead, the true victim of the violence.

On the table before her the datum showed the signal notation WORKING. The algorithm had been running for nearly two hours now, searching for a series of connections which, if there, may only be tenuous, insubstantial coincidences. The tenuousness of her hunches had made her reluctant to even begin such a search, but some of the names on the lists generated in the last two days struck her as odd. She doubted anything would turn up, but for lack of any other ideas and a dependable leg it seemed worth the trouble. In her studies at the academy it had amazed her how many crimes in recorded history had been solved due to serendipity. All this training went for nothing if chance failed to manifest. The good investigator was one who knew how to take advantage of the coincidences that presented themselves.

For instance, the fact that not one of the DyNan Manual Industries people had been shot.

Going over and over the recordings from the newscams, Mia returned to that oddity time after time. She had had Bogard run trajectory analysis several times, and she could not explain away the curious fact that no shots had been directed at any member of the DyNan party. There had been only three executives and one security, but they had been right alongside Imbitek and Porvan-StandardMech, another company that built supplemental technologies like conveyors, lifters, tractors, and a variety of other moving equipment. Two people in the Imbitek group had been wounded and three people in the PSM group, plus one dead. In spite of being sandwiched between these two, Rega Loom's people had survived untouched.

Unable to go to them to ask her questions, Mia worked the data.

Now that she was satisfied that none of the injuries and deaths had been accidental, that indeed the assassins had been good enough to hit exactly what they aimed at, she found herself trying to figure out what each victim meant in the scheme of cause and effect.

Humadros and Eliton represented the primary targets, obviously. Without them, the conference died, even though several parties worked valiantly to keep it alive. There would be a meeting, certainly, but how much could realistically be accomplished now? The bulk of Humadros's legation had died. Those remaining were junior members, more diplomats-in-training and gophers than real negotiators. Of course, there was the anomaly of Ariel's acquaintance, Tro Aspil, being both dead and en route back to Aurora, but even he had not been a significant member of the legation, not in the larger schema.

All of Eliton's security people.

Including her.

Why? Did they represent the only honest group within Special Service? As easy as it was to think that way, it was unlikely. But Mattu and Gel and Mia were the most likely to figure out the inconsistencies in the cover-up. It had been a matter of expedience to close off that avenue of trouble immediately. They had missed Mia in the Gallery, possibly the only shot that had gone wild.

Or maybe not. Maybe they had wanted her alive to frame, along with Bogard. Easy enough to do.

Then why the attack on the hospital? Second thoughts? Correcting a mistake?

Safer to believe that she was a target all along.

Eliton's staff—two people—were dead. Along with five members of Humadros's team killed, that totalled thirteen. One dead in the PSM party. Fourteen. The other seven?

Crol Dushek, head of the Solarian Legation, and two of his aides. Seventeen. The three Aurorans from the embassy here. Twenty.

The last one still seemed anomalous: a woman named Viansa Risher, who at first had no apparent reason to be on the platform. She had been a member of the Settler's Transport Committee, a division of the Settler's Coalition, a bureaucrat with no direct connection to anyone else. It looked like a token invitation.

When Mia called up newsnet articles, though, she discovered that Risher's presence had been significant indeed. The Settler Worlds had demanded a seat at the table from the first announcement of the conference and had been consistently ignored by both Terran and Spacer governments. Risher was the Settler Coalition's spokesperson on Earth and had made a good case for inclusion. Trade relations between Spacer Worlds and Earth *did* potentially impact Settler Worlds, and they certainly had an interest in the piracy issue since everyone privately believed that the pirates were Settlers or at least used a Settler world as a base. The exclusion made little sense and none of the reasons given had been convincing. Finally, in the last month, Eliton's office issued an invitation to Risher and the conference committee certified her for inclusion. But only her.

Twenty-one officially dead (or twenty, depending on Eliton's actual status). Thirty-three wounded. Fifty-five actual shots fired. Who among the thirty-three had they intended to kill?

And why no one in the DyNan Manual Industries party?

The screen on her datum continued to show WORKING. Mia finished her water, staring at it, waiting.

Ariel's com registered another call. Mia hobbled over and sat down. She had scrolled through the growing list of messages, worried. Three from Ambassador Setaris, two from Delegate Korolin, five from her aide, Hofton, one from Senator Taprin . . .

This one was from Coren Lanra, the security for the DyNan group.

Mia killed the visual and pressed ACCEPT.

"Ariel Burgess."

"Oh, Ms. Burgess." Lanra's voice was nasal and a little

rough. "I tried your office already but they told me you weren't in—"

"So you called me here. How did you obtain this number?"

"I'm Coren Lanra, security for DyNan Manual Industries."

He said it as if it explained everything. Mia felt herself smile despite her annoyance. "I'll take that to mean it's none of my business? What can I do for you, Mr. Lanra?"

"Well . . ." He sounded unsure now. This was not the kind of response he had expected, obviously. "I had hoped we could discuss the incident at Union Station."

"Is there a reason you want to discuss it with me?"

"I've tried to talk to several other people at your embassy, but no one seems to have the time. Understandable, with three of Ambassador Setaris's immediate staff dead. But I've been working down the list. I thought I'd give up when I reached the maintenance department."

"Our maintenance is handled by robots, Mr. Lanra."

"Yes, well, as I said."

"I still need a reason."

Lanra said nothing for several seconds and Mia began to think he would simply excuse himself and go away.

"There are certain . . ." he said finally, ". . . irregularities . . . about what happened."

"Concerning?"

"My employers, for one."

Mia chewed her lip. "You mean like the fact that none of DyNan's people were injured?"

"Like that, yes."

"Do you think that needs explaining?"

"It will."

"And you'd like to explain to us. Why? It seems to me that you ought to take this to Terran authorities."

"Right now they aren't very receptive to explanations."

Mia did not doubt DyNan would be high on the list of suspects. Even without the anomaly of no injuries, Rega Loom, DyNan's owner, was also the untitled head of the Church of Organic Sapiens, a rabidly anti-robot faction. But not only anti-robot—DyNan manufactured ergonomic and organic multiplier tech, tools that allowed a person to do the work personally; in fact, *required* a human to operate it. Their philosophy was a modified form of self-reliance: any tool that operated independently of human control, they claimed, sapped something vital from the human condition. Positronics topped the pyramid of technologies DyNan found inimical to their concept of humanity, but it certainly did not stop at robots. Imbitek, they declared, made things that were little better. Imbedded tech quietly did things humans did not even know about, hidden and forgotten. Humanity had no idea what capabilities it lost to machines that did work for them. Nothing DyNan made operated on its own. The Church of Organic Sapiens extended that belief into the religious, claiming that the true nature of humankind was pretechnological, that Eden had contained no machines, and that the only true state of grace was a state wherein human beings required and possessed nothing but their own bodies and minds.

But, Mia reasoned, if they *had* been behind the attack, then it was stupid of them to have not at least offered a token victim.

"I suppose listening couldn't hurt, Mr. Lanra," she said finally. "What do you have in mind?"

"If we could meet somewhere . . ."

"Give me a code where I can reach you. I have to juggle some things, but I'll get back to you."

"Ms. Burgess, please don't avoid me. I think this is very important—"

"I have no intention of avoiding you, Mr. Lanra. But I still have responsibilities to attend. I *will* get back to you."

Lanra sighed unhappily. "All right. You can reach me here."

A number appeared on the com. "Thank you, Mr. Lanra. How late will you be there?"

"As late as necessary."

"I'll be in touch."

Mia stabbed the disconnect with a trembling hand and leaned back in the chair, thrilled and frightened.

Something, she thought. *Finally something!*

Now the only problem was finding Ariel.

"Bogard," she called.

"Yes, Mia?"

"Can you still tap directly into security com lines?"

"I have not attempted to do so since our arrival here," the robot said. "It may be that I have been isolated from access."

I doubt it, she thought, *especially if they think you're gone . . .*

"Try it now. See if there is any local security chatter concerning Ariel and Derec."

Bogard moved up to the com console and extruded a thin cable from its left hand. The cable connected directly to the I/O port. Data flashed rapidly across the screen.

"No," Bogard reported.

"Send an anonymous report concerning them."

"Through central coordination, or shall I find a field unit in the area?"

"A field unit, of course, if you can."

A few seconds later, Bogard said, "There is a cruiser within the grid around the garage Ms. Burgess is investigating. I have sent a simulated dispatch directing it to the site."

"Very good, Bogard. Thank you."

"Do you wish me to continue monitoring?"

"Yes, Bogard. No further communications, but let me know if anything happens."

"Yes, Mia."

Mia limped back to the couch, leaving Bogard connected to the com. She had not thought Bogard could do this, but, thinking about it now, it was only logical. She stared at it, wondering what other capabilities it possessed to which she—or anybody else in her department—had given no thought.

She stared at her datum screen for several seconds. It no longer said WORKING. Instead, the words SEARCH COMPLETED glowed green.

Hesitantly, she pressed ACCESS.

TWENTY

D erec touched pavement at street level, relieved to finally be off the rooftops. He looked back up the length of ladder, toward the distant ceiling of D.C. Some of those roofs ended at that ceiling, forming part of the support for the cap that covered the city.

He shook his right arm to ease the burn. He had climbed down the entire length of this building—about fifteen meters, he guessed—with the crate under his left arm. His muscles ached.

"You know," he observed, "it's been a long time since I did any serious climbing, but this really isn't a very good substitute."

Ariel was looking around, her face pulled into an annoyed scowl.

"What?" he asked. "You've been looking like you lost something since we got to this sector."

"It's—I don't know, I can't quite put my finger on it. I should know something else about this area."

"What does your datum say about it?"

"A warehouse district, some small assembly plants, mostly merchandiser's storage. I—"

Ariel snatched out her datum and tapped it quickly. She turned and pointed. "That way."

Derec followed, irritated afresh. "You have an appointment?"

"Actually, yes."

"Have you ever been here before?"

"No, but it's part of my duties to know certain areas."

Derec waited for more explanation, but none came. He resigned himself to following and waiting for a bit longer.

Ariel went down a narrow gangway and out into a broad service alley that ran between loading docks. She glanced left and right and went left. At the fourth dock she stopped, referred to her datum, then pointed.

"That's the place."

"*What* place?" Derec asked.

Ariel climbed onto the dock apron and tried the employee door. When it did not open, she looked expectantly at Derec.

"Don't overuse this," he said as he joined her and inserted his decrypter. The lock was simple and the door opened within seconds.

Inside, they found a small, neat office. Business licenses hung on the walls.

"This is Auroran," Derec noted.

"I know."

"What are we looking for?"

"Contraband."

The warehouse proper was filled with rows of ceiling-high shelving containing crates of a similar dull grey as the one beneath Derec's arm, though much larger. Ariel stepped up to the nearest one and studied it, then looked around.

She found a small handheld device hanging from the end of the shelves and ran it along the length of the crate.

The lid unsealed and swung out. Within stood a humaniform robot, minus the head.

"A DP-8," she said. "Porter model drone."

"A bit too human for here, isn't it?" Derec commented dryly.

"Just a bit." Ariel checked three more and they all contained headless DP-8 drones. "Now, where do you suppose the heads are?"

They wandered among the shelves. Derec saw cases containing a variety of drones—factory assembler units, agromaintenance, cleaning drones—but only one section with the humaniforms, and every one of those that they opened they found headless. He began to suspect now what it was he carried under his arm.

"Derec," Ariel called.

He followed her voice to a wide door leading into another, smaller storage chamber. He saw machinery and workbenches.

"How come no one's here?" he asked.

"The embassy ordered all our nationals to close their businesses for the duration of the crisis."

"There's a crisis?"

She gave him a warning look.

On one of the benches sat a row of humaniform heads. Not absolutely human, but broadly so—caricatures of human faces. The backs were open. Derec turned one to peer into it.

"Empty."

"And . . . ?"

He looked at Ariel. "It's easily adaptable to a positronic brain, if that's what you mean."

"I do."

He looked at the crate he carried, then back at Ariel.

"This place is only a short distance from the garage," she said. "Proximity doesn't usually mean much, but in this case I'd have to say the coincidence is a little too much."

"I think we'd better leave before another incident."

Ariel nodded vaguely and let Derec lead her back to the small office. She went to one of the three desks, though, and switched on the terminal. She took out her datum and connected it to the I/O.

"Ariel—"

She held up a hand and Derec pressed his lips together tightly. It was futile to argue with her when she had her mind set on a goal. He waited while she riffled the system and transferred data.

Finally, she shut down and pocketed her datum.

"Let's go."

Relieved, Derec stepped out onto the loading dock.

"PLEASE STAND STILL. PLACE ALL OBJECTS ON THE PAVEMENT AND RAISE YOUR HANDS."

Derec looked sharply to the right. A police cruiser squatted in the alley and two officers stood behind it, weapons aimed at them.

"Shit," he muttered and slowly placed the crate at his feet.

"Just what were you looking for?"

Ariel stared angrily at the back of the cop's head. Her voice was controlled and reasonable, completely at odds with the frustration Derec saw in her face.

"Convention space," she said. "There's going to be a trade show of Spacer manufactures. That's what I do, I'm the commerce liaison with the Auroran Embassy."

"Convention—? There aren't any convention facilities in this area, Ambassador, and that was a private warehouse—"

"But it's called Convention Center District on all the maps."

"Yes, it is," the cop said agreeably. "But there really aren't any convention facilities there."

"So why is it called that if that's not what it contains?"

"It's always been called that," the other cop said. "You must be new on Earth."

"So it must be a practical joke, is that it? Leave outdated names on all the maps so the new tourists end up over their head in a bad neighborhood. Of course, that's a joke, too, since the Terran Tourism and Visitors Department swears there are no bad areas in D.C. or in any other major urban center on the planet."

"Tourism doesn't ask the police, Ms. Sorry."

"Someone should ask someone," Ariel went on, her voice acquiring an edge now.

Derec watched appreciatively as she gradually amplified her rant, over the course of the several kilometers back to the Auroran embassy, irritating and then enraging the two police officers who had, in fairness, just done their jobs. She picked on every explanation they offered until they clammed up and gave her only monotone answers and clearly could not wait to get her out of their cruiser. They had not arrested them because Ariel had her embassy ID on her and had convinced them that she had had business at that warehouse. Derec still had the crate, secured by the same explanation, though the policemen were clearly not happy about it. They were not willing to risk the trouble, though, in arresting an ambassador. Now she had gotten them to the point where they cared about nothing other than returning them to the Auroran embassy, which they had been more than willing to do, no doubt under orders to make sure no more Spacers got harmed or killed in the aftermath of Union Station. Ariel took advantage of that to so thoroughly outrage them with her petty slurs against Earth that they did not bother asking for Derec's ID, nor did they ask the questions that would have opened the door to answers Ariel did not wish to give.

On the landing pad, fifth floor of the embassy, they climbed out of the transport. Ariel strode off in a huff. Derec looked in at the two cops.

"Thanks, I really appreciate it," he said.

The nearer one glared at him. "Your boss needs to learn a little circumspection."

Derec shrugged. "Well . . ."

"Have a good day, sir."

They lifted off and Derec staggered back from the wash of hot, compressed air. He wondered how much of a report they would file.

Derec caught up with Ariel at the elevator.

"That was—"

She shot him a look. "Unnecessary?"

"—masterful."

She frowned briefly, then laughed. "Those poor . . ."

The elevator door opened, letting three people out. Ariel did not finish her thought.

"All the log recorded was date, destination, and distance," Derec announced. "It was used once in the last eleven months."

"Union Station?" Mia asked.

"Correct. And directly back to that garage. There's no record of the driver, the medical technicians, or the patient."

"No surprises, then," Ariel said.

"But it's confirmation," Mia said, nodding. She pointed at the crate on the end of the table. "What's in that?"

Derec felt inexplicably reluctant to open it. He looked at Ariel, his heart pounding. "Do you still have that key?"

Ariel handed him the seal key from the warehouse. Derec switched it on and ran it along the seam. The crate lid popped open.

Nestled within padding lay a plastic-wrapped mound of silver-and-gold webbing, wrapped tightly and mingled with darker nodes.

"Damn," Ariel hissed.

"What is it?" Mia asked.

"A positronic brain," Derec said. "Absolute contraband."

"Close it up," Ariel said.

Derec complied, then looked at Mia. "You called the police, didn't you?"

Mia nodded. "Something came up. I had Bogard issue a dispatch through their channels. Not much, just a cruiser to go look-see."

"Bogard is just full of tricks," Ariel said icily. "Pity it couldn't do its primary job as well."

Derec looked at her. She was staring at Bogard, arms folded, an expression of unconcealed resentment on her face.

"You sent me a message," Derec said, "after the Incident. You said 'I see you got your wish.' What did you mean by that?"

"You knew it was from me. Can't you figure out what it means?"

"Eliton's death was—"

"Beside the point. You got what you wanted by being able to create a dangerous robot. I don't think you wanted to kill Eliton. I think you wanted to build robots, any way you could, any way you wanted."

"How does that follow?" Derec asked. "With Eliton's death, *no one* will be able to build robots on Earth."

"I don't think it matters. Someone will hire you to build bodyguards now, no matter what."

"Excuse me, but I failed to do that."

Ariel waved her hand dismissively. "Glitches. No one on Earth would buy it, but Spacers understand that prototypes always have bugs to be worked out. It brought back three of the assassins. That's the point that won't be missed. You've got your opportunity to build your special positronics now. More leeway, more freedom of action, more humanlike. Hell, they'll even make mistakes."

"Ariel—"

"Pardon me," Mia said. "I feel like I've come in at the tail end of a very complicated argument."

"Derec and I disagree fundamentally over Bogard. What it represents."

"I gathered that much. Why?"

"Derec's robot here is the product of an attempt to circumvent Three Law programming—"

"That's a complete mischaracterization!" Derec shouted. "You never understood what I was after!"

"Really? Tell me something—why is that robot still functioning?"

"What? I don't—"

"It failed," Ariel snapped. "It let a human in its care die. It stood witness to dozens of fatalities and injuries. It should be a mass of collapsed positronic gelatin. Instead, it is fully functional."

"What good would it be if it *had* collapsed?"

"It would be inert. It would pose no further threat."

"What threat?"

"The threat of negligence!"

"It wasn't negligent! Look at how it performed for Mia."

"Then why is Eliton *dead?*"

"We don't *know* he's dead!"

"As far as Bogard is concerned, he is! Why?"

Derec did not know. Of everything he had intended in designing and building Bogard, that was precisely the thing which ought never to have happened. He looked at the unmoving, unmoved machine and wondered what had gone so profoundly wrong that it had allowed the human it was programmed expressly to protect to die.

"Would someone please explain this to me?" Mia asked.

"Derec built it, let him try," Ariel said in disgust.

"Under normal circumstances..." Derec started. His throat caught, and he coughed. "Normal circumstances... whatever that means... the Three Laws are built into every positronic brain, part of the core template. They represent the First Principles for a robot, the foundation on which all its subsequent learning and experience rests. The initial designers set it up so that almost all the secondary programming requires the presence of those laws in order to function. It would require a complete redesign of all the manufacturing methods as well as the basic pathways themselves to build a brain without the Three Laws. They aren't just hardwired into the brain, they are basic to the processes of constructing one."

"Is that what you did? Redesign everything?"

"No. I'm not that good. Nor am I that irresponsible. All I did was set in place a new set of parameters for the application of the Laws."

"You circumvented them," Ariel snapped.

"I did not. I took an accepted standard practice and stretched it."

"What practice?" Mia asked.

"Setting conditions of when the robot perceives that *it* is responsible for a violation," Derec explained. "Think about it. According to the First Law, if a robot followed it absolutely, all robots would collapse. 'A robot may not injure a human being, or, through inaction, allow a human being to come to harm.' Consider that as an absolute. Human beings are always coming to harm. Time and distance alone guarantee that a robot can't act to prevent that harm in all cases. If some kind of buffer zone, a hierarchical response, weren't in place, the instant robots realized how many humans came to harm because they weren't doing something to prevent it, we would have no functional robot population. So we establish a reasonable limitation for its application. If a robot does nothing to stop the human it is standing right next to from being killed—say, by a speeding vehicle, out of control—then it fails and collapse follows. If that same robot *can* do nothing to prevent the same fate happening to a human a kilometer away from it, the only way it fails is if another human forcefully asserts that it was at fault. It does not automatically perceive itself as responsible."

Mia nodded. "That makes sense."

"Practical engineering," Derec said. "But then we run into a functional brick wall when it comes to certain tasks. Law enforcement, for one. Most positronic brains cannot cope with violent crime. A few have been programmed to dissociate under very specific circumstances so that, say, witnessing dead humans at a crime scene won't create a Three Law crisis. But they still can't make arrests because that offers the potential of harm to a human being."

"But a criminal—" Mia began.

"Is still a human being," Derec insisted. "What a human *has* done by violating a law does not mitigate the robot's adherence to the Three Laws."

"Unless you redefine harm," Ariel said. "Which is how you got around the Three Law imperative."

"That's an oversimplification," Derec replied. "What I redefined was the sphere of responsibility. Bogard is just as committed to the Three Laws as any other robot, but it has a broader definition of that commitment. It can make the determination that limiting a human's freedom action, even if it results in a degree of harm—bruises or strained muscles, for instance—may prevent harm from coming to other humans."

"You're telling me you gave it a moral barometer?" Ariel demanded.

"Sort of. It relies on the human to which it is assigned to make that determination. It also recognizes a human prerogative to go in harm's way should circumstances require risk to prevent further harm."

"And when confronted with a clear case of Three Law violation?"

"It has memory buffers and a failsafe that shunts the data out of the primary positronic matrix. It prevents positronic collapse and allows for the opportunity for further evaluation. In a proper lab debriefing, the cause-and-effect of a situation can be properly explained and set in context. The robot can be reset and returned to duty."

"You gave it selective amnesia," Ariel said. "It can allow a human to come to harm and still function because after the fact it doesn't remember doing it."

"That's why Bogard left data out of its report," Mia said.

"That's why I have to take Bogard back to Phylaxis to debrief it."

Mia nodded thoughtfully. "So why don't you approve, Ariel?"

"A robot is a machine," she said. "A very powerful machine. It is intelligent, it can make decisions. I want them inextricably joined to the Three Laws so that they can never—*never*—circumvent their concern for my safety. If they fail to protect me, I want them shut down. I don't want them thinking it over. I don't want to ever be considered a secondary or tertiary concern by a robot who may decide that I ought to be sacrificed for the good of the many. Or of a specific individual. I think loosening the bonds like this can only lead to operational conflicts that will result in unnecessary harm."

"That's the only way to construct a robot bodyguard, though," Derec said.

"There should be no such thing, then!" Ariel shouted. "It didn't work! Somewhere in its sloppy brain it made a decision and sacrificed Senator Eliton! Explain it to me how that was for anyone's greater good!"

Derec stared at her, ashamed. He could think of no answer to give her. In fact, he had no answer for himself.

TWENTY-ONE

Mia watched the argument escalate, amazed at Ariel. She had always seen her friend as impatient but controlled, usually even-tempered, never enraged and irrational. But this was a side of Ariel with which Mia had no experience. The unreasoned hatred she directed at Bogard reminded Mia more of an anti-robot fanatic than of a Spacer who ought to be at ease with robots.

"Ariel—" Derec said tightly, obviously reining in his own anger.

Ariel left the room.

Derec closed his eyes, leaning back in his chair.

"You two have known each other a long time?" Mia asked.

Derec gave a wan smile. "Too long, I sometimes think. In a way, I've known her all my life."

"You're not—"

"Related? No. It's just I—we—both had amnemonic plague. Burundi's Fever. We've been complete amnesiacs.

When I had my bout, Ariel was the first human I came into contact with."

"And you were with her when she had hers?"

Derec nodded.

"So . . . why don't you explain this dispute to me. I didn't understand half of what you were talking about."

Derec drew a deep breath, clearly uncomfortable. "Well. I started investigating the way positronic memory works, especially in the aftermath of collapse. Sometimes you can recover a collapsed positronic brain—not often, but it can happen. There's something . . . unpredictable . . . in the way they collapse. I was curious about that."

"Having been an amnesiac have anything to do with this?"

"More than a little. What differs between human and robot is in the way we're locked into our perceptual realities. The way we interface with the world. Humans have a plasticity robots lack—we can indulge fiction, for instance, and know the difference, even when it's a full-sensory entertainment that is designed to mimic reality in the finest detail. A robot can't do that. Tell its senses that what it is perceiving is 'real,' and it acts upon that stimulus. It can't make the intuitive distinction. If what it perceives causes a conflict with its Three Law imperatives, collapse is likely unless quickly resolved."

"Even a fictional crisis?" Mia asked.

Derec nodded. "Exactly. Convince a robot a lie is real, and it has no way to treat the lie as a conditional reality pending further data, like a human does. Now in either case, unacceptable realities can cause breakdowns. Humans still suffer nervous collapses, psychotic amnesia, reactive psychoses—a variety of disorders in which the brain tries to deal with an emotional or physical shock that the mind cannot accept. It happens faster and under more concrete conditions to a robot. But in the case of humans, the attempted resolution is also an attempt to circumvent the trauma to allow the organism to continue functioning."

"Amnesia victims can still carry on living even if they can't remember who they are or where they came from."

"Simply put, yes. I wanted to see if some sort of the same mechanism could be duplicated in a positronic brain."

Mia looked over at Bogard. "It seems you succeeded."

"Not completely. What I established was a bypass, true. The memory is still there, but inaccessible to the primary matrix. I shunted it over to a buffer. Eventually, it has to be dealt with or Bogard will start suffering from diagnostic neurosis."

"What's that?"

"It's what I tried to explain to you before. A positronic brain runs a self-diagnostic every few hours. At some point, Bogard's diagnostic will register the absence of a specific memory node as a chronic problem. It won't be able to fix it, so Bogard will start feeling the need to be serviced. It can impair function."

Mia felt a ripple of anxiety. She still did not want to release Bogard. "So tell me why Ariel doesn't like this."

"Anything that tampers with the full function of the Three Laws she sees as a step away from heresy," Derec said. "In her view, by giving Bogard the ability to continue functioning in the wake of a Three Law conflict that should shut it down, I've created a monster." He grunted. "It was *her* work that gave me the direction to go, though."

"How's that?"

"Her doctoral thesis from Calvin. 'Three Law Conflict Under Alternative Concretizations.' Basically, she proposed the possibility of an informational loop that is created when a robot has incomplete data which strongly suggests the necessity of action." Derec frowned. "Unfortunately, it can't make the determination of which kind of action because the information is incomplete. It starts running probability scenarios, to fill in—basically by Occam's Razor—the blanks in its information so it can make a decision. But it still can't. It can theoretically create its own delusional scenario wherein collapse is imminent based on an unreal situation. One of Ariel's inferences was that a positronic brain could be lied to on a fundamental level and thus create a false standard of reality for it. The hierarchical response to perception would be distorted. And it would be stuck in it, the loop causing a cascade of alternative perceptions."

"How would you do that? Just walk up to it and say 'By the way, black is white, and people can fly'?"

"No, the hardwiring prevents the brain from accepting that kind of input. It would have to be a more direct interference, like a virus that could change pathways in the brain structure. Something that would directly affect the positronic pathways themselves."

"Doesn't that describe what happened to the RI at Union Station?"

Derec looked worriedly at her. "Yes. That's what I wanted to see by doing the physical inspection. There's evidence of a direct intervention at certain sensory nodes, but we can't tell which ones they were."

"Could anyone have accessed your research?"

Derec shook his head, but Mia saw uncertainty in his face. The notion had occurred to him, but he did not want to give it too much consideration.

"If I understand everything you've told me so far," Mia continued, "that means that Bogard could only have malfunctioned if it had been ordered to do so. If it had been given a set of operational parameters that allowed it to perceive reality a little bit differently."

"I suppose . . . yes, that's logical. But—"

"So someone told it to fail. That's the only way it could have. Correct? Because it's been performing flawlessly for me."

Derec shifted uncomfortably. "I'm not sure I completely follow."

"Somehow, someone convinced Bogard that Eliton was in no danger. Someone programmed it to ignore the real situation."

"But it went into full protect mode. It enshielded Eliton."

"Bogard was linked to the RI's sensory net at the time."

Derec stared at her for a long time, then nodded. "Bogard would have been affected by the same thing that altered the RI's realtime perception. But it still enshielded Eliton . . ."

"It looked to me like Eliton had ordered Bogard to go protect Humadros."

"Eliton would have needed the override codes. He didn't have them, did he?"

"No . . . unless someone gave them to him." Mia rapped her fist on the arm of her chair. "I have to get access to the Service datum."

"There may be a way to do that. But I have to debrief Bogard before we go much further. You *have* to release it to me."

Mia knew he was right. Bogard carried information they needed and she did not have the skills to get to it. But she still walked painfully and badly, and she felt more vulnerable than she ever had in her life.

Bogard could not protect her forever, though. The only way to feel safe again, on her own, would be to solve this.

For that, Derec needed Bogard. She had to hand it over to him.

Do Spacers feel this way all the time? she wondered. *Vulnerable without their robots? Lost, insecure, incapable? Maybe it wasn't such a bad thing to get rid of them . . .*

The thought shocked her. Robots were tools. If people had allowed themselves to become so overdependent on them that they could no longer function without them, was that the fault of the tool? Hardly. But it was always easier to change an environment than change the people who lived in it. Getting rid of robots was far easier than making the necessary—and probably beneficial—changes in people.

But what do I know? I'm just a cop, not a philosopher.

"Very well, Mr. Avery," she said. She turned to the robot. "Bogard?"

Mia knocked on Ariel's bedroom door. She heard nothing and nearly returned to the living room when it opened. Ariel had changed her clothes. She had an appointment with the representative from the Settler's Coalition this afternoon, Mia remembered.

"Sorry," Ariel said.

"For what?"

Ariel shrugged, smiled, scowled, and turned away with a look of disgust, all within the space of a second. "I get a little irrational on certain subjects. I hate losing control in front of people."

"You enjoy it in private?"

Ariel looked startled, then laughed. She came out and went into the living room. She stopped and looked around. "Where are they?"

"I, uh, turned Bogard over to Derec. It was time."

Ariel nodded thoughtfully. "You know, this is the only thing Derec and I have ever disagreed on."

"I'm sure."

Ariel smiled wryly. "You're very politic. But I'm talking about serious issues, not the annoying debris that clutters up anyone's life."

"Besides bodyguard work, what else would such a robot be good for?"

"Good for? Nothing." Ariel paused. "No, that's not fair. Quite a few situations would suit a robot that was able to more loosely interpret the Three Laws. Starships rarely have mixed bridge crews. Usually, the robotic contingents are on stand-by till needed. It's still dangerous to travel space. Exploration, certain kinds of lab work, some heavy industries. It's feasible that where now we have to either leave it all to robots or all to people, a robot like Bogard would make it possible for a mixed presence. Police work, certainly. Forensics robots are lab technicians that are specifically programmed to ignore the fact that a corpse was once a human being in the sense of a *person* in need of protection. But those are very limited refinements, nothing like what Derec has done."

"You really disapprove," Mia said.

"It really scares me."

Silence stretched between them. Mia could find no worthwhile response to her friend's admission. She shrugged.

"We have plenty to keep us busy. You got another interesting call while you and Derec were gone."

Mia ran a query through the public datum on the garage. The place was serviced under general contract by a maintenance firm called Cyvan. Cyvan Services did upkeep on a variety of storage facilities and a few government buildings. They were owned by a holding company, though: Glovax Diversified. It took time to find out who owned Glovax, but the answer, even though she would have guessed another, did not surprise her.

"Imbitek. Just like the ambulance."

"Imbitek bought the ambulance?" Ariel asked.

"Not directly. It took me the whole time you were gone to track that one down. The bid was submitted by Holden Transport and Combined Services, who took possession. But the credits came from Lexington-Siever Financial. Holden Transport banks with them, but it's not their primary account, just a short term cache for incidental expenditures. It was certainly large enough for this purchase, but the credits were replenished the next day from another in the same institution—a private account for one Nis Garvander, who sits on the board of directors of Glovax Diversified. Three days after the transfer of funds, Garvander closed his account down."

"Glovax . . ." Ariel mused. "So we're right back at Imbitek."

"Looks that way."

Ariel tapped her lips. "But this is still circumstantial, isn't it? After all, Imbitek suffered casualties. How come DyNan didn't?"

"Good question. Rega Looms certainly looks like the more obvious suspect."

"Which might be exactly why DyNan took no hits."

Mia looked at Ariel. "You're thinking they were set up."

Ariel nodded. Mia respected Ariel's perceptiveness. She would have made a good security specialist.

"But," Mia said, "we shouldn't discount DyNan completely. I'm trying to find out if there have been any funds exchanged between the two companies. It's still possible that DyNan engineered everything and left this trail just so we'd find it."

"I could never be a cop," Ariel said, shaking her head. "It must drive you crazy to suspect everyone all the time."

"Oh, it's not that bad. I don't suspect you."

Ariel grinned. "Thanks. It would help if we knew why this happened."

"Motive. Both those firms have motive. Positronics could directly impact their markets, and in DyNan's case there's a moral aspect."

"I don't believe anyone seriously thinks positronics will ever have the presence on Earth it once had. I've talked to Alda Mikels a couple of times. He's far too sensible to think that way."

Mia gestured at the crate with the positronic brain. "What about that?"

"Certain people will always buy things that are illegal, just to be daring. There's no doubt that Earth has enough of a market to sustain an illicit trade in positronics, but it would never support a legitimate traffic."

"But it would have an impact on interstellar trade, wouldn't it? I mean, Mikels wants to export his products. Competition with positronics isn't a big deal here, but on Settler worlds and Spacer worlds?"

Ariel pursed her lips thoughtfully. "Hmm. But the conference would have addressed those issues."

"If he trusted the outcome."

"And Rega Looms?"

"He doesn't even think we should *be* in space."

Ariel fell silent, deep in thought, and Mia turned her attention to the datum. The ambulance log Ariel and Derec had retrieved gave little enough information, but it was sufficient for them to construct the scenario. The false ambulance team arrived, got hold of Eliton's body, and took it back to the garage. The travel time recorded allowed for no other possibility. So they at least knew that the body lying in the morgue adjacent to Reed Hospital Complex was not Eliton's.

But, then, where was the real body?

Or was Eliton really dead?

Mia cleared her throat. "There's something else. I did a public data search on the connections between the various people in this and . . ." She hated her own reticence. "I found something that shouldn't be. Derec mentioned that Imbitek was doing the refit at Union Station. They started the next morning, after the attack, which is incredibly fast. I thought it had been an emergency appropriation that had been rushed through to meet the crisis, but I checked and found that the contract for the refit was part of the original deal for Union Station. When the contract was drawn up two years ago, Imbitek was the first company signed for work. There's a clause that gives them exclusivity in case of a failure."

"That sounds unbelievably foresighted. Or . . ."

"Or collusive. Senator Eliton—it was his committee that vetted the contract."

"Of course," Ariel said.

"It turns out that Eliton and Mikels have another connection. Mikels' son died in the military. At Ganymede. Eliton was the Brigade commandant on that action."

Ariel's eyebrows rose. "I had no idea that Eliton had been in the military."

Mia nodded. "Eliton and Mikels knew each other then. Eliton had arranged for Mikels' son to be transferred into his unit. Shortly afterward, Mikels gave him a significant share of stock in Imbitek. As far as I have been able to determine, Eliton never divested. There are nondisclosure restrictions on private actions dating back over fifteen years."

"Convenient. So Mikels and Eliton knew each other. And Eliton got Mikels' son killed. So what is this? Revenge?"

"I suppose that depends on whether or not Eliton is still alive. But if they hated each other, why would Eliton give this kind of a concession to Imbitek on Union Station?"

"Blackmail?"

Mia shrugged uncomfortably. "Which reminds me. You have an appointment to make."

Ariel looked at her quizzically. "Hmm? Oh, your acquaintance. Coren Lanra?"

"Correct."

Ariel went to the com. "Tell me about him."

"He used to be Special Service. He quit last year in protest over Senator Eliton's pro-positronic leanings. He's a committed anti-robot humanist."

" 'Flesh, not steel'?"

"He wasn't quite there when he quit, but he works for Looms now."

"Why do you think he contacted me?"

"That's what we need to find out."

Ariel entered Lanra's code and waited.

"Lanra."

"Mr. Lanra, this is Ariel Burgess again." Mia started at the sound of Ariel's voice; she was making it rough and gravelly. "Where would you be comfortable meeting?"

There was a long pause. "Are you sure you want to? Your voice sounds—"

"It's been a long day and I've been talking most of it,

Mr. Lanra. That's the kind of job I have. Now, if you please?"

"I see. All right. Um . . . do you know *Sullivan's*?"

"Very well."

"In . . . four hours?"

"How will I know you?"

"I know you. I'll meet you."

The connection broke and Ariel cleared her throat.

"Why'd you do that?" Mia asked.

"You and I don't sound that much alike. Now what?"

Mia looked at the assortment of devices Ariel had gotten, some from a specialty dealer Mia knew, others from her own embassy security people, and wondered if it would be enough. She picked up a transceiver pair and rolled the small beads around in the palm of her hand. They were good for several kilometers. She sighed and held them out to Ariel.

"We meet him at *Sullivan's*."

Sullivan's occupied three floors of the Lexington-Coriolis Hotel and offered a view of the Mall just south of the ancient Lincoln Memorial. Mia could not remember now if the Memorial was one of the reconstructions or the original. A good part of the old Washington D.C. had been destroyed in the Riot Years, during which, among other things, robots were banned from Earth. It looked crowded and out-of-place beneath the enclosing roof that now covered all urban habitats on Earth. The Mall itself was an anachronism, a holdover of a time known now only to professional historians and a few antiquarian enthusiasts. It served more as a reminder that there had *been* a past than what that past meant.

Mia sat by the terrace on the second level, alone at a

small table. She had been terrified when she stepped out of the embassy. Her leg still ached, but Ariel had gotten her painkillers and an adrenal analog in case she needed to move faster than she should. Still, she was not one hundred percent and she felt open and vulnerable.

But the terror subsided and it felt good to be out. She was Doing Something and it surprised her how much she had missed that feeling.

She absently scratched her left ear and pressed the small bead more firmly in. Ariel wore the other of the pair as a pin on her jacket.

The other tool Mia had brought along rested inside her jacket—a short, blunt tube that projected a jolt of electricity, enough to stun. She had wanted to bring a sidearm, but decided against it—this time.

"Ms. Burgess?" said a male voice through the transceiver.

Mia casually looked toward Ariel's table, in the center of the main dining room. Lanra stood there now, introducing himself.

"Yes?" Ariel said.

"I'm Coren Lanra, chief of security for DyNan Manual Industries."

"Pleased to meet you." Ariel gestured for him to sit.

"I appreciate you coming to talk. I realize that you've got a busy schedule."

"I do, Mr. Lanra, so please make the time count."

Lanra grinned slightly, apparently surprised by Ariel's abruptness. "Yes, well. My employers are concerned at the reaction over the Union Station incident. Certain charges are being made. They fear arrests are imminent."

"And why would that be?"

"You saw the recordings? No one from our group was

injured. Every other group suffered casualties, but not one of our people was shot."

"You make that sound like a bad thing."

"In this instance, it is. We look very culpable."

"Are you?"

"No." Pause. "You don't believe me."

"I think I could accept that *you* aren't culpable, Mr. Lanra, at least not directly," Ariel replied. "But Looms has been railing against Spacers and robots since I've been here and, I'm assured, long before that. He's been very explicit in his desire to cut off all contact between Earth and the Spacer worlds and to stop the exodus of Settlers. Now, on the eve of a conference which would strengthen all those ties and possibly enable an even freer exchange of immigrants and ideas, he and his entourage are the only ones untouched by assassins, who themselves may be affiliated with a group in sympathy with Mr. Looms' own Church. Tell me that doesn't make a persuasive case against him."

Lanra nodded. "It does. It's almost perfect. And that should tell you that it's not true. How often does reality match up so well with appearances?"

"You have a different view, of course."

"Looms is on record as being opposed to any kind of technology that isolates people from direct control."

"True."

"Then why would he use that very technology to commit a crime for which he'd be likely to be implicated? And where would he get the expertise to implement it?"

"Expertise can be bought," Ariel noted.

"To what end? Close down a conference that might give him the best platform he's ever had from which to be heard?"

Ariel shook her head. "All you're doing is arguing mo-

tive, Mr. Lanra. There is as much motive to implicate him
as there is to exonerate him."

"All right, what do *you* think was accomplished by this
assassination? What was there in this conference that was
so threatening that someone would commit murder to stop
it?"

"A lot of tradition, a lot of credits, a lot of territorial
imperative."

"All that, yes. But it's the money. Now ask yourself:
what part of the proposed treaty was most likely to pass
that would cost the most money."

"Cost who?"

"Answer the first, you answer that."

"There were a lot of elements—"

"Let me give you a hint. *Tiberius.*"

"The boarding incident?"

Lanra nodded. "That almost triggered a war, yes."

"I'm not sure I follow, Mr. Lanra."

Lanra leaned toward her, folding his hands on the table.
"A year-and-a-half ago, Mr. Looms was approached by a
group of industrialists to join an investment portfolio being
funded by certain shipping lines. Mr. Looms declined, since
he disapproves of interstellar settlement and, although the
money looked very good, he could not afford to appear
hypocritical on this issue. Most of his own investors are
members of his church and they invest in DyNan as much
from ideological conviction as out of the hope for potential
profit. The fact is, DyNan doesn't perform nearly as well as
its closest competitors, so that loyalty is significant. We
make a lot of money, but our profit margins are narrower
than average. This group assured him that his participation
would be entirely anonymous. In fact, all of their participation in it was anonymous and completely off-record. The

profits were funneled directly into the mutual fund, loaned out, and returned as interest free payments, at which time the funds could go into any account without the hint of taint. When Mr. Looms inquired into this shipping line through other channels, he found no such line existed. Officially."

"Black market," Ariel said.

"Exactly."

"The pirates."

"Who are not, strictly speaking, pirates," Lanra pointed out. "The thefts are all prearranged. The part of the treaty that would put a damper on it was the clause concerning robotic inspection of all ships, coming or going, to any recognized colony or Spacer world."

"I'd considered that, of course. How does this let Looms off?"

"He has no investment in this enterprise and, in fact, would not mind seeing such inspection. He feels that Terrans would resent it so much that it would significantly reduce trade. In time, it could curtail colonization. Hurt both enough, and you might see the day when Earth can extricate itself from involvement with Spacers and Settlers."

"That seems a bit optimistic, don't you think?" Ariel asked.

"Maybe. All I'm concerned with here is that it reduces Rega Looms' culpability."

"Disrupting the conference could accomplish the same thing, though. Give me something more concrete."

Lanra shook his head. "I can't. I'm looking into it, but right now I can't. I needed to see you to find out what you intend to do."

Ariel raised her eyebrows. "Me?"

"Spacers."

"We're hardly a monolith, Mr. Lanra. My own people are taking a wait-and-see approach. When and if the Terran authorities make arrests, then we can see."

"They're likely to arrest Rega Looms. What then?"

"It's a question of evidence."

"Look," Lanra said. "Mr. Looms is not especially liked here, either."

"What do you mean, 'either'?"

"Like Spacers. See, people want stability, they want comfort, they want reassurance. They *don't* want disruption. Change scares them. The way things are right now, it's fairly comfortable. Both you and my employer advocate changes. Whoever is setting this up will give the people something they want—two avenues of unwelcome change closed down. Who's going to be on Rega Looms' side in this when he's been telling people for years what lazy bastards they've been because they won't peel their own potatoes or make their own clothes? He sees the average technological environment today as no better than one with positronics. People resent it—enough to not care that he might not be guilty."

"He's the perfect scapegoat, in other words," Ariel said.

"As you say."

"You still haven't given me an alternative."

"Alda Mikels."

"Imbitek? Why would he?"

"You should look at his finances. And you should look at your own people. This didn't happen entirely here on Earth. The black market exists to serve Spacers and Settlers as well as Terrans."

"You're very good at making broad claims that you can't back up," Ariel said dryly.

"There's a very, very old saying on Earth, Ms. Burgess: 'Follow the money.' "

Lanra stood then. "Thanks for meeting with me. I hope it wasn't fruitless."

Mia watched him cross the dining room. Halfway toward the entrance, he did a casual turn, sweeping the room. A very professional move, one she should have seen coming, but did not. She froze in place as his gaze swept past her, then returned, briefly. She thought she saw a faint frown of puzzlement, followed by a quick smile.

Then he was gone.

TWENTY-TWO

The embassy limo pulled into the Phylaxis garage. Derec told it to wait and ascended to the main level to see who was present. He found Rana in the cafeteria, making coffee.

"Anyone here?" Derec asked.

"No. Stu came by today, filed his reports, then went home. No one else. Listen, this has been quite a day so far. You received a call you will *not* believe and the work-ups on that stuff you found—"

"Later. Prep Bogard's niche."

She blinked at him, momentarily uncomprehending. Then her eyes widened. "Right."

Derec returned to the limo.

"Bogard, come with me."

The robot unfolded out of the rear seat, its body flowing liquidly and resuming its standard form alongside Derec. Derec told the limo to return to the embassy. He watched it back out of the garage and drive away. The door closed and Derec led Bogard up to the lab.

"Do you remember this place, Bogard?"

"Yes, Derec. I was constructed and programmed here."

"That's correct. Do you know why I've brought you back?"

"Debriefing and recalibration."

"Correct. Are you aware of a gap in your primary memory?"

"Y-yes—yes," the robot stammered.

"Fine, Bogard, don't focus on it," Derec said calmly. "That gap represents a potential conflict. That's what we're going to fix."

"Y-esss, Derec."

The abrupt distortion in Bogard's speech execution worried Derec. He had expected a slight hesitancy, not such a clear sign of imminent collapse. It had been over four days since the Incident, so perhaps it was not unreasonable to expect problems like this.

"Oh, my." Rana stood at the door to a separate chamber, staring at Bogard. "I thought—"

"I know," Derec said quickly. "Is everything prepped?"

"Uh, yes."

Derec led the robot through the doorway into the small room. The space contained two workstations, cousins to those in the main lab. Against one wall stood a robotic niche, modified to link to a third console off to the left. A wide table hung from the right-hand wall; tools and half-constructed components covered it.

Rana went to one of the workstations, Derec the other.

"Bogard, please enter the standby module," Derec said.

Bogard obediently backed into the niche. Derec activated the module. The niche extruded hundreds of wire-fine I/O probes and linked Bogard into the system.

Derec relaxed then, surprised at the amount of tension he had carried all the way from the embassy. He realized at that moment that he had been uncertain of Bogard's cooperation. Perhaps Ariel was right and tinkering with absolute Three Law restrictions was a mistake.

Too late . . .

"All right," he said to Rana, "start the alignment. Bogard's buffer is holding a major conflict at bay. I think the internal barriers are about to yield to the diagnostics."

"It's been what? Four, five days?" Rana asked, working her console.

"Close enough. I thought we might have a little more time, but it's already showing symptoms of collapse."

Derec watched the screens at his station. The buffer transfer was the most complicated part of the debriefing. A duplicate positronic brain received the contents of Bogard's buffer, allowing for a full assessment of its impact. Simultaneously, a simple memory cache received a verbatim record of those same contents.

"Thales, please monitor the positronic transfer," Derec said.

"Yes, Derec," the RI replied.

"Alignment ready," Rana said.

"Begin."

Several things happened at once. All the screens on Derec's board showed sudden changes, most especially the three showing activity in the receptor brain. Where there had been the trace readings of a functioning but unprogrammed positronic net, now the scales indicated a rapidly adapting set of personality algorithms, basic memory notation, and program parameters. Within less than two minutes, the receiving positronic brain became Bogard.

And the trouble started.

"Derec," Thales said, "there is a rejection algorithm working."

"What?"

"The receptor is rejecting the contents. It carries an unassimilable paradox."

Now Derec saw it: a discontinuity starting in the memory pathways and spreading into the personality. The two aspects were drifting out of sync with each other. The receptor brain was trying to refuse the information. Positronic brains carried certain self-protects in their initial make-up which prevented them being programmed in any way that conflicted with the Three Laws.

"How about the memory dump?"

"Reception and encoding nominal."

"Bypass the personality sectors," Derec told Rana.

Rana nodded, her fingers dancing on her console. Gradually, the discontinuity flattened out and the transfer proceeded. By circumventing that part of the positronic brain which manifested as a robot's personality, the information could now load as simple data.

"Once it's all transferred," Derec said, "then we'll try adding the rest."

Rana frowned, but continued working. "Set and working. This will take some time—maybe ten minutes. Fifteen."

"Good." Derec ran a hand over his face, feeling all the weariness from the day. Had it all happened in less than five days? Yes, and he had been working eighteen out of every twenty-four hours since the Incident. Even so, he knew he should not be this tired. Then again, arguing with Ariel always drained him.

"Was that coffee I saw?" he asked.

"Absolutely," Rana replied.

"I'll be right back."

He wanted to go upstairs and stretch out on the cot, but he walked into the cafeteria instead and poured a cup of coffee. The past few days seemed to both contract and expand in his memory, at once too short a time and too long. He was worn from the distorted time sense.

But he was excited, too. He felt close to an answer. Maybe not *the* answer, but an important one just the same, and once he had a handle on one relevant fact the rest could be dragged out into the open through sheer persistence.

Unfortunately, right now he could make no sense of anything he had learned.

The com chimed. Derec wandered toward it, intending only to hear who it was.

"Mr. Avery, this is Tathis Kedder. From Union Station? I, uh—"

Derec stepped up to the com and pressed ACCEPT. "I'm here, Mr. Kedder. How can I help you?"

"Well, I'm not sure." Kedder laughed nervously. "I was going over some old logs and, um . . . there are some inconsistencies in the way the RI was reporting certain things that, well, in light of everything else that's happened, they made me wonder."

"What sort of inconsistencies?"

"I'd, uh, rather not discuss it over a comline."

"I see. Where would you like to talk, then?"

"My apartment? Tomorrow afternoon?"

"Send the address. I'll be there, Mr. Kedder."

"Thank you, Mr. Avery. I, uh, I appreciate this."

The connection broke and Derec grunted. What was *this* all about now? Reminded, he touched the reconnect for Joler Hammis. The line still came up UNAVAILABLE.

"How come Kedder isn't looking for new work?" he wondered aloud. "Maybe he is."

"Derec," Rana called from the main lab. "I need to show you this."

Derec returned to the lab. Rana was leaning over a workstation.

"Those flakes you gave me the other night? Look." She pointed to one of the screens.

The image showed a six-sided lattice structure. The pattern spread over the entire screen . . . except in three places, where the hexagonal form splintered around an octahedron.

"What . . . ?" Derec said.

"The vertices," Rana said, "are oxygen atoms. They're bonding aluminum atoms throughout most of the matrix except here—" she pointed to the octagonal forms "—where they're bonding faujasite analogs."

"Analogs . . . you mean they're synthetic."

"As far as I can tell, the whole thing is synthetic. What I mean is, the faujasite molecules are composed of similar components, except instead of electrons in the constituent atoms, these have positrons."

Derec felt his scalp ripple. "Positrons. You're telling me this is a brain construct?"

"It's a construct, but I wouldn't call it a brain. The basic shape is a zeolite."

"Zeolites . . . filters, industrial filters." Derec shook his head. "Huh?"

"I said the basic shape," Rana explained. "Those faujasite analogs have one other component that I don't recognize. The positrons are interacting with the aluminum atoms and transferring themselves like an electrical current from octahedron to octahedron. The aluminum ends up 'borrowing' electrons from the oxygen atoms. The resultant oxide sort of follows the current, passing the positrons along. No normal atom wants to keep the positron, so it just travels."

"Ending up where?"

"It's looking for another positronic matrix."

"Why?"

Rana shrugged.

Derec studied the screen. "Industrial filters . . . zeolites are used in food processors, for reconstituting certain molecules into different combinations . . . they're used in gas exchangers. All they're really designed to do is pass other molecules and recombine them or strip out electrons to make isotopes. What would this be used for?" He chewed his lip. "This is incomplete, isn't it? Were there any other atoms?"

"A few scattered ions, nothing coherent."

"Like what?"

"Platinum, a few pyroxenes, stray carbons . . ." Rana's voice trailed off.

Derec looked at her. "And?" he prodded.

"Well, there were a few large fragments of long chain carbon atoms—I can't swear to it, but it looked like a fullerene."

"A buckyball?"

"No, bucky*tubes.*"

"Superconducting?"

"There wasn't enough of one left to test, but that would be my bet."

"Buckytubes . . . with positrons instead of electrons?"

"No, but the fragmenting looked like it had occurred at that level, like the binding electron shells had been disrupted."

"As if a positron had been passed through it?"

Again, she shrugged, but now there was a small grin on her face.

"So what we're looking at," Derec mused, "is a material designed to find and link with a positronic matrix and pass material into that matrix. A conduit that—what?—attaches parasitically and sets up a single point feedback loop?"

"Fullerenes grow under the right circumstances. If this material permeated the RI—"

"There'd be no way to tell without examining the RI itself." Derec shuddered. "Clever. Somebody has created what amounts to a positronic parasite."

"But all it could do would be to pass positrons into the system. The charges are opposite for anything else and if it's a positronic matrix, then it's still functioning as its own brain."

"Unless this thing can be used to feed it new information."

"What kind?" Rana asked.

"Perceptions?"

Rana's eyes widened. "The game."

Derec nodded. "The RI took itself off-line during the assault to play a game. The game was loaded into the system to begin with, but it knew it was a game."

"But if it came through a secondary matrix that substituted one set of sensory parameters for another—"

"The RI wouldn't be able to tell which one was reality. At least not right away. It might have reset itself."

"Or this might have just switched off."

"Either way, it wouldn't be able to tell that the false information was coming from outside. This would appear to be just another branch of its own system."

"Damn."

"Absolutely damn. I—"

A chime sounded. Rana peered at another console. "Bogard's finished transferring."

Derec put Bogard on standby before he brought the receptor brain up. "Thales, I want you to run monitor. Keep the receptor brain from collapsing till we get a complete picture."

"May I remind you, Derec," Thales said in its calm way, "that a conflicted positronic brain on the verge of collapse is a chaotic system? I will do what I can, but I guarantee nothing."

"Do your best, Thales." Derec touched a contact and watched his screens.

"Would you like me to run a recalibration on Bogard?" Thales asked.

"Can you handle both?"

"Of course."

Derec glanced at Rana, who smiled at the hint of injured pride in Thales' voice.

"Go ahead, then." He studied the readouts. He keyed a set of commands. "Bringing up the surrogate . . . now."

All the realtime graphs warped radically.

"What? What? What?" came sharply over the speakers. Derec turned down the decibels.

"Bogard," he said.

"Y-yes. Who are—what?"

"This is Derec Avery, Bogard. Pay attention to my voice. Center on my voice."

"D-Derec, yes. I acknowledge—I know—I—yes—"

"Calm down."

"I am. I—am."

"Listen to me. Are you listening?"

"Yes, Derec."

"I require a report. Can you give me a full report of the operation at Union Station?"

"Yes, I—will."

"Begin report."

Several seconds passed in silence. The fluctuations displayed on the screens continued.

"Thales?" Derec asked.

"The brain continues nominal for the circumstances," Thales said.

Derec nodded. "Bogard, report."

"*I cannot!*" The response came as a shriek.

"Bogard, center on my voice," Derec said calmly. "Pay attention to my voice."

The robot paused. "Yes, Derec."

"I require your report."

"Yes."

Again, the silence stretched. As Derec was about to make his request again, Bogard's voice finally responded.

"I failed!" it shouted.

"*Report*, Bogard," Derec insisted.

Suddenly, the chaos on Derec's screens seemed to settle down slightly.

"Report on security operation," Bogard said. "Subject: Eliton. Theater: the Gallery at Union Station, Washington, D.C."

Derec looked at Rana, who seemed surprised.

"Continue," Derec said.

"All telemetry reports optimal. Crowd control is in effect. Communications and sensor telemetry established realtime through Resident Intelligence. Surveillance reports zero infiltration of threatening subjects. Police have blocked admission to several protestors who appear on their trouble list. Robotic security maximum. Crowd density acceptable, assessment acceptable, the word from One is GO.

"The limo stops at main entrance. We are met by Eliton's field security team. I am assigned operational control to Agent Mia Daventri. She indicates that the situation, while apparently chaotic, is acceptable. I allow Senator Eliton to emerge from the limo first per prearranged program. I follow immediately and perform an on-site scan. The crowd is noisy and hostile, but belligerence is kept at the level of verbal protest. No indication of immediate threat. Per scheduled conditions I uplink to Resident Intelligence for optimal security coordination. The security team moves ahead. I stay one meter behind Senator Eliton all the way to the ceremonial platform.

"I—mission parameter amendment—tier four, level B-nine—proceed sublevel sixteen—"

"Bogard, stop," Derec ordered. "Clarify last sentence."

"Mission parameter amendment."

"Understood. What is the nature of the amendment?"

"Circumvention tactic. Request movement to tier four—"

"Bogard, stop. Clarify. Circumvention of what? You are performing observe and protect duties for Senator Eliton. What circumvention?"

Bogard paused. "I do not know. Missing modules, data incomplete."

"Very well, Bogard. From whom have you received this amendment?"

"Source—direct-link, Resident Intelligence, Union Station."

Derec leaned forward. "Proceed with report. You followed Senator Eliton to the ceremonial platform. What happened then?"

"I continue monitoring security channels. Everything is

continuing optimal. There is movement in the audience, but floor security indicates that everything is acceptable. RI reports everything under control. The assembly is informed that the Spacer legations are arriving. Senator Eliton takes his prearranged position to greet Ambassador Humadros. I—"

The robot fell silent.

"Bogard?" Derec prodded.

"Mission parameter amendment to defence standby, level twelve—"

"What's it talking about?" Rana asked. "We don't have any routines that run by levels like that."

"Bogard, reset," Derec said. "Report events, bypass further program modifications."

"They are shooting. They are shooting. They are shooting." Bogard repeated the sentence, almost mantralike, until Derec interrupted.

"Who? Bogard, follow report protocols. Sequencing—"

"Explosions occur all around the outer wall of the gallery. They are harmless, smoke and noise, no fragmentation. Loud. The humans are frightened. Then the shooting begins. I see several people rush from the crowd carrying weapons. They begin shooting at us. Telemetry from RI indicates situation normal. I step forward and enshield Senator Eliton. My primary concern is Senator Eliton. Other humans are falling from injuries. My primary concern is Senator Eliton. Ambassador Humadros is my secondary, but she is out of my reach. Senator Eliton is demanding that I secure her as well. I see her, frightened, four-point-six meters away. I cannot be responsible for other humans outside the limits of my priority. First Law violation. I alert the nearest human security, Agent Daventri, and indicate Ambassador Humadros's situation. I shunt response to hierarchical buffer. My primary concern is Senator Eliton—"

"All right, Bogard. You are tending your primary. What happens next?"

"I perceive that the majority of the shots from the assailants are illusions, part of an internal scenario run by the RI. There are no projectiles emerging from their weapons. This is inconsistent with my own sensor telemetry. I count nine whose weapons are dangerous. I cannot locate Senator Eliton. I cannot locate Senator Eliton. My primary is changed. I am to protect Ambassador Humadros. I retract enshielding and proceed to cover her, but I am not fast enough. Ambassador Humadros falls from a puncture to the throat."

"What happened to Eliton?" Rana asked, dismayed.

"I don't—" Derec began.

"I search for my previous primary," Bogard continued. "I see Senator Eliton. He is in the open. He is vulnerable. I move to enshield him. I am not fast enough. He falls from a puncture to the chest. I move to administer medical attention, but I scan no pulse, no respiration, falling body temperature. Senator Eliton is dead. Senator Eliton is—I failed—I have—"

"Bogard, stop. Back up. What happened just before you lost Senator Eliton?"

"I receive a mission parameter amendment."

"From who? The RI?"

"The Resident Intelligence, yes."

"What is the nature of the amendment?"

"Respond to verbal command, reset identification specifications. After that, the communications link goes down. We lose all contact with the RI."

"What is the verbal command?"

"Zed-slash-repatch-one, reestablish, local parameter, verbal command 'I am not here. Protect Ambassador Humadros.' Omega-five catalogue reset. Responding."

Derec exchanged a startled look with Rana. That was the command code to override Bogard's preset priority, the command used by Mia Daventri to save the robot at Union Station.

"Who gave that command?" Derec asked.

"I do not know."

"Was it a human?"

"Yes."

Derec felt a chill. "Did it originate from within your en-shielding?"

"Yes."

"Do you know who gave the command?" Derec asked again.

"No one."

"Someone had to. Bogard, reset parameters. Follow the logic. You perceived a threat?"

"Yes."

"You enshielded Senator Eliton."

"Yes."

"You received an amendment from the RI."

"Yes."

"The command to reassign your primary concern came from within your enshielding."

"Yes."

"Who was the last human within your enshielding?"

"Senator Eliton."

"Conclusion?"

"Senator Eliton gave the command." There was a long pause. Then: "But he was no longer there. I lost him. I could not perceive him. The RI had a positive track on him and he disappeared. He could not have been there to give the command."

"Bogard, were you using the RI's telemetry the whole time?"

"Yes, as an augmentation to my own, until the link went down."

"You were relying on the RI for identification and location?"

"Yes."

"Who instructed you to do that?"

"Standard procedure within Union Station. I was told to conform to the required protocol."

"By whom?"

"Agent Otin Cupra, pending verification."

Derec slammed his fist down on the console. "Damn! That son-of-a—" He took a deep breath, exhaled raggedly. "Bogard, did the RI lose track on Senator Eliton at the time of its last amendation?"

"Yes."

"I don't understand," Rana said. "What's going on?"

"Bogard was linked into the RI during the entire assault. When the RI went off-line, it took Bogard with it."

"That's not possible—Bogard wasn't *slaved* to it. Besides, Bogard claims the RI communication net went down."

"True, but until that happened, for all practical purposes, at least half of Bogard's sensory net was being used by the RI. It was sharing data realtime. Bogard never got drawn completely into the illusion that took the RI off-line, but it was sufficient to impair Bogard's ability to sort out reality, at least for a short time. Long enough. Bogard was relying on the RI to keep informed of everyone's whereabouts. And why not? One positronic brain to another, what was there to worry about? They both had the same interests, the same standards, the same basic imperatives. Why would the RI intentionally distort data? So when Bogard lost track of Eliton—"

"It was because the RI had," Rana concluded. "Then the link went down and all that remained was the last amendation. But what about this command that Eliton gave? That doesn't make any sense. Bogard didn't know he was within the enshieldment, but still accepted the command? And how did Eliton know it? The primary should *never* know how to do that, otherwise what good is it having an incorruptible agent as bodyguard. That was the whole point—"

"Rana, it's *me*, Derec. I know. I designed it."

"But none of this is making any sense. Who's Agent Otin Cupra?"

"One of the pair that threw us off the job at Union Station."

"What authority did he have issuing protocol instructions to Bogard? And why would Bogard accept that instruction when it didn't have to?"

"That's a damn good question. Agent Daventri had field control of Bogard, but within Special Service I suppose anyone could give it orders that don't run counter to its priorities." Derec sighed heavily. "It could take months to sort out all the numbers, but I think Bogard had become—for an instant—part of the game the RI was absorbed in. The command could have come from anywhere. Since Bogard couldn't locate Eliton, it only made sense for it to shift priority to another primary. Left to its own, it might have realized its mistake and covered Eliton again. But it was given a new primary."

"And failed to protect her."

Derec nodded. "At which point Bogard was probably in

the process of severing its connection to the RI. Then it found Eliton."

"And failed to protect *him.*"

"And should by any normal expectation have collapsed on the spot. If Agent Daventri hadn't had the presence of mind to reset its priority again—"

"Daventri. The one that died in the hospital later that night?"

"She didn't die. Bogard got her out. Bogard performed faultlessly in protecting her."

"If she's not dead, why are they claiming that her body is in the morgue?" Rana asked.

"Who's claiming that?"

"I saw it on subetheric, oh, yesterday? Newsnet program. The usual interviews with officials, meaningless answers. They did, however, suggest a conspiracy between renegade agents within the Service and the Managins."

"Managins . . ." Derec winced. "Well, there's a conspiracy, all right, but Daventri isn't part of it. That's why she was killed."

"You said she wasn't."

"It's not her body in the morgue. I know. I saw them both. I also saw Eliton's body, with three wounds in it. But at Union Station he only received one wound."

"What does that mean?"

"It means that Eliton didn't die at Union Station . . . if he died at all." Dreec looked toward the ceiling. "Thales, did you record all that?"

"Everything, Derec. How much longer do you wish me to maintain the receptor's integrity?"

"Talk to it until you're satisfied you have everything of use from it, then let it go."

Rana looked pale. "Now what?"

"Now we get Bogard back up to spec. I have to call Ariel. I think I have a job for it."

"You might want to answer the call you got today."

"You did say something about that. Sorry. Who was it from?"

"Alda Mikels of Imbitek."

external diagnostic complete, buffer nodes P-Seven and P-Eight purged, protect encryption reset, internal overrides reset, initiate internal diagnostic for corrupted sequencing, system purged, internal diagnostic complete, potential First and Second Law violations negated, memory download complete as nonvolitonal data, status report generating, complete, initial task designation as personal security to Senator Eliton, Clar, terminated due to death of subject—

death of subject Eliton, Clar, analyze relevant data, resume status report—

death of subject Eliton, Clar, occurred during task designation, responsibility primary, analyze—

associational data relevant to death of subject Eliton, Clar, indicates a potential Three Law conflict, buffer nodes purged, memory secondary, function secured, analyze context—

death of subject Eliton, Clar, primary responsibility per initial data analysis—

death of subject Eliton, Clar, conditional pending analysis of all contextual data—

death of subject Eliton, Clar, nonverifiable, responsibility secondary—

death of subject Eliton, Clar, result of conflicting priority, responsibility tertiary pending verification and validation of coded instructions—

report complete, death of subject indeterminate, respon-

sibility potentially primary pending location of subject, context of disappearance, condition of subject upon recovery, conclusion must determine circumstances of primary failure and disposition of subject
   end report

TWENTY-THREE

Mia watched Bogard stumble away from the transport and felt a twinge of optimism. The plan did not amount to very much, an act of desperation, but it was action nonetheless, and after days of waiting for her body to recover, hiding out in Ariel's apartment, it seemed to her the zenith of plans.

Bogard moved hesitantly, as if uncertain that it could or should walk. The scarring and pitting over its shell, the way one arm hung inoperatively at its side, gave a convincing account of the aftermath of horrible trauma. Its coppery gleam was mostly hidden under a charred black. Anyone seeing it would know that it had been through a conflagration.

Even so, it looked new compared to the ancient walls, columns, and beams of the alleyway. Graffiti formed palimpsests over the corroded, mildewed surfaces, attesting to the centuries of ambivalent residence. Pocked walls, undifferentiated litter softening corners and accruing in shallows mounds, half-open doors, and a smell born of machine,

stale breath, yeast, and sweat accentuated the lack of attention the district received. Most of the buildings here stood
empty, long abandoned. They were deep in the sublevels of
D.C., near where Bogard had brought her on that first
night's flight from the infirmary.

Bogard staggered against a wall, turned with comic
grace on one foot, and lurched toward the opposite wall.
Mia found herself inexplicably worried for the robot, even
though it was a machine just doing what it was told.

What Derec had told it to do.

"You're sure it'll be all right?" she asked.

He gave her a curious look, then shook his head. "It's
risky. Any number of things could go wrong. TBI could pick
it up, local police, a corridor gang, even a salvage crew. Are
you changing your mind? You said this was the only way
to get inside."

"Yes . . . it is. Only . . ." She glanced at her feet, avoiding
his gaze. *Only Bogard is the only thing I feel absolutely con-
fident in right now . . .* She sighed. "All my backdoors into
the Service databases have been shut down, all my passwords have been discontinued. We need access."

Derec nodded, then touched the com unit on their vehicle's dash.

"Ariel," he said, "we're ready. We let it off in Corridor
93, sublevel ten, MacMillan Sector."

"Got it," Ariel replied. "I'll wait two minutes, then call
it in."

"Good."

Bogard disappeared around a corner and Derec started
the transport. "Car, proceed to second preset destination."

The transport—an ordinary maintenance vehicle from an
embassy garage, unmarked and anonymous—pulled away
from the alleyway.

"Don't worry," Derec said to Mia. "The least we can do is fail."

"Hah! Mattu used to say that failure wasn't even part of our vocabulary."

"Mattu was your team leader?"

"Since the first day I was assigned personal security for Senator Eliton. He and Gel had been working as a team for four years. I replaced a retiring agent, Starns. She'd been team leader. Mattu was next in line. He was very good, Mr. Avery."

Mia looked at him and saw surprise in his face and wondered how harsh she had sounded. Her eyes burned; time to stop talking about it.

"You feel guilty," he said quietly. "You're alive, they're not. Bad enough if it had been some bunch of mad fanatics, outsiders, but you don't know how to make sense of it being your own people."

"Are you a frustrated psychoanalyst?"

He laughed briefly, without humor. "That would be convenient. No, I just—I don't really understand human nature that well. I try. I pay attention. It seems that's more than most people who don't believe they have a problem with it do."

"Is that why you work with robots?"

"I told you—"

"You told me why you built Bogard."

"Touché." Derec looked out the opposite window for a time, and she thought he intended to drop the subject. But then, not looking at her, he said, "I'm the son of a genius. I lost . . . memories. I've made up for a lot of them, but I can never know how much I'll never recover. I don't know why I'm as good at robotics as I am. Parental influence? Maybe. Probably. But that answer is common, easy, and unsatisfying. Maybe you're right. Maybe I work with robots to . . . to understand." He turned to her. "They make more sense than people do. Most of the time."

Mia felt uncomfortable under his gaze, as if he expected more confession or perhaps confirmation.

The transport turned onto an ascending ramp.

"Do you think Senator Eliton is alive?" she asked.

He blinked at her, surprised again. He nodded, though, accepting the change of subject. "If he is, then where is he?"

"I'm more interested in why. If we know why he's still alive, then we can figure out the rest. Why will give us who."

"Maybe we can find out from Bogard."

"From the Service database? Why would it be there?"

"Two agents, a senator, who knows who else?"

"I can't accept that the entire Service is culpable. Can you?"

"Can you accept that Eliton might be part of it?"

"I don't know."

Derec shrugged. "This is Earth."

"What is *that* supposed to mean?"

"When something inexplicable happens, Spacers like to say 'Must be Terran.' It's a joke. A bad one. But there's some truth in it. Something inexplicable happens here, they say 'This is Earth.' Less of a joke."

"What is so inexplicable about Earth that isn't about Spacers?" Mia asked.

"Hate. Hatred is a tradition here. Terrans hate robots. Most of them have never even seen one except in bad vids with rampaging robot villains, but they hate them anyway. It doesn't make sense, but it's the truth. Even sensible people hate them. How can you tell the difference between them and the fanatics?"

"We don't have a monopoly on hatred."

"No. But it seems to be better done here than anywhere else."

Mia fought with her resentment, surprised at her sudden anger—it proved his point, after all, especially since she found it impossible to disagree with him.

"If hate is driving this," she said, "then why the pretense of a conference at all? Why not just reinforce the restrictions already in place and shut the Spacers out even more?"

"Too much money at stake to stand on principle," he said.

"For some, not all."

"Like Rega Looms?"

Mia nodded. "He's one example."

"Maybe. But it may still be a money issue. If the conference succeeded, what would that do to DyNan's P & L statement?"

"You're suggesting he's the one most motivated to see it fail because of profit?" Mia shook her head. "Even without Spacer competition, he would never be able to outperform the others. Imbitek could buy DyNan out of petty cash."

"Then it's hate."

"Coren Lanra suggested that it's the black market. The pirates."

"Greed again. Take your pick. Hate versus greed. In the middle, Eliton."

Mia found it too simple. Credits dictated life throughout the vast moral middleground of Terran politics and industry, yielding at the edges to the passions. But she had never known a truly passionate fanatic who could move in those middle terrains and not be seen clearly for an outsider. Even Looms, radical as his personal philosophies made him, gave unto Caesar and was deemed dependable by all the rest. Somehow, he did not fit this crime.

But she found Derec's simplistic reasoning compelling. What had she learned at the academy? The simplest motives explain the most? Complex behaviors could often be rendered down to very basic emotions. The complexity only obscured the driving force.

So what was it? Hate or money?

Or both?

The transport pulled onto a broad, brightly-lit thoroughfare. Derec climbed into the back and returned wearing a stylish blue jacket.

"Personally," he said, "I'm hoping it's greed. That can be understood as a matter of logic, simple numbers. If it's hate—"

"Then why would Alda Mikels personally invite you to see him?"

"One can only wonder. Wish me luck."

"Luck better have nothing to do with this."

He grinned at her. Presently, the transport pulled off the main road and slowed to a stop in a service corridor. Derec opened his door and stepped out.

"Be careful, Agent Daventri. After all, you're supposed to be dead."

"The dead are tough, Mr. Avery," Mia said. He started to close the door. "Derec." He paused, waiting. "Good luck."

"Thanks. You, too."

He closed the door and she watched him cross the corridor in front of the transport. They had stopped half a kilometer from the corporate offices of Imbitek.

Derec and Ariel were not professionals and although so far everything they had done had turned out well, Mia wondered how much longer they could operate without incident. Now they were confronting people, digging where they could be discovered. This would have been a difficult enough investigation with trained agents, but with amateurs . . .

She would have to get used to it, there was no choice. When Derec was out of sight, she touched the contact on the dash.

"Car, proceed to destination three."

The transport rolled on.

DyNan Manual Industries maintained a large suite of offices far out in the Arlington District, away from the majority of its fellow corporations. Looms evidently believed in making statements whenever possible, and his choice of location spoke of his deliberate dissociation from everyone else.

Coren Lanra, however, kept private offices closer to the heart of D.C., on the fourth floor of an old but well-maintained structure just off the Southwest Corridor, at the outskirts of the Infant District. The area was popular for lawyers and lobbyists and supported a large community of service industries that catered to the wealthier residents. In the mix one found research agencies, professional witnesses, independent forensics labs, physicians, therapists, a variety of technical experts, and private security firms. Mia had never learned why it was called the Infant District.

The transport parked in the garage opposite, and Mia stepped out onto the pavement. Her leg hurt like an old bruise, but she could walk normally again. The only thing holding her back was fear.

She crossed to the entrance, sweeping the immediate area for any sign of Service attention.

Lanra's office was in the middle of a row of eight along

the hallway. No one sat behind the reception desk. Mia stood very quietly in the middle of the foyer, listening for signs of occupation, and slowly searching for evidence of an arrest. But everything was orderly, as if those who worked here had simply stepped out for a few minutes.

She went to the door marked COREN LANRA, I.S.I. and nervously pressed her hand against it. The door swung in soundlessly.

Seated behind a desk, Coren Lanra watched her, a vague smile on his lips. Casually, he gestured for her to enter, then put a finger to his lips.

When the door closed behind her, Lanra reached across his desk and pressed a contact.

"There," he said. "Now we've got maybe ten minutes before their AIs untangle my encryption." He smiled, a combination of genuine pleasure and opportunistic anticipation. "It's not every day the dead walk. How are you, Mia?"

"I've been better."

"I don't doubt it. Please, sit down. Since we're on a timer, we should skip the reminiscence and move to the important issues. Agreed?"

"Agreed. I have one question."

"Only one?"

"The only one there is. Who killed Senator Eliton?"

Lanra spread his hands, then folded them together. "I wish I knew. The TBI wants to hang it on Looms. They've always had a fondness for morally committed outsiders."

"You're sure Looms had nothing to do with it?"

"Please, not you, too. No, Mia, it wasn't Looms. Let's not waste time on a false lead. Besides, I'm fairly certain you've looked into enough of the peripheral evidence to have another suspect. Am I right?"

"The assassins were Managins."

"Predictable. You think they did it on their own?"

"No."

Lanra nodded. "They haven't got the resources. The people, sure. The means, no. I'm still trying to figure out how they got inside Union Station with those weapons."

Mia hesitated, wondering how much to reveal, how much any revelation might tell a trained ex-Service agent by what it left out or implied. There was just too little time to be as careful as she wanted.

"The RI was subverted," she said.

He covered it well, kept his expression as neutral as he could, but there was a moment of puzzlement in his eyes, replaced almost instantly by surprise, then masked. He had not known. Lanra, at least, was not part of it.

"That's what we get for playing with this positronic crap." He glanced at his hands for a moment. "I thought it had just failed. So that definitely leaves out the Managins. They were the weapon, not the wielder. So, how are you pursuing this?"

"First, I want to know why you contacted the Aurorans."

"Process of elimination. I knew it couldn't be the Managins and I knew it *wasn't* Looms. Once the TBI started looking at us, I wondered where the Service was. They haven't asked a single question of Looms. When you were killed—" he cocked his eyebrows and grinned "—it started to look like someone on the inside. That meant someone in the Service was involved, so I couldn't go to them. The TBI won't listen, the local authorities could care less once the TBI take over. The official statement from the Spacers is basically wait-and-see, but one of the Aurorans is staying here to try to conduct the conference. I checked on her—a junior member, no experience and almost no authority. The rest of the survivors have returned home, leaving the embassy staffs here to clean up after the mess is finished making. All their actions indicate that they never knew this would happen—confused, disorganized, trying to put a good face on it. I decided not to talk to the Solarians because of their involvement with the RI. The Aurorans are as close to an objective party as we can find right now, and when I asked around to find out who was talking the Spacers living on Earth to stay put and not run, I hear the name Ariel Burgess. Calvin Institute. I started trying to talk to the Aurorans."

"You didn't call Burgess first?"

"No, I started at the top. I wanted to see who would be willing to speak to me as much as anything else."

"What about other corporate security?"

"Our competitors?" Lanra shook his head. "Besides, they're all amateurs."

"Underestimating your enemies?"

"No, keeping a handle on leaks. The biggest problem with amateurs isn't that they aren't good at the job itself, but that they brag about it. Usually to their employers."

"You think it's corporate."

"Don't you?"

"I can't see a motive. As far as I can tell, everyone stood to make a lot of money from this treaty."

"Legally, yes."

"I don't follow."

"You're looking at the wrong flow of capital."

"The piracy?"

Lanra grunted. "One of the things I miss about working for the Service is all the alternate labels the government puts on things. 'Piracy,' they call it, as if ships in space chase each other, shooting, and the bad guys seize a hapless freighter against its will. Crap. It's tariff dodging, pure and simple, and if the treaty goes into effect, that ends. Frankly, as much as I hate robots, I can't say I'd be sorry."

"You're saying major corporations are behind it?" Mia asked. "There can't be enough money in it to make it worth the risk."

Lanra gave her a mock incredulous look. "Really? Mia, *think* about it. Earth exports to fifteen of the fifty Spacer Worlds and another twenty Settler colonies. Leaving out the Settlers for now, do you have any idea how much we're talking about? On average, ten to twenty billion credits per world annually. Now that's the legitimate trade. Out of that, the so-called piracy bleeds off about five to eight percent. Just to average that out, let's say that comes up to one-point-two billion a year that never gets to its destination. The current set-up prohibits Earth from directly trading with the other Spacer Worlds—the fifteen we export to are licensed to distribute to them, we aren't—and there's a stiff tariff system in place between them, not to mention the contractual arrangements on those Settler Worlds where there are also Spacer colonies. Black market merchandise easily commands twice to three times its legitimate market value, especially on merchandise not on the approved export list. So that eighteen billion credits' worth of 'lost' merchandise ends up on the black market fetching fifty to eighty billion in sales. And if the Spacers react predictably over these killings, you could see *that* figure double when they start raising tariffs and putting on more restrictions. And I haven't even mentioned the *import* black market or the fact that those 'stolen' shipments are insured. In total, I'd guess that you're looking at a two-hundred-plus billion credit illicit trade volume that could dry up if this treaty goes into effect. Now you tell me that profit isn't a motive."

Mia had known the black market was large, but not that

large. Officially, it was estimated that the total volume came up to less than thirty billion credits. Still a substantial amount of money, but hardly enough to jeopardize a treaty that would have lowered tariffs and increased exports. But if Lanra's estimates were true, there was simply too much money in it to give it up easily. In fact, worsening the situation would seem even better.

Lanra was nodding sympathetically. "We're too parochial here, we don't see things in terms of entire star systems and trade routes extending dozens of light years," he said, following her thoughts. "It's too much to take in. We're willing to believe the official numbers because we can't imagine past them."

"So how have *you* managed it?"

"Not easily, I'll tell you. Looms has been wanting it exposed for a long time. It's one more reason, he says, that we don't just turn our backs on space and be done with it. But letting people know how much money can be made at something . . . that's not always the best way to convince them to leave it alone. So he's been waiting and paying attention. He's got a big file on it."

"Does he have a favorite suspect?"

"No one person could do this. It has to be a consortium, and not just of Terrans."

"Spacers?"

Lanra nodded. "And a few Settlers."

"The Settler representative—" Mia began.

"The Settlers are getting the worst end of the whole enterprise. A lot of Settler colonies have a real start-over-from-scratch attitude and set up their charters to limit trade with Earth. They aren't well disposed to deal with Spacers, either. As a consequence, a lot of Settler Worlds are austere. The black market for them is like a drug—people buying stuff that doesn't even exist on the open market. It also makes them an easy scapegoat. Most of us believed that the pirates were Settlers."

"You don't think so?"

"A few individuals, I'm sure. Have to have agents on the ground for something like this. But state sanctioned? No."

"How do explain the fact that not one member of DyNan's party was injured?"

"What better way to paint us the villain? It's simple, clear, obvious—all it takes is for someone to point out the fact at the right time in the right way."

"It's *too* obvious," Mia said.

"For who? You, maybe? A judge? Does it matter? This will be a political trial. It's not too simple for the masses and it has the added benefit of discrediting anything Looms might reveal about the black market before he can say word one."

"You're a cynical one."

Lanra nodded. "I've learned that expediency is the only constant. When you live like that it's easy to lose faith in anything else."

"I don't suppose you have any proof of any of this?"

Lanra pursed his lips. "What is it you're trying to do, Mia? You're supposed to be dead. What can you do?"

"I'm . . . trying to find out who set us up."

"Someone on the inside, obviously. Do you have a name?"

"Cupra and Gambel."

Lanra's eyes widened briefly. "Well, well. Three surprises in less than a day."

"I don't know them."

"Service all the way. If they're involved, you can be certain someone higher up is, too. I can't imagine them doing this on their own." He opened a drawer in his desk and took out a disk. He slid it toward her. "This is a synopsis of my conclusion from the last three years. My logic trees, my numbers, guesses. I—"

He glanced at his desk top and scowled. "Time's up. You need to leave. Now."

"One more question."

Lanra glanced nervously at his desktop. "Quick."

"The guns, the assassins. I need a name, a supplier."

"Look at Kynig Parapoyos. Now you *have* to leave."

Mia tucked the disk inside her jacket and stood. She looked at Lanra an extra moment—an exchange of sympathies, a way of acknowledging a debt without saying anything—then hurried out of his office.

running chameleon program, tactical parameters imitate severe motive impairment, isolate memory node to selective disclosure pending coded release, proceed to predetermined retrieval point, avoid undesignated humans, defensive protocols at minimum, corridor uninhabited, continuing continuing continuing, designated humans approaching, two, both armed, assuming wide field, defensive posture

"I thought it was vaporized?"

"Well, it's tougher than we thought. Look at it, though—it hasn't worn well."

"Bogard, confirm command recognition, Agent Gambel."

processing command recognition, partially impaired protocol, response limited, confirmed voice recognition "c-con-confirrrr-con-firm . . ."

"Oh, that's good, he'll love this. Listen to it."

"Knock it off. That device should have rendered it down to its component molecules. It's still walking around."

"I'm impressed. Can you imagine body armor made out of this stuff? Bogard, command imperative established, Agent Gambel and Agent Cupra. Confirm?"

". . . con-firrrrm-ed . . ."

"Bogard, you will accompany us. We are your field retrieval. Confirmed?"

". . . field . . . re-field-retrieve-field . . ."

"Confirm, Bogard."

"Con-firrrmed—field retrie-retrieval."

"Great. Come with us, now, Bogard. We're going to take you back to headquarters for debriefing."

"De-de-debrief—retrieve—rebrief—"

"This is going to be a nightmare."

"Just so long as what we see is what we get, I don't care. Bogard, come with us."

command recognition confirmed, Cupra Gambel, initiate secondary protocol, conform to request

"That's good, Bogard. Come with us. Everything will be just fine. We have a lot to talk about."

TWENTY-FOUR

Imbitek occupied a good portion of the Navy District. Derec had heard stories that its manufacturing facilities went all the way down to the ancient Anacostia River, although these in D.C. were not Imbitek's main works. The largest plant was somewhere on the other side of the globe, near Kiev Sector.

Derec entered a high archway into a maze of walkways that wound among the offices. The entrance lay on the opposite side of a large fountain. A series of canopies at various heights obscured the towering bulk of Imbitek while letting light diffuse delicately onto the corporate mall. The result was an impression of Imbitek as warm, considerate, and human-scaled, most of it hidden from sight, like its products.

He walked through the broad doors and up to the reception desk.

"Derec Avery to see Mr. Mikels."

"You're expected, Mr. Avery," the receptionist told him. "Please wait a moment and I'll have someone take you up."

Another woman arrived, smiled pleasantly, and asked him to follow her.

Behind the reception area, they entered a wide hallway lined by doors. Derec was led to one at the far end. His guide pressed a contact and waited. The door opened and she waved him into the small cubicle.

"This will take you directly to Mr. Mikels' offices, Mr. Avery. He's looking forward to meeting you."

"Thank you."

Derec stepped into the cubicle. A bench hung from one wall. The door closed and he felt only the briefest of movements. A few seconds later, the door opened again to admit him into a spacious office.

Alda Mikels stood before an immense desk, smiling. He was a broadshouldered man, slightly shorter than Derec, with a thick mane of nearly-white hair. His eyes were a muddy brown and he tended toward overweight, though his tailored dark suit hid it well.

"Mr. Avery."

"Mr. Mikels."

"My apologies for the way my man Kusk brushed you off. We were rude. I am sorry."

"Contract restrictions often leave little room for cordiality, sir. Don't worry about."

Mikels laughed, a deep, pleasant sound. It could be easy to like this man. "Nevertheless, I wanted to make amends. Thank you for coming. Can I get you anything? A drink?"

"Water would be fine, thank you."

Alda Mikels gestured to the opposite end of the office where a bar covered most of one wall. It was not the kind of office where work got done, at least not the hands-on sort Derec thought of as work. He imagined meetings here, drinks or smokes offered, and talk designed to prepare the way for work. Clients met Mikels here, if they were important enough, and perhaps enemies as well. Derec wondered in which category Mikels placed him.

Mikels filled a tall glass from a crystal pitcher and handed it to Derec. He poured for himself a tumbler of brandy from an ornate decanter. Every move exuded a kind of pride: *look what I have.*

"Your original call concerned Union Station," he said, lifting the tumbler in a half salute. He sipped.

"Phylaxis Group was supposed to have the exclusive service contract on the RI. I was concerned that everything be handled the best way possible. And Phylaxis was able to get operations back online within hours. We were running all the operations before we were excluded. I'm curious—"

"You're curious if we had anything to do with shoving you out of the way." Mikels shrugged. "Depends how you look at it, Mr. Avery. We'd been lobbying to displace positronics in Union Station since the proposal to go that way first came up. Now, I understand as well as you that having positronics there was political, not practical, so our lobbying was directed at those people in government responsible for deciding such things. Good business. When it failed, Imbitek wanted to be able to take advantage of it."

"You were certain it would fail. That's why you convinced Senator Eliton to write you into the contract two years ago, so you could step in at once."

Mikels looked momentarily surprised. He smiled. "We'd already warned the Senate that positronics would not work there and that when it went wrong it would go very wrong, either technically or politically." He frowned. "We had no idea it would be this costly."

"You don't blame positronics for Eliton's death, do you?"

"Being a non-Terran yourself, perhaps you wouldn't understand. Yes, indirectly or otherwise. Without positronics—the issue and the fact—Eliton would never have made himself a target."

Derec was surprised at Mikels' bluntness. He stared at the man, wondering what would follow such an observation.

Mikels smiled again. "But that's politics. No one does it successfully without making enemies, and Clar was very successful."

"I suppose it's also difficult losing a friend this way."

Mikels blinked at him. "I knew Clar, certainly. We were as close to being friends as two people in our positions can be. We had lunch at least once a week. He was the main target of our lobbying efforts." He finished his brandy and poured another. "He'll be missed."

The words came out flat, empty of emotion. A mistake, Derec realized.

"So, how can I help you now, Mr. Avery?"

"Can you get me inside Union Station to look at what you're doing?"

Mikels looked surprised for a moment, then laughed. "What do you need me to do that for?"

"I've been barred by Special Service."

"In that case, why would I risk their displeasure to help you?"

Derec shrugged. "Just a thought. You asked." He drank his water and set the glass down, half-finished. "Who do you think engineered the assassinations?"

"Fanatics. Zealots. Patriots."

"Former employees?"

"And why would you say that?" Mikels asked.

"You aren't the only one with lobbying interests, Mr. Mikels."

Mikels nodded as if he had just had something confirmed.

"Since you're here, Mr. Avery, can I offer you a tour? Do you know much about imbedded technology?"

"Honestly, no, I don't."

"Well, let me show you. I think you'll find it amazing."

Mikels crossed to his desk and leaned over it. He spoke briefly, his words indistinct to Derec, then smiled and gestured for Derec to follow.

Derec's scalp tingled. *I should leave now*, he thought.

Instead, he let Alda Mikels take him by the elbow and lead him into his empire.

"This," Mikels declared, one arm outstretched, as they stepped out of a transport cubicle, "is our bench test lab. One of them, anyway."

Derec slowed as he approached the enormous window that ran the length of the oversized hallway. Beyond stretched a maze of tables laden with equipment, tended by dozens of people in pristine white coveralls, working under shadowless light. It dazzled; he found it difficult to focus on any one point, all of it fascinated him. No sound came through the glass.

"I understand your main manufacturing facilities are elsewhere," Derec said, as much to break the long stillness as anything.

"Our largest factory is in Kiev, but it's not much larger than the ones in Denver and Singapore. R and D happens here, and we build the prototypes. There's some jobshopping that gets done as well—special requests, custom-fitted pieces, things like that."

This was what Aurora and Solaria had hoped to obtain from the new treaty, Derec knew—the methodology to do manufacturing on such a scale. The Fifty Worlds were wonderful places and their tech was awesome in many respects, but in a way they were simple tinkerers compared to Earth. Here, humans knew how to create places where tools and machines could be made in the millions. The ability to do so, to conceive of the techniques and construct the mechanisms, both human and machine, to produce in those quantities was an art that somehow had never made the transition from Earth to the stars. Aurora built excellent robots, but in small lots of a hundred or less. If Earth decided to build them they could flood the trade lanes with absolutely identical models by the tens and hundreds of thousands. Spacer tech was "handmade" compared to the mass manufacturing culture of Earth.

Current trade law forbade the exportation of key technologies. It gave Earth an edge. Even black marketeers would be inclined to want it to stay that way. Their profit came from inequities in systems.

"I didn't realize the need to do new research was so important," Derec said. "I mean, the basic design of a positronic brain has remained largely unchanged for—"

"And the culture stagnates, doesn't it?" Mikels interjected. "Nothing new, nothing grows. Why change perfection? But perfection is only real for a given time, place, and person. Tomorrow, it's not perfect anymore, is it? And usually never for your neighbor." He smiled at Derec, enjoying himself. "But don't take offense. The basic *idea* of imbedded tech hasn't changed for almost as long. I like to think it began with burnt toast."

"Pardon me?"

"Way back when, people had to toast their bread over an open fire. Lay the slices on a plate, suspend it over a flame, and watch it so they could turn it at the right time. Too little time, it was just warm bread. Too much and it was blackened grit. Had to be a better way. So someone devises a box with heating coils and a thermostat attached to a springlock that retracts when enough heat has been applied. The box knows exactly how much heat is necessary and toasts the bread the same way every time. Imbedded tech. Since then, if people want something done and they don't want to tend to it with one hundred percent of their attention, someone else has found a way to make a device that will do it for them. It finally got so sophisticated that some of these devices are the intellectual equivalent of small children. Then they got so that they weren't even visible and hardly ever broke. Paradise."

"Perfection?" Derec chided.

"Not at all. People change, needs change, technology has to keep up. Take that toaster. It's so good now that it even makes the bread, assembling molecules in just the right way and shaping the result before heating it. But what if you also want it to make sweet bread? Or cake? It doesn't have the programming for that and the device simply isn't important enough—or expensive enough—to warrant having a reprogrammable feature. What do you do?"

"Throw it out and buy a better model."

"Wasteful. But we've gotten around it." Mikels waved at the lab. "Penetrating polycollates."

"I'm not familiar with the term."

"Not many are. We can introduce augmentation through the surface of the device, reprogram it the same way a virus reprograms a healthy cell. It's a complex filtration system that can work its way through the interstices of a material—"

"Like a zeolite."

For the second time in their talk, Mikels seemed surprised, although he masked it well. "Yes, that's right. You're familiar with zeolites, Mr. Avery?"

"Only slightly. I've seen some work done on positronic matrices with them."

"Indeed. That's very interesting. Where was this?"

"Aurora."

"Now that's surprising. I wouldn't have thought Spacers would have much need for such primitive tech."

"Is it primitive?"

"The idea is."

"Like your imbedded devices?"

This time Mikels' smile did not seem warm, but predatory. He studied Derec for a few seconds, then turned his gaze toward his lab, his left hand playing absently with the cuff of his right sleeve.

"You have an interesting perspective, Mr. Avery. Have you ever considered—"

"Mr. Mikels."

Derec started, surprised. An aide stood behind Mikels, leaning forward slightly at the waist, solicitous and apologetic. Mikels frowned at him.

"Sorry to disturb you, sir, but you're needed in Section Four."

"What? Damn." Mikels sighed loudly. "Forgive me, Mr. Avery. I have to tend to something. Kobbs here can finish the tour for you. It has been a pleasure making your acquaintance. Perhaps we can get together another time."

Mikels gripped Derec's hand firmly and shook it twice.

"Thank you for taking the time," Derec said.

Mikels gave him a last cordial smile and stalked off, leaving Kobbs waiting for Derec.

"There really isn't an emergency, is there, Kobbs?" Derec asked. "You just came to rescue him. What did he do, summon you somehow? His cuff?"

Kobbs looked uncomfortable. "If you'd like to follow me, sir, we can continue the tour in—"

"No, thank you, Kobbs. I feel that I've already gotten the tour. If you'd just show me the way out . . . ?"

Tathis Kedder lived just north of the Navy District, off the Southeast Corridor in the Garfield District. Derec left the strips near the apartment complex a little before twelve, an hour early for his appointment with Kedder. He had given himself plenty of time.

The complex was a collection of blocks arranged at different levels, heights, and orientations. Walkways, stairs, and balconies threaded throughout the mass like complicated three-dimensional mazes. Derec had once considered taking rooms here. It was an enclave for midlevel professionals like Kedder. He had been unsurprised to discover that Joler Hammis also lived here.

After receiving Hammis's résumé, Derec had been unable to get in touch with the man. He had left messages asking Hammis to call him back, let him know if he had found other employment, or just to talk. Ariel's insistence that no one at the Calvin Institute had issued any such directive about "transition errors" made Derec curious about where those orders had come from. Kedder had obviously not questioned them, but Hammis had struck Derec as the sort who might question anything.

He went to Hammis's apartment first. He mounted the steps and went up to the third level of Hammis's block, found the number, and pressed the bell. He waited nearly a minute before pressing it again.

"It's probably available if you want it."

A man stood at the open door of the next apartment, a few meters further down the walkway. He was neatly dressed and carried a small case, large enough for a custom datum. Derec thought: *Lawyer.*

"Mr. Hammis is no longer living here?"

"Moved out three days ago," the man said, punching a code into his own door. "He complained about the job market, but Joler didn't strike me as the type to stay unemployed for long. He probably found something and *swee–*" he made a flying gesture to go with the half-whistle "*–gone.* Check with the housing authority."

The man smiled and walked past Derec to the steps and descended out of sight.

Derec punched the code for the complex housing authority into the scanner beside the door. The small screen came up with a bright pink MAY I HELP YOU? Derec entered the apartment number and pressed ENTER. A menu came up: RESIDENT, AVAILABILITY, OTHER. Derec touched AVAILABILITY.

NOT CURRENTLY AVAILABLE.

Derec stared at the door for a time, debating if it would be worth the trouble to break in. He checked his watch—he still had forty minutes till his meeting with Kedder—and pulled out his decrypter.

Within two minutes, the device unlocked the door. Derec did a reflexive inspection of the walkway, then entered Hammis's apartment.

It did not look vacated so much as abandoned. Clothes

lay scattered over the floor, a plate with days-old remains set beside a cup with a few centimeters of coffee on a table covered with disks and scraps of paper. The comline contained several calls in the message queue. Even to Derec it was obvious that Hammis had not moved out.

He walked from room to room, stepping quietly and carefully, touching nothing.

The place was disheveled, but it did not quite look ransacked. Derec returned to the living room and examined the scattered paper on the table. He recognized algorithms, a few scribbled notes on pathways—could be positronic, could be AI—and a pair of pamphlets half-buried under the disks. He eased one out and opened it.

Derec felt his scalp tingle coldly as he read.

> ORDER FOR THE SUPREMACY OF MAN AGAIN
> The ancient and honorable struggle to
> free Humankind from its own delusions
> and the chains such delusions become
> has never been more difficult and demanding
> as it is today. Now the battle must
> be fought with information systems and
> the very tools we have created to aid us
> in overcoming nature itself.
> To this end, OSMA has dedicated itself
> to the cause of resisting wherever
> possible, and by whatever means seem
> most appropriate, the subjugation of
> humans by machines, systems, or the
> seductive and pernicious ideologies such
> seeming-innocuous constructs require
> to come into existence in the first place.

Derec dropped the pamphlet back on the table and looked around the room for any other sign of Managins. After a few minutes, he picked the paper up again, folded it, and slipped it into his pocket.

He checked that no one was on the walkway when he left, then headed quickly to the other side of the complex, to his appointment with Kedder. The two had worked together. Maybe Kedder knew something about Hammis. Perhaps he suspected Hammis of being the method by which the Managins had gotten into Union Station with weapons. In any case, Derec felt relieved to be out of Hammis's apartment. He made himself walk at a normal pace, conscious of his quick, adrenalized strides.

Calm down, he told himself, *it could mean anything. Millions of people probably have these pamphlets, it doesn't mean they're all Managins.*

But what did it really take to be one? Perhaps most people were not officially members of OSMA, but certainly most of people on Earth sympathized with them—at least where it concerned robotics.

He was still ten minutes early when he knocked on Kedder's door. The scanner came on.

"Yes?"

"Derec Avery, Mr. Kedder."

"Oh. Um, yes. One moment."

The door slid aside and Kedder blinked at him. He was barefoot and looked as though he were still waking up. He smiled sheepishly at Derec, then stood to one side.

"Please."

Derec stepped into the apartment. It was much neater than Hammis's.

"Your coworker seems to have moved out, Mr. Kedder," Derec said. "He lost his job, I understand." Derec turned.

Hammis stood by the door, looking frightened and apologetic. Beside him were two men, dressed in black, hoods covering their heads.

"I'm sorry, Mr. Avery," Kedder said.

Derec bolted for the back of the apartment and the rear exit.

Something caught his shins just through the first doorway and he slammed heavily onto the floor. Before he could stand, bodies crushed him. He struggled until something cool touched his neck and numbness spread throughout his body.

TWENTY-FIVE

Ariel disliked using Derec's robot. She made the call to Special Service—anonymously, routed through a comline far from the embassy—with misgivings. They were sending a robot to lie to humans. There was no other way to look at it and her absolutist soul chafed at the idea.

Hofton looked briefly surprised when she walked into the reception area, the crate with the contraband brain under her arm. He smiled and followed her into her office.

The door closed. "The keeper visits the zoo," he said. "I trust you've been well?"

Ariel looked at him. "It's been busy?" She placed the crate under her desk. She was not really sure why she had brought it, other than she did not feel comfortable leaving it in her apartment anymore.

"Moderately."

"I've been handling some of it from home," she said, sitting down behind her desk. It had only been a couple of days and yet it seemed much longer. "What have you got?"

"Setaris has called at least eight times a day. Most of her questions I've been able to handle, primarily to do with the migration of Aurorans off Earth."

"How many?"

"Nearly six hundred in the last two days."

Ariel stared at him. "I thought—"

"It seems that the TBI interrogated a few of our key citizens. They decided to leave immediately after. Others, not unexpectedly, followed."

"Who in particular?"

"I have a list . . ." Hofton fussed briefly with Ariel's terminal. "There. And at the top—"

"Guviya Tralen. Damn!" She stabbed at her comline. "What business did the TBI have interrogating her?"

"Her complaint was quite specific. They wanted to know who she knew among 'her kind'—I quote—who would want to disrupt the conference."

"Get me a schedule of everything else I need to tend to, Hofton. This call is private."

"Of course."

Hofton retreated from the office and Ariel stared in rage at the screen until a secretary appeared.

"I want to speak to Jonis Taprin."

"I'm sorry—" the secretary began.

"This is Ariel Burgess from the Auroran Embassy. He will want to take this call. Trust me."

"One moment, Ms. Burgess."

TBI . . . ? I thought Special Service had assumed complete authority? Well, never assume anything on Earth . . .

Nearly two minutes elapsed before Jonis appeared; even at that, Ariel was surprised. Under other circumstances, she would have been pleased.

"Ariel," he said, smiling broadly. "How very good to hear from you, I've been—"

"What the hell is going on, Jonis? The TBI is rousting Aurorans."

Jonis's face seemed to ripple, settling finally into a wary frown. "I'm not sure I understand . . ."

"Don't play politic with me, Jonis, you know damn well what I'm talking about. I've got a list of prominent Aurorans in front of me who've been interrogated over the last two days by TBI agents. Most of them are leaving, which was something I worked very hard to prevent not four days ago, if you'll recall, because they don't like being called conspirators."

"Ariel, wait—"

"Guviya Tralen, Jonis! They asked Guviya Tralen who she knew who would want to see the conference stopped! She's a pain, she's obnoxious, I sometimes wish she had never come to Earth, but she's a fashion icon, not a killer!"

"Calm down, Ariel. TBI was just doing its job."

"What job is that? Safeguarding Terra from bloodthirsty Spacers?"

Jonis reddened. "That's not fair. We've lost one of our most important citizens. You can't expect—"

"I can expect a little more attention to who really killed *our* people when they were *invited* here and a little less Spacer-baiting. Especially from you."

"Me? I don't have any say over how the TBI conducts their investigations."

"No? Maybe. But you *do* have a responsibility not to feed public fears over positronics by suggesting a positronic robot intentionally killed humans."

"Those men were dead on arrival—"

"That's not true and you know it," Ariel shot back. "And even if it were, don't you think it would have been responsible to keep it to yourself and check with me first? After all, I know more about what positronics can do than you or your descendants ever will."

"How do you know it's not true?"

"It's a positronic robot. The Three Laws would forbid—"

"Three Laws, Three Laws, Three Laws!" Taprin glared at her. "It was built by *people*, Ariel, and as long as people hold to no law absolutely, their machines won't, either. I don't give a damn about your sacred Three Laws because I don't believe them. As for the TBI, they're doing their job and once they're finished, we'll all be better off for it."

"Who will be?"

He looked puzzled. "What do you mean?"

"Who will be better off? They keep insulting Aurorans and they'll start an exodus I won't be able to stop. Six hundred have already left or booked passage. They've undone everything I tried to do, Jonis."

"They have killers to find."

"Among *us?* Those were Managins, Jonis. What would Aurorans have to do with Managins?"

"We have to trust that they know what they're doing," Taprin said.

"No, we don't. Your police agencies have already made more mistakes than I'd tolerate from a janitor."

"Such as?"

"Such as barring Derec Avery from doing his job," Ariel replied. "Special Service has no roboticists, they won't have a clue what to look for. Or does this come under the category of looking for killers among Spacers?"

"Why would you know about that?" Taprin asked after a moment, his voice now cautious.

"Jonis, it's me—Ariel. Calvin Institute. Anything to do with robots?"

He seemed to relax then, which Ariel found unsettling.

"I've already looked into that," Taprin said. "Mr. Avery called me, I've taken care of it."

"He's getting reinstated?"

"I can't discuss it, Ariel. Suffice it to say that Special Service clamped down on everything related to the killings, including that, and your Mr. Avery did not have the necessary security ratings. He was automatically barred."

"Does he know that?"

"He's been notified." He sighed. "Look, Ariel—it's been a lousy week and it isn't over yet. When I heard it was you, I thought that for two minutes I'd be able to talk to someone who didn't want a liter of my blood and a position statement. Where've you been, by the way? I've called a couple of times, but Hofton kept telling me you were unavailable."

"As you say, it's been a lousy week."

Taprin nodded. "Touché. Look, what do you want me to do?"

"Talk to somebody, get them to stop. Or do you want to see the Spacer community leave *en masse?*"

"It might actually be safer for them. But I'll see what I can do." He gave a wan smile. "Maybe this Saturday? Dinner? I'm not sure what I'll be doing, but if you say yes, I'll make time."

"I'll have to see, Jonis. This situation was unexpected. I might not have any Saturdays for a while."

He was visibly disappointed, but he nodded. "I understand, believe me."

"While we're talking, what *has* been found out? And how did the TBI get involved? I was under the assumption Special Service was handling this exclusively."

"For the most part they are, but the TBI has its own mandate."

Ariel frowned. "Mmm."

"Well, as you said, the assassins were Managins, but so far there doesn't seem to be a clear connection between them and anyone else. Unlikely as it sounds, it may turn out to be that they did this on their own."

"You can't possibly believe that."

Taprin shrugged. "Special Service knows what they're doing. They've been keeping me fairly current, though I'd like it to be hourly rather than daily."

"What about the people who murdered my friend?"

He frowned thoughtfully. "Oh. I, uh—frankly, I haven't asked specifically. I assume it's part of the same investigation. I'll ask about it next time I get a report, all right?"

"Fine. Now please, call off the hounds. I'll be doing damage control until I retire after this."

Taprin winced, but nodded. "I have to return to the arena now and face the lions. I'd like to see you . . ."

"I'll be in touch, Jonis. I have my own lions to fight right now."

Ariel broke the connection. Her anger thrummed at the back of her head.

What had he said? *I don't give a damn about your sacred Three Laws because I don't believe them.*

That pretty much said it all, she thought. Jonis had put into words what likely powered all the fear Terrans held for robots. To them, a robot seemed to possess will, and anything with a will was potentially corruptible. Terrans relied on automatons, mindless machines with no will at all, but that could kill or injure purely by accident or if wielded by another human. Their machines could not refuse to be misused that way, could not make a decision to protect a human. They just did their tasks and if flesh got in the way, too bad. An accident. Or a human's fault. They no more trusted that a robot with evident capacity to decide would never harm them than Ariel trusted that Derec's "variation" on robotics would never harm her. Perhaps for the first time she really understood Terrans and their unreasoning fear of positronics and robots.

"Thank you, Jonis," she mused. "Your last act as my lover was at least beneficial."

If Taprin believed that, though, after all their time together and having worked so closely with Clar Eliton for several years, then how could he possibly represent Humadros's and Eliton's beliefs? She thought back over the interview she had seen, and his comments about Bogard.

He's not, she realized. *It's over . . .*

"Ariel," Hofton's voice came over the intercom. "Ambassador Setaris is on the link."

Ariel touched ACCEPT. Setaris winked onto her screen.

"Ariel, where have you been?"

"Working," Ariel said, more sharply than she had intended.

Setaris frowned slightly. "Are you aware of the flight?"

"Yes, I am. I've spoken to Senator Taprin about it. I think it should be taken as given that nothing will be done. Special Service has assumed complete authority over the investigation and the TBI is upset about it. They're having a territorial dispute and they somehow think that entitles them to harass our citizens. I don't think we can stop them any time soon, certainly not quickly enough to do any good. I'm going to make the rounds again and see what I can salvage, but with Tralen—" she glanced at the list Hofton had provided "—Shorit, Klasina, Prattek, and Qurvis leaving, I don't expect to have much success."

Setaris was quiet for a time. "I see. Legate Korolin is being put off over when the conference will actually take place, as well. Negotiations have snagged on venue. Once they start arguing about *where* a meeting is going to be held, it's a guarantee that there will *be* no meeting."

"It's coming apart."

"It looks that way, yes. Unless arrests can be made in the next day or two, our brief will probably be to sever relations."

"It's that bad?"

"The credits, Ariel," Setaris said wearily. "You have no idea how much money is in play here. Without the conference and some kind of treaty . . ."

"I see. Then whoever did this has won. Even if they're captured, they did what they intended."

"Who knows what was intended? Yes, you're probably right in the main, but—I have a meeting to attend with the other ambassadors in six hours. I doubt any of them will stay if Aurora pulls out. It would be pleasant if you could give me good news before then."

"I'll do what I can, Ambassador, but—"

"I won't expect miracles, Ariel."

Setaris broke the link.

"How generous," Ariel said to the blank screen.

She resisted the urge to call Mia. They had put Bogard into play, a gamble Ariel had been reluctant to take, and now all they could do was wait to see if it paid off. She surveyed her desk. She had more than enough to keep her occupied, but just now she could not summon the interest to begin.

"Ariel," Hofton broke in again.

"Yes?"

"I wouldn't bother you with this normally, but under the circumstances I think you should take this call. Mr. Udal?"

"Udal . . . ?"

"The vendor who filed a complaint of vandalism with us early in the week?"

Ariel felt a wave of annoyance. "What the hell does *he* want?"

"As I say, I think you should take the call."

Ariel banged her finger against the ACCEPT contact.

"Yes, Mr. Udal, how can I help you?" She managed only a hint of strain.

"I, uh, request an intervention. I need asylum."

"What? From what, Mr. Udal? Have the vandals come back to smash the rest of your illicit stock—"

"Please, Ms. Burgess! I'm quite serious. The Terran Bureau of Investigation is threatening me with confinement."

"For what?"

"Contraband. I swear I didn't know, I swear it, but—"

Ariel felt a solid lump form just below her throat. "What sort of contraband, Mr. Udal?"

"Positronic robots! I swear, I've never handled—"

"Mr. Udal, come to the embassy at once. I want to speak with you in person."

"Do I get asylum?"

"We won't know that until I talk to you. Please come in at once."

"Yes, yes. I'll be there within the hour."

"Sooner." She paused. "In fact, Mr. Udal, stay where you are. I'm sending an embassy limo for you. Is that clear? Don't leave where you are. I'm sending a limo."

"Yes," Udal spluttered. "Yes, I—thank you."

"Hofton, do you have Mr. Udal's location?"

"Yes, Ariel."

"Go there yourself, personally, and pick him up and bring him here. Immediately. Take—what's his name down in security? Michensol? Take him with you. I want Mr. Udal in my office in half an hour."

"Thank you, Ms. Burgess," Udal said. "Thank you."

Ariel broke the connection, more annoyed than when she had answered it.

Contraband. Damn and damn. What next? All she needed was for the TBI to announce the arrest of an Auroran smuggler and the presence of an unknown quantity of illegal robots scattered who knew where on Earth.

I should have stayed home this morning . . .

"I'm not at liberty to discuss the specifics of our investigation, Ambassador. Please understand our position."

Ariel tapped her index finger impatiently on her desk, out of sight of the com screen. The TBI agent had been very polite, very receptive, and very uninformative.

"I understand perfectly," Ariel said. "You've decided that the assassination was directed at Senator Eliton exclusively and Ambassador Humadros simply got in the way . . . not to mention all the other Spacer nationals killed or injured. They had nothing to do with the fact that only Terran nationals were the target."

The agent—Royan—almost frowned, appearing puzzled more than offended. Ariel tried to imagine Mia like this after several more years in the Service—professional and cynically unresponsive.

"We don't disregard the losses to your people, Ambassador Burgess, but we are conducting our investigation the way we think best. Again, I apologize if this has inconvenienced your people."

"Your people." We're human, aren't we?

Ariel made herself nod, matching Agent Royan point for point with politesse. "If you had come to us before you started rousting Spacers, we might have been of assistance. You could have gotten better results, saved us all time, and possibly moved on to a more productive avenue."

"Ambassador—"

"Let me put it to you this way," Ariel said, hearing another obfuscation coming and losing patience. "If you don't desist from harassing Aurorans I'll file an injunction through the Senate and block you at every step. I've been less than impressed with Terran law enforcement over this. Five days and not one arrest? How hard can it be, Agent Royan? Nine armed assassins charge into Union Station, in front of thousands of witnesses on site and millions more through subetheric, six of them are dead, and you can't find the last three? My government is patient, but with limits."

Agent Royan was openly frowning now. "We're pursuing every likely avenue, Ambassador Burgess. You will just have to be content with that. I'm sorry—"

"If this inconveniences me, yes, I know, you've said that a dozen times since this conversation began. I am curious about one other thing, though."

"Yes?"

"It's my understanding that Special Service has assumed jurisdiction over this matter."

"Technically, that's correct."

"Then what exactly is it the TBI is investigating?"

"I'm not at—"

"—liberty to discuss that. Very well, Agent Royan, I'll let you get back to your job. You've been notified of our objections. The next time you hear from us will be in the form of a court order. Thank you for your time."

MIRAGE

Ariel stabbed the disconnect.

The com chimed. "What?"

"Excuse me, Ambassador," the robot receptionist said, "but there is a call—"

"If it can wait, tell them I'll get back to them."

"She insists on speaking with you *now*, Ambassador."

Ariel wondered if she would ever grow used to being called "Ambassador." Coming from the robot, it sounded so formal; from humans, it just sounded odd.

"Who is it?"

"A Rana Duvan."

Rana? Derec's specialist. She touched ACCEPT.

"Ms. Duvan, this is Ariel Burgess. How may I help you?"

"Sorry to call you, Ms. Burgess, but I have a problem I'm hoping you can help me with. Do you know where Derec is?"

"I—he had an appointment this morning with Alda Mikels of Imbitek. Hasn't he checked in?"

"No, but—well, I don't think he could help, but he should know."

"Know what?"

"We've been shut down."

It took Ariel a few moments to understand what Rana meant. "Phylaxis? What do you mean, shut down?"

"I mean I have an order here from a judge, cosigned by the Chair of the Committee on New Technologies, revoking our license and ordering us to cease all operations."

Ariel's ears grew warm as she took the news in. "Who's the Chair of the Committee?"

"Senator Taprin."

"Hell . . ." She remembered then that the New Technologies Committee was a sister committee to Eliton's Machine

372

Intelligence Committee. So had Jonis done this on his own, or bowed to pressure?

Does it matter? she thought bitterly.

"It's worse than that, Ms. Burgess," Rana continued. "I've been ordered by the TBI to hand over all our material, including our RI. In fact, there's an agent standing in the lab now, who says he's going to remain here until I comply."

"How long do you have?"

"Not long."

"Can you—?"

"That's what I need to talk to Derec about. What does he want me to do?"

Ariel drummed her fingers, thinking frantically. If the TBI got hold of the illegally downloaded RI matrix, they could charge Derec and derail everything.

"Have you finished everything that needed finishing?" she asked.

"Except for a few minor details, yes."

"I'll see to it that they can't take Thales—that's your RI's name?—and get a team over there to remove it to the embassy. In the meantime, I'd just clean some things up. I'll be back in touch."

"Thank you, Ms. Burgess."

The screen went blank again, and Ariel closed her eyes.

Never wonder what could be worse, she thought wryly. She touched the intercom. "Let me know the instant Hofton gets back—"

"He has returned, Ambassador," the robot replied.

"Get him in here."

A minute later, the door opened and Hofton came in with Mr. Udal in tow. Udal looked embarrassed and contrite. A security guard followed them both.

Ariel held up her hand. "Have Mr. Udal wait outside for a few minutes."

Hofton raised his eyebrows, but turned to the embassy security guard and nodded. Udal left the office.

"You have that look," Hofton said. "More fires?"

"Things may be falling apart faster than we can patch them together. You know where the Phylaxis Group is?"

"Yes . . ."

"TBI is there to impound all their equipment and data. I'm having a claim drawn up declaring their RI—its name is Thales—exclusive jurisdiction of Aurora as a positronic entity. I want you personally to get it signed by the appropriate bureaucrat, take it to Phylaxis with a team of our roboticists, and get it out of there before they destroy it. If possible, get a restraining order, and try to extract Derec's assistant, Rana Duvan."

"Shall I shift any planets from their orbits while I'm at it?" Hofton asked dryly.

"This is a bit more pressing than gravity, Hofton. I *need* Phylaxis and its material secured. Thales definitely, everything else as a can-do-if-possible."

"How soon?"

"An hour ago. Now, send Udal in here and get on it."

"Your wish, etcetera," he said with a slight flourish of his hand as he backed away from the desk.

The security guard brought Udal in.

"Sit down, Mr. Udal." Ariel entered commands into her terminal and the tri-d image of his mangled robot came up. She reached under the desk and brought up the crate containing the contraband positronic brain, gratified at the sudden amazed fear in his eyes.

"I'll talk," she said, "you listen. This isn't just a human-iform drone. This is a positronic robot and here is the brain.

You receive the drone bodies through normal trade routes and buy the brains from a black market source. The result is an illegal positronic robot, contraband, forbidden by more laws here than I can remember. The people who vandalized your establishment weren't there to simply damage your business, they were there to give you and us a warning. You've been trading in black market robots, Mr. Udal, and some of the local fanatics have found out about it. I admire the nerve to make a complaint to me—"

"But—"

"*I'm* talking now, Mr. Udal. This is causing us a lot of trouble and if you want to come out of this with a whole skin you will begin cooperating with me. First, by telling me the truth. I want to know who you're buying them from and where you're picking them up. I want to know how long you've been doing this, and I want to know who else is doing it and what else is being marketed illegally."

Udal's face began to distort. "I can't—"

"You *can,* Mr. Udal. Don't tell me you're afraid of reprisals. I assure you there's nothing they can do to you that I won't, and I can do it legally."

It took Udal several minutes to reach the point of decision. Ariel waited. She could see it coming, see him wrestling with the options, and finally realizing that he had none.

"Kynig Parapoyos," he said finally. "It's all through him."

Now, Ariel listened while Udal talked.

TWENTY-SIX

tactical parameters, security enhanced facility, path map in place, sensor log consistent with template, sublevels sealed, primary levels combined AI and organic surveillance, interconnected access between areas minimal, laboratory isolation standard, tentative probability escape assigned high seventy percentile, factors dependent on direct observation

Bogard recognized the place as the headquarters of Special Service. Agents Cupra and Gambel stood on either side, guiding Bogard as if it were an invalid who needed careful attention.

"Damn thing is tougher than I thought," Cupra said. "Look at this scoring. Shouldn't even be here."

"Amalloy," Gambel commented quietly. He looked around. "Lock it till we get to the lab."

They continued down to the third sublevel and brought Bogard into a room filled with familiar-looking equipment. Mostly diagnostics, but a standby niche stood against one wall. They brought the robot to it, turned it to face the room, and eased it back into the depression.

"Doesn't quite fit right anymore," Cupra said.

"Yes, well, if we melted part of you, I imagine your clothes would need altering."

Cupra grunted, moving to a console to the left of the niche. "Ready?"

"Let's try it," Gambel answered.

standby mode disabled, connection utilization protocol open, tier three data ready for dump, connection complete, standby command inoperative, tier three data delivered, trace feedback through system diagnostic/interrogatory, bypass feed overload, bypass polarity gate, bypass directional bias, connect to diagnostic/interrogatory AI, reroute interrogatory, bypass security buffer, locate output to accessory diagnostic systems, bypass isolation buffers, connection established

"Maybe it looks better than it should," Gambel said, studying the console, "but it's a mess internally. I'm amazed it could move. Look at this—"

"I can't decipher this stuff."

"You should learn."

"Why? Are we going to get another one?"

Gambel gave his partner a critical look, then returned his attention to the readouts.

"There's no brain left here," he said finally.

"You're sure?"

"Pretty sure. I think we should get Kedder in here to be sure, but . . . Bogard is not much anymore. The radiation must have burned out most of his pathways. Sixty, sixty-five percent degradation."

"I love it when you sound like you know what you're talking about."

"If you'd paid attention during the briefings then *you'd* know what I'm talking about, too. Look." Gambel tapped the console. "See this? It indicates volume of positron transmission through the matrix. It should be higher. That means Bogard's running on about one-twentieth of what he should be. That's the equivalent of a major stroke in you or I. Well, in you, anyway."

"Ha ha. I'm going to call Kedder."

"Do that. I won't feel safe until this thing is shut down completely."

"You don't know how to do that?" Cupra asked.

"Not now. Most of Bogard's failsafes look just as crippled as the rest of him."

"*I'd* feel better if we hadn't used a nuke."

"Why? Anything smaller and Bogard might be more functional."

"But we'd have had a body."

"And more questions. Go call Kedder."

tactical analysis, zero surveillance, sealed lab, comline on security routing, analyzing encryption, code entered, call established, recorder on, searching searching searching, no external surveillance verified, unsecured facility, escape probabilities increased to eighty-plus percentile, analyzing available equipment

"There's a problem," Cupra said. "They took Avery."

Gambel frowned. "Who took him?"

"Golner. Kedder set it up."

"Damn. Idiots. Where are they?"

"The garage."

"Tell them to do nothing with him till one of us gets there."

"Already did. But the word came from the top floor. Avery was at Imbitek this morning."

Gambel blinked at his partner. "Oh." He shrugged. "Let me finish here. Is Kedder coming?"

"I'll bring him back."

"You're going?"

"I don't know what *you're* doing here. *I* might as well do something useful."

Gambel nodded. "Check with One before you go."

"Yes, sir, boss." Cupra turned to leave.

"Cupra?"

"Yes?"

"When this is over, I'm requesting a new partner."

Cupra grinned. "I like you, too."

Cupra left the lab and Gambel shook his head. "Idiot." He checked the readouts again, then looked up at Bogard. "The only question I have is, how come it took so long for someone to call you in? You must've been wandering around down there ever since. Where were you?"

interrogatory parameters referent primary instructions, negative violation, negative obligation, reply not required, refer program buffer sublevel C-two, continue analysis of supplemental systems

Bogard said nothing.

Gambel shrugged. "As far as I'm concerned, you are gone, my friend. I'd rather you had burned up in the blast, but . . ." He worked the console. "We'll let Kedder take a look at you. He's our positronic man, but I think I know enough to tell. Meantime, we don't want you wandering off, so . . ."

Clamps extruded from the sides of the niche to secure Bogard.

"Gambel?" a voice called.

The agent went to the comline. "Yes, sir?"

"I want to see you in my office. Now."

"Yes, sir. Be right up." He walked up to Bogard and studied it for a moment. "You know, I could get to like working with robots. I don't really see the big problem." He shrugged. "Oh, well, not my decision. One calls, have to see what's going on. I'll be back."

Gambel gave the monitors one more look, then left the lab.

niche locks bypassed, command override initiated, survey internal surveillance, continues zero, sealed lab, initiate second tier program

Bogard's body seemed to ooze out of the niche, leaving the locks in place. The connections retracted from their contacts automatically once the unit detected activity, and Bogard reformed itself, adopting a smooth, seamless configuration with a very shallow sensor shadow, and a dull, dark color.

resume functions, full positronic access, initiate third tier program, load data, load memory, analyze, sort, configure, reset, function optimal, situation nominal, initiate search parameters, accessory buffer online to receive data

Bogard shifted from station to station in the lab, extruding direct contacts to link into each piece of data storage equipment and copying what it found into the prepared space. It moved fluidly, swiftly, making the entire round of the lab in less than a minute. It stopped finally at the intercom terminal and inserted a probe.

analyze security, decode primary and secondary restriction algorithms, set and establish access protocols, direct system interrogatory, scan complete, search and copy protocols initiated

Mia waited with growing anxiety. Bogard had been "in the field" for nearly three hours and she could not help but doubt everything was fine.

The transport sat at the end of a long alley within sight of one of the maintenance accesses to the Special Service HQ. The building alongside which she had parked contained an extension of the government law library, and her vehicle ID transponder offered, when requested, a permit for a pick-up from the library. Mia was unsure what exactly she would be picking up, but Ariel had assured her that the permit was routine, and so far no one had challenged Mia's presence. It was sloppy of the Service not to, though. An Auroran embassy vehicle, parked for nearly an hour just down the way from a high security complex, for no apparent reason.

She had spent that hour going through the disk from Lanra. In many respects they had duplicated each other's efforts. He had gone through the same lists, rejected the same names, kept many of the same possibilities. At the top of his list of suspects was Alda Mikels of Imbitek.

But he also considered Gale Chassik, the Solarian ambassador, as a possible. As evidence he cited several meetings between Imbitek people and the Solarians at the embassy. But that meant little to Mia—it had been a Solarian company that had installed the RI at Union Station, and Imbitek had installed a good part of the accessory systems. Cooperation at some level was to be expected.

There had been three meetings between Chassik and Mikels.

"So what?" Mia asked aloud. "Ariel probably knows Mikels, too . . ."

Another name on the list was Bok Golner. "So you came up with him, too . . ." Lanra had a slightly more extensive file than she. Golner had been with almost all the larger anti-robot, Earth-firster organizations, some for only a few weeks. She had expected that. But he worked as an environmental service tech for Cyvan. So through a long chain of corporate connections, he worked for Alda Mikels. But the chain was long enough that it would not support the conclusion in court. Lanra had appended Golner's military service record, as well.

He had also included a section on an investigation of his own client, DyNan Manual Industries. Lanra was thorough; he had no intention of working for anyone who he would otherwise find culpable. The file contained the usual statistics on personnel, profits, distribution, customers. Then it opened into a file on the Church of Organic Sapiens. Lanra found much of the dogma as unpalatable as Mia, but he noted several policy statements advocating nonviolence and patience and the general principle that to reject something it was vital to reject it completely and not even copy parts of it. To Lanra, this meant that Looms would never stoop low enough to do what he despised in others.

Mia was not so sure. She had seen the way people compartmentalized their ethics—things they would never do at home, they did effortlessly at work; politics they would never advocate in their personal relations, they applied ruthlessly in public affairs—so a "policy statement" from the head of a fundamentally revolutionary organization did not impress her.

But then Lanra returned to business and Mia saw what must have intrigued him. The consortium Lanra mentioned had approached Looms a year-and-a-half ago. The committee had been headed by Mikels. Till then, Looms owned stock in Imbitek. After the meeting, Looms divested—at a loss. Mikels and others in the consortium had evidently initiated a program to hurt DyNan. Looms had been forced to buy back majority control in his own company very quickly to defend against a takeover. It had cost Looms a good portion of his personal wealth, but as of two months ago DyNan was seventy-two percent owned by Looms.

It did seem that Looms was unpopular with Mikels and the others in the consortium. Nothing Lanra had been able to find told anything about the meeting or what it was Mikels had proposed that had so disturbed Looms.

But he noted that a politician had been in attendance. He had been unable to learn which one, only that it had been a high-ranking person, maybe a senator or vice-senator.

All right, Coren, let's take it as given that Looms had nothing to do with this . . . Mia thought.

Then the fact that none of DyNan's people had been injured looked very much like a set-up.

It occurred to Mia that someone would have to know who they were in order to make sure they would not be hurt. A list had to have gotten to the assassins, but the final list had not been completed till the day before. Last minute changes were even expected that morning. Who got the lists? Who made them? Who would have been in a position to get that information to the assassins?

And on the Spacer side? Had those been random or had there been a list for that, too? She remembered that on the morning of the Incident, Mattu, Gel, and she still had no idea how many Spacers were coming down from Kopernik. They would not have known till the Spacers walked out of the concourse . . .

Ariel's friend, Aspil. Was the corpse the real Aspil? If there had been an informant in their midst to send down the list just before they descended . . .

"Just how many people are involved in this?" Mia groaned. She looked down the alleyway and wondered where Bogard was.

Take it logically. It was beginning to appear that ten, twenty—a hundred?—people were involved. Perhaps there were a lot of *bodies* concerned—nine assassins at the very least, someone in the civic morgue, newsnet people maybe—but did they know anything about the larger conspiracy? Not necessarily. How many people need be involved? There must be a coordinator, someone to find the right people, the right data, and monitor everything. There must be a resource, for money, equipment, transportation. There must be a killer. Three people. The conspiracy looked manageable at that level.

Who would fill all those requirements, though?

Someone leaked the list of guests. Someone subverted the RI and otherwise circumvented security. Someone hired, prepared, and unleashed a team of assassins. Someone led those assassins.

And afterward? Someone was cleaning up loose ends. Could be the same someone who had leaked the list . . .

Movement attracted her attention and she looked down the alley.

The service door opened and an oversized drone rolled

out. It was little more than a collection of boxes on tracks, moving in fits and starts. It seemed confused, almost comical. Then it came trundling down the alley toward her. Mia's pulse picked up.

Ten meters from the transport, the drone began to change. As Mia watched, it liquidly unfolded, rising in stature, slimming, losing the treads, becoming recognizably Bogard. She opened the back door and the robot slipped into the transport.

"Car, resume to fourth destination," she said.

The transport started up and backed down the alley, to the main corridor, and pulled into the light midafternoon traffic.

"Hi, Bogard," Mia said pleasantly.

"Hello, Mia," Bogard replied evenly.

"How did you do?"

"I believe I have acquired everything requested." Bogard paused. "There is a problem, however. Derec has been abducted."

TWENTY-SEVEN

A faint smell of burning plastic brought him awake. Derec kept his eyes closed, remembering almost too late that he was a prisoner.

He concentrated on his other senses. After the smell, he noticed that his hands were bound—by a thin cord, from the way it bit into his flesh—and he was lying on his stomach on a pad of some kind. The air was cold. He heard distant sounds, like water dripping or the delicate rattle of tools in use, distorted by the space and the consequent echo. Then he heard footsteps, drawing nearer. The soles clicked on a hard surface, like concrete. He wondered . . .

"Hey, Bok," someone very near said, his voice tense with a forced joviality. And it sounded familiar.

"Shut up," the other—Bok, Derec guessed—said flatly, as though he expected to be obeyed.

There was silence.

"He's awake," Bok said then. "He didn't get that much. Mr. Avery, I expect you can hear and understand me. Go ahead and pretend to still be unconscious if you want, it doesn't matter. Soon you won't be my problem anymore. But until then, let me inform you that if you try to escape, I will kill you without a second thought. The only reason you're alive now is because someone wants it that way. He could just as easily want it the other way. If we're clear on this, just continue to lie there as if you haven't heard a word I've said."

Bok walked away.

"Asshole," the other, familiar, voice said softly. Then: "Are you awake?"

Derec did not move.

"This is unbelievable," the other said. "Absolutely unbelievable." He sounded strained, barely in control. "All this was supposed to be . . . damn. No one was supposed to get hurt and after the station they told me it was over, no one else would get hurt, and then . . . this is unbelievable."

Now Derec opened his eyes. He lay on a thick pad, several centimeters from the floor, in some kind of stall. The light was dim and came from outside the small area, spilling over the contents unevenly. Across from him, sitting against a wall, was Tathis Kedder, his legs drawn up against his chest, one hand pressed flat against the floor, the other hovering by his mouth. He was staring out of the stall.

Derec recognized the space, then: the garage with the ambulances.

Kedder looked around and saw him. "You *are* awake." Kedder stared at him for a time, then seemed about to crawl across the stall to his side. He made the first move, then changed his mind and pressed his back firmly against the wall and shook his head. "This isn't my fault."

"What isn't?" Derec asked.

"This." He waved a hand at Derec, then at the garage around them. "None of this. I had nothing to do with this."

"Of course not. You only set me up to be abducted. Now it looks like you're in about the same position I'm in. Except *you're* not bound."

Kedder swallowed loudly and started shaking his head in desperate denial. "I am not like you. I didn't ask too many questions. I didn't scan where I wasn't supposed to. I did what I was told and nothing more. *I shouldn't be here!*"

Derec waited for Kedder to calm down. "So, why *are* you here?"

"I don't know."

"Yes, you do."

"I *don't*." Kedder glared, his eyes wide and moist. He rubbed a hand over his mouth and looked away. "All I was asked to do was to modify a couple of reports. It was research. That was all. Basic research, they said, the installation of a few extra components, nothing vital, attached to a couple of maintenance nodes. In the interest of—the money was very good."

"Who asked you? Imbitek?"

Kedder nodded. "I looked over the specifications—there didn't seem to be any harm, and it takes forever to get clearance for some of the simplest changes. Did you know that three years ago, we needed an upgrade in the lavatories? A new processing unit had to be installed specifically to handle the increase in Spacer traffic. A few new microbes had gotten into their systems and the standard purification filters just didn't clean it all out anymore. Nothing serious, mind you, but it was a concern that should any of these flora get into the general sewage system, there could be a problem or two, so the request was made to upgrade. It took three months for the clearances. Do you have any idea how many people use the station facilities in a *day?* In three months, when you consider all the traffic, well, a major plague could have gotten started before the bureaucrats made up their minds. So when I was asked to help with this, well, you understand, it was with that in mind—"

"You were thinking of toilets and took the money. I understand. Makes perfect sense."

Kedder blinked at him, frowning. "The money was very good. And frankly, I didn't think I'd have a job for that much longer."

"At Union Station? Why not?"

"Things . . . it's a positronic unit—was—and I just couldn't see it lasting. When I'd tell people what I did, most of them thought I was weird. A few called me a traitor. If the idea was to get people used to the idea of positronics it wasn't working. And I was tainted. It occurred to me, Mr. Avery, that I might have trouble finding employment after the program shut down."

"You were certain it was going to shut down?" Derec asked.

"Be serious. Did you think it would last as long as it did?"

"Senator Eliton—"

"Would do what his constituency told him to do. That's his job, that's what he's paid to do. His numbers were dropping. If this conference succeeded as advertised, I imagine he'd be voted out of office. People don't want positronics. They don't want robots. They don't want—"

"So why did you study it if that's how you felt?"

"What? Oh. I—well, I didn't always feel that way. But after working there and—I lost friends, Mr. Avery. I was a pariah among certain people."

"Find new friends. Not everyone on this planet is a bigot."

Kedder grunted and lapsed into sullen silence.

Derec licked his lips; his mouth felt dry and numb— leftovers from the anæsthetic. "So let me see if I guessed correctly. Imbitek paid you to allow them to install a few experimental components. Since they were already an authorized contractor on the project, you couldn't see a legal problem, certainly not an ethical one. They offered enough money to assuage any other doubts you might have and, besides, they convinced you that the RI was temporary and afterward, if everything went well, you could have a position with them. So you agreed. You also helped them with locating the nodes they wanted. They even had a Solarian consultant to convince you that nothing would go wrong. You know your training in positronics isn't on par with a specialist from Solaria, so this makes perfect sense. All you have to do over the course of the next several months is log any glitches that crop up and route the reports to the Solarian consultant rather than to the authorized service contractor—me."

Derec tried to shift onto his side to make breathing a little easier, but without success. " 'Adjustment errors,' they told you—happens from time to time, nothing to worry about. Then it all blew up in your face when the attack on the conference delegates happened. You knew something to do with those systems had interfered with the RI and compromised security. You didn't know what, you probably didn't even know that it was supposed to do that. You only knew that something you had allowed to happen had caused a major disaster. I show up and you decide, on the spot, to say nothing. Maybe I'd conclude it was Imbitek's fault, which I did. It never occurred to me to question you or Hammis, not till I found out that no directive had been issued by the Calvin Institute to route those 'adjustment errors' to them instead of me. Even then, I didn't really think it was you. I thought you'd been lied to. I wanted to find out who'd done that. But now . . . let me guess, it was pointed out to you that your continued cooperation was necessary or the facts of your violation of protocol would be made public. You'd be lucky to escape imprisonment."

Kedder sniffed. "It wasn't supposed to happen this way."

"What about Hammis? Was he part of it?"

"No, he—I trained him. Sometimes I think he was better than me, but—he never knew. I think he suspected."

"So you had him fired."

Kedder shrugged. "Yes."

"Where is he? His apartment's been searched."

Kedder gestured with his thumb toward the wall at his back. "In the next stall. Dead."

Derec felt a chill grow down his back. "That means you're next, Tathis."

"Maybe." He looked at Derec. In the half-light his tears glistened. "You're only half correct about the Solarian. There was one, but he wasn't introduced to me as a Solarian but an Auroran, someone on staff at the Calvin Institute. Later I checked because I found his name on the roster of the Auroran legation en route."

"Tro Aspil?"

Kedder nodded. "The one I talked to was Solarian."

"How do you know?"

"Accent. During my training and during the installation of the RI I talked to both Aurorans and Solarians. They sound different. It's hard to define, but . . . I didn't think anything of it at the time . . . Solarians work for Aurorans, there are Solarians at the Calvin Institute . . ."

"But none on Earth."

"Not with the Institute, no."

"So who was this man?"

"I don't know. Just not Tro Aspil."

How far does this go? Derec wondered. Imbitek, probably Mikels himself—no, certainly Mikels himself—and at least two Special Service agents. And a Solarian? It would make the installation of those growths easier, certainly. Then there were his present captors—Managins. Maybe.

"I'm sure they know I'm awake now," Derec said. "So, could you help me sit up. This is a very awkward position."

At first, it seemed Kedder would not move. Then he unfolded from the wall and quickly turned Derec onto his side and helped him up.

"Thanks." Derec saw then that he was on an ambulance gurney.

Kedder resumed his position on the floor against the wall.

"So," Derec said, "who's Bok?"

"Bok Golner."

"Am I supposed to know him?"

"He's . . . dangerous."

"So I gather. Managin?"

Kedder nodded.

"All the gunmen at Union Station?"

Another nod.

"All nine of them?"

Kedder shot him a startled look. "How—?"

"I wanted to ask the same question. Do you know?"

"Part of the . . . modification . . . to the RI. They carried holographic projectors, tied in to the RI communications network, just like all the robots and other security systems."

"Everything became part of the game the RI was playing."

"It couldn't discern game targets from reality. The sensor feed was completely subsumed into the game, except for a couple of satellite systems. The trick was getting it to play the game long enough. It could go through a high order scenario in seconds. They needed minutes."

"The adjustment errors."

"Testing different games, different levels, different difficulties."

"You figured this all out later?"

"In the last few days." Kedder looked at him. "You've got to believe me—"

"You never intended it to turn out this way. Of course I believe you. It doesn't matter. Any way it turned out, it would have been your responsibility. Even if no one had been harmed, what you did was wrong."

"Damn it, Mr. Avery—"

"Find absolution somewhere else. I'm not interested."

Kedder looked stunned. "You—but I thought—"

"You thought what? That confession brings instant forgiveness? I understand what you did, Kedder, but people died."

"I didn't know! They told me no one would get hurt!"

"And the money was good, so you believed them."

Derec was not sure what reaction he expected, but Kedder suddenly launched himself off the floor. He slammed into Derec and both of them plus the gurney went over. Derec hit the floor solidly across the shoulders, his arms complaining sharply. Kedder tried to get to his knees but he could not stop himself from punching ineffectually at Derec, hitting the floor more than his face.

Running feet filled the stall, then grunting, and suddenly the weight was off him. Three men held Kedder while a fourth shifted an impatient gaze between him and Derec.

"Get him out of here," he said, and Derec recognized Bok's voice. "Put him next to his friend."

Derec rolled slowly off his bruised wrists. Bok grabbed his shirt and hauled him to his feet with astonishing strength. He held Derec with one hand and righted the gurney with his other, then sat Derec down on the edge.

"Welcome back to the world of the waking," Bok Golner said. "What did you do to piss him off?"

"Told him he was a killer."

Bok Golner stared at him for a few seconds, then laughed. "No. He's just a scared fool. I, on the other hand, *am* a killer, Mr. Avery. I'm very good at it. Now, you be good. I won't be far away."

As Bok Golner walked away, Derec let out his breath, not realizing till then that he had been holding it. He shuddered once, rolled his shoulders to ease the pain, then turned to examine the contents of the stall. Now that he was alone, he might be able to find a way out.

tactical parameters, multilevel facility, modifications from standard include unidentified internal security array, status standby; three additional access conduits, two in sublevels, one on topmost level; coded access monitor security level eight, recent manufacture, inconsistent with age of structure or registered usage; present status of structure occupied, census required, stealth mode active, surveillance initiated, defense mode on, census acquisition minimal First Law Violation, nominal Second Law Violation within acceptable parameters, negative Third Law Violation, proceeding maximum covert imperatives

sublevels, main level, second level, third level unoccupied, all stored equipment connected to maintenance systems on standby, four individuals on fourth level, armed, decommissioned military style stunners, model APS-47, comlink active and open, fifth level unoccupied, eight individuals on sixth level, one decedent, armed, APS-47 stunners, two nine-millimeter projectile rifles type unknown, identical to type previously noted, two military style blasters, model SIB-90, current standard issue, two operational transports, two individuals under restraint, one unidentified, one identified Derec Avery

First Law protocols assigned to primary, Derec Avery, initiating analysis for optimal retrieval

Besides a few odd bits of machinery, Derec saw nothing that could be easily used to cut his bonds. He curled his fingers palmward as much as he could and managed to brush against the cord around his wrists. Thin, probably a carbon-fiber analog, likely as not a molecular seal. Even if he had a knife it would be useless.

"Why did you bring him here?" demanded a brusque voice outside the stall.

Derec sat still and listened to the new voice.

"We were told to obtain and hold him," Golner answered. "Where else would you suggest?"

"Try Manassas."

"We weren't told to move them that far."

Derec recognized the newcomer—Cupra. The puzzle was assembling itself. Too bad he might not survive its completion.

"All right, let me talk to—"

"We were told to wait for instructions. We didn't hear anything about circumventing the chain of command."

"Be current, will you? We'll be lucky if this doesn't—"

"Doesn't what? Cause an incident?"

The other Managins laughed.

"You could as easily," Cupra went on, speaking a little louder, "have kept him at Kedder's apartment. Why move him?"

"We brought Kedder, too."

"You brought—you ass. We need Kedder."

"I don't see why," Golner said.

"He's our roboticist."

"So?"

"So we have a robot. We retrieved the bodyguard."

"What? How?"

"It was called in, wandering in the sublevels. Badly damaged."

"It shouldn't even exist anymore. That was a bubble nuke you used. Everything should have been—"

"It survived. Now we need Kedder to do a full vetting."

"No one leaves till we hear word."

"I'm going to get you word, Golner. Where's Avery and Kedder?"

"Over there."

"Captain," another voice cut in. "There's a problem. Point isn't responding to check."

"Perimeter?" Golner demanded.

"No breaks. Comlink is down. We—"

Derec heard a soft impact, like someone flopping to the floor for a nap. Then running.

"Hey—"

"Left! Left!"

The clatter of boots diminished, one pair at a time.

Derec tried to stand.

"No, no," Golner whispered from behind him, his arm suddenly around Derec's neck. The barrel of a pistol pressed against his right temple.

"I can't run with my feet hobbled," Derec said as calmly as he could.

The barrel shifted to the small of his back and the arm retracted. A second later the bindings around his ankles fell away. He put one foot forward and slammed the other back. It impacted with concrete, though, and Golner jerked him back and forth twice before wrapping his arm around Derec's neck again.

"Very good, you have nerve. You'll never be fast enough." The barrel returned to Derec's temple. "What's out there? Nothing human could get past our perimeter surveillance. Is that your toy?"

"I have no idea. You heard what Cupra said."

"Cupra's an idiot. You built that machine out of amalloy. I watched what it did at Union Station. Imitating damage wouldn't be much trouble for it, would it?"

"How'd you have time to notice? You were so busy slaughtering people."

"That wasn't slaughter, Mr. Avery. That was surgery. Like any competent medic, I pay attention when I operate."

"I don't know where Bogard is," Derec insisted.

Golner was silent for a time. The garage was still now. Derec heard nothing but a distant ventilator.

"It's definitely not human," Golner said. "We're getting out now, Mr. Avery. You move when I move, stop when I stop. You mean nothing to me but a shield. Clear?"

Derec nodded.

"Good."

"But you won't make it. You aren't fast enough."

"You hope."

Golner urged Derec forward, out of the stall. Derec tried to turn his head left to see down the aisle, but Golner jerked him to the right and frogmarched him toward the far wall.

"I'll kill him!" Golner shouted. "You can't stop me!"

"No?" a woman answered, off to the right.

Golner reacted. The barrel left Derec's head to aim toward the voice. Derec bent forward against Golner's arm and tried kicking him again. He missed again, but suddenly Golner released him, and Derec sprawled face down on the cold concrete.

He rolled left, quickly, until he came up against a wall.

When he managed to sit up, he saw Mia Daventri across from him, leaning on the divider between two stalls. Between them lay Golner—unconscious, limbs sprawled. Standing over him was Bogard, almost invisible in the dim light, the trace of its optical array slicing across its head, brilliant and white.

TWENTY-EIGHT

Bogard laid the unconscious Managins in a row, moving in a blur. When it finished, Mia walked along them, slowly, still favoring her sore leg, and collected their weapons. Bogard paced her, a portion of its torso shaped to receive each one as she finished inspecting it. Derec sat on the opposite side of the aisle, massaging his wrists and shaking every so often, face pale.

Mia hefted one of the rifles. "This is definitely a custom job," she said admiringly. She dropped the clip and cleared the chamber, then raised it to her shoulder. "Nice weight, balance . . ." She closed the slide with a loud snap. "The rest of these are a combination of old military and new, but standard issue all the same." She picked up one of the blasters. "This is current issue. Inappropriate for anything short of open combat. You could burn this whole place down with it."

Derec watched her, eyes fixed, expressionless. Shock, she decided. He had very nearly died.

"Is this all of them, Bogard?" she asked, waving a hand at the row.

"There is one decedent, Mia," Bogard said.

She shot it a look, startled.

"Not Bogard," Derec said quietly. "The body was already here. Dead."

"Where?"

Derec pointed and Mia went to one of the stalls. Within she found a portable stasis tube with a man inside.

"Do you know him?" she called.

"His name is Hammis. He was one of the positronic techs at Union Station."

Mia came back to the Managins. She stopped at the feet of the one who had held Derec.

"Bogard, identify this one."

"Bok Vin Golner, age forty-one, born Earth, Atlanta Sector, retired military, rank Captain, Space Tactical, surviving family—"

"That's fine, Bogard." Mia kicked Golner's limp foot. "I think he's the leader. I think he led the assault at Union Station."

"He's awfully strong," Derec said.

"He was Space Tactical. They were involved in all kinds of special projects—body modifications, advanced biotech systems, experimental field trials. Super soldiers, literally." She thought about that. "Bogard, the trank you administered. How long will it remain effective on him?"

Bogard knelt beside Golner. Two thin tendrils snaked out from its arms and connected to Golner's neck and lower back. "His system is already purging. We have twenty minutes."

"He should be out for a couple of hours," Derec said.

"Not to worry," Mia said. "We'll be long gone before he comes to. Bogard, secure them."

The robot moved almost too quickly to follow, pausing only to gently turn each man over and bind wrists, elbows, and ankles. Within seconds, the entire row lay face down, arms behind their backs.

"Can you administer another dose of trank to Golner?" Derec asked, his voice a little nervous.

"I cannot be certain of the effect on his system," Bogard said. "Two doses within such a brief time period are contraindicated for a normal human. I cannot guarantee a nondestructive reaction, therefore I cannot administer a second dose, Derec. I am sorry."

Mia felt her patience yield. She took out her own weapon and walked up to Golner's head. She aimed it and thumbed off the safety.

Suddenly, Bogard was right in front of her, its hand encasing the barrel of her pistol. She jerked back, but Bogard did not let go.

"What are you doing?" she demanded.

"I must assume that your intention is to kill or permanently incapacitate Bok Vin Golner."

Mia tugged at her weapon. "I had something like that in mind."

"He poses no threat."

"He won't be unconscious for long. He will pose a threat then."

"There are other actions to assure our safety."

"This action would ensure the safety of many people. Golner will do damage if he survives."

"Turn him over to the authorities. They will incarcerate him, and he will pose no threat."

"Bogard, release my weapon," Mia demanded.

"Only if you will assure me you will not use it to cause harm or death to Bok Vin Golner."

Mia stopped struggling and looked over at Derec. He still looked shaken, but there was a thin smile on his face.

"What is it doing?" she asked.

"Obeying the First Law."

"I thought—"

"You thought wrong. You thought Bogard had some sense of good guys and bad guys and that the bad guys are always dangerous."

"Doesn't it?"

"Sort of. But the bad guys are also still human. Bogard is assessing its responsibilities according to the Three Laws. It won't let you simply kill a human being if there are alternatives."

Mia frowned. "That's . . . inconvenient."

Derec shrugged.

"All right," she said. "I give you my word, Bogard, I won't harm him."

Bogard's hand unfolded from around the pistol. Mia staggered back slightly. For a moment, she considered her chances of taking the shot now, before Bogard could react. Almost at once she felt a pang of shame. She holstered her weapon.

"If we have twenty minutes," Derec said, pushing himself to his feet, "we should use it. How did you get here?"

"I'm still using the embassy transport."

Derec came up alongside her. He pointed to two of the sleeping figures. "Cupra. And that one is the other positronic specialist from Union Station, Tathis Kedder. He set me up for this."

"I think Bogard is right," Mia said. "We *should* turn them

over to the authorities. But not all of them." She turned to the robot. "Bogard, I want you to send in a report to the local police. Trespassers. And we'll leave several of the weapons. And the corpse. Then I want you to rig to carry two bodies."

She walked over to Agent Cupra and Kedder, then looked at Derec. "I think we need to have a sincere conversation."

A small contingent of Auroran security met them in the embassy garage. Mia stepped out of the transport warily; she did not know any of them. One man stepped forward, dressed in a formal embassy jacket.

"Ms. Daventri? I'm Hofton, Ariel's aide."

Mia relaxed. "Good. And these others?"

"Embassy security." He looked past her to Derec. "Sir?"

"Derec Avery, Hofton. We met once . . ."

Hofton nodded. "Yes, sir, I remember you. I'm pleased to see that you're all right. There have been further complications. Ariel wishes to see both of you as soon as possible. What needs tending here?"

From the rear of the transport, Bogard emerged, carrying the still-unconscious men. Mia watched the expressions on the faces of the security team. They looked briefly startled and a little wary, but accepted Bogard at once.

"We need these two placed in isolation, under guard," Mia said.

Hofton frowned. "The embassy doesn't have a jail as such . . ."

"I don't care if it's a closet."

"That we can provide." Hofton gestured to the Aurorans. "Take them to the secured briefing rooms."

"Keep them separate," Mia added. "Bogard, go with them and assist in observation."

"Is open movement advisable, Mia?" Bogard asked.

"This is the Auroran Embassy, Bogard."

Bogard seemed to consider that for a moment, then moved to follow the security guards, Cupra and Kedder cradled on either side of him.

Hofton watched the robot as it went on. "Remarkable." He looked at Derec. "Do you need medical attention, sir?"

"No, thank you, I'm just bruised up."

"I could use some pain blockers," Mia said. She rubbed her right leg.

"I'll see to it. Please, come with me."

As they headed for the lift, Hofton filled them in.

"Several things have occurred simultaneously that have changed our situation here. The TBI have been interrogating Spacers throughout the district. No arrests have been made, but the confrontations have been such that many more Spacers are leaving Earth than before. Ariel's been working all morning to stem the flow before it becomes a general rout. One of her constituents is here after being threatened with arrest for dealing in contraband. On a more personal note, sir, your firm has been shut down by the TBI."

Hofton hesitated, and it seemed to Mia that he was embarrassed. "I attempted to extricate your assistant, Ms. Duvan, but I'm afraid she's been arrested. There are warrants for your other employees as well. I don't know if they've been found. There is also a warrant for your arrest."

Derec sighed wearily. "Great. And we've just kidnapped a Special Service agent." He shrugged. "Well, if you're going to go to prison, go for something worthwhile." He smiled weakly.

"I did my best, Mr. Avery," Hofton said quietly. "It's my

impression, though, that the TBI have an agenda not stated in their warrants."

"TBI . . ." Mia said. "Not Special Service."

"Significant?" Derec asked.

"I don't know. Possibly. There's a strict code of territoriality between us. We don't encroach on each others' investigations. If Special Service takes control of something, TBI stays out, and vice versa."

"Unless this is an unrelated investigation," Derec said.

"What are the chances of that?" Hofton asked.

Mia grunted.

They rode the rest of the way up to the embassy offices in silence. The doors opened and they stepped into a scene of restrained chaos. Staff huddled by office doors down the corridor, while others flitted from room to room. In the reception area, Ariel was bent over the desk, going over something with a secretary while three other aides talked tersely among themselves. Two security guards stood at the main entrance.

Ariel looked up at them and gestured for Hofton to take Derec and Mia into her office.

"Can I get either of you anything while you wait?" Hofton asked. He pointed at Mia. "Pain blockers, yes, I'll see to it. Anything else?"

"I could stand something to eat," Derec said.

"Nothing for me," Mia said.

"I'll return as soon as I can," Hofton promised and left.

Almost immediately, Ariel came in, shutting the doors behind her.

"Are you all right?" she asked Derec. She stopped short of arm's length from him. "I was—"

He raised his hands and nodded. "I'm fine, I just—it—"

Ariel started to back away, then winced visibly and

pulled Derec into a hug. He hesitated, his arms extended as if unsure what to do next. Then he closed them around her and they stood like that for a long time.

When she did break away, Mia saw her eyes glint wetly. Ariel sniffed once, loudly, then seemed to seize control of herself.

"Your prisoners are in two of our debriefing rooms," she said. "They're for high security conversations, completely shielded. Who are they?"

"One is a positronic tech," Derec said. "Tathis Kedder, one of the two at Union Station. The other . . ."

"Otin Cupra," Mia said.

Ariel stared at her. "You snatched a Service agent?"

"Chance encounter," Mia said. "He showed up just when we were about to rescue Derec."

"The garage," Derec said with emphasis.

"I see," Ariel said, folding her arms. "Well, I doubt it could worsen the situation in the long run."

"What's happened?" Derec asked. "Hofton said my people are in custody."

"Phylaxis has been shut down and seized by the TBI. I tried to get the personnel declared Auroran nationals, but they weren't backing down. They want you, too. Now that you're actually here, I can reinstate your Auroran citizenship and grant asylum, but you can't leave the embassy at this point. At least, it wouldn't be a good idea to go shopping."

Derec almost laughed. He looked around the office and moved to a couch. He dropped into it, sprawling, and put a hand to his face, gently rubbing his eyes.

"What happened?" Ariel asked. "You were vague on the comlink."

Mia described the events in the garage, watching Derec

as she spoke to see how he reacted. He did not move. As Mia finished, Hofton returned with a tray bearing food and a small plate with pills which he offered to Mia.

"I gathered you wanted something stronger than a med robot would permit."

Mia gave him a smile and scooped the pills from the plate. There were four. She took two and pocketed the others.

Derec sat up as Hofton opened the legs under the tray and set it before him. "Thanks," he murmured and examined the contents. He took a piece of bread and started eating it.

"Why the local police?" Ariel asked.

"To complicate things. However far this conspiracy goes, I doubt it includes the D.C. cops. Those men we snagged will go into the system and will be explaining themselves to a local judge, effectively out of reach of higher authority . . . at least, for the time being. It will be a matter of public record by morning, and maybe some questions will be asked that aren't being asked now."

Ariel scowled. "I wonder if this could be made to constitute 'arrests' in the eyes of Aurora."

"What's happening here?" Mia asked.

"Solaria has officially pulled out of the conference. They jumped the gun on us; we had no response. I haven't gotten word from Setaris and as far as I know she hasn't gotten word from Aurora."

"Then it's over. They won."

"That's not clear yet. Aurora can pressure Solaria to return to the table, but we have to have a reason."

"All you're going to do is push Solaria further away," Derec said. His words came out muffled around a mouthful of food. He was eating heartily now. "Maybe that's exactly what they want."

"What do you mean?" Ariel asked.

"Solaria's involved. Your friend, Tro Aspil? He was introduced to Kedder as a representative from the Calvin Institute, an Auroran, but Kedder says the man he met was a Solarian."

"When was this?"

"Over a year ago."

"That's not—he was introduced *as* Tro Aspil?"

Derec nodded. He took a long drink, then started telling them about Kedder's confession.

Cupra struggled against Bogard's grip on both his arms until they entered the lift. Michensol, the embassy security man, accompanied them. Mia noted that he looked distantly disapproving of Bogard, but he said nothing. Cupra resigned himself once they were in the small car and kept shifting his gaze between Mia and Michensol, wary but helpless and resentful.

"Where are we going?" Cupra asked finally.

"A new experience," Mia said.

The lift came to a halt and the doors opened onto a small chamber. Opposite the lift was another door. The lift closed, leaving the four of them, three humans and a robot, in the quiet, almost intimate space.

"Have you ever seen a sunset?" Mia asked conversationally.

Cupra blinked. "Of course—"

"I mean a real one." She touched a contact and the door opened. A breeze swept into the chamber and Cupra's eyes widened slightly. "Bring him, Bogard."

Mia stepped out onto the observation platform.

"What are you doing?" Cupra demanded, his voice tinged with anxiety.

"Giving you a treat," Mia said.

She felt a few moments of apprehension herself, standing suddenly beneath an open sky, walking across a wide terrace to the railing, and gazing west toward a distant, uneven line of bluish mountains. By the time she reached the rail, she had control and began to admire the view.

The roof of D.C. stretched before her, multileveled, aerials and dishes and towers forming a kind of forest-in-abstract all the way to a point where it blended with the landscape. The green of actual forest became, finally, the blue of the mountain range, and above them the sky was yellowing as evening approached. The wind was cold and came in gusts; some of the roof's protrusions waved slightly.

"I remember the first time I came up like this," she said as Bogard brought Cupra to the railing beside her. "I was four and my parents were Settler hopefuls. They had to prove that they could tolerate the open, so they started making excursions outside the city. Naturally, they brought me. We went to the Smokey Mountain Preserve—you had to get a permit and there was a time limit. They let you out in stages. First, there was a shuttle ride to the visitor's center, then there was the orientation lecture, then a covered area with wildlife that opened at one end and let onto the forest proper. My parents wanted to stay back under the canopy, but I got loose and ran for the open. All of a sudden I was Outside. I looked up at the trees reaching above me. The tops broke into thousands of little shapes. Leaves. And through the breaks in the leaves was all this blue. Somehow I realized that it was sky. And I screamed."

She looked back at Michensol, who was listening intently. "I think—I remember—that it was a scream of delight. But my parents must have thought it was something less wonderful and came rushing out to save me. My father swept me up, stopped, and looked up himself. Then he ran with me back under the canopy. We never came outside again. My parents didn't emigrate. But I've never gotten over that experience. Every time I come outside, it's exciting. The fear goes away pretty quickly and then it's just . . . intense. I love it. What do you think, Otin?"

Cupra hung in Bogard's hands, head lowered and eyes squeezed shut. He was pale now.

"I take it you don't share my enthusiasm," she said.

"You've made your point," he said tersely. "Do you mind if we go back?"

"No, not at all. After you tell me who gives you instructions."

"Damn it—!"

"We can stay out here all night," Mia said pleasantly. "If you think a sunset is something to see, wait till you experience dawn."

Cupra drew a deep breath, then raised his head and opened his eyes. Mia was impressed. He gazed at the distant horizon for several seconds before finally looking at her.

"What do you want?"

"Answers."

"I can't tell you. You know how it works."

"Sure, I do. But it only counts when it's legal. Last time I checked, covering for a murderer and conspiring to conceal evidence were not things for which we were trained to indulge."

Cupra's eyes closed. He trembled.

"We are going to stay out here all night if necessary. I want to know who's running you."

"You don't know anything. You haven't got any evidence."

"I don't know about that, but if you want to play it that way, fine. Bogard?"

"Yes, Mia?"

"You accessed Service files earlier today."

"Yes, I did, Mia."

"Do you have those files relating to the Service investigation of the Union Station assassinations?"

"Yes, I do."

"Physical evidence. Forensics."

"Fifty-five bullets, nine-millimeter, were recovered from the bodies and surrounding area. Ballistics matches them to the type of weapon recovered from Bok Vin Golner and his associates, which match the rifles recovered from Union Station in the aftermath of the assault."

"Provenance?"

"Specially-built rifles, no traceable provenance. However, the basic frame closely matches weapons seized in a raid two years ago on Mars. The shipment was about to be sold to a buyer from one of the Settler colonies."

"The seller?"

"An agent was arrested and later confessed to being in the employ of Kynig Parapoyos."

"Where were the weapons stored?"

"Standard policy is that all such contraband be destroyed after use as trial evidence. In this instance, no record of such destruction exists. According to the files, the weapons were stored at the Special Service impound facility. A check of the internal log of the impound facility shows that they have not been present for at least six months."

"Interesting," Mia mused. "So the rifles were removed from impound and modified and issued to Managins; namely, Bok Golner. Who does Bok Golner work for, Bogard?"

"His last recorded regular employment was as an environmental technician for Cyvan Industries, a subsidiary of Imbitek."

"I just got done doing a deep background on the bodies of those Managins at Union Station. Every one of them has, at one time or another, been employed by either Imbitek or a subsidiary."

"Very interesting," Cupra said through clamped teeth. "So?"

"Imbitek manufactures imbedded technologies, like the kind found permeating the maintenance nodes of the Union Station Resident Intelligence. An interesting substance. It relays positrons, according to Derec Avery. I didn't understand it very well, but it was fairly clear that whatever it is and however it works, it had something to do with disrupting the entire security net of Union Station. That allowed Golner and his people to get inside with their rifles—rifles that seem very similar to weapons once held in a Special Service impound. Now, all that may be circumstantial and may mean nothing."

"That's right."

"But then you and your partner show up and stop Derec Avery from investigating what went wrong with the RI. Then you show up at the clinic where I was being treated and reassign the agents who *had* been there. And later, you came in and bombed my room."

"You can't prove that!" Cupra bellowed.

Mia ignored him. "Finally, you show up at a facility where contraband has been found, and the very same Managins involved with the assassinations are holding not only the chief roboticist from Union Station and his dead partner, but Derec Avery." She shook her head in mock sadness.

"You seem to be in all the wrong places at all the right times, Otin. And you haven't disputed the fact that it was Golner who did the killing. If you knew that, then why didn't you arrest him? Unless you both take orders from the same source. So, I ask again: Who's giving you instructions?"

Cupra shook his head.

"Bogard, suspend him."

In a swift movement, Bogard let one of Cupra's arms go and grabbed his ankle, then stepped up against the railing and stretched that arm out over the drop. He let the agent's other arm go, and Cupra swung free.

He screamed.

"All the texts tell us that torture doesn't work," Mia said. "But I'm not so sure."

"You bitch!"

Mia frowned. "Oh, *that's* not what I want to hear."

"Bogard won't drop me!"

Mia raised an eyebrow. "You're sure? Bogard is different from other robots. It's already left details out when you asked it questions, and, of course, a robot isn't supposed to be able to do that."

Cupra screamed again. He stopped flailing and let himself go limp. Mia's estimate of his courage went up again.

"Bogard, how many files are there pertaining to the Union Station assault?" Mia asked.

"Forty-seven, Mia."

"Are they available through the general Service data pool?"

"No. Fourteen are open files. The rest are security locked and coded to specific agents."

"Which agents?"

"Cupra and Gambel."

Mia smiled. "Gets better and better. Maybe we don't need you to talk at all, Otin. Seems like Bogard got all the data we need."

"Please." The word came out as a thin whine. Cupra started trembling again, then tried to curl himself up to grab Bogard's arm. He could not quite make it and fell back.

"Who's running you?" Mia barked. "Who set it up?"

"I don't know!"

"Wrong, Otin! You and Gambel have been running around putting out fires. You *have* to know what you're protecting in order to know what fires to smother."

"Lemme up. Please. Mia, I—please!"

"I want a name, Otin. And it has to be the right one. If it isn't, we do this again until it is."

Cupra waved his arms desperately. Suddenly, he said, "Mikels! Alda Mikels!"

"Old news, Otin. Mikels couldn't sabotage security. Who else?"

"Please, for pity's sake!"

"A *name*, Otin."

The silence stretched. Cupra flapped his arms again. If Bogard had not been holding him, he might have worked himself loose and into a fatal fall.

Then: "One! One signed off on the security!"

"Bogard, retrieve."

Bogard brought Cupra back over the rail, snatched his arm, and righted him. The robot stood the agent on his feet and kept a hand on the shaking man's shoulder. Drool ran down Cupra's chin. He glared at Mia with open hatred and terror.

"One," Mia repeated. "And Alda Mikels. How does that work? Make it sing, Otin."

"Can we go inside?"

"After you convince me."

Cupra swallowed, closed his eyes, and nodded. "There's a consortium of patriots. Mikels heads it. One is a member. When Eliton first proposed this conference, Mikels approached One to discuss ways to stop it. One came to us."

"Us? You and Gambel?"

"Yes."

"Why you two?"

"History. We were in the military with Golner."

"Mikels gave Golner a job. How did Mikels know Golner?"

"His . . . son . . . was in Golner's unit. He died in the Ganymede action."

"I'm going to check this, Otin."

"It's true! I swear!"

Mia watched the man for a few moments. "All right, Otin. We'll continue this below."

He nodded gratefully.

"Bring him, Bogard."

The robot moved Cupra toward the lounge. Mia caught Michensol's eyes then, and saw the mix of respect and disgust. She felt bad enough without his reproach, so she gave him nothing.

"Shall we?" she asked.

"Of course."

Michensol went first. Mia gave the approaching sunset another look before following.

TWENTY-NINE

A riel stepped into the foyer of Gale Chassik's offices and stopped, baffled by the scene of calm. The receptionist looked up and smiled.

"Ambassador Burgess," he said. "Ambassador Chassik will be with you in a few minutes."

"Yes, thank you . . ."

Besides the receptionist, two robots occupied niches. No one else was in the room, and while she waited only two com messages came through. It was very much business-as-usual, as orderly as her own offices were chaotic.

Chassik's door opened and a man came out. He crossed in front of the reception desk and glanced at Ariel. He nodded politely, and left.

"Ariel," Chassik called from his doorway. "Good to see you. Come in, come in. I've been meaning to send you a formal congratulations on your promotion. I've been remiss."

"It's only temporary, Gale, nothing to get ceremonious about."

He smiled. "Who can say what's temporary these days? I've been a diplomat almost fifty years now, and I've seen far more 'temporary' changes become permanent fixtures than I care to think about."

"In that case," Ariel said, walking past him into his chambers, "I accept your apology and thank you for your sentiments. I—"

Jonis Taprin stood by one of the two chairs facing Chassik's desk. "Ariel." He smiled hesitantly.

"I believe you know each other," Chassik said as he resumed his own chair.

"Yes, of course," Ariel said. "Senator Taprin."

Jonis's smile faltered. "Ambassador."

Chassik seemed amused, but he said nothing. Ariel took the chair opposite Taprin and sat down.

"Forgive me not telling you that we'd have another party to our discussion," Chassik said. "Senator Taprin, being the successor to Senator Eliton, I think has a special interest in the events of the past week."

"Likely as not," Ariel conceded. "But what I have to discuss with you is confidential."

"Even from—?"

"Right at the moment," Ariel cut in, "I don't see that Senator Taprin has our best interests in mind."

"That's unfair, Ariel," Jonis said.

She looked at him evenly. "No? Your state police are still harassing Auroran nationals. I asked for a word from you to put a halt to it until we can sort out what's going on, and all I got was Terran phobias."

"Senator Taprin," Chassik said, "has come to me with a proposal for putting an end to the harassment."

Jonis's face was slightly red, but he held his temper. "I *did* talk to the head of TBI after our earlier talk. The investigation is not gratuitous, Ariel. A few of your people have been trading in illicit goods. The TBI is following up on an inquiry that began over a year ago."

"Let me guess. Just after the *Tiberius* incident."

"There are very specific laws concerning the possession of positronic robots on Earth," Jonis continued. "The TBI has found a number of violations."

"Are they looking into the same violations on the part of Terrans?"

"Ariel—" Chassik began.

"Why now? If this has been an ongoing investigation, why push it now? All they're doing is fueling a panic that could drive most of the Spacer population off Earth. With them goes any hope of improved trade relations, and with that, Earth stands to lose a great deal of money, not to mention risking future conflicts."

"Is that a threat?" Taprin asked.

"No, just a statement of fact. Don't pretend you don't understand me, Senator. Nobody wins from this. The only reason for the TBI to do what it's doing right now is to drive a wedge between Terrans and Spacers. They could just as easily carry out their investigation quietly and *later,* after we have the people in custody who have committed murder. Murder, by the way, against Spacers as well as Terrans."

"Yes, well . . ." Chassik pursed his lips. "There's the complication, Ariel. It seems that arrests are imminent."

"Oh?"

"It seems," Taprin said, "that the assault—the conspiracy—was Auroran in origin."

Ariel stared at him. "You have got to be joking."

"He's not," Chassik said. "What's more, they apparently have some evidence connecting you to it."

"Evidence? *What* evidence?"

"I'm not at liberty to—"

Ariel stood and glared down at Taprin. "Don't give me that, you son-of-a-bitch! Any evidence they claim to have is manufactured and you damn well know it!"

"Please, Ariel," Chassik said, "calm down. You're certainly in no danger, at least not from them. As long as you remain within embassy grounds they can't even question you."

"Question me about what? How *dare* you believe this, Gale! The assassins were Managins! Order for the Supremacy of Man Again! What possible connection can you make between them and me?"

"It concerns the contraband," Taprin said, marshalling himself. "Now sit down and I'll tell you what I can."

Reluctantly, fighting rage, Ariel made herself resume her chair. Taprin shifted in his own seat, as if physically trying to recover lost dignity.

"The TBI were looking at a man named Udal," he explained. "He operates one of the largest retail outlets for drones and automatons. They've suspected him of dealing in illicit positronics for some time. Earlier today, a facility was seized in the Convention Center District that contained a large stock of undeclared imports, including a cache of positronic brains. The shipment was linked to similar ones that have been traced to Udal's warehouse where he apparently has an operation to switch nonpositronic AI plants with these, converting an otherwise legal drone into a fully positronic robot. In the same facility was found a number of people who have been connected to the same group that did the killings at Union Station. Before Udal could be arrested, you had him picked up by your security people and brought under diplomatic cover to your embassy. You've had dealings with Udal in the past. You knew about the facility in question. You basically rescued Udal from imminent arrest. What else are we to conclude?"

"That possibly I was trying to shut down the same illicit trade?"

"If you were doing that," Taprin said quietly, "why didn't you come to me? I thought the whole point of this conference was to increase cooperation between us."

"Why?" Ariel snorted. "Quite obviously because I couldn't trust you."

"Ariel," Chassik said, "we can help—"

"Help with what?"

"The repercussions."

Ariel grew still. Not calm, no, but clear, understanding. "Perfect. This is perfect. I'm implicated in covering for the black market and in one stroke you discredit me, Aurora, and the Humadros-Eliton treaty. The political fallout reduces Aurora's influence on Terra, and Solaria steps forward to become the new broker of agreements, the defender of Earth-Spacer relations. And I walked right into it. I thought I was doing everything I could to avoid this kind of incident and I walked right into it. Very elegant. Neat."

"Ariel," Taprin said, "what are you talking about?"

"I suppose Derec Avery is implicated, too?"

The senator looked troubled. "Phylaxis has been servicing the illegal robots. Collusion at best. But—"

"Perfect. You know, if you worked this hard and this well to solve problems and do the right thing, the universe would—oh, hell, what am I saying? There's no profit to be made from *that*, is there?" She got to her feet.

"Ariel—" Taprin began.

"Ambassador Burgess to you, Senator."

Taprin snapped his mouth shut and paled. He shook his head and looked away.

"My offer to help remains open," Chassik said.

"I'm sure it does, Gale. I'll let you know later what you can do with it."

Ariel felt a slight trembling in her legs as she walked out of his office and left the Solarian quarter. She had badly wanted to tell them what she now knew, how elegantly they had not only compromised her entire position but given themselves away as well, but she did not know yet if that information could be used to her advantage. The parts assembled themselves neatly now. They could not have known that she would recognize the visitor who had left before Chassik had ushered her in to hear the sentence they handed her on her career. They could not know that she held his partner and that Mia Daventri, whom they also did not know was still alive, was interrogating him.

No, she was right to keep it to herself. A name was still missing—the keystone, the node that connected Taprin and Chassik to the man she had recognized as Special Agent Gambel.

"Very clever," Mia agreed. "A perfect trap."

Ariel nodded dreamily. It did not seem real, not back in her own office, amid people who knew her, trusted her, and depended on her. She was not letting them down, not Ariel Burgess, not *Ambassador* Ariel Burgess. That promotion was now a hideous weight. Had she remained only the Institute liaison, the political consequences of all this would never, bad as they might have been, amounted to the catastrophe before her.

"I spoke with Setaris already," she said, subdued. "She wants me to confine myself to the compound. The embassy offices or my apartments. If I go out, she can't guarantee my safety."

"Safety?" Mia said. "You're a diplomat. You can't be arrested."

"I think she was more concerned for the image of the embassy."

"It always bothered me a little," Derec said abruptly, "about the ambulance. Why hadn't they changed the ID markers? It seemed a stupid oversight."

"They wanted it followed," Mia said. "Somebody would have, eventually—probably a newsnet investigator—and it would have led to the same TBI discovery of contraband. It was just a bonus that Ariel found it."

"It's a good assumption that our little excursion there was recorded," Ariel said.

"Traps within traps," Derec mused. "But then, where's Eliton's body?"

"It might never be found," Mia said. "Even if it is and the cadaver in the morgue is announced as a fake, it still points to Spacers."

"How does that follow?" Ariel asked.

"The biotech. Cloning. We only do a little of it here; it's mostly illegal. Exceptions are made for rare blood groups or certain organs with high rejection factors—exotic stuff. But Spacers . . ."

"Ah. It doesn't explain the switch, though."

"Does it have to? The more layers we peel back from this, the more solid the conclusions become that Spacers were behind this. All it took was one good connection to the black market, and Udal handed that to them. What I don't get is the Solarian's connection."

"Oh, that's simple," Ariel said. "They can use this as a political fulcrum to lever themselves into the dominant position in the Fifty Worlds. For them, this is a perfect opportunity to become the primary Spacer world."

"But the RI," Mia insisted. "They allowed the corruption of a positronic brain. I thought that was a sort of blasphemy to you."

"Anywhere else but Earth," Derec said. "Prejudice cuts both ways. When Chassik offered to let me have the RI, it would have been a perfect way to get rid of it before it was shipped back to Solaria. I'm sure they could lose it anyway, but if I'd accepted it, then it would be one more bit of incriminating evidence linking us to the murders. And Chassik could deny all knowledge, since I was supposed to be the legal service for that system anyway. At best, Phylaxis was negligent. At worst, collusive."

"And if they had managed to take out Eliton's personal security and implicate Bogard . . ." Mia shook her head. "No one would be able to give a credible alternative account. The Spacers set up the conference to kill Eliton and damage Earth's position in all future trade negotiations. It would look like they had tried to make it appear that it was a Terran plot and they botched it."

"What about Cupra?" Ariel asked. "Has he told us anything worth while?"

"He hasn't stopped talking," Mia said. "But it's all verification of what we already knew." She frowned. "With one exception. The head of Special Service is involved. One signed off on everything they did, ran interference from other agents, and encrypted a lot of data under his personal seal. It made sense once I heard it. Someone had to compromise the external security links at Union Station, and since we were overseeing it . . ."

"You sound dissatisfied with that," Derec said.

Mia held up her hand and counted off points on her fingers. "We have Alda Mikels—the funding, the personnel, and the tech to undermine the RI. We have the head of

Special Service—equipment, communications, and security, plus the cover-up afterward. We have the Solarian ambassador—collusion, diversion of legitimate Spacer interests, and the source of the final list of targets."

"That's a guess," Ariel said.

"Are you inclined to argue?"

"No."

"All right. We have all these people, plus a few fringe players—Kynig Parapoyos is an obvious choice for the contraband—and Udal, and maybe even Senator Taprin."

"I'm inclined to think that he's going along with what he's being handed by everyone else," Ariel said. "I've known him a long time. He's not fundamentally a bad man."

"Whatever." Mia shrugged. "But which one is the prime mover? They still all look like parts of the conspiracy to me. Which one came up with the plan and initiated the operation and organized it?"

"Cupra says it's Mikels," Derec said.

"I don't think Cupra knows. Why should he?" Mia shook her head. "Mikels makes a good figurehead for something like this, but the primary? I don't think so."

"Sounds like your One could do it," Derec said.

"At first glance, but why would the Solarians listen to him? For that matter, why would he listen to the Solarians? And why would either of them listen to Alda Mikels? Money? Does Gale Chassik need money? Influence? What could Mikels offer the head of Special Service?" She shook her head. "Something's missing."

"What about Golner?" Ariel asked.

"No, he's just muscle."

There was a knock on the door. Ariel turned in her chair. "Yes?"

Bogard entered the room.

"Your pardon, Ms. Burgess," it said. "I have a question."

"Yes, Bogard?" Derec said.

"I would like to know if your investigation is concluded."

"We're determining that now, Bogard," Ariel said.

"If I may offer my help. I have concluded that the conspiracy is composed of a pyramidal arrangement of persons. Several were hired for specific tasks without knowledge of the whole plan. Tathis Kedder, for instance, and Shor Udal. I imagine that many of the actual assassins knew little of the overall strategy. Above them were Agents Cupra and Gambel, who knew more but still not everything. Their counterparts would be people like Bok Vin Golner. At least three knew the entirety of it."

"We've just reached the same conclusion, Bogard," Mia said. "Our candidates are Ambassador Gale Chassik, Alda Mikels of Imbitek, and the head of Special Service, One."

"I concur," Bogard said. "With the arrest of those three, the entire conspiracy should be exposed. That being the case, I must ask if I may be allowed to resume my primary obligation."

"Which is what?" Derec asked.

"I was assigned to protect Senator Eliton."

"Senator Eliton is dead, Bogard," Ariel said.

"Your pardon, Ambassador, but there is no evidence on which to confidently base that conclusion. My assessment is that a high probability exists that Senator Eliton is still alive, and it is my duty to find and protect him. If it is all the same to you, I would like to pursue that responsibility."

THIRTY

Among the weapons we confiscated at the garage," Bogard explained, "we recovered two sets of personal documents. I have run a check through civic records and determined that they are forged. However, both also included passes for above-ground access to the Manassas Preserves."

"Cupra said something about Manassas before you rescued me," Derec said.

"There is a section of the Preserve operated by a Settler colonial recruiting organ and leased by OSMA. They run a nature camp. There was a report filed the day after the Union Station assault that the OSMA camp was investigated and searched. Nothing was found."

"Who filed the report?" Mia asked.

"Agent Gambel."

"Imagine that," Ariel said.

"So why do you believe Eliton is there, Bogard?" Derec asked.

"It is a matter of probabilities. Managins, apparently under control of Bok Vin Golner, staged the assault at Union Station. During the aftermath, Senator Eliton's body was switched and the legitimate one was taken to the garage where you found the ambulance used, contraband positronics, and were then taken as prisoner by the very same Bok Vin Golner. The Managins run a camp in the Manassas Preserve, which was investigated by one of the corrupt agents who have exerted an inhibitory influence on this entire matter. Obviously, there is something there they wish to keep undiscovered. Given all the possibilities, it is the most likely place to begin a search for Senator Eliton."

"Why hold him prisoner?" Ariel asked.

Derec shrugged. Mia pursed her lips.

"I have no conclusion on that matter, Ambassador Burgess," Bogard said.

"Call me Ariel, Bogard. 'Ambassador Burgess' is clumsy and, right now, problematic."

"Yes, Ariel."

"So," Mia said, "we go look and see. Bogard, are you game for a little open-air field work?"

"I am prepared to do this alone," Bogard said. "This is my responsibility, the risk is high, and I am capable of—"

"Bogard," Derec interrupted. "We're going."

"We?" Mia said. "Me and Bogard—"

"Of course we're going," Ariel said. "There's no question. It would make me crazy now to sit and wait while you two thrashed around in the woods."

"But—"

Derec shook his head. "Don't bother, Agent Daventri."

Mia looked at them, then shrugged. "I won't argue too much. Let me brief you on the weapons. Ariel, we'll need Hofton to get us some things. Bogard, whether you approve or not, we're going with you."

* * *

Bogard bypassed the security lock on a Solarian embassy transport. They loaded a pair of packs in the back and piled aboard. Mia programmed the vehicle for their destination and sat up front during their exit from the garage.

"I only see one TBI vehicle," she called back as they rolled onto the main avenue. "There are more, I'm sure."

"If everybody keeps a level head," Ariel said, "we might get through this without starting a war."

The transport left the Anacostia District unchallenged. Mia came back and started changing her clothes, pulling on the same nonreflective, graphite-black suit they all wore. Bogard's surface was even less reflective; it made an ominous, cloudy presence by the rear doors.

"Anything else you need to go over about your weapons?" Mia asked. "The suits are invisible to most sensor arrays and give back no heat or light. If you're standing in the open under bright illumination you will be visible, but if you keep to shadows, close to larger structures, and avoid direct line-of-sight, we should be able to get in and out without being seen. I've set all your sidearms on heavy stun."

"What about yours?" Derec asked.

"Never mind that. If any killing has to occur, it's on my head."

"I thought with Bogard—" Ariel began.

"Bogard can't be everywhere at once," Mia interrupted. "We learned that. It also has limitations that we don't have; we found that out, too. I won't risk any of us over an ethical qualm. But it's my decision."

"How are you doing?" Derec asked. "Your leg—"

"Hofton got me some painblock that makes me feel like I could run a marathon. I feel wonderful."

"All right," Ariel said, "one more time. What is it we're looking for?"

"Any place where someone might be hidden or confined that wouldn't be obvious on a casual visit. So I'm thinking a storage facility or an underground bunker of some kind. We have the ground plan from the camp's registration file, but obviously that's not going to have anything new or illegal. We'll just have to do a thorough sweep."

"Bogard could do it a lot faster," Derec said.

"Bogard *will* do it, but I want us in there looking as well. Bogard might miss something we wouldn't."

"Unlikely."

"What I really want Bogard to do is sweep the perimeter, nullify as much security as possible, and plot us an escape route. Can you do that, Bogard?"

"Of course, Mia. That was my first intention."

"Excellent. Getting out might be a lot harder than getting in."

"You sound like you expect this to be an armed camp," Ariel said.

"If Golner had any say in setting it up, it will be."

"Overtly?"

"At night, what difference would it make? We assume the worst and hope for the best. Now, until we reach the transition point, go over the maps, memorize them."

The Manassas Preserve occupied a vast area of land roughly fifty kilometers from the heart of D.C. Townships once dotted the countryside, all of them now gone or abandoned to wilderness. Densely forested, the Preserve had been one of the surface areas set aside for the Settler's program. Over time, other groups interested in "open" experiences had come to use it, and a couple had requested and received special licenses for continual use. To most Terrans, those who chose to spend long stretches of time outside the warrens of the cities were weird. They were watched occasionally, but largely left alone.

A main throughway, a major traffic artery that connected D.C. to Cincinnati, ran just north of the Preserve. A trunk line split off for the few transports that went directly to Manassas.

Mia directed their vehicle off the trunk line and into the service tunnels alongside. Most of the traffic here was automated and sparse. She found a garage for local technical vehicles and parked the transport among them. Unless an audit occurred in the next few hours, the system would log their vehicle and file the data, but would alert no one.

Bogard unfolded from the back of the transport. A jagged patch of night, he looked menacing and unpleasantly efficient. The white line of the optical array dimmed to a smokey grey.

Mia pulled her night veil over her face and the others did likewise. The garage sprang into full detail from the combination of radar, infrared, and neutrino-shadow-amplification the veils interpreted for them. Even with all that enhancement their suits showed almost no detail; Bogard gave even less.

"Ready?" Mia asked.

They nodded.

Bogard led the way back into the trunk line and they headed south.

The road ended at a vast parking lot. Several transports clustered against one end, but it was mostly empty. Steps led up to the entrance to a wide pavilion in which booths and galleries provided a history of the area and related data.

During normal hours, it was easy to imagine tours coming this far, people winding their way through the displays, still safely under a roof, and going no farther, retreating to the safety of the warrens after a brief, dissociated brush with wildness and the Outside. A few, perhaps, might later come back to take the last few steps into the open air.

But now it was deserted, testament to the circadian of day and night from which the retreat underground had failed to free humans.

"Do we just go through the front door?" Derec asked.

"There is an employee entrance," Bogard said and moved off to the right, skirting the wall of the garage.

They had no cover now, but had to rely on the suits Mia had obtained for them to hide them from any surveillance. They followed Mia's lead and scurried along quickly in Bogard's wake.

The door Bogard opened for them led into dark corridors that connected a set of offices, a food service plant, a machine shop, and laboratories. One of the labs offered access to a tunnel that ended at a door marked CAUTION: BEYOND THIS POINT IS UNCANOPIED AREA.

"Nice of them to let us know," Derec said. "Bogard, is the door keyed to an alarm?"

The robot pressed itself against the door for a few seconds. Suddenly, it slid open.

"No, Derec," Bogard said.

"Thanks," Ariel hissed.

Beyond, a poured concrete apron ended at dense underbrush, through which a ground stone path led into a tangle of towering trees. Mia sucked her breath loudly.

"What?" Derec asked.

"Nothing," she said. "It's just . . . been a while. It's beautiful."

"The OSMA enclave is this way," Bogard said and headed for the trail.

After walking for nearly a kilometer, Bogard stopped.

"We should leave the path here," it said. "There are sensors further along."

"How far from the camp?" Mia asked.

"Three hundred meters."

"Find us a way in first, Bogard. Let's go."

They plunged into the woods, off the trail. The foliage stood out sharply in the general wash of sensor impressions. Without the depth provided by the radar it would all have appeared to be a senseless array of meaningless detail—wrinkles and lines and textures cobbled together with only a kind of vertical tendency to suggest any order. It was easy to imagine people who had spent all their lives in artificial environments—the tunnels, chambers, and warrens of Earth's cities—becoming instantly and horribly lost out here simply because nothing made visual sense. It was not only the agoraphobia that came with vast, open spaces that hobbled Terrans—there were large spaces within all Earth's inhabited areas—but the fear of disorder, the unpredictability of organic chaos, the *alienness* of the life of their own world which they had so carefully built to deny.

And yet there were parks within the cities, though they were tame places, manicured and confined. This wilderness overwhelmed and obeyed no geometry.

Bogard seemed to shift between obstacles, the shapes oozing around it as if they did not exist. A mirage, like heat rising off a flat surface, looked like that, rippling and indistinct. Bogard made no sound, disturbed nothing, passed through like a breeze. Derec had not known such movement was possible. Then he realized that Bogard's amalloy body was twisting and distorting and reshaping constantly to accommodate its passage. He glanced toward Ariel, but he could not see her face through the night veil. He imagined her staring at Bogard, impressed and a little frightened.

Bogard stopped a few meters from a break in the tree line.

"Wait," it said, and oozed slowly forward. It returned in less than a minute. "The boundary is a perimeter sensor. There is no physical barrier, but the sensor will trigger an alarm. It is possible that it can also release a mild electrical shock, but it seems unlikely. Please wait one full minute, then follow me out."

Bogard faded through the underbrush again. Around them, the forest hummed with rhythmic, organic sounds. Derec's pulse pounded in his ears.

"Now," Mia said quietly and he started.

They came out of the trees at the edge of a cleared strip of land. Across from them stood prefab barracks in neat rows. Walkways ran among them. A larger structure dominated the center of the compound—a kind of community center, Derec thought—and glowed more brightly than any other building, most of the windows illuminated from within.

Bogard was wrapped around a post. At five-meter intervals stood identical posts, each with a knobby crown—the sensor array—and all of them giving false readings back to whoever monitored them. Bogard was using its body to deflect and reroute connecting signals.

"Make sure you pass below one-point-seven-five meters," Bogard said. "I am maintaining a carrier signal above that height."

Mia crouched low and sprinted across the invisible boundary. Derec and Ariel copied her and hurried after. A few moments later, Bogard was among them, a silent, lithic presence.

"All right," Mia said. "Take your sectors of the camp, do your search, and rendezvous at the main building. Bogard, do the perimeter, secure what you can, guarantee us a way out."

Bogard vanished.

"I wish it wouldn't do that," Ariel said.

"Go," Mia said and scurried away.

"Good luck," Derec said.

"Be careful," Ariel answered.

tactical parameters, standard field sensor perimeter, motion sensor capacity damped to ignore thirty kilograms and below, internal monitoring at entries and exits only, two human patrols walking perimeter equipped with nightvision, limited to infrared only, armed with stunners, garage containing five unmodified terrain vehicles, no surveillance, six barracks, three unoccupied, three containing eighteen individuals each, one barracks provisioned with supply of lethal weapons, three blasters and eight projectile rifles, all personnel in barracks currently asleep, monitoring links fed to each barracks, connections to perimeter sensors, patrols, and main building, generator housed in main building supplying camp power, dedicated line to feed shock field keyed to perimeter sensor, thirty-thousand volts, zero amperes, non fatal charge, direct line disconnected, monitor connection to barracks' disconnected, patrols tranquilized, UTVs depowered by removal of battery packs, internal security nullified, external security unknown, potential estimated low threat

I must locate Senator Eliton

Primary responsibility, automatic reset
I must locate and secure Primary
I must locate Senator Eliton
First and Second Law violations minimal, camp secured,
risk potential low, competency level, Daventri, Mia, suffi-
cient, competency level, Avery, Derec, sufficient, competency
level, Burgess, Ariel, unknown, tentatively assigned suffi-
cient based on available data and observation, threat man-
ageable
I must locate Senator Eliton

Aside from the barracks, the camp contained a communal
shower, a communal mess with its own kitchens, and a supply shed. Ariel had checked the shower and mess. The
supply shed did not appear locked.

She had passed two guards not fifteen meters back who
had been tranquilized—by Bogard, she hoped—and she had
removed their stunners and tossed them into the trees, over
the range of the perimeter. She did not know where Bogard
was and wished she did, but she did not risk calling for it.

She adjusted her grip on the stunner. The blaster nestled
against the small of her back, but she did not want to pull
it yet. If it came to that, then they would probably have to
burn the entire camp down, and she did not know if she
could do that.

She pushed open the door of the shed and a light winked
on inside. She pulled it shut immediately, pulse racing, and
surveyed the camp, waiting for a rush of angry Managins.
When they failed to materialize, she slipped quickly into the
shed.

On one wall hung a variety of hand tools, most of them
worn and dirty from use. Against the opposite wall stood

boxes of pamphlets. She opened one and pulled out the slim sheaf of paperlike plastic, amused at the novelty.

IDENTIFYING AND ANALYZING WILDNERNESS SPOOR the title read. Ariel leafed through it quickly. A wildlife guide. She checked through others—CLEANING AND DRESSING OF INJURIES IN THE WILD, CAMPSITE ERGONOMICS AND ECOLOGICAL AWARE-NESS, PERSONAL HYGIENE IN UNMODIFIED TERRITORY—impressed despite herself at the evident attention to the details of living outside an urban environment.

She followed the line down to the end. On top of each crate one of the pamphlets had been placed in an attached sleeve. Except the last one.

Ariel pried the lid up and found another stack of pamphlets. These contained a picture of Clar Eliton below a banner that declared ELITON FOR TERRA FIRST. She pulled one out and opened it.

Mia reached the first-floor veranda of the main building at the same time as Derec. They sat next to each other below one of the few unlit windows.

"Anything?" he asked.

"No. Where's Ariel?"

"I don't know. I thought she was over there." He pointed toward the west end of the enclave. "This is the last building."

"That we know about."

He shrugged.

Mia began crawling along the veranda, keeping below the windows. Derec followed.

The veranda encircled the building. At each window, Mia risked a quick look inside, then continued on. Derec trusted her that she saw nothing important in any of these rooms.

They climbed the stairs to the second floor balcony on all fours.

Immediately, they heard voices.

Mia moved carefully but faster than Derec could match and still keep quiet. He caught up to her beneath a broad window. Voices came from within and when Derec looked up at the opening he, saw that, instead of a solid surface, it was only screened. Mia knelt before it, her head just above the sill so she could see in.

"—a mess. Should've stayed arrested—"

"—not my style—"

"Style be damned!"

Derec felt his scalp tingle; he recognized the voice. He raised himself up to Mia's level.

The room was large and comfortable, with heavy divans and thick armchairs scattered about. Lamps cast conflicting though warm and pleasant shadows over the tables and walls and the three men facing each other in a loose triangle.

Agent Gambel held a glass. Across from him stood Bok Golner, still in his black fatigues, scowling at the man seated before them. Derec's unease multiplied at the sight of Senator Eliton, sitting in a low chair, a drink at his elbow, dressed in an evening jacket.

"It shouldn't make any difference at this point," Gambel said. "We have the robot, the TBI have seized four Spacer warehouses containing contraband, and Phylaxis has been shut down under a warrant based on illegal service to contraband robots. The Spacers are looking worse and worse. All we need to do now is drop the last bit of evidence on Taprin's desk and there'll be a general outcry to throw the Aurorans off Earth."

Eliton sighed wearily. "I don't know what you think this

accomplishes. Anything could undo the whole thing, like finding *him—*" he stabbed a finger at Golner "*—here*, when he ought to be in jail with the rest of his goons."

"I don't do that," Golner said.

"Do what?" Eliton demanded.

"Serve time in an institution. I already did that once."

"You should remember how to follow orders," Gambel said.

Golner's face reddened. He opened his mouth to speak.

But the door opened behind him, and suddenly Bogard was in the room with them.

"Shit," Derec hissed.

Several things happened.

Eliton stood abruptly, knocking his drink off the table.

Golner drew a weapon and began to turn. Bogard touched Golner's hand, but the Managin flinched away, letting the pistol fly. He ducked under Bogard grasp, so *fast* that Derec almost could not follow his turn as he twisted around Bogard's left flank and bolted for the door.

Gambel dropped his glass and reached for his sidearm.

Mia threw herself through the screen, weapon drawn. "Bogard!" she cried.

Bogard, reaching for Golner, hesitated.

Eliton dropped to his knees and came up holding Golner's pistol.

"Thank god!" he shouted and shot Gambel.

Bogard's entire body seemed to unfold and suddenly refold around Eliton.

Golner staggered from the room.

Mia ran to the doorway, leaned out, and fired twice.

Derec got to his feet.

It all too place in a few seconds.

Derec stepped into the room and went to Gambel. His face was distorted, the eyeballs pulped and oozing—the effects of a heavy stun at nearly pointblank range. Derec looked away.

"Time to leave," Mia said. "Bogard, do you have the Senator secured?"

"Yes, Mia."

"Don't let him out unless absolutely necessary and not on his command. Clear?"

"I understand, Mia."

"Escape route."

Bogard swept out of the window and down the outside stairs.

"Platoon!" Golner shouted from somewhere below. "Compromise! The perimeter has been compromised!"

"Move," Mia urged Derec.

They followed Bogard down to the ground and hurried across the enclave. Behind them, people were spilling from two of the barracks.

"Where's Ariel?" Derec asked.

Ahead, they saw a figure running to intercept them, barely a shadow against larger shadows. She waved and Derec knew it was Ariel.

Bogard stopped at the perimeter. "Please step against me," it said.

"What—?" Mia began.

"Like this." Derec pressed himself to Bogard's side. The amalloy skin warped around him. A few moments later, he felt Bogard begin to move.

Bogard ran directly through the perimeter. The voltage discharged against it, but coursed around the robot and grounded harmlessly. Just within the tree line, the shielding retracted and let Derec, Ariel, and Mia out.

"This way," Bogard said, and plunged through the underbrush.

The distant, distinct pops of gunfire sounded behind them. The whiz and snap of bullets tearing through leaves and branches overhead made them duck involuntarily.

"The shots are random," Mia said. "They can't see us."

The rate of fire increased.

"Eventually one of them will get lucky," Ariel complained.

They were running now, arms outstretched to fend off the whipping branches.

Suddenly, Bogard stopped and let them catch up and pass.

"Bogard, what—?" Mia called.

"I cannot accept the level of risk to you. Please take Senator Eliton in your care."

Derec stopped. Bogard opened up and Eliton stumbled out from within the enshielding. He looked around frantically, eyes wide, still holding Golner's weapon.

Mia stepped up to him. "Senator," she said, and deftly took the pistol from him. "This way, please."

"It's a miracle you showed up," Eliton said and looked around, puzzled that he could barely see his rescuers. "Whoever you are."

"Talk later, move now," Mia said and took his elbow.

They continued on.

Derec looked back to see what Bogard intended. Bogard followed, but its body seemed to grow even as Derec watched. Bogard had dispensed with its stealth shielding. It was a bright coppery target now, making itself wider and higher. Beyond, the gunfire resumed and Derec heard the bullets impact on Bogard. Then he heard the wash of a blaster.

Bogard's entire body seemed to shudder and glow.

"Run, Derec," Bogard ordered.

Derec ran.

They reached the path and sprinted back toward the orientation center. It sounded like a small army attacking Bogard, and Derec winced at the staccato sounds.

Just as the door came into sight, a dozen men poured onto the path, blocking their way, all armed and converging on them. Derec skidded to a stop and backpedaled.

"Sir!" someone shouted, but Derec did not stop.

He crashed into the woods and tried to find a place to hide. Before him now rose an eerie specter, a sheen of gold through the foliage, rippling and moving. As he stared at the sight, he realized that it was Bogard, stretched out like a blanket between him and the Managins in pursuit. Derec understood the potential for Bogard to manage this, but it still amazed him.

But it was too much. Holes were appearing in the skin. They rehealed almost at once—except in a couple of spots where they were ragged, the edges flapping uselessly. Bogard was losing integrity and could no longer absorb the impacts.

As he watched, Bogard seemed to shred into fragments.

"No!" Derec screamed.

Then the second group caught up to him.

Instead of seizing him, though, they passed him, driving into the woods, and firing at the Managins.

Derec backed away.

Something closed on his neck painfully. He tried to turn, but could not. Then he hit the gravel on his back.

When he looked up, someone knelt on his chest, aiming a pistol at his face.

"Let's see who we have now," Golner said and lifted Derec's veil. "Spacer boy. Great. Are you worth my trouble? Will you get me out of here? It's a good question, isn't it?"

Derec swung at Golner, aiming to knock the weapon aside. Golner just held it out of harm's way, then punched Derec in the sternum—a short, hard blow that knocked the wind from him.

"No chance," Golner said. "You'll be more trouble than you're worth."

He aimed again.

A coppery tendril snaked around Golner's body, encircled his wrist, and jerked the gun up. It went off, a loud crack of thunder that set Derec's ears ringing.

Golner struggled briefly, then tried to turn the pistol in the direction of his assailant. The barrel came around, the wrist still held by Bogard's tendril. Golner tried to twist so he could see; the barrel of the gun came close to his head. Bogard flexed to turn the weapon away, and it went off again.

Golner's head burst open in a spray of blood and bone.

Derec screamed and pushed himself away.

People surrounded him, but their guns were aimed at Golner's corpse.

It lay now, half its head gone, a copper strand wrapped around its waist and wrist. Derec followed the line of the strand into the woods to a shapeless mass of material that glowed dimly in the first vague light of approaching dawn.

"Violation . . . violation . . ." The voice was weak and tinny. "First Law violation . . . unacceptable . . . vio—vi—vi-olation . . ."

Gradually the voice faded away, and the forest was still.

* * *

Agent Sathen knelt before Derec and offered him a cup.

"I don't understand," Derec said.

"It's coffee," Sathen said.

Derec shook his head. "I mean you. What are *you* doing here?"

Sathen gave him a wry grin. "Did you think none of us were doing anything?"

"Does One know you're here?" Mia asked. She pointed past him. "With TBI agents?"

Sathen looked at her. "Good question for a corpse. No, One doesn't. Or maybe he does. He's gone. We moved to arrest him when this phase began."

Mia nodded as if the answer meant everything.

"—woke up out here, I had no idea what had happened," Senator Eliton's voice drifted over to them.

Sathen looked toward the group of agents surrounding the Senator and shook his head. "I'm amazed. I really expected—"

"That he was really dead?" Ariel asked.

"No. But that he'd be off the planet."

Ariel cocked an eyebrow. "You believe Spacers were behind this?"

"Not all of you. The fake bodies in the morgue are Spacer biotech—"

"Which can be purchased easily enough," Ariel said.

Sathen shrugged. "But we have him back."

"For better or worse," Ariel said.

Sathen frowned. "I thought you'd be pleased. We found the assassins, shut down their operation, and recovered Senator Eliton. He's the best friend you people have."

"Is he really?"

Sathen stared at her for a time, then stood. "Whatever. You politicos can sort it out from here."

He walked off. Eliton continued to talk, describing his ordeal among the fanatic Managins.

Ariel pulled a pamphlet out of her jacket and passed it to Mia. "You might find this instructive," she said.

Mia opened it and silently began to read.

Another agent came up to Derec. "Are you Avery?"

"Yes."

"We gathered up what was left of Bogard. Nothing seems to be working anymore. What do you want us to do with him?"

"Deliver it—him—to Phylaxis."

The agent nodded and walked away. Derec sat quietly for a moment, staring off into space, Bogard's last words echoing in his head. He felt numb. Then he suddenly started, his mind clearing. –

"Phylaxis," he muttered, then groaned. "Rana."

"Don't worry," Ariel said. She placed a consoling hand on his shoulder. "We'll work on getting your people out of confinement in the morning."

Derec nodded and sat there then, listening to Eliton drone on, and watched the company of agents try to sort out prisoners and bodies and logistics. He drank his coffee and tried not to think.

After a while, Mia stood and walked over to Eliton. Derec heard her speaking, but could make out none of the words. Then she held out the pamphlet Ariel had given her and tossed it in the senator's lap. She walked off. Eliton stared at the pamphlet. The other agents watched Mia.

EPILOGUE

Record module CF942 attach log sequencing file "Zealots Inc." running virtual conference Maui Overlook fill visual fill audio status on

T his will be our last meeting under these circumstances," the thick man with amber-tinged white hair announced. Only three others sat around the table. "I'm arranging for another medium, which I will let you all know about in due course. Circumstances have forced me to remove myself from easy access. However, I think we can agree that, in spite of a wrinkle or two we didn't foresee, things have worked out neatly."

"A wrinkle or two? We damn near started a war."

"But we didn't, did we? We aren't at war. Yet. The conference ended without a treaty, the Aurorans have been thoroughly compromised, and in six months we can resume traffic with even less interference than we had before now that Risher is out of the way. I already have commitments from two Settler colonies for new bases."

"What about Eliton? He's fighting a losing battle."

"In your opinion. I think he'll manage to win reelection. Taprin is just not as good a campaigner."

"But he's untainted. We might do better to back him. Those files that agent spilled into the public database on his past associations with Mikels and Golner are doing a lot of damage. Even if he wins he may be a spent force."

The chairman considered that for a time, then nodded. "You have a point. Let's see how the numbers fall out for a time. If it turns out that people believe all that data, then maybe we should switch to Taprin. Of course, there was that matter of his relationship with that Auroran ambassador."

"It's over. He stood on principle, she left him. I have that on very good authority."

"Usable."

"What *do* we do about the Aurorans now?"

"That's up to the Fifty Worlds. Our friend Ambassador Chassik is making tremendous political capital out of their apparent indiscretions. The damage is done, we just have to wait and see how much. Once Solaria displaces Aurora as de facto head of the Spacer Worlds, then business will be even better. Agreed?"

The three attendees nodded.

"It has been an interesting campaign," the chairman said. "We won most of what we wanted. No robotic inspections of Earth transports, no lowering of tariffs here or among the Spacer Worlds, although the easement among the Settler worlds might do some small damage to our profits. However, that should be offset by the tighter controls that Solaria will propose once they assume the dominant role among the Fifty Worlds. All in all, a good year's work. You should all congratulate yourselves. You did very well."

"It cost you quite a bit."

"Yes, well . . . I always did consider emigrating." He paused for a time to let them all think about that. "Anything else?"

"What about Alda? Are we going to leave him in prison?"

"Alda won't spent any time in prison, I assure you. The charges are circumstantial, the evidence corrupted. This will cost him a little out of pocket, that's all."

"And Looms?"

"Yes, well, we missed that one, didn't we? A pity he won't even be charged. But maybe next time." Again, a pause. "No further business? Good. In that case, I'll be in touch some time in the next ten months with the new arrangements for our meetings. Be careful to purge your files of any hint of this place. Thank you all. I'll look forward to our next talk."

One by one the attendees winked out. The chairman went to the transparency and gazed out at the simulation. The ocean, the waterfall, the trees, the beauty. He wondered if where he was going would have anything to compare.

Well, if it did not, then he would simply have to build it. What else was money and power for?

"Flesh, not steel?"

The chairman turned to find a ghostly form standing behind him. He was only mildly surprised.

"I didn't expect you to chance coming back here," he said.

"The meeting's over? I missed it?"

"It's all over."

"No, I don't think so. You'll resume in some other medium. I just wanted to say good-bye. I couldn't have done this without your help."

"No, you couldn't. But then we've been dependent on each other, haven't we?"

"I wondered if you noticed."

"I never get overconfident."

"Good."

"Will you be all right? Will you win?"

"I think so. The fight will do me good, but ..."

"Well, then. Good luck to you."

"And to you. See you around."

The ghost faded. The chairman scowled. That should not have been possible. It was just as well he was closing this place down. Holes must have developed.

"Recording complete?" he asked.

"Recording complete. Decoding routines in place, descrambler active."

The chairman sighed, gave the place a last look.

"Transfer all relevant data to hard copy and disassemble construct."

Bit by bit, Maui disappeared. The chairman did not stay for the end of the destruction.